THE
nobleman's
DAUGHTER

THE *nobleman's* DAUGHTER

A REGENCY ROMANCE

JEN GEIGLE JOHNSON

Covenant Communications, Inc.

Published by Covenant Communications, Inc.
American Fork, Utah

Printed in the United States of America
First Printing: November 2017

23 22 21 20 19 18 17   10 9 8 7 6 5 4 3 2 1

ISBN 978-1-52440-429-1

To my parents, Dana and David. To Amanda, Sarah, Benjamin, Andrew, Audrey, and Noah. And to Dustin. To all those who stand up for the downtrodden.

ACKNOWLEDGEMENTS

I HAVE ALWAYS READ ACKNOWLEDGMENTS and wondered how so many people could be involved in writing one book. And now I understand. So, with great joy, I must begin my own stream of gratitude. Dustin, you make my every dream a possibility. Thank you, children, for happily eating all of your favorite easy dinners and for being proud of me. Amanda, you freed all of my caged characters and told me when it was boring. My parents, David and Dana Geigle, read my very first draft with unending faith in me. Sarah Eden's specific encouragement lifted me at just the right moments. Jennifer Moore read an early draft and steered me gently and carefully. And then Annette Luthy Lyon's edits chipped off the rough and helped transform it into something beautiful. I still hear her voice in my head when I write. I would be remiss without mentioning awesome critique groups and Adrienne and John Burger for their clarity and insight; as well as Cheryl Callison, David Christiansen, Matt Sullivan, Jessica Bell, Lisa Fenley, Nuha Said, and Michelle Pennington. I also acknowledge Kathy and Kami and the great team at Covenant for their faith in my manuscript and in me as an author. And finally, Paul Fitzgerald and the Peterloo Memorial Campaign deserve a mention. We have the same goal: to ensure these peaceful freedom fighters in St. Peter's Fields are never forgotten.

CHAPTER ONE

Taunton, England, 1819

THE CANDLE FLAME QUIVERED, DANCING, and the wind moaned through the window of her small bedroom at the inn. Footsteps creaked the floors in the hall, and the sound of the very roof shaking overhead caused delicious shivers to course through her and a slow delighted smile to light Lady Amanda's face.

I am living in a gothic novel.

With a tiny laugh, she pulled the covers up closer around herself and turned the page of the book that was keeping her up hours into the dark of night.

Tomorrow they would be home. She leaned her head back, relaxing into pleasant thoughts. This trip to London had been thrilling: new gowns for her first Season, the opera, family dinners. But she missed running about on her grounds, volunteering with the children at the local school, and, admittedly, she missed Charlie.

Maybe she didn't miss *him* so much as the freedom she had when they were together. After his stable hand chores, they had gone fishing with the children from her class before she had left. But outings with Charlie would be curtailed, and much sooner than she liked to think about.

She returned to her book. No need to address uncomfortable subjects yet.

> *Unaware of a dark presence above him, Mordaunt ran through the forest. The wind whipped his cape, and a bat swooped down, brushing the top of his head.*

The window rattled and she jumped, fisting her blankets and pulling them closer to her chin. The resulting silence unnerved her for a moment, but when nothing more happened, she relaxed and smoothed down her coverlet. Laughing at herself, her eyes found the page again but couldn't read even one more sentence.

A crash at the window sprayed tinkling glass across her floor. She screamed when something heavy landed near her feet on the bed. Her breath coming fast, she jumped up, whimpering and dancing on her toes to avoid shards of glass. A brown object indented her covers in a single welt. *It might be alive.* She lifted her blankets to dislodge it from the bed, ready to leap off if it jumped at her. A gaping hole in her window let in the bitter cold from outside and brought gooseflesh to her arms and legs. And the dratted thing was so heavy it wouldn't move. A strange yellow powder spread across her coverlet, and the room filled with a pungent, burning odor of sulfur.

"Gah!" She pulled folds of her nightdress up to her face to block the smell. Pulling back the covers by inches, trying not to puff any more of the powder into the air, she peeked at what had been hurtled into her room. A rock. A note attached and written in scarlet read, *Freedom for all or none.*

Ominous. Curious. Bizarre. She had never seen the like. Noting she was not in any danger of being attacked by a creature, she peered closer. A small yellow satchel, dusting its contents onto her bed, was tied to the note. She lifted it and dropped it again, gagging. She'd discovered the source of the smell.

"Molly." She choked out just as her maid ran into the room from the adjoining closet.

"Lands of mercy! Are you all right, my lady?"

Amanda held her hand up, signaling Molly to wait. Gagging and gasping for air, she tried breathing through her mouth, but the smell stung her throat and she tasted it on her tongue. She knelt and grabbed the blankets, pulling them close, to cover her mouth and nose.

Muffled by the blankets, she coughed. "Wait, there's glass everywhere. Walk around and alert a footman." Molly carefully left to carry out her instructions.

Wind whipped her lovely green drapes high up to the ceiling, leaving a sharp, icy cold but clearing some of the odor. Heart pounding, she tried to pull the blankets tighter around her body, but the rock weighed them down.

Dizzy, trying to slow her breathing, she forced herself into motion.

Still holding a part of the blankets up to her face, she rolled to her stomach and slid a foot down to the floor. Glass cut through her skin, a sharp pain stinging her big toe. She flinched and pulled her foot back into bed. A bright trail of red followed and a new thin slice in her skin dripped blood down her foot.

Blast.

Wrapping another portion of blankets around her toe, frustration rose within her, challenging her fear. She loathed feeling helpless. But what could she do with glass all over the floor? Molly had left with the footman.

"Papa!" she shouted. "Molly! Someone, come quick!"

Footsteps and doors slamming sounded in the halls. Within moments, her door burst open. Her parents' faces paled immediately.

"Good heavens!" Her mother's voice cleared some of the fog in Lady Amanda's brain.

Father will be very angry.

But William, the Duke of Devonshire, ran to his daughter, worry all over his face, glass crunching under his house slippers, and cradled her small sixteen-year-old frame in his arms, hurrying toward his own room.

Her mother ran at his side, reaching over to place a hand on her head. "Are you hurt, my dear?"

"A little, but I couldn't walk on the floor. My toe . . ." The blood started dripping again the moment she pulled away the sheet. It was a mess of red.

"Amanda, you're bleeding. Oh, my dear." Her mother waved her hand at a footman. "Summon the innkeeper's wife."

He nodded and broke into a run.

"It's just a small cut. I am fine now, truly. But what a thing to happen." The corner of her mouth lowered. "What was that? The rock . . ." Amanda's eyes still stung from the smell, and she blinked back tears.

Her father squeezed her more tightly to him as they reached his room, his lips firming into a tight line. His features stern, lines etched in his face, he shouted at the nearest footman, "Someone discover the meaning of this!"

"Yes, Your Grace."

The duke shut his bedroom door with a snap. Hurrying to his large bed, he lowered Amanda as if she might break. Kissing the top of her head and holding her hands out to look her over, he asked, "Did the rock hit you?" His hands enveloped the sides of her face. "Are you quite all right?"

Amanda had never seen her father so unraveled. "Yes, Father. I am well. My hands still shake, but that is all." She held them out, palms down.

The duke covered both her hands in his own.

A scratch at the door interrupted them, and her father rose to crack it open. Amanda strained to hear bits of a hushed conversation. Mother moved to sit next to her, taking her hand.

"Bender," Simmons, her father's valet, said in an undertone.

Her mother gasped, and Amanda searched her face. That name meant nothing to Amanda.

"Can you be sure?" Her father's voice had a higher pitch. He sounded almost frightened.

She studied her father's back. *Who is Bender?*

Simmons nodded. "The worst miscreants of all time, preying on such lovely people as yourselves—we should involve the magistrate."

Her father nodded, his fists and teeth clenched. "Do what we have to— the gallows, if we must. I want him out of our lives, forever."

The gallows? Amanda turned to question her mother. Everyone seemed to know something and the common frustration of not knowing that very something everyone else knew rose inside her. But she bit the words back before they left her lips, her mother's face a sickly gray.

"Jack is back?" Her mother's voice cracked, and she cleared her throat.

CHAPTER TWO

FIVE MILES AWAY, IN AN old hunter's cottage, Jack Bender sat drumming a scratched old table with his fingers, smoke from his cigar curling up to the ceiling. He should be feeling victorious. No mistakes. A flawless execution that had appropriately brought terror to the house of Devonshire. He'd made sure of it himself.

But the rising swell of victory eluded him. If only he had not seen Marian. By some sick twist of all the fates, he had crossed around to the back of the inn and looked through the very window where she stood. Ten years had only enhanced her beauty and his desire. He had almost aborted the plan in that moment, his feet frozen to the ground. His eyes, glued to the window, had stared at a repulsive scene inside. Marian was laughing, smiling up into the face of her duke. And they were dancing, sure of no audience and laughing louder and louder, faces flushed and exhilarated. The duke had spun Marian in a wide arc around him, grasping her hand in his, and then he'd brought her up close to kiss her.

The sight had brought bile into Jack's throat. He hadn't been able to turn away, the pain as horrifying as it was addicting. The duke had looked into Marian's face with such tender attention there could be no doubt of his feelings. He loved her. Jack searched Marian's face, hoping she did not return the feeling; hoping to see friendship, camaraderie, anything but love. What he'd seen there had stolen his breath: a heart-stopping expression of pure joy. It brought his whole life of effort in a mad parade before his eyes, and all of it was found wanting. What could he ever do to be worthy of such a look from such a woman?

Jack Bender's throat closed, obstructed by a shard of conscience, a poignant regret for all the many awful things he had done choking him. As was want to happen, however, remorse was quickly replaced by a sinister reminder. *That joy could have been yours. Her lips on yours.*

This rush of thoughts and emotion had sped up his heart, fueling his anger and spurring him to move forward with the plan to throw the awful-smelling linens and rock into their daughter's room.

His fingers drummed the tabletop again. Here, in this old and musty cottage, he realized he expected a little happiness of his own, some sort of triumph knowing he had stripped theirs. He waited for it to come, for even a bit of satisfaction. It did not. Instead, he felt hollow. And he felt alone. His fist crashed down onto the table, and he dropped his cigar onto the floor, grinding it deeper into the dirt with the toe of his boot.

Amanda's eyes watered as she tried not to sneeze. Dust had gathered in the passageway behind the wall in her father's study. If her parents weren't going to tell her anything about the rock, then she'd use her own methods. She adjusted her body so that she could see better out the small peephole in the wall.

Her father toyed with Cook's biscuits on his tray, staring unseeing out the window. A stack of unanswered correspondence sat in front of him, and his brow was deeply furrowed.

Her uncle Ethan had just arrived up the front drive, and she hoped they would finally discuss the rock in the inn and whoever this Jack Bender person could be.

A sharp knock made her jump.

"Enter."

In the doorway, nearly filling it with his bulk, stood a man near in age to her father and, except for his lighter hair, almost identical in appearance as well. The duke arose to greet his brother, the Earl of Norfolk, with a shake of the hand and a pounding on his back. "Oh, it's good to see you brother!" her father said.

"I got here as quickly as possible. Your express was so cryptic. I hardly know what to think," Ethan responded.

A maid brought in the tray with sandwiches, and the earl helped himself to some brandy from the sidebar. He brought a glass for the duke, who swirled his glass and stared at the amber color for a minute before speaking. "It's Bender. He crossed the line, Ethan, at the inn in Traunton—threw a rock through the window. It was a calculated threat against my own child. In Amanda's bedchamber no less. He had to have known." He paused then looked up at Ethan as he said, "He sent a written message this time."

Ethan raised his eyebrows in surprise.

Her father reached into a drawer and drew out the cloth bearing the written threat.

Amanda swallowed and wished for a larger peephole.

"*Freedom for all or none.* What does that mean, precisely?" Ethan asked, exasperated. "And what in the blazes does he hope to gain by threatening a child?"

"She's sixteen, Ethan. Which in some ways concerns me more than if she were still in leading strings. We are looking into it. I have a few Bow Street Runners on the hunt as well as a couple of men Simmons knows. I hope to have some answers by the end of next week. But from what I learned just listening at White's last month, Bender and his gang are terrorizing other families as well. They want common rule."

"Common rule! The uneducated and inexperienced ruling England!" Ethan stood and started pacing. "What would they have us do, vote your dear Simmons into Parliament?"

"Ethan, lower your voice." The duke paused. "Apparently Bender himself isn't too keen on the idea of nobility as a whole. Wishes to do away with all of us."

"And who, may I ask, would take care of all of these good common people in England, if not the nobles? Who would make sure they have food during harsh winters and offer them employment in our houses? Are they suggesting landownership for everyone?"

Amanda's father cleared his throat. "Some of the more radical groups are. Bender is. Our very existence stands as a threat to his idea of a free society of universal opportunity, including landownership for all who can afford it and equal votes across the country. I'm not opposed to the idea. But even the factory workers should have equal rights, says he. Poorhouse inhabitants. Prisoners! He is beyond the pale."

Boring political talk between her father and uncle was not what she expected, and Amanda struggled to understand it all.

"But what does this have to do with Amanda? Why a rock through a young lady's bedroom window?" Ethan rubbed his hand across his forehead.

Amanda stilled her breathing.

The duke's brow furrowed. "I can't make sense of it. The Bender we know doesn't care about this stuff and nonsense: freedom, equality, any of it. I fear he means us ill will, our family in particular."

Ethan grimaced. "A form of revenge." He shook his head. "And now our Amanda, a victim of his depravity. How is she?"

"Right as rain." The duke chuckled. "She has quite a lot of gumption, that one, and courage too. She is pacing in the library this minute, bemoaning how we won't include her in the Bender discussions."

Ethan laughed. "I've always admired her pluck."

"I need your thoughts, brother, about my instructions to Simmons. He is handling the Bender situation for me."

"That sounds ominous, Will." Lord Ethan stilled his cup. "Just what did you ask Simmons to do?"

"Return him to prison and ask that he be sent straight to the gallows. No mercy this time. I should have done it years ago." The duke's face was rigid with stress. "We are to blame, you know. If it weren't for us, there would be no threat of Jack Bender. There would only be Jack Bender the barrister, or Jack Bender the solicitor. We created this monster, you and I and the boys at Eton."

CHAPTER THREE

Devonshire, England

HOME. A HINT OF THE ocean in the air, skies the shade of her mother's eyes, and the greenest pastures in all of England. Lady Amanda drank it all in, smiling as she watched the horses graze near the stables, east of the estate entrance.

"Still longing to ride the stallions?" Charlie murmured close to her ear.

She turned her head in surprise and found his eyes, inches from her own. Her heart sped up, and she stepped back a little in surprise. "Oh, Charlie!" She looked at him with a bit of reproach then sighed in resignation. "Must you always startle me?"

Charlie smirked. "You'd think you'd be used to it by now, eh?" He gently bumped her shoulder with his own. "How are you, Lady Amanda? Not hurt, I take it? That was a long drop from the tree this morning."

"Some crazed lunatic throws a rock through my window, and all you can think about is the tree? You were there—you saw for yourself I am just fine." She frowned at him and stepped farther away.

Laughing, he reached for her hands, pulling her to walk beside him. "Whoever it was throwing the rock just wanted to make a point. I'm sure he never planned to hurt you." He avoided her eyes, then he cleared his throat. "Let's see if he did any damage." He made a show of looking her over for any bumps or scrapes, turning her this way and that, one eyebrow quirked up. He stopped, face close to hers again, looking into her eyes, and said, "I'm sorry about the crazed lunatic. But you look perfect, my lady. Just right."

Amanda allowed her eyes to meet his. She was about to respond when they were interrupted by Jerome shouting, "Charlie! Let's get these horses in their paddocks. Horatia is arriving this morning—four years we've been waiting for this horse. Get to work, lad!"

Charlie bowed his head to her and, with a wink, raced off to the stables.

Jerome reined in his horse in front of Amanda and tipped his head. "Lady Amanda." A cheerful and demanding stable master, his grin always urged smiles in return. She hoped Charlie would not get into trouble for stopping to chat. She knew Jerome hoped his son would one day fill his shoes.

"Hello, Master Jerome. How are our gentlemen this morning?" Amanda grinned in welcome.

Looking over at two stallions tied to the fence, Jerome answered, "They're the best sort of horseflesh, you know. But that makes 'em mighty difficult to saddle." Jerome's mouth quirked into a wry smile. "And how are you, my lady? I hear you've had quite a fall already today and a scare yesterday besides." His eyes filled with concern.

Amanda sighed. "I feel perfectly safe with all the guards Father has placed about." As if summoned by the mere mention of their presence, two footmen replaced those who stood through the night at the entrance. "Except for a bit of embarrassment that everyone now knows I was up in a tree and silly enough to fall out, I am well."

Jerome chuckled at her response. "You have pluck, my lady, mountains' worth of pluck. The household staff admires you for it."

Amanda laughed. "Grateful I am to all of you for keeping me out of trouble these many years."

Jerome chuckled and tipped his hat. "A good day to you, Lady Amanda. I best get these horses out to pasture before her majesty, Horatia, shows up." He shook his head. "Never thought I'd live to see one of the foals of the famous Eclipse." Master Jerome headed in the direction of Socks, who looked as though he would start kicking the fence in his irritation to still be tied there. Jerome tensed, turned back to her, and said in a low voice, "And don't be listening to everything Charlie tells you. Some things are just best left the way they are." He turned and continued toward Socks.

What a curious thing to say.

The sound of horse hooves interrupted her thoughts. Charlie called from the stables, "She's here—make ready."

A carriage with a large ducal crest entered the long drive and made its way toward the house followed by the beautiful chestnut mare, ridden by a tall man, broad across his shoulders. He looked familiar and as he drew closer, Amanda's mouth slowly opened. This could not be Lord Nathaniel who came a few summers past to visit. That scraggly boy would hardly have filled out those riding clothes so well. Her face warmed as she recognized the direction of her thoughts.

Jerome dismounted, tied up his horse, and prepared to greet the newcomers. Lady Amanda joined him, watching as the carriage pulled in front of the estate entrance. The duke opened the house door and met his guests out front.

Amanda shook her head in amusement. *Answering the front door, is he?*

After a brief handshake and greeting, the three men headed in her direction, followed by a stable hand leading the lovely mare. Amanda stepped forward to greet her father and meet the others.

"You may remember my daughter from your visit a few summers ago. Allow me to introduce Lady Amanda Alexandria Cumberland."

Amanda dipped a low curtsy.

"Amanda, this is His Grace, Edgar, Duke of Somerset, and his son, Lord Nathaniel," her father said.

"Pleased to meet you both and welcome. Do I understand correctly that you are from Bath?" Amanda asked.

Nathaniel answered, "We are. Have you ever been to Bath, Lady Amanda?"

She liked the sound of her name and title coming from his lips. He smiled at her with a knowing grin. Oh, but he was handsome. Her eyes wandered along his firm jawline to his thick dark hair—a portion fell onto his forehead—to his eyes, which were a cloudy blue, like the sea on a misty morning. They lit with a new spark and the corners crinkled.

She realized with a start that he had asked her a question. Clearing her throat she said, "I have not had that pleasure yet, no. But I do hope Father will allow a visit someday soon. I hear the whole town is lovely."

"Indeed it is, and if Bath is ever so fortunate as to have your company, I do hope you will call on us."

She nodded, beginning to feel overwhelmed by his attention. She could not remember ever being so intrigued by him. "Thank you, my lord. It would be our pleasure, I am sure." Turning toward the mare, she said, "And might I ask, is this lovely animal, Horatia?"

Her father laughed. "I am anxious to get to know her myself." The duke noticed Jerome waiting a few steps behind Amanda. "And here is another who is chomping at the bit, so to speak. "Ho, ho! Jerome, allow me to introduce the newest addition to our stables."

With that, the mare dipped her head, rubbing her teeth on her forward flank.

"And lovely to meet *you*, Your Highness," Jerome responded with a gallant bow and a dip of his hat, earning laughs.

Charlie's laugh carried as he walked back across the mud on the other side of the fence.

Amanda's eyes flitted to Lord Nathaniel, who seemed to be enjoying only her. She smiled and moved over to the horse to hide from his gaze. Stroking the mare's shiny coat, she shared a look with Charlie over Horatia's shoulder. He raised both eyebrows a couple of times then led Socks back to his stall.

Lord Nathaniel joined her. His hand brushed hers as he reached forward to stroke the mare's muscular back, and a thrill of tingles rushed up her arm. She turned to him and Nathaniel paused for a moment, searching her face. Then he winked at her and stepped aside to allow her father room to approach them.

The Duke of Devonshire examined his new mare. He ran his hands down her legs and lifted each hoof. "She's perfect." He handed the reins to Jerome and patted her on the shoulder. "Go with Jerome now, young girl. He will take good care of you." To the others he said, "Gentlemen, shall we go inside to draw up the final papers with my solicitor? I'll have Mrs. Gibbons send tea." The dukes turned toward the house, and Amanda stayed behind so that she might follow Jerome.

Nathaniel tipped his hat to her. "A real pleasure to meet you, Lady Amanda." She dipped a slow curtsy in return, grinning at him through her lashes, which she fluttered a few times. She didn't know what else to do. She liked him but was unaccustomed to flirting. Lord Nathaniel chuckled in response and shook his head as he too turned toward the house.

But he stopped and turned toward her again, and she swallowed as he approached.

Standing close enough that her skirts brushed his knees, he stared into her eyes as he brought her gloved hand to his lips and placed a lingering kiss on her fingers. With his back toward their fathers, Lord Nathaniel's large frame blocked their view, but Charlie, who must have been watching from the barn, coughed loudly. Nathaniel's eyes flickered up over Amanda's head toward the sound and back to her again.

"I hope to see you again someday." He found the skin just above her glove on the underside of her wrist and gently, covertly stroked it with his finger. "If not in Bath, perhaps at your coming out. Will you have a Season in London?"

Her fingers still burned from his attention, and though she could feel her mind clouding over, she hoped her voice would not fail her.

"Yes, I am but sixteen now though, you see." She felt her face heat. Surely he would dismiss her as only a child.

"Sixteen. Hmm." His eyes traveled across her face, lingering on her lips for just a moment, long enough for Amanda to laugh and look away. He waited a moment for her eyes to meet his again, and she saw sincerity and kindness apparent there; it surprised and warmed her.

His voice soft, he said, "Soon then."

She could not speak. Her heart still pounded in her chest. Lord Nathaniel stepped back, still locking her with his gaze. Then he tipped his head and turned to walk toward their fathers, who waited near the house with pleased smiles.

She watched him walk away, strong and purposeful in his tall boots. He looked fine in his tailcoat. He was everything a gentleman should be, she decided, still studying his retreating figure. Nathaniel turned his head slightly back to her, his knowing look and grin melting her insides. She whirled around, chastising herself for ogling.

Not fully recovered, her gaze found Charlie observing her closely. She called to him, "Let's see this horse then, shall we?"

Charlie grinned in response, dropped the pitchfork he had been holding, and walked to meet her and Jerome, whom Amanda followed to Horatia's stall.

Charlie and Amanda spent the rest of the morning helping Jerome acclimate the new horse. As it was nearing time for her afternoon lessons, Amanda frowned. "I had better get back inside."

"Lady Amanda, can I talk to you for a minute first?" Charlie closed the distance between them and watched her face closely.

She took a small step back. "Of course, but we've been talking all morning, haven't we?" she teased.

"I saw you with Lord Nathaniel." Charlie ran a hand through his hair. "He was . . . friendly."

Her eyes darted away in surprise. "Yes, I suppose he was." A blush crept onto her cheeks. She forced herself to return his gaze.

His eyes lingered on her cheeks and with a tighter jaw he continued. "You let him kiss your hand."

Amanda sucked in her breath.

Charlie asked, "Do you feel some sort of regard for him?"

"No! I mean, I don't know. He was attentive, that's all." She waved her hand in the air. "It means nothing. I will probably never see him again."

"You cannot give men such liberties. You are but a child. And he . . . well, he is *not*."

A great fire of indignation rose inside her.

He must have noticed because he added in a more placating tone, "He is obviously a rake. What proper gentleman would play with the affections of a girl so young?"

Her mouth opened and then closed, and her eyes narrowed. "Maybe he is interested in getting to know me. And even if *you* haven't noticed, I am not a child any longer. At least, *he* obviously doesn't think so." She folded her arms across her chest and turned from him.

Charlie placed a hand on her shoulder, gently rotating her to face him. "I'm sorry. This is coming out all wrong. That's not what I meant to say at all. I saw the two of you standing so closely, you staring at him with those eyes of yours."

She could feel her cheeks heating up again. *Could this conversation get any more uncomfortable?*

He looked away, his foot kicking the dirt.

A moment passed. Amanda waited for her confusion, anger, embarrassment, and all the myriad emotions rushing through her to slow and calm.

He stopped fidgeting and stepped closer to her. "I felt like someone punched me in the gut. It seemed all sorts of wrong, him standing so close to you, and it was all I could do to stop myself from threatening him with my pitchfork!" A bitter tone edged his laughter.

Amanda's heart warmed. "But why should you care at all? We didn't even say anything important. And you and I talk for hours and have all sorts of fun. You are the best friend I have."

"But that's just it. I saw him with you and realized I don't want to be your best friend."

She wrinkled her forehead and squinted her eyes. "What?"

Charlie moved even closer, pulling her back into a corner of the stables, his face full of hope. He reached forward and rested the palm of his hand on the side of her face.

A delicious sort of anxiety filled her. Teetering on the brink of something dangerous, she was equal parts enticed and afraid.

Step away, she told herself, but her feet would not move.

"I *do* want to be your best friend, but I am hoping—that is to say, I would really like it, if you would consider me to be *more* than a friend."

"You would?" she whispered.

Charlie leaned closer until his lips were almost touching hers.

She breathed in slowly, searching his eyes. She should step back, at least one step. She knew she should.

"I'm saying I care for you, Amanda." He pressed his lips to hers softly and quickly, and backed away a half step, ready to retreat.

"Oh!" Amanda breathed. A soft thrill ran through her. She looked up at him hesitantly. "I care for you too, Charlie." She reached her fingers up to touch her lips. A horse whinnied and stomped his hoofs. Reality cleared her fog. And something close to alarm pounded through her. She searched the stables. No one near. Jerome busy inside. "But, Charlie, you know that we can never—"

"Lady Amanda, I know." He sounded almost desperate, and he began talking faster. "But things are changing. I know some people who say reform is on the way. We could make it work, maybe . . . someday." He pulled her close again, leaning down to kiss her one more time.

"What is the meaning of this?" her father thundered. "You will unhand her this instant."

They both stepped apart, and Amanda wished to sink away, hidden. She hoped her father had not seen their kiss. Dread filled her at the thought of the consequences. Charlie's face turned a bright shade of red, but fire lit his eyes.

The duke's eyes flashed. "Amanda, I did not raise you for this!"

"But Father, surely you see there is no harm. It is just Charlie."

"What I see is far more than you can see. Charles, I want you to limit your activities on this estate to those for which you are in our employ. I have been too lenient with the both of you. And you have betrayed my trust." Looking meaningfully at Charlie, he said, "It is time you remembered your place and station in life."

Amanda grimaced. "Father—"

Ignoring her, he continued. "Charles, you will meet me in my office with your father tomorrow morning, and we will discuss your placement elsewhere."

"No!" Amanda grasped her father's arm.

"And Amanda, if you wish to come down to the stables, or anywhere else for that matter, you will do so with a chaperone. Do I make myself clear?"

"What! On my own grounds? I shall feel as though I live in a cage!"

"It is high time you begin to act your age and your station. You are my daughter and as such . . ." The duke began pacing in front of them. "Cavorting with stable hands . . ."

Amanda gasped and Charlie sucked in a breath.

He stopped in front of them and placed his hand on Charlie's shoulder as he looked them both in the eyes in turn. "As good a friend as Charles may be—I know he has been like a brother to you—spending time with a stable hand and being viewed in an"—the duke waved his hand in their direction— "intimate manner reflects poorly on both of you. This is not the way things are done."

She thought her mortification complete. But her father continued anyway. "I blame myself. I see I have let you two run freely long enough. Charles, please see to my horse. He needs an extra washing this evening. And Amanda, come with me into the house. Your mother would like you to join us as we entertain the Duke of Somerset and his son."

She looked over her shoulder as they walked away. Charlie kicked the dirt again, but he headed back toward the stable to find the duke's horse as requested. She turned her head to look at her father, his worry lines deeper than usual. She could feel the tension rolling off him.

"I'm sorry, Father."

He stopped and sighed, facing the house. "I know, my dear. Let us not speak of it." Then he took both her hands in his and looked into her eyes. The strength of his obvious love and its constancy moved her. He spoke softly. "But prepare yourself, my Amanda. Things will be very different for you now. You are growing up. Men and boys are starting to notice you. Lord Nathaniel certainly expressed an interest." The duke looked at the house again and grunted in amused displeasure. "I came out myself to summon you because I wanted to tell you before we return to the house. He is a good man, and he has a sincere desire to know you better."

Wonder filled her. She could not stop her smile.

The duke shook his head and brought one of her hands up to the side of his face. "This is all happening much too quickly for me. I thought surely I had my little girl a while longer." He pulled her into a gentle embrace, and she felt the security she had always known. She allowed herself a moment to simply enjoy it.

"Oh, Father, I'm not going anywhere. And I'm certain Charlie will be back to normal by morning. Truly, we skip rocks. He has *never* . . ." She blushed, flustered. "What is left for me now? Sit and do needlepoint? You know I cannot abide—"

"Amanda, Amanda, my dear. Let us hope Lord Nathaniel did not witness your embrace." His eyebrow raised, and the look he gave her stopped her resistance and brought more heat to her face. "There will still be time for fun. But you must now work harder and spend more time obeying that governess of yours and following the fine example of your mother in your education and decorum."

She sighed in reluctant acceptance and nodded. Turning back toward the stables, she said, "I think you have hurt Charlie terribly." She felt indignation rising again as she thought over the conversation. "Employment elsewhere? How could you say those things to dear Charlie?" She couldn't stop the tiny sob that escaped from her throat while she spoke. She clenched her fists and blinked back her tears.

"How can you not understand? If he had kissed you, if anyone had seen the two of you in such an embrace—you could well be ruined."

She forced her expression not to change.

"Even as far from London as we are, people talk. Servants talk."

She understood, of course. Society's strictures had been drilled into her as a young child. But none of those rules ever seemed to apply where Charlie was concerned.

He reached for her elbow, guiding her in the direction of the house. "I care for the lad, of course I do. I know I hurt him. But it cannot be helped. He is a servant. Though we have allowed him much freedom here on our estate, what with Cook doting on him as she does, and you and he playing together like siblings . . . none of that changes his station in life. Better to hurt him now than for disaster to happen later." He ran a hand through his hair. "I delayed too long in separating the two of you. You were born to be a lady, to marry nobility, to help care for people on an estate, and to continue our ancient family line. There is no room for a stable hand in your future, except to groom and care for your horses."

An awful clenching tightness filled her chest. The loss of Charlie sat at the center of a much broader ache and sense of failure. She grasped inside herself for any carefree childhood feeling, but the elusive memories flitted away, replaced by an overwhelming sense of duty and responsibility pressing in upon her. What if she could never master the proper behavior and deportment of a duke's daughter? And if she did, what if she loathed it?

The blue sky, instead of feeling vast, bore down on her with so much pressure that the air around her felt thick, and she struggled to fill her lungs. With a cry, she broke into a run, her father calling after her; she did not stop.

Amanda ran as far and as fast as she could. With no destination in mind, she ran across the lawn, around the house, across the back gardens toward the pond. Her lungs and side aching, she stopped to rest in the cool shade of the white gazebo. She sat on a stone bench, staring at nothing, waiting for her breathing to slow; the cold from the stone seeped through her thin gown and chilled her.

She ran a finger along her lower lip, reliving Charlie's kiss. She wished to hide under the bench. How could she have let him do that? And then Lord Nathaniel's touch still tingled. She wrapped her arms around herself. She enjoyed his attention too much. Was Charlie right? Was Lord Nathaniel just a rake, toying with her? And now, to never run free on her own estate? Charlie dismissed? Too much emotion coursed through her.

The rock's message entered her mind. *Freedom for all or none.* Amanda agreed with her assailant.

She closed her eyes against too many thoughts, blocking them all. Numbness settled, and she just sat.

A bird's chirping startled her out of her stupor. To her right, sparrows eyed her from their cage. Mrs. Gibbons, the housekeeper, often asked the footmen to place the birds outside on days with lovely weather.

They usually brought her great comfort: caged, but cheerful and active. Except not today. This afternoon, they mirrored her own feelings. Instead of singing brightly, they remained eerily silent. She watched with concern. All eight of them clutched the bars on the side of the cage with their feet, some tilting their heads so one eye could look upward at the sky, others watching the woods.

Movement to her left distracted her, and she frowned. One of Father's promised footmen had found her and he stood guard down the path.

A sparrow made another small chirping noise. From the woods, the sound of an answering bird reached them. Wild sparrows sang to each other and jumped from branch to branch in the small copse of trees near her gazebo. And then her sparrows started chirping and calling from their cage. One of the birds flew at the bars, knocked her head on the side of the cage, and fell to the bottom in a daze.

"Oh, you poor dear." She understood their desperation and their longing. Her own heart felt caged, and she yearned to fly free. Moving as if in a dream, sluggish at first, then faster and deliberately, she took the remaining steps to the cage. With one swift movement, she threw open the door and stepped back, her arms stiff at her sides, fists clenched. The birds burst out, flying into the open, higher and higher, dipping and diving in circles and flying higher yet again. She closed her eyes for a moment and imagined she was with them, flying high with no limits, as if she could break the sky.

When she opened her eyes again, she spread her arms and ran across the grass, swaying and dipping and curving as she had when she was a little girl. Time passed unnoticed by Amanda, her awareness consumed by a delirious sensation of freedom. The world around her invisible, she finally stopped and watched intently as all of her sparrows returned from the sky to settle in the branches of a tree. She breathed out the tightness and tension in her shoulders.

And she felt strangely at peace.

☞

Unseen, closer to the house, Lord Nathaniel watched. He had seen Lady Amanda run blindly from her father, seen the caged expression in her face.

Curious, he had moved from his position in the library so he could slip out the door leading to the gardens, unnoticed. He smiled, amused when she let the birds go, but as his gaze followed their progress, he understood—he too exulted in their freedom. As the sparrows soared into the sky, a restless desire filled him, a longing to be free.

CHAPTER FOUR

"Shall I grab the smelling salts, Father?" Nathaniel chuckled. "You look about to swoon."

The wheels dipped and struggled through the ruts and holes in the road. His father gritted his teeth and gripped the window ledge to stay upright.

Nathaniel put aside his pleasant thoughts of the beautiful Lady Amanda and focused on his father.

The duke grunted and eyed him. "Blast this awful conveyance. I will mount Smoke the next time I travel, Dr. Wilson or no."

Nathaniel reached over and squeezed his shoulder. "The venerable Duke of Somerset. If the biddies of the *ton* could see you now."

"Heaven forbid."

"Not to worry. Only three more hours until we rest at the inn."

The duke pinched the area between his eyes. "I could put up with a few biddies, as you call them, in exchange for a good night's rest somewhere closer. Victoria Annesley's house party is sounding more appealing. Shall we stop, just for the night?"

"I can think of nothing better. Lords Castlereagh and Tilleroy will be there and a whole mess of the men from Oxford. I would like to join their hunting party in the morning."

"To the Annesley estate then." The duke sat back in his seat with his eyes closed.

Nathaniel rapped on the ceiling.

A small hatch opened up above them and half of the coachman's face appeared, framed in the small rectangle. "My lord?"

"Turn at the next crossing. We will be stopping at the Annesley estate for the evening."

"Very good, my lord."

What a perfect turn of events. Nathaniel needed to stop at the estate. One of his contacts desired a meeting and further direction. Also, Lord Castlereagh's presence interested him. He hoped to learn more of the prime minister's plans for the poor and working classes. And more than anything, to get a sense of his temperament. The man remained a mystery. If they were to ever sway him, Nathaniel needed to understand him. Lord Castlereagh, who worked so closely with their venerable Lord Liverpool, would be one step closer.

⌒

Morning broke early, but Nathaniel dressed in time to meet the hunting party out by the stables.

"Nathaniel. Good to see you, man. Glad you could join us." Lord Tilleroy stood a hand shorter than Nathaniel and was stouter around the middle.

Lord Annesley grunted. "You are not at all glad to see him. None of us are, really."

"Honesty becomes you." Nathaniel chuckled and cuffed his friend on the back.

Annesley grunted. "I'm the only one who will admit it. Every female eye turned in your direction when you joined us for cards last night and they haven't broken their gaze yet." He stood a couple of inches taller than Nathaniel and balanced his dark looks with fair features and blond wavy locks. Nathaniel knew more than a few of the ladies remained with eyes fixed solely on his friend.

"Not so, Annesley. You know my purpose is not to woo the ladies. This hunt is just the thing. I'm needing a bit of a run through the thickets of your great estate."

Annesley grinned and winked. "But if a lady just happened to pay you a bit of attention . . ."

Nathaniel ran a hand through his hair and shrugged. "Well now, who would complain about that?"

Annesley clapped him on the back in return. "It's good to see you, Nathaniel. Whatever your reasons, I am glad you made an appearance."

When the others joined them and they were all mounted, Annesley signaled the servants, who turned the dogs loose.

While waiting for the hounds to catch a scent, Castlereagh sneered. "I find I am in great need of a new valet."

"I thought this one was new." Tilleroy turned his head to eye Lord Castlereagh.

"Look at this cravat. Limp already. The man is incompetent—hands shaking like a scared woman while he tied it."

Nathaniel frowned. "Why would he be shaking?"

"Scared of your wrath, no doubt." Tilleroy laughed. "You dock wages for mistakes, do you not?"

"I do, but I've done nothing of the kind to him yet. His reasons are selfish, personal. Caught him crying in the dressing room this morning."

Annesley frowned. "But did you find out why? Perhaps it is not some trifling matter."

Nathaniel shared a look with his friend. "I remember my Phillips truly struggled when his mother fell ill. Turned out limp cravats and ill-pressed tailcoats for a week. Aghast I was, showing up before the jewels of the *ton* in such a state." Nathaniel waved his hand in the air with a dramatic flick of his wrist. "But after going to visit his family, he returned much better for it. And no one would question my presentation now. Look at this cravat. It is perfection." Nathaniel raised his head so all could see, holding his profile for a moment.

"Ridiculous. You would reward poor behavior with a holiday." Lord Castlereagh's smug smile tightened a string of irritation beginning inside of Nathaniel, and the man's laugh rankled him further. "If it hasn't to do with the ladies, you are at a loss, man. Have you a logical thought in that head of yours more than twice in a day?"

Nathaniel willed his face not to burn. He knew he must play along. "If the thought brings with it a beautiful lady or a mad romp through the woods on a horse, then yes. I string together many a coherent thought." The others laughed.

Castlereagh would not be put off. "You need to go about this whole servant business differently. If you give them the tiniest bit of leeway, they will take a pound more. Follow Liverpool's example. This new Corn Law will work wonders to keep them in line. Just watch. They'll be too worried about where to find their next meal to go attending any rallies or the like."

Tilleroy joined him. "He's right, I dare say. Some say we are headed for our own storming of the Bastille. Best be careful while we can—keep them tight and under control." Tilleroy nodded as if he had decided the fate of the world.

Nathaniel gritted his teeth. If Castlereagh represented any of the prime minister's thoughts, Lord Liverpool had not listened to his warnings. The man could not be reasoned with. So worked up about a possible uprising in England, he reacted more out of panic than reason. Cooling his features and shrugging, Nathaniel said, "Talk of politics bores me. Are we in the drawing room or on a hunt? Come, man. I do believe the dogs are doing all the work here." He indicated with his head that they should move forward.

The others leaped ahead of him, racing off on their horses. Shouting in the air, they called back over their shoulders.

Annesley stayed behind. "You could defend yourself."

Nathaniel grinned. "I thought I did."

"No, you proved him right. He's left thinking you have wool in the brain. You have one of the most brilliant minds of our time, man. Your research at Oxford remains uncontested. You could put some of those principles to work here. Further your theories. Work for change in the House of Lords."

Nathaniel felt the familiar sadness tighten his throat. "What makes you think I am not?"

His friend sighed. "I hope you are. I can only wait for the day." Shaking his head, he took off, calling over his shoulder, "But this is the year I will best you in our hunt!"

With that challenge ringing in his ears, Nathaniel spurred his horse in a different direction, laughing to the forest around him when he heard the dogs begin baying in exactly the place he had predicted. He knew, racing toward the sound, with his head start he would beat every rider.

CHAPTER FIVE

AMANDA STILLED HER BREATHING AND placed a hand across her stomach to calm the fluttering. She stood at the top of the stairs, waiting for her father and mother.

Her brilliant white dress flowed down to her feet, hair done up in piles of auburn curls on top of her head, a few placed carefully to frame her face. She willed her heart to slow. Her mother had chosen the guest list to help ease and comfort. Most attending her come-out were dear family and friends. Her aunt and uncle, Lady Amelia and Lord Ethan, Countess and Earl of Norfolk, had graciously offered to host her first ball.

In one week's time, she would be presented at court. And then her first Season would begin. She closed her eyes and smiled.

Her mind drifted to Charles as she awaited her parents. These last eight months she had seen very little of her old childhood friend, who was dismissed from their service. She did see him time and again because a neighboring estate employed him, but when they crossed paths, he nodded his head with a restrained, "Lady Amanda." She had missed him dearly, but more and more, preparations to be a lady and run an estate replaced her childhood activities.

She loved her visits to the tenants and her help with the local school in the vicarage. She'd relished studying from master poets. She loved to read history. She had quickly grasped French and Italian. Needlepoint was still a chore, but drawing and painting were a joy.

Her days of childhood play and Charlie were becoming increasingly distant, although pleasurable, memories. The night before she left for her aunt and uncle's estate, completely unexpectedly, she found one white rose with a note in her horse's stall.

Dear Amanda,
My heart remains with you. I hope one day for the change that can set
us free.
Charles

Could he really still harbor hope? Remembering his words now, a vague
sense of unease settled over her. She should have taken the note directly to her
father. But after everything that had happened, she hadn't dared. Charlie would
have been dismissed immediately from his new employment, and she couldn't
do that to an old friend.

His note brought with it disturbing memories of another note, tied to a rock
thrown onto her bed. *Freedom for all or none.* So different in tone: one filled with
hope and the other a threat. As her mind turned again to Charlie's note, the uneasiness worked its tendrils through her mind and tightened her chest. She vowed
to have an uncomfortable conversation with Charlie when she returned home.

She shook her head slightly. Away with her troublesome thoughts. She would
not allow them, not tonight when everything had been planned so carefully. She
determined to enjoy every moment of the evening: the gowns, the flowers, the
friends, the men. The familiar sound of her father's shoes on the stairs behind her
increased her happy anticipation.

He cleared his throat. "You look beautiful, my darling girl. I am so very
proud of all you have become."

Amanda felt her throat tighten and her eyes mist. "Thank you, Father. I
owe so much to so many, but most of all to you and Mother." She leaned in
and kissed him on the cheek.

The duke's eyes shone with love. "Your mother and I could not imagine
a better daughter. This dress, your beauty, all of this merely an adornment for
the stunning woman beneath. He held up a necklace of sapphires. "We want
you to have these."

Amanda's eyes widened in delight. "They are exquisite! Thank you." She
fingered the stones.

"They match your eyes, you know; brilliant blue, just like your mother's."
Amanda smiled and turned so that he could fasten the clasp, securing the
sapphires resting at her neckline.

"Now we are ready. Shall we?" he asked, holding out his arm. Together they
descended the stairs until he paused as his eyes moved toward the landing, where
Amanda's mother stood. "She still takes my breath away."

Marian returned her husband's gaze with adoration of her own and then
moved her eyes to rest on Amanda, love filling her face.

Amanda didn't think she could be any happier than at that moment, basking in the love of her family. Its strength gave her confidence, and a thrill of energy coursed through her. "Let's go, then," she said and kissed her mother's cheeks then hastened their pace down the hallway toward the ballroom entrance.

Her mother laughed good-naturedly and nodded to the footman. When the doors opened, the musicians stopped, and everyone in the room turned in welcome.

Amanda looked out over her friends and family and smiled. A few of her mother's dear friends turned to her with tear-filled eyes, hands on their hearts. Amanda held her chin held high as she proudly stood with her parents.

"His Grace, William Cumberland, Duke of Devonshire," the master of ceremonies announced. "Her Grace, Marian Atwater Cumberland, Duchess of Devonshire, and their daughter, Lady Amanda Alexandria Cumberland."

The duke bowed, and the duchess and Amanda curtsied low. The music began again, and people resumed their conversations.

Flowers filled the room, cascading off tables, crowding vases in every corner and overflowing from wall sconces. Echoing Amanda's dress, the white floral adorned the ball and turned every thought to her. Candles filled the hall. Tables with bowls of lemonade and bites of tarts lined one wall. In Amanda's mind, the greatest adornments in the room moved about inside it. Brilliant dresses and brightly colored tailcoats shifted in intricate social patterns, approaching and fading and circling each other in conversation. Amanda grinned in anticipation.

After greeting her uncle and aunt, Amanda and her parents walked a few more steps into the room, where they were met immediately by a tall gentleman with light-brown hair. His friendly, open face and engaging, intelligent eyes put her at ease and sparked her curiosity.

A kind-looking woman with many smile lines approached at his left, and Amanda's father made the introductions. Apparently Lord Jonathon Needley had become an earl at a young age. Besides the misfortune of such a name, Amanda found much to be pleased with in this new acquaintance; but when he bowed over her hand, she felt no rush of energy or excitement, only mild curiosity. He secured two dances on her card and then stepped aside as others worked their way forward to greet her.

Her father held out his arm. "Well, my little flower. Shall we dazzle them with our excellent dancing?" Walking out to the floor as the music cued for their first dance, he winked at her.

With a spark of challenge, she said, "Dazzle them, Father? They shall all be made blind, I am sure of it." The duke laughed his great belly laugh, and several people turned in curiosity. The nearest matrons shared indulgent smiles and then whispered together with hands on their hearts and their fans fluttering.

Amanda began the steps with a teasing glint in her eye. She loved the freedom of movement across the floor. She could express so much with her body—with a simple gesture, with the manner in which she held her head or her hands.

She and her father shared this love of dancing, and the pair of them drew many eyes from the crowd at the end of their set.

When they finished he approached the duchess next, bowing over her hand with a schoolboy excitement. Amanda smiled fondly at them. She hoped—no, she *longed*, for the kind of love they shared. *Could it be found with someone here, even in this room?*

Lord Needley's hand, reaching for her own, interrupted her thoughts. "I do believe this set is ours, my lady." His warm, kind smile, full of brilliant white teeth, made her grin. He seemed to be left speechless for a moment as he stared in wonder at her face. She blushed and looked at her shoes. *Must he stare at me so?*

"I apologize, my lady. I quite forgot what I was about. Shall we dance?"

Amanda, relieved, returned her eyes to his.

Lord Needley, although a good dancer, could not compare to her father; she wondered if Papa would be glad to know the other gentlemen in the room would be found wanting.

She enjoyed her time with this new handsome earl very much. Their fathers shared a close camaraderie at Oxford and had maintained close contact, although their estates were not in easy travelling distance of each other. That thought troubled her for a moment. And then she stopped herself. *Must I analyze every partner as a future husband? Can I not simply enjoy the dance?* She determined to do so. To the earl she said, "What a wonderful night this is turning out to be. I am afraid I am quite overwhelmed by it all, really."

"Yes, it is easy to see how one could be completely overwhelmed, especially gazing into eyes such as yours."

She willed her face to maintain a neutral expression. "Oh, Lord Needley, I hope many women have heard those kind words from you. There are so many beautiful faces. I dare say, a room full of them."

When she had circled around through the other dancers in their line and they came back together in the dance, he replied, "And I have eyes only for one."

She searched his face. He seemed sincere. "Then, I thank you." She dipped her head in acknowledgement and wondered at his intensity. *Have I not just met the man?*

She was not unaffected by him, for certain, but if he kept on in this fashion, he might squelch anything she *could* feel in return.

Women from all directions looked with envy at the pair of them. And why wouldn't they? He was a kind and handsome earl. She imagined he sat at the top of more than a few debutantes' lists of hopefuls. As her gaze continued to wander around the room, the intense stare of another captured her attention. She swallowed, her mouth suddenly dry, and hid a smile of excitement. But she could do nothing about the added pink to her cheeks. Lord Needley's lip curled into a small smile and he held her a bit closer, his hands lingering a bit longer as they moved past each other through the dance. She hardly noticed, her eyes seeking out and catching the new face again.

She had not forgotten Lord Nathaniel this past year, or his lingering kiss on her hand. Her hands trembled in anticipation. She dared another look in his direction. His eyes still followed her. And now he stood just off the dance floor, in obvious declaration of his intent to approach as soon as she was free.

Lord Needley followed her distracted gaze to see the cause. Concern flickered across his face. "Are you acquainted with the infamous Lord Nathaniel?" he asked.

"Infamous? For what is he infamous?" she wondered aloud, full of curiosity.

At this question, Lord Needley fumbled about a bit and seemed to look for an appropriate way to respond. "He . . . well, that is to say . . . he is a bit of a rake, that is all."

She blushed deeper. "Oh, I see."

The dance came to an end, and Lord Needley held his arm out for her to take as he moved to escort her to the top of the line for their next set.

Lord Nathaniel intercepted them before they had walked more than a few paces. "Lord Needley, how are you, fine man? Captured the loveliest girl in the room I see. I am enchanted." He bowed in Lord Needley's direction but looked only at Amanda. He was more handsome than she remembered, his hair more tousled, his eyes a deeper blue, his shoulders broader.

Lord Needley interrupted her thoughts. "Yes, I was fortunate enough to secure her hand for this next set as well. If you'll excuse us, it is soon to begin."

Nathaniel put his hand on Lord Needley's shoulder, stalling his intended escape. "Well now, a slight detour will not distress anyone unduly. Lady Amanda." She raised her eyebrows in surprise at his bold tone. "Might I say, you look ravishing. Quite took my breath away. You are not sixteen any longer."

Lord Needley stiffened next to her. But Lord Nathaniel took her hand and gallantly bowed over it, gently bringing it to his lips in the process. The familiar tingle remained after he stood and released her hand, a mischievous glint in his eyes. He quirked an eyebrow, waiting for her to say something.

She cleared her throat. Feeling her temperature rise, she wished for her fan. "It is good to see you again, my lord." She dipped a low curtsy, slowly rising, looking up at him through her fluttering lashes. Would he remember? His laugh carried to the couples nearby at this repeat performance. Then he nodded once more at her and turned to walk away in the opposite direction.

Amanda's mouth opened, watching him swagger off and greet friends on the other side of the room. "How abrupt of him," she gasped before she could stop herself. Lord Needley gently restored her hand to his arm and led her back onto the floor to join the line of dancers.

Before they began, he said, "Thank you for our dances. I don't know that I have enjoyed one quite so much as I did ours. Would you do me the honor of allowing me to call on you this week?" She was not yet fully paying attention but awoke from her stupor when she noticed that Lord Needley was looking down at her expectantly, awaiting a response.

"Oh yes! Yes of course, Lord Needley. I would be honored to receive you." She liked this young earl. He was a good sort of man, she could tell. Kindness lit his eyes. Hopefully she could summon within herself something more than friendship for him, something that left her skin tingling as a certain other young gentleman just had.

After their second set, they arrived to stand with her parents. Lord Needley chatted with them all for a moment, and then he and the duke excused themselves to talk to a group of men a few feet over.

Her mother smiled warmly at her and Amanda felt a bit of the sun enter the room. Her mother's words were a balm. "Amanda darling, you look simply stunning. Your face just glows. Are you as happy as you seem?" The duchess's face also glowed with happiness.

"Oh, yes, Mama, everything is absolutely lovely. Was it this wonderful for you when you had your Season?" She knew her mother had met her father at a ball similar to this one.

Her mother's hesitant tone surprised her. "Mostly, yes. I was immediately drawn to your father. He had such a presence, quite dominated the room—just like now, I suppose." She smiled fondly at him and he, feeling her gaze, grinned in return. Her mother continued. "All the women in the room were drawn to him, it seemed."

Amanda inserted, "But he was drawn to only you. He's told me so a thousand times."

Her mother nodded. "And it was true. He danced two sets with me and then, as propriety wouldn't allow more, he glowered at all my other partners who came for their sets for the rest of the evening. Men were quite intimidated by him, but I didn't mind."

Amanda loved this story.

"It couldn't have been any more wonderful, up until . . ."

Her mother's face drained of color as she stared toward the entrance to the ballroom. There stood a man with a long scar on the side of his face. His gaze so fixed on her mother, Amanda wondered if he blinked.

Then her mother finished her sentence. "Until *he* showed up." She turned immediately toward her husband, but the duke faced the other direction now. This strange new man made his way slowly, the crowd parting curiously around him as he moved like a snake in their direction.

"Who is that, Mother? He makes me nervous." Amanda's heart pounded and she gripped her mother's hand in her own.

He stopped in front of them and bowed. "Marian."

Amanda looked in surprise at her mother. Who was this eerie man who dared call her mother by her first name? She searched for her father. He had noticed them and was quickly making his way in their direction, a look of steel in his eyes.

Her mother said, "Mr. Bender."

Amanda gasped. *Bender.*

The duchess glanced at her daughter and continued. "What are you doing here? You know His Grace . . ."

The duke arrived at their side. "Bender. What is the meaning of this?" With a lift of his finger, two footmen appeared. One stood at each side and placed their hands on Bender's arms, ready to escort him out. With slight pressure, they started moving toward the door. It was obvious to Amanda that they were hoping to leave the room without creating a scene and marring an otherwise lovely evening.

But it seemed Bender would have none of that. "Unhand me this minute!" he shouted.

The conversation in the ballroom stopped.

"What's the matter, *William?*" Jack sneered. "Afraid I might sully your brother's home? Embarrass you in front of your guests?"

The Duke of Cumberland waved his hands, and the footmen more forcibly grabbed Bender's arms and began to drag him out. Two more footmen rushed to aid, and the four of them dragged a kicking Mr. Bender toward the door;

the man shouted all the way, "You know, you don't control everything! A duke is not God. People are growing tired of your airs and nobility. Tired of the lot of you!" He strained his neck, indicating everyone in the room. He cackled a screechy laugh, setting all the hairs on Amanda's arms on end.

Bender deepened his voice. "If you can't learn to share, we will take it *all* from you." The footmen moved more quickly toward the back part of the house, where, Amanda was certain, he would be contained until a Bow Street Runner could be summoned.

However, just as they turned toward a hallway out of sight, chaos ensued. A huge crowd of rough-looking, tattered, and boisterous men poured in through the ballroom entrance. They knocked servants to the ground and pushed their way in, in one large mass. Threadbare, unclean clothes and disheveled hair stormed the room all around Amanda. Women screamed and fell, swooning, to the floor. Gentlemen moved to catch them and waved fans in their faces. Window glass shattered and flew across the floor as a linen-wrapped package slid to a stop at Amanda's feet. Similar packages broke more windows and crashed all around them.

Amanda read the message: *Freedom for all or none.* Her heart beat wildly in her chest. Her mother, who had been watching Bender, wrapped her arms around Amanda as Lord Needley showed up at their side.

Her father said, "Oh good, Needley, please take Lady Amanda and the duchess into Lord Hamilton's study, now!"

"Papa! Where are you going?" Amanda cried.

"I'm going to make sure the rat doesn't escape this time."

Her father took off at a run in the direction of the straining group of men. Others continued to burst into her aunt and uncles' home. Soon their guests would be completely overtaken by the mob. She caught a glimpse of the duke just outside the ballroom, pulling Bender by the back of his collar and yanking him down, the footmen trailing and securing Bender's arms.

The burning smell of sulfur overpowered the lovely floral scent. Added to that were the odors of whiskey and human sweat and waste coming from the invaders; Amanda felt the urge to retch. She covered her mouth and nose with a handkerchief.

Lord Needley tugged gently on her arm and applied gentle pressure to her lower back with his other hand, leading her through the chaos toward the ballroom door.

London's worst, the awful dredges of the city's population, ripped at the draperies and knocked over the vases with the gorgeous flowers. They grabbed at women and tore their dresses, ripping jewelry from their necks, planting wet kisses on disgusted mouths. The intruders tipped tables and drank from the punch bowl.

Women in the room scattered and screamed. A short, pudgy man tried to steal cakes from the refreshment table while a lady from Her Grace's charity organization swung her reticule madly at his face and neck, shouting with each successful impact. Except for the brave woman's interference, very few stood in the way of these street ruffians at first. Most guests attempted to clear the room as quickly as possible, her mother, Amanda, and Lord Needley included.

"Going somewhere, swell?" A huge mass of a man completely blocked their retreat.

"As a matter of fact, yes. Now kindly get out of our way!" Lord Needley shoved the man aside.

Amanda eyed her friend with new respect, but the intruder was not deterred. He stepped back in front of them with anger in his eyes. Reeking of whiskey and vomit, he pulled back his fist, ready to let it fly into Lord Needley's face. Before he made impact, Lord Nathaniel surprised him from behind and swung a fire poker at the side of his head. The huge oaf fell forward and would have landed on the duchess had Amanda not pulled her in the opposite direction and started running.

"Lady Amanda! Wait!" Lord Needley called.

But Amanda was finished waiting. Seeing their way to the entrance door was barred by the crowd, she ran to get herself and her mother to safety. A tall vase crashed to the floor directly behind them, and two men fell at their feet, swinging fists and rolling on the ground. Amanda and her mother yelped in surprise and ran faster. Amanda dodged a man as he swung his fist in rapid succession into the faces of three others who surrounded him. Leading her mother, she worked their way through the ballroom to the other side and out onto the balcony overlooking the gardens.

"Where are we going?" her mother looked around in confusion. Then comprehension dawned. "No. Amanda, you cannot possibly think . . ."

Amanda's childhood adventures were finally paying off. "What other choice do we have, Mother?" Amanda hitched up her gown, sat on the stone railing and slipped one leg over to the other side, where she knew there was a trellis. She held a hand out to her mother. "Come, Mama, we have no time." The duchess looked around in all directions.

Amanda said, "No one is watching."

With a worried expression, her mother hoisted up her skirts as well and followed Amanda over the banister. They clung to the trellis as they both slowly climbed down to the grounds below.

Relief at having reached the ground without falling was quickly replaced by renewed fear when they realized their mistake. As they backed up against the stone wall of the house, sounds of the rough crowd and fighting filled the gardens in front of them. They cowered in the shadow of the balcony, peering out toward the grounds. Four unsavory men ran past, shouting words Amanda knew the definitions of but had never heard strung together.

"We must hide." Her mother clutched her hand, pulling her farther back under the balcony, but one of the men had seen them and stopped abruptly, pulling on another's arm. Soon all four had turned their attention to the women.

"Well, would ya look a' tha', Ernest. Would ya look a' tha'?"

Amanda froze with her mother. A dark, evil sensation rippled through her. The men hungrily searched their faces with crazed eyes, their gazes running up and down the lengths of them. One stepped closer, his hands opening and closing. His hair stuck to his scalp with grease, large lumps of white matting strands of hair together. Pockmarked and red, he leered at them, his mouth full of brown, chipped teeth.

"Leave us alone," Amanda's mother commanded, her imperious tone every bit the duchess.

The men only laughed. The one apparently called Ernest said, "You are in no position to be taking any tone with us, Your Mightiness. Now come a little closer so we can get a good look at you."

Amanda and her mother pressed their backs to the wall behind them, and Amanda trembled in fear. She looked around, desperate for an idea, anything that would get them away and safe.

"I said come closer." The man stepped forward and grabbed Amanda's arm, bruising her with his fingers, she was sure.

He yanked her closer, and the duchess called out, "Stop! Don't touch her." She ran at the man, pulling on his arm, trying to step between them.

Amanda struggled against his grip while she scratched and clawed him, kicking his shins; her mother pulled at his fingers, trying to pry them from her arm—all to no avail. He brought his hand up and knocked her mother on the side of the head, sending her toppling to the ground.

Horror filled Amanda, her lungs tightening. Desperately, she looked at her mother, willing her to move. Ernest laughed, his breath and drops of saliva spattering one side of Amanda's face. Nearly gagging from the rotten stink coming from his mouth, Amanda set her jaw and forced herself to look at her captor. "What is it you want? Reward? I am sure my father will pay handsomely for our return."

His free hand began stroking her other arm. Amanda stiffened and tried to pull away. "That's not the kind of reward I'm looking for, little miss. I'll be taking you home with me, I will." His hand moved to her waist, pulling her against him.

She turned away, his hot breath all but melting her hair. The dark tightness in her chest intensified. Amanda desperately tried to wiggle free, stomping on his feet, but her soft slippers did little to harm him through his big, solid worker's boots. What else could she do? Powerless, terror gripped her.

She screamed, loud and long. "Help us! Oh! Please help us!" She tried to push away from his loathsome body.

The other men laughed. One hitched his pants up and goaded, "Come on, Ernest, can't control that little slip?"

She pummeled him across the chest. She did not think; she struck out, clawing his face, hitting any part of his body or clothing she could reach.

But he stopped her with one hand sent across her face, nearly knocking her to the earth. "There will be no more of that, do you understand?" He clamped her mouth so tightly she could feel bruises beginning where his fingers pressed into her skin. She nodded. Madly, she searched their surroundings. Nothing. No one to see or to help ventured near.

Her breath coming faster, she tried to slow it. Squinting in the darkness, she sought her mother. The duchess lay absolutely still, but as Amanda's eyes focused, she saw that her mother's eyes were wide open, watching the balcony above. She subtly gestured upward with her head, and then she winked. A drop of hope lessoned the tension in Amanda's chest. She tried not to alert her captors, and the corner of her eye caught movement on the balcony.

Before she could move out of the way, a body hurtled down onto them from above. Knocked to the ground and dazed, she blinked two or three times before she picked herself up and ran to her mother's side. Carefully helping her mother rise, Amanda embraced her.

Her mother winced, holding her head with one hand, leaning on Amanda. She raised a hand to her mouth. "Oh."

Amanda turned in the direction of her mother's gaze.

Lord Nathaniel sat astride the belly of their captor and delivered a swift and strong blow to the side of his face, knocking him unconscious. Ernest sprawled on the ground near them. The others had deserted their friends.

Lord Nathaniel pulled an arm back, ready to hit him again.

She called to her rescuer, "Lord Nathaniel. LORD NATHANIEL!" She shook his shoulder. "Stop."

Lord Nathaniel stilled, looked down at the man below him, and lowered his arms. His head dropped. After several long breaths, he looked uncomfortably at her mother and then back at her. His gaze intense, he asked in a low voice, "Did he hurt you?"

Her heart went to her throat. She shook her head. "Not really."

Nathaniel's eyes burned a path to hers through the air. She felt the force of his fierce protection deep inside and it warmed her; a new feeling of wonder crept in. He held her gaze, searching, and then after a moment he nodded.

Rising to stand, he paused and flexed his fist, staring at the man at his feet. Amanda could almost see a wave of sorrow roll over him. But when turning back to face her, his mouth turned up in a sheepish smile. "So, do you think he's out?"

Amanda couldn't help the nervous giggle that escaped her mouth. "Yes, I think you got him."

Nathaniel tilted his head to the side. "His nose is straighter now. Perhaps I made an improvement?"

She shivered. "He had much room for improvement." Looking into Lord Nathaniel's eyes as he stepped closer, Amanda said, "We thank you. I don't know what we would have done . . ." Her mouth turned down and her face pinched in pain, tears threatening to fall, and she looked between her mother and Lord Nathaniel. "Why would anyone do this?"

The duchess moved forward, pulling Amanda into her arms. "I don't know, my sweet. I just don't know." She paused. "But you can be sure your father will not rest until he finds out."

The sound of broken glass gave them little warning of the man who crashed through the upstairs window and landed not six feet from where they were standing. Amanda shrieked as splinters of glass fell all around them and landed on her slippers.

Lord Nathaniel moved quickly, favoring his knuckles, and led the ladies away. "We must get you to safety." At that moment, loud whistles and the sound of dozens of boots on the stone floor filtered out through the open doorway on the balcony above. Nathaniel took a deep breath. "Sounds like the magistrate has arrived, finally." They hurried to the side of the London home and through a servant's entrance. Navigating the servants' hallways, they entered Uncle Ethan's study through a panel, just as the duke charged through the other door looking for them.

"Oh, thank heavens you are safe." He rushed to his ladies, pulling them both into his chest, his arms encircling them in a protective and grateful embrace.

Amanda enjoyed the pounding of his heart against her cheek and felt him shift as he spoke over her head in Lord Nathaniel's direction.

"What happened?"

But it was Amanda who answered from her protective cocoon inside her father's arms, her voice a bit muffled as she spoke into his chest. "We were down in the garden. I think they would have taken us away. And they hurt Mother!"

The duke pulled back a little in alarm to look his wife over. "Where? Are you all right, my dear?"

She rested a hand on his arm. "Just some bruises, I think. Although I would be happy to have Dr. Fielding examine us both."

The duke nodded. "He has already been summoned."

"I'm afraid he might be much needed tonight." Her eyes filled with sorrow and worry. The duke and duchess shared a long look.

Amanda's muffled voice again spoke from her father's embrace. "And then Lord Nathaniel jumped from the balcony!" The duke's eyebrows rose in surprise and Lord Nathaniel shrugged his shoulders. "He landed on the men and fought them—rendered them both unconscious. He saved us. I . . . I didn't know what to do or how to get away. They were so strong."

Feeling completely powerless in the hands of another had been one of the worst feelings of her life. Even thinking of it now, her breathing picked up again, and she started to feel dizzy. "I couldn't get away. Couldn't move, even." She squeezed her father around his middle and buried her head in his chest.

"My sweet Amanda. You are safe." He rubbed his palm up and down her back in a soothing rhythm. She felt his head turn. "Thank you, Lord Nathaniel."

"Maidens in distress and all that, you know . . ." Amanda peeked out. Nathaniel shrugged. "I cannot resist a good rescue."

A slight pinch pulled at her new-found peace. The moment between them had felt important.

"You are to be commended. If anything had happened to my dears, if they had been hurt . . ." The duke paused, clearing his throat. He continued with much emotion. "It just doesn't bear thinking of. You have my deepest gratitude."

Lord Nathaniel smiled and nodded in acceptance, a pleased light in his eyes. "Hopefully the magistrate and his watchmen will have taken care of everything by now."

"They are clearing out the place, hauling miscreants off to jail while footmen help our guests find their carriages. I must go and talk to one Hucklebee, if I'm not mistaken. Would you please stay with them, Lord Nathaniel?"

Amanda felt Nathaniel's gaze. She tilted her head again so she could meet his eyes.

"Of course," Nathaniel said.

The duke continued. "And I will send Dr. Fielding in to you directly to see to your hands." Nathaniel held his bloodied and cracked knuckles and raised his eyebrows.

The door banged open to reveal a flushed and agitated Lord Needley. Amanda jerked her head up. With great relief on his face, Lord Needley said, "I have spent the last half hour trying to reach you, my lady, Your Graces." He bowed to them. "I hope you are well?"

"Yes, they are well," the duke responded in their behalf. "Thanks be to God and Lord Nathaniel, here."

Still in her father's arms, Amanda looked up into his face. "Lord Needley helped us as well. We would have been dragged away from the house directly had it not been for him and Lord Nathaniel both."

The duke smiled. "Well then, more gratitude is in order. Would you both stay here with my ladies and stand outside the door when Dr. Fielding tends to them? I will take no risks."

Both men nodded. Lord Nathaniel answered, "Of course, Your Grace."

The duke looked with love at his family one more time before closing the door behind him.

Amanda and her mother sat together on a settee under the window. Lord Nathaniel found them a blanket from the trunk in the corner, and Lord Needley stoked the fire. Soon it was blazing cheerfully in the grate, and the group began to relax. Amanda rested her head on her mother's shoulder, their hands clasped together in the duchess's lap. They could still hear the sounds of police and footmen cleaning up and helping their guests be on their way.

Shouts and frenzied movement out on the street drew Amanda's attention, and she looked out the window. An authoritative-looking man—probably the magistrate—and his men pushed some of the intruders into a strange box-like carriage lined with bars. A group of the prisoners resisted, and she was unable to look away as the police clubbed any resistors to near unconsciousness.

Amanda gasped as she saw familiar chestnut curls and a strong jawline. *It can't be.* Charlie looked up, and their eyes met for a long moment. She brought her hands to her mouth in astonishment. He nodded as he pretended to tip a hat in her direction and then broke free, running off into the darkness. The night watchmen let him go, more concerned with the others who were still resisting.

Amanda turned toward her mother, who shook her head sadly. "I am sorry, my dear. We have both been greatly disappointed in our friends, it seems."

Amanda felt the eyes of Lord Needley and Lord Nathaniel watching her closely. Numbness settled. She could think of nothing to say. But her mind raced. Every reason she could conceive for Charlie to be out on the street flashed through her brain. *He could have been caught unawares. He was visiting some of her family's servants.* Not daring to face the most obvious, she rested her head again on her mother's shoulder and closed her eyes.

CHAPTER SIX

AMANDA FELT THE SUN ON her face before she opened her eyes. All the horror of her first ball rushed back in one heartless flood, and her first thoughts were of Molly, her maid. Amanda could not remember seeing her in the carriage ride home. She sat up quickly in her bed. "Molly!" And when Molly didn't answer, she called again more urgently, "Molly!"

Hurrying from Amanda's dressing room, the maid stood at the end of her bed with several garments in her hands. "What is it, my lady? Are you unwell?"

Relief filled Amanda. "Oh, Molly, thank you. I am so glad *you* are well. I wasn't sure what had become of you last night. I think I fell asleep in the study. The carriage ride is hazy. I barely remember it."

"That will be the laudanum they gave you, my lady."

Amanda frowned. "I detest the stuff. How odd, to not remember the happenings of one's own life. How is the rest of the staff? Thomas and Paul, and the other footmen who came with us?"

Molly came to sit at the edge of her bed and took Amanda's hand in her own. "We are all well, my lady, and don't you be worrying about us. It's you with the scrapes and the bruises and who knows what else."

"I feel perfectly well." She smiled at her friend and squeezed her hand in gratitude. "Surely there is talk downstairs. What are they saying?"

Her maid stared at her for a few moments, her eyes showing her reluctance.

Amanda pleaded. "I'm no more a child than you. I have to know what's going on. I was nearly abducted from my uncle's home twice in one evening."

Molly brought a hand to her face. "So it's true? How did you survive it? I would have fainted dead away, I'm sure." She ran a hand through Amanda's hair. "The whole staff is talking about it, they are. We don't know what we would've done had anything happened to you." Molly's voice caught, and she started to pull away, but Amanda pulled her back and into her arms.

"I'm so happy you and the others are well. Now, let's begin our day, shall we?" She pulled the blankets back and moved to sit at her dressing table. The feel of the brush gently tugging through her hair calmed her mind.

Molly asked, "Is it true you were rescued by not one, but two of the handsomest lords of the Season?"

Amanda's eyes widened and then she smiled as she remembered. "It is true, yes."

Molly clasped her hands together, nearly dropping the brush. "Are they as handsome as everyone says?"

Amanda laughed. How nice to talk of something diverting and feel the tension leave her neck. "They were. Tall, both of them, and very pleasing to gaze upon."

Molly said, "Hmm."

"*Hmm?* Why do you say, 'hmm'?"

"Pleasing to gaze upon? Surely Lord Nathaniel is more than simply pleasing to gaze upon. Why, I have heard he has caused many a young debutante to take to her room in fits of desperation, that one."

"Has he now? Well, you will see no fits of desperation from me, I can assure you."

Eyebrows raised, waiting, Molly said, "And?"

Amanda leaned back in her chair and turned toward her wonderful maid. "And nothing. He is distractingly handsome, but that is all I know about him. I will admit, I do have an irresistible curiosity to learn all there *is* to know about him, but for now, you have heard the whole of it."

Molly nodded with a satisfied smile. She moved to pour water into a basin and then laid out clothes for Amanda to wear. Amanda watched her for a minute, not wanting to change the lovely tone of the conversation, but questions weighed heavily. Questions she knew would fester and torment her all day. She turned in her chair. "Why attack my uncle's home? Can anyone make sense of why this happened?"

Molly thought for a minute and then replied, "Because your uncle's a noble, isn't he? Lots of folks just don't like nobility anymore. But I heard some talk downstairs, and I don't think it was anything personal against your uncle or you either for that matter. It seems this Bender person has been targeting many of the homes in the area. Although this is the largest attack anyone has seen."

Amanda said, "But he knew my parents."

"What?" Molly turned, shock showing on her face.

Amanda nodded. She and Molly shared a closeness over the last few years; Amanda trusted her. Molly knew when to keep things to herself, and she was a valuable resource of news from the servants.

"Well, that is something." Molly tapped her chin with her finger. "There's something else that's curious, too."

Amanda moved to the basin and splashed water on her face, gently rubbing it with her towel. "What's curious?"

Molly gestured for her to return to the chair. She separated sections of Amanda's thick auburn hair. Molly's face scrunched up as she thought. "I cannot make heads or tails of it myself. But some of the footmen swear that not all of the men from the street were fighting against us. James claims he saw many of them fighting amongst themselves."

"But half of them had too much to drink. Maybe once the fight started they became confused."

Molly shook her head. "We talked about that, and Thomas and Paul both swear they saw street folk in there, deliberately fighting against the intruders."

"You think some of them came to defend us?"

"That's the feeling from downstairs, miss. They all feel we never could've made it out of there unharmed if not for those that came to our aid."

Tears came immediately to Amanda's eyes and spilled down her cheeks. "How incredibly kind."

Molly smiled at her through the mirror and squeezed her shoulders in understanding. "Her Grace wishes to see you in her bedchamber when you're ready. She said to tell you she hopes you'll take breakfast with her."

A burst of hope brought a smile. Maybe she would get some answers to all of her many questions. "I was about to pay her a visit anyway. I feel we have much to discuss."

The duchess sat at her favorite chair by the window. She radiated beauty. Once, Amanda had heard the vicar talking about angels among them, helping, guiding, and serving; and she had immediately thought of her mother and the sweet watch-care she gave the Cumberland tenants. In that moment, with the sun shining through the stained glass, she had vowed to try to be as kind as the woman sitting next to her on their family pew.

When her mother noticed her in the doorway, she arose with hands outstretched. Amanda stepped into her embrace. "Oh, Mother, did that really happen yesterday?"

Her mother held her another moment and then sat her down in the chair opposite her next to the window. "England is changing, my dear." The duchess sighed and squeezed her hands. "Unspeakable, harsh things happen in London all the time; even now, as we speak, someone out there in London is suffering." Amanda felt the sorrow in her mother's tone. *Surely something could be done, could be fixed.*

"That reality, though depressing, has weighed upon us for years. But never has it crossed the threshold into my, or your uncle's, home as it did last night." Amanda waited. She absently fingered the exquisite fabric of her morning dress.

How do the common, working people in England live? she wondered for the first time in her life. She thought of their tenants. They seemed happy enough, clean and fed. They received regular baskets from the estate and gifts around yuletide. *If given a choice, would they want a different sort of life?*

Her mother squeezed her hands again. "Do not despair, my flower. Never forget that amidst all the awful circumstances that you may see, if you look, you will always find the good. Where suffering shows its persistent face, heroes always rise."

Amanda drew in a hopeful breath and nodded. "Even last night, people came to our aid: Lords Nathaniel and Needley, and others."

"Yes, you see?" Her mother continued. "Now, I asked you to come this morning so I could tell you a story. And I hope when I tell it, you will not think too harshly of me, but learn from my mistakes."

Amanda bit her lip and leaned forward in her chair.

"Oh, it's not as bad as all that. My mistakes were those of a young girl, nothing too serious, but I fear much harm has come from it.

"When I was a child, the son of our steward was permitted to roam the estate freely. Father doted on him, and the servants loved him. I remember Cook saved biscuits for him in a tin that he indulged in often. He was very much like a member of the family, the entire estate's family. Which is, I suppose, where the problem really started."

"What do you mean?" Amanda asked, thinking of one Christmas when Charlie opened presents with her. She had been but five years old at the time. He had never done so again, but at the time she had thought it one of the best Christmases in her young life because they had played with all the toys together.

Her mother sighed. "The familiarity became his downfall. He grew to expect what was not rightfully his; this measure of entitlement tainted his expectations and created a dissatisfaction with his life and station. It also complicated our relationship."

Amanda looked up in surprise. "You had a relationship?"

Her mother smiled sadly, her expression hesitant and regretful. "We were dear friends, he and I. We spent many hours playing outside together as children often do. But as we grew, our feelings naturally matured. I was irresponsible, I admit, in my actions toward him. I knew that he and I did not have a future, and I enjoyed what I thought was a harmless flirtation with a good friend. What I didn't know, what I couldn't possibly realize at my young age, was that he was developing much more than a harmless crush on the daughter of a duke. He had begun to make plans for our eventual life together."

"Oh no." Amanda raised her hands to her face. "What did you do?" A certain amount of gratitude filled her that she and Charlie had never progressed to this point.

"Father sent him to Eton with the boys, hoping to give Jack Bender the education he needed to one day be a barrister or clergyman. It was a wonderful gesture and a blessed opportunity for the son of a steward. But he had a difficult time at Eton. He never felt accepted by the boys, which is to be understood. Instead of seeking out those from his station, of which there were a few, he trailed behind sons of dukes and marquesses and other lords, hoping to be accepted as one of them."

"Jack Bender." The connection clicked in Amanda's mind. "The man we saw last night was the steward's son?"

Her mother nodded. "I remember one holiday they were all home. Your Uncle Andrew and his friends, including your father and Uncle Ethan, were spending a week of the holiday together at our estate; and of course Mr. Bender arrived home as well to visit his family.

"One afternoon, I was practicing my pianoforte, preparing for an upcoming concert. When I finished playing, I heard clapping behind me. Mr. Bender had always listened to me play as children, but I felt a new discomfort being alone in our front parlor with him.

"He approached me, and I stood up from my bench. I remember the conversation clearly. He said he had something he would ask of me, and I felt all the more uncomfortable for his saying so and for seeing the doors were closed.

"He said that he had been setting aside money and furthering his education in hopes that in two years' time he could be employed as a barrister in London.

"He seemed so flustered, I was getting more worried each moment we were together; he looked different, agitated. His eyes were almost wild. As I've reviewed our conversation in my mind over the years, I wonder if those were not the first signs of the mental distress that he would show later. I took pity on him even in my discomfort and smiled."

Amanda began absently playing with the ball of ribbons on her mother's table.

"I suppose that smile gave him the courage he needed, because to my utter shock and dismay he went down on one knee and began a proposal of marriage right there in the parlor. And in the middle of his asking, my brother and his friends walked in; they saw it all."

"No!" Amanda listened with rapt attention to all her mother was saying.

The duchess nodded sadly. "It only gets worse from there, I am afraid. At first the boys stood silent in shock at what they were witnessing and then, as one, they all burst into laughter.

"Mr. Bender looked up at them and then at me. He must've noticed my embarrassment, because he ran from the room. They teased him that holiday at home, and I suspect through all the rest of their years of education together."

"Did he ever return and ask an answer of you?"

Her mother shook her head. "He was called into your grandfather's office. They remained locked in there a long time with Mr. Bender's father. When they finished, he walked out the front door without even looking at me or anyone else.

"I never really saw him again after that. And Father would never tell me what they discussed behind that closed door."

"That is so sad for poor Mr. Bender."

Her mother nodded. "I'm not proud of the way I treated him or the way I handled that situation years ago. I look back now and realize I was but seventeen and lacked experience, but I am afraid I may feel regret all my days." She sighed and studied her hands. "I did not consider that a flirtation when we were young would have such consequences even now, many years later. I fear I broke his heart and with it, his courage and desire for success."

"What do you mean?" Amanda asked.

"Well, he did finish his education, but he never went on to any form of employment that we heard of. He stopped coming home to see his father, probably in an effort to avoid me."

"Surely it is not all your fault, Mother. My uncles and their teasing friends were more a problem than you were."

"That is most likely true, but I do bear a large part of the blame. We must be very careful with the hearts of others. We do not always return the ardor, that is true, but we must guard the portion of their heart that is ours and try to return it whole."

"So what's become of him for all these years? Why was Jack Bender at Uncle Ethan's house last night?"

Her mother paused before answering. "I am not sure, Amanda dear, but your father seems to think he is behind much of the trouble going on in London these days."

"Could he really be bitter and angry after all this time?" Amanda could not believe it.

"I do not know what fuels the anger now, but I do believe its beginnings were kindled under my own roof, and that my brothers and I might have prevented it."

CHAPTER SEVEN

Jack Bender thoughtfully chewed on the end of his unlit cigar. He should be reveling in his escape, should be glorying in the damage done to *Ethan's* home. Instead he was reliving one of his worst memories. Peace would never be his until *William* suffered.

It felt like only a few short months ago Jack stood in the dormitory hallway at Eton; he had happened upon a room where a group of boys all sat together in a room laughing uproariously. He had wanted to slink away, unseen and unheard, but they stopped him before he could turn back and hide around a corner.

"Jack, come in here, my friend," Andrew, Marian's older brother, had called to him.

With dread, he had inched into the room and looked at each of the boys present. "What do you want, Andrew?"

"Oh come now, don't be so angry all the time. If you are to be family . . ." They had all burst out laughing. "If we are to be brothers . . ." The laughter had increased, the boys clutching their sides.

"Did you really think she'd say yes?" one of the boys had asked. Robert, *Earl of Lambton* he was called now.

Seamus, the most pompous one of the lot, had made the comment Jack would never forget. "What on earth made you think you had any right to kneel before the daughter of a duke and petition her hand? What do you have to offer her? You"—Seamus had sneered—"The son of a steward." They had laughed even harder, their voices echoing down the hall and drawing a crowd from other rooms.

The more people who pushed into their small apartment, the more nervous and agitated Jack had become. His face had begun to twitch. He'd felt his eye blink uncontrollably. *No!* Flashbacks of his mother's face twitching through the carriage window, on the road to bedlam, her body wrapped and tied to itself, had blinded him. His eyes had darted all around, seeking an escape. A crush of boys had blocked the door behind him. He'd tried to push through them and leave the room. But they'd pushed him back inside, laughing. Fireworks had gone off behind his eyes. The window had beckoned to him as an open door, freedom. *If I could just get out that window . . .*

"What's the matter, Bender? You look a little flushed; embarrassed, are you?" Robert had nudged him.

Seamus had added, "Not as embarrassed as Marian would be if she were married to you. She can have any man in all of England to wed, you fool."

Jack had shoved his way through the crowd toward the only other exit available. He had picked up speed and dived through the window, breaking the glass and thundering to the ground two stories below.

His arm had felt the brunt of the impact. He had lain on the cobblestones, stunned, for several seconds; then hearing students begin to gather, he had risen dizzily, tottered to the right and left and tried to run, cradling his arm as he went.

After stumbling along, tilting to one side for several minutes, a large man holding a club had stopped him. "Jack Bender, is it? I'll need you to come with me. Destruction of school property is not a minor offense." Jack had swayed and fallen into a blessed blackness.

The memory of that night haunted him still. Jack put down his unlit cigar and ran his fingers along the scar on his face: the only lasting physical evidence. Jack's morose thoughts were interrupted as Charles Lemming sauntered into the room.

Jack steeled himself, hiding any hint of vulnerability. He wasn't sure what to think of this young man so closely tied to the duke's household and yet seemingly loyal to the cause of freedom. Perhaps Lemming would benefit from a history lesson. Jack narrowed his eyes. He let Lemming remain standing and said, "I spent ten years in prison, you know."

The man, too young, raised his eyebrows in surprise.

Jack nodded. "I was forced out an upper-story window—crashed to the ground, narrowly avoiding death. And do you know what they did?" Lemming shook his head. "They threw me in jail for destroying a window."

Lemming frowned. "Let me guess, the window in a noble's room."

Jack laughed bitterly. "Not just any nobility—a future duke, earl, and marquess."

He closed his eyes and leaned his head back. Long ago, before prison, he would have used peaceful and political means to make change. He could have become a barrister. Even after the window incident, he had planned to make something respectable of himself. But the boys had testified of his violent behavior, which had increased his sentence. Ten years to ponder his hatred had fueled a pulsing venom within him that nothing could quench except for the absolute misery of the Cumberland family. Even that seemed insufficient. *Every noble.* The thought made him smile. He now ran the largest crime ring in London, using his vast resources to bring terror and unrest.

But Lemming didn't know that. He thought Jack wanted freedom for the poor families of the working class. *Those helpless whelps.* He cared nothing for them. A man who could not help himself was a worthless man indeed. Jack walked a careful line with Lemming and all of the idealistic fops in his gang. Many of his followers fought solely for the causes of freedom: for landownership, for a new system in England in which everyone had an equal chance. The ones he did not control with blackmail, he moved with passion. A nobler bunch Jack had rarely seen.

Lemming definitely fell in with the altruistic set. Lifting Jack away from his memories and back to the conversation, Lemming said, "Naturally they pushed their suit against you. Sorry lot of spoiled soft hands with nothing better to do."

He stepped farther into the room and rested his hand on the back of a chair. Jack flipped two fingers open toward the chair and nodded his head. Lemming sat down, and Jack changed the subject. "Our team made some serious mistakes this time."

Lemming looked directly into Jack's eyes and comfortably answered, "Almost everything went as smoothly as we planned. Everybody was in position. The timing was perfect."

"And yet, Amanda remains at home safe in her bed! The purpose of the night has not been met."

Alarm and confusion crossed the whelp's face. "You meant to harm Lady Amanda?"

Jack considered him for a moment and answered slowly, "I asked you to come today because I feel you are ready to be taken into my confidence. You have proven yourself dedicated to the cause and completely loyal."

Lemming leaned forward in his seat as Jack continued. "We had hoped by the end of the evening to have Lady Amanda in an old cellar under guard."

Lemming's face went white but maintained a neutral expression. He said, "I was not aware that this was the goal of the evening. Perhaps if you had told me . . ."

"Others were tasked with that responsibility. Unfortunately, they failed."

Obviously treading cautiously, Lemming cleared his throat. "May I ask, sir, what did you hope to gain by abducting the daughter of the most powerful duke in England?"

"That's just it, isn't it? The most powerful duke in England would have a lot of influence to support our cause, wouldn't he?" Jack's smile curled slowly.

"The duke wouldn't rest until he found her, sir, and punishment would be the most severe . . . Lady Amanda and the Duchess Marian mean everything to him, and they love him—"

Jack's fuse suddenly became short. He slammed his fist onto the table and shouted, "I mean to make him suffer as I have!"

∙

Charlie swallowed and stared at the man in front of him for a few long moments, and then Jack Bender continued in his eerie mock-calm voice. "And then, after leaving him to agonize over his lost child for a time, I would've written a letter explaining our mission and petitioning his help. Surely a duke on our side would be a major victory for freedom and equality in London, would it not?"

Charlie stared at the man and wondered at his sanity. *What duke would ever support the cause of anyone who had abducted his daughter?* "What went wrong?" he said aloud.

Bender grunted and sifted through the papers on his desk. "That's not your concern. What I need you to do is to keep a close eye on the duke's household."

Dread filled him. "I am not entirely sure I am the right person for this assignment. They know me too well. I would need a viable reason to give them for my presence in London so close to their town house."

Bender studied him for a moment. Charlie hoped his face didn't show his concern. Bender finally replied, "I have arranged a position of employment for you nearby in the home of one Lord Nathaniel. His father is Duke of Somerset."

"Yes, I know him. He wouldn't remember, but we have crossed paths before."

This assignment was getting worse and worse. To be employed in the service of that rake and to be so close to Amanda was almost more than he could stomach. It would be a sore trial indeed. And yet for the cause of freedom, he knew he needed to maintain a close relationship with Bender. Charlie nodded. "When do I start?"

"They are expecting you two days from now. Report to the servants' quarters and speak with the housekeeper there. She will direct you further. If it's any consolation, Lord Nathaniel is reported to treat his servants very fairly." Bender smirked.

Charlie grunted and rose from his chair, ready to leave the room. Acting as though it was an afterthought, he turned and asked, "Who is the next target?"

Bender shook his head and waved him out of the office.

With a deep sense of foreboding, Charlie made his way back through London toward his small lodgings. At least he would now have a better source of income and a more comfortable place to sleep, excellent food to eat, and likely good company.

⌒

Early in the morning, hoping to avoid the crush of all her neighbors prancing about, Lady Amanda sought the peace of a park near her home.

A familiar figure, eyes on the pavement startled her.

"Charlie? Charlie, is that you?"

He turned and stopped, seemingly speechless for a moment. Clearing his throat, he said, "Lady Amanda." He bowed to her as she arrived in front of him. Molly followed her at a distance, and Amanda knew she was curious. Charlie's face flushed, and she wondered if he too was thinking of the rose and note he had left her. "Lady Amanda, I . . . How are you this morning? Out early as usual, I see."

"A good walk helps me think." She smiled, her gaze flickering to his face. She said, "It always has."

"I remember."

Amanda wrinkled her forehead, sighing inside. "The rose was beautiful, and I thank you. But it was risky and wholly inappropriate, and you could've gotten yourself and others in a lot of trouble." She had never been comfortable putting other people at risk.

"I know it was unwise," he said. "But I couldn't let you leave without doing so, knowing I won't be there when you return."

"Not return? What do you mean?"

"I have come to London in search of work here. I am saving, and as soon as I am able, I will study to become a barrister."

Amanda felt sparks of admiration and pride for her dear friend.

She thought he stood a little taller as he said what he'd told her many times before, "England is changing. It might be a different place for us someday." His voice seemed to bubble with hope.

But she weighed her words carefully before she spoke next, and noticing her pause, Charlie stiffened. He seemed to brace himself.

"This change you speak of . . . I don't know if there's a change big enough to merit any kind of hope that you—that we—could ever make anything work.

What change could be so grand? You have never explained it to me. Though I have asked countless times."

"I am not at liberty to give details . . . but our social system, our habit of nobility, our rule of government are all under attack."

"Attack? Surely you don't mean Jack Bender and his attack on my uncle's home? Is that why you were there?" She stepped back in alarm, swaying a bit.

Charlie reached his hand out to steady her. "No! Lady Amanda, no. That is not the method of change—I am talking about votes, landownership—*civilized* ways to make a difference right now. What if Father and Molly and I could choose elected representatives? We could vote for laws that served us as well as them, or I mean you—the nobility. England could become a free nation. Much like what they've started over in the Americas."

"The Americas?"

"Anyone can own land there. They all vote to determine their form of government and leaders."

"That sounds wonderful." She knew nothing about America's form of government or this freedom that Charlie described to her now. But she had to admit broadening freedoms appealed to a part of her soul, a part she had forgotten more than eight months ago. As she thought of the ramifications of such a government for the poor people in England, her heart rose in hope by degrees, and her mind was taken back to her days of pretending to be a sparrow at the top of a mountain. Did a part of her long for that freedom still?

Charlie searched her face, understanding her expression and the emotions that flitted through her eyes all too easily, she feared. A sigh left her lips as the wisps of freedom vanished from her thoughts. "Freedom is a precious and elusive blessing. Even now, how many in England are truly free? The nobility of which you speak—the power that you seem to feel they hold—how much of it is available to me?" Amanda thought of upcoming marriage vows. Her future husband would be given her dowry and then assign her an allowance in return. "Others in England lack freedom besides your poor or working classes."

She hesitated, reluctant to deliver what would surely be a blow to his heart. "I need you to understand something." She paused, looking intently into his eyes. "We were close, growing up." His face clouded a bit. "You were a true friend to me, Charlie, and I will never forget all of our time together and all that you did for me as a young girl. But you must know, in our separation over the course of the last year, I have changed. My mind has been opened to a larger world than the beautiful acreage of my ancestral home." She smiled at him and reached for his hand. "There's so much more I wish to know and do and understand! I feel I can make a difference in this world. I can help others. I will have tenants and servants and others in my care. I have my work in the children's home and with the parsonage. And I hope to travel someday and continue my education."

He took a step back from her. "And those are things I cannot provide you."

She watched his face closely, shook her head, and said, "It is not only that. My feelings have also changed. I feel the warmest *friendship* . . . but nothing more." She hated to say it.

Hurt moved across his eyes in a great wave. His conflicted expression would be a source of pain to her for many years to come, she knew it. But even though he still caused her stomach to leap, she could not allow herself to explore minor fluttering with so much at stake.

Clearing his throat, he shifted from foot to foot and looked into her eyes. His mouth pulled down on one side. "I see." And then his brow seemed to clear a bit. "I understand. Please know you always have a friend in me. And if you do ever think of a way I can help you or if you find yourself truly in need, in danger even . . ."

"Danger?" She remembered her earlier question and narrowed her eyes.

He must have noticed her change of expression immediately. "You are wondering what I was doing at your uncle's home. You saw me from the window the other night."

"Please tell me you are not with the group who attacked Uncle Ethan's house. I've been arguing within myself day and night, grasping for a reason that you would've been there that did not involve attacking his home." She looked imploringly up at him, feeling certain betrayal would break her heart.

Charlie stepped closer to her, held both her hands in his own, looked deeply into her eyes, and said, "I know it looked—I know it seemed just the opposite, but I promise to you, I did not attack your uncle's home that night."

"But Charles—"

He shook his head. "There is much going on you do not understand, and I cannot explain it to you. Please, trust me. You and your house have nothing to fear from me, and I will see that no harm comes to you. I swear it." He stepped closer to her, their faces inches apart.

Amanda's head spun. He would give her no explanation. But how could she not trust Charlie? The intensity she saw in his eyes spoke of truth.

Molly cleared her throat.

Charlie stepped back. "I must go. Farewell, Lady Amanda." Then he turned on his heel and walked quickly in the other direction.

Molly approached her, and they both watched the back of his tailcoat until he rounded a bend.

"Did you hear our conversation?"

"That I did, my lady. And I was right proud of you, I was."

She smiled at Molly. "Do you believe him?"

She took a deep breath. "I don't know." Molly looked at her mistress. "Do you?"

"Yes, I believe I do."

CHAPTER EIGHT

WHEN AMANDA ARRIVED BACK AT her town house, Mr. Parsons, their butler, met her at the door. He smiled warmly, unable to maintain the typical butler persona with her. From the day he caught her sneaking up the stairs with some of Cook's pilfered biscuits, they had been a bit chummy. She had winked at him, held a finger to her lips, and shared one.

"You've had callers already this morning, my lady."

"Callers? At this hour?"

Parsons nodded. "They are in the drawing room waiting for you. One Lord Nathaniel and one Lord Needley."

Amanda paused, hands frozen on their way to handing over her bonnet and wrap. She quickly rallied and turned to the right, down the hallway to discover why two very eligible lords were present in her home this morning at the same time. Surely they were calling to ask after her health, but so early? She could not account for it, and she hastened her pace to reach them. Both men rose when she entered, inquiring and anxious looks on their faces.

Lord Needley rushed to her side and asked, "Are you quite recovered, Lady Amanda?" She smiled and curtsied, noticing Lord Nathaniel standing farther back in the room. His eyebrow quirked, his expression showing disdain for Lord Needley's immediate hovering.

Irritated with Lord Nathaniel, she sweetened her smile to Lord Needley as she responded, "Thank you. I admit to feeling shaken, naturally, but I awoke refreshed this morning with a great many of my own new thoughts keeping me company."

He placed her hand on his arm as they entered the room. "I am sure your father will make quite certain that nothing further disturbs your safety."

"Oh, you are so right," she responded quickly. "But I find I have very little concern for myself. My thoughts are centered more on other things."

"Oh? And where are your thoughts directed?" Lord Needley waited expectantly.

She frowned slightly. "I am most concerned with *why*. Are people's lives so terrible that they feel they must strike out in such a manner?"

A new interest lit Lord Nathaniel's face. He took several steps forward, reached for her free hand, and bowed over it. "You look lovely this morning. Refreshed, just as you said. I find your statement curious. Shall we sit, and might I hear more?"

Amanda's interest piqued at his sudden sincerity. Gone was the bored and lazy expression previously present. His attentive look of intelligence intrigued and attracted her.

"Yes, please, won't you sit down?" She rang for tea, and the three of them turned to sit. She chose a low settee with room for only two. Lord Needley hurried to her side, sitting as close as was acceptable. Lord Nathaniel chose a seat opposite her, which allowed her a good view of his face.

He leaned forward, arms resting on his thighs, and asked, "Now, if you wouldn't mind humoring me with a bit of droll conversation, I am most interested in your thoughts. Do you feel that somehow the intruders in your home are responding justly to something wrong with their circumstances?"

"Surely not!" Lord Needley said.

Lord Nathaniel's gaze did not leave her face.

Refusing to be unnerved, she allowed herself a moment before she said, "Not exactly, no. Nothing justifies such violence and destruction of another's home, of course. But I do feel that, were they not hurting in some way, they would have no reason to lash out as they did."

Lord Nathaniel seemed to appraise her. Admiration, and what looked like agreement, shone in his eyes.

She smiled in the glow of feeling understood, heady with the confidence in feeling heard and being taken seriously.

He leaned back in his chair, gave a short laugh, and smiled with an air of condescension. "Very pretty thoughts, my dear. We shall call it, 'An Ode to the Poor Commoners and Their Plights.' I daresay a basket to the orphanage or some such gesture will do the trick."

Her warm ember doused immediately.

Amanda's eyes narrowed, and she was mortified to feel her throat tighten up and tears threaten to fall. Lord Nathaniel quickly looked away, his face coloring slightly. Did he notice her discomfort? She would not give him any further satisfaction.

She turned her entire attention back to Lord Needley. Giving him her most brilliant smile she asked, "And how are you faring? I don't think I can tell you enough how much it means to us that you would bring us safely from harm last night. To think I could be in such harm's way in my own uncle's home. Why, if it weren't for you, I might this very minute still be in the greatest peril. What can we ever do to thank you?"

Lord Needley's handsome features brightened under such praise. He straightened his shoulders, smiled down into her eyes, and said, "It was my pleasure, one I hope you never need again but will happily perform at any time."

Lord Nathaniel coughed.

Amanda ignored him.

At that moment, Duchess Cumberland entered the room. The men stood and bowed to her. She nodded to them. "Gentlemen, might we deprive you of my daughter's company for a moment?" She reached her hand out. "Amanda, my dear. Your father would like you to join him in his study, if you don't mind."

They hadn't yet spoken today. She was anxious to see him and hear his thoughts about their evening. She rose, curtsied to the room, and left quickly in search of the duke.

She had seen her father so infrequently these last few weeks. The Season, as exciting as it was, left precious little time for her favorite hobby—curling up with a book next to him in his study. She smiled again at Parsons when she passed him and turned down the hallway to knock at the door.

"Enter," he called from inside.

She stepped into his warm and cheery study, admiring the full bookshelves, the maps tacked up to the wall, the fireplace and mantel along one side of the room, and the plush carpet rug.

Her father stepped around from behind his desk and came toward her with open arms, smiling broadly. "Amanda, my dear. How are you faring?"

She stepped into his embrace, face pressed to his chest, and allowed herself a moment to be a young girl again. "I am well," she answered. "It was quite a coming-out ball, was it not?"

The duke's mouth turned in what could have been a smile but looked more like a grimace. He rubbed a hand over his face before looking down at her again. "Sit with me, my Amanda." He led her to her favorite couch by the fireplace, keeping her hand in his. "London is changing. We will continue forward as best we can, but the whole idea of a Season is not what it once was. Our friends are afraid. Many are already on their way out to their country estates. They feel the threat on their families is too great to remain."

Amanda considered this information. "I have heard that there have been other attacks on families, on children."

The duke eyed her knowingly. "I should not be surprised you know such things." He paused, looking out the window in thought. "Yes, Amanda, others have been threatened, many others, and not just here in London. It seems no place is safe. Remember the rock in your window?" Amanda nodded, hoping her father would keep talking. "We believe it is all from the same gang, the same man."

"Jack Bender," Amanda said.

Her father nodded. "Your mother told me you know a bit of his history."

Amanda squeezed her father's hands. His face lowered, studying the floor, and he looked years older than even the previous evening when last she had seen him. She hoped to reassure him. "I am not afraid, Father."

His head snapped up. "And that is what scares me most. Your headstrong ways and independent spirit could bring you more danger than you understand."

Amanda pulled back in surprise, trying to keep back the tears welling up in her eyes.

He continued. "I admit, I have always loved your fire, your curiosity. I enjoyed watching you learn to shoot an arrow, fence even, climb trees."

He seemed more intent the more he talked. "But sometimes, it is important to know when to back away, to hide. We are an obvious target, and I need to know you are safe and cared for." He paused, running one hand through his hair. "These recent events have pushed me to ask you to rush your decision."

She felt a ball of uneasiness begin to grow in her stomach. "What decision? Surely you don't mean—"

"Marriage, Amanda." She began to protest, but he held up his hand. "I need to see you happily settled and secure and away from your mother and me. It is more important now than ever. I would like to get you out of harm's way in the happiest of circumstances possible."

Amanda tried to interrupt, but her father stayed her again. "Not only do I want you happy and safe, but you know if you have a son, he is to be my heir. Passing on our family title and generations of responsibility weighs heavily on me. I have made special arrangements with our solicitor. I do not want the dukedom to go to your cousin Percival, or Uncle Ethan if he outlives me. As dear as Uncle Ethan is, your son is dearer than his could ever be. I am young enough still for your child to grow to adulthood."

For a moment, Amanda was too stunned for words. *Make a marriage decision? After one ball? A ball that ended in violence?* Her mind desperately searched for something that would distract her father, dissuade him.

Clearing his throat, he continued. "Happily . . . and I do hope you are happy with my news . . ."

News? Amanda began to panic.

"Two men have come to me already, expressing sincere and, dare I say, heartfelt interest in pursuing you."

Amanda forced herself to say something, anything. "But Father, who could possibly?"

"Don't you know? Why, Lords Needley and Nathaniel, of course. They came to me this very morning; arrived almost together." He chuckled. "Humorous moment, that, when they politely attempted to be the first at my door."

Before she could stop herself, she vocalized her immediate thought. "Lord Nathaniel can't be serious, Father. He looks at me with disdain and hardly lowers himself to talk with me." She didn't for one minute believe that he held any sincere interest in her or her happiness. She had seen evidence enough of that this morning. "Just now, in the parlor, he proved himself unable to take me seriously at all."

Her father chuckled again. "He takes you seriously, Amanda. You can take my word for that. He is quite sincere; has been for years, I believe."

Her heart jumped a little at that revelation. A smile threatened, which she squelched. She needed to respond to her father, and quickly. "Father, this is all quite a shock, you must know. You cannot possibly think that I could make any kind of marriage decision right now. I had hoped another Season at least—some time, years even, as a grown woman, to consider my tastes, my goals. I don't know these men or anything about them."

Fear entered her heart as she considered all she would give up with marriage. *What if the man turned out to be a cruel, overly domineering person? What if she could never come and go as she pleased?*

The duke patted her hand. "I've done my research on all the eligible men this Season. These two are some of the best. They are both good men and come from good families. They aren't given to much drink or gambling. They aren't, dare I say, free with their attentions to women."

She scoffed. "You think not? Lord Nathaniel has a reputation—"

"I am well aware of the manner in which Lord Nathaniel presents himself, but I assure you, my dear, there is no truth to substantiate the rumors surrounding him. I am unsure why he allows them to continue, and it does give rise to questions, but all other evidence is so much in his favor I very much hope he is the man you choose."

Amanda rose quickly from her seat and began pacing, her voice rising. "Father, I could never. I loathe the man! We have barely spoken three words together, and danced only once."

"And he saved you from ruin and possible death."

"Yes, there is that, but I cannot account for it—a desire for glory and heroics, I suppose." Her arms flailed about in agitation as she spoke and paced the room.

"Open your heart to these men, for you must choose one of them." She froze, felt her face go pale, and slowly turned to look at her father. He gently smiled.

"What can you mean?"

"I want you to allow them both to court you, unofficially of course."

"What, at the same time?"

"I have asked them for a time of informal courtship. I know it isn't usually done, but as I said, many have left town, others are sure to follow. And at the end of the Season, you will choose which you would like to ask for your hand."

"Father! No! Where is the romance in that? What about the discovery, the fun? It is all so decided, so formal." She felt her world closing in and felt as though the ceiling were getting closer; her heart constricted with pressure. She could not bear it one more moment. She turned to run, but her father's hand gently held her for one moment more.

"They both came to me at once. I wanted to give you time to choose for yourself." He looked so kind, his eyes smiling at her in pride. Then the light turned to concern. "I need this, Amanda. I need to see you safe. And I need to know I will have an heir. I owe it to generations of Cumberlands and to all of our tenants. I will not tolerate your defiance in this." She looked into her father's loving, kind eyes and saw steel.

CHAPTER NINE

Breaking free, Amanda ran from the study out into the hall, desperately looking for a wrap, a pelisse—anything to be outdoors, to see the sky. The nearest cloak off a hook served her purpose. She ran through the entry and out the front door, dragging it behind. Following her, the warning shouts and immediate sounds of running footmen went unheeded. She pulled on the cloak as she ran; it drowned her small frame and dragged at her feet. When she managed to pull the hood over her head, it covered her face and hair, hopefully hiding her identity from the curious eyes of the London *ton*.

Faster and farther, fighting to escape familiarity, she ran through London's streets. Seeking a hiding place, somewhere, anywhere, she turned blindly around corners, ran behind town houses and through alleys until she became more aware of her circumstances.

The smell hit her first. Rotten waste and filth lay before her on the street. She lifted her skirts and stepped with care. A slushy gurgling splat landed behind her. The new odor of day-old chamber pot crawled into her senses and encouraged her into another run, out of that alley and across a busier street.

Her tired feet brought her to a square, at the back of which was a church, well-worn and small, and she slowed to a walk toward what she hoped would be a peaceful place to ponder her next move. A comforting pleasure brought light to her face. An open green area in front of the church welcomed her. The trees felt like an oasis in the desert of London's gray and tan.

The location perfect for reflection, already her mind began sifting through her options. She could not survive the rest of her life if it was merely a form of captivity, one not even of her own choosing. Her father could not force her into a marriage choice. He must be brought to see reason. And she must appeal to her mother's kindness. Surely they would understand that she wanted a love match like theirs.

She considered Lord Needley. He was a nice enough man. She knew he would be kind. But she had not developed any sort of attraction to him. When they had danced, there was no fire or spark or pull. Rushing into marriage with him might very well ruin any chance that something could develop between them besides friendship.

Her mind turned to Lord Nathaniel, and immediately her heart picked up—treacherous territory for her. Her physical fascination with him consumed her at times. What if he continued to treat her with the disdain he'd displayed in the drawing room? Could her heart bear such rejection? She suspected she would be happier marrying a man she did not love than one she might love who did not return her regard.

Blast her reaction to this man! She could not account for it. Intellectually, she loathed him. He disdained the poor. He probably broke half the hearts of the new debutantes each year. He had appeared interested when she spoke of the rights of the working class and then completely dismissed her thoughts as trite, childish fancies. She could not imagine she would ever have a true marriage of the minds with Lord Nathaniel.

She approached the church, yearning for the peace she hoped to find inside, but a noise from the opposite street caused her to jump behind a copse of trees on the edge of the square. A small rank and file of people marched toward her, jeering and calling out. The men were loud, swaying, probably drunk; the women, dirty, with tattered dresses. She sunk back into the shadows, daring not to move. Angry faces; drunk faces; daft, ridiculous faces marched together in a mock processional. One woman shouted, her eyes bulging, and then fell backward into the arms of the laughing, teetering men behind her. A man swayed with a bottle in one hand, singing an old folk tune as he stumbled forward. From behind them a voice called, "Move along! Out of the way!"

Surprised, Amanda stepped forward involuntarily at the sight before her. A carriage with bars, a human cage, being pulled by two men rolled slowly in front of the church. In its horrific splendor, filled with captives, it reigned as the focal point of this bizarre, regimented march. As it drew nearer, Amanda's heart constricted. A young girl, not yet ten, sat in the arms of a woman—surely her mother—face tight with fear. A boy hunched in the corner, resting his arms on his knees, which were bent to his chest. He noticed Amanda in her hiding spot and stared at her with such a look of want, or despair, it seared her heart. She would never forget those eyes.

Another mother sat with a vacant, hollow expression, unashamedly giving suck to her infant. The cart also carried two men, neither looking anywhere but their own bare feet.

Encouraging the carriage onward, a constable of sorts mocked his own profession. Perhaps a bit in the cups himself, he called, "Move along!" Riding his horse, he watched the side streets lazily, every now and then a yawn escaping.

Amanda returned her attention to the eerie prison. The wheels went down into a rut, and the people fell against each other in a garbled mass of limbs. She watched as they slowly righted themselves again.

Someone bumped into her, teetering on his feet. "Oh, beg pardon." He moved away, shuffling his feet.

She swallowed. "Wait." Stepping nearer, she asked, "Could you tell me why those people are locked up in there?"

Swaying on his feet, he burst out laughing. "What manners ye have. Puttin' on airs, are ye?" He leaned closer, and she stepped back, the smell of him sharp at the back of her throat.

"Ye ain't from around here." He jabbed a filthy finger in her direction. "They are going to Marshalsea Prison, they are. 'Cause they can't pay what they owe. Mind ye, none of these have the means to pay anyone, they don't. That woman there, with the babe—her husband drowned in the Thames and left her owing all his money." He swayed toward her, losing his balance. "And once they go in the Mashalsea, they don't ever come out."

She gripped his sleeve to steady him, pushing back when he tipped too much in her direction. He righted himself and stumbled away from her. And then her own shackles paled as she worried about theirs. The injustice of everything she saw filled her with an anger she hadn't felt since she was a young child. People, caged like animals. *Caged. Children.* The baby with her mother, unjustly shackled with someone else's debt.

A great rise of emotion surged through her. All the struggle from this morning, the raid on her house, a forced marriage decision combined with the endless hopelessness of these people before her, the injustice of their lives with no one to speak for them. Fiery emotion burned inside and she rushed forward without thinking, throwing back the hood of her cloak, whose ends dragged in the dirt of the street. She pointed an arm, completely covered by the sleeves of her cloak, at the man on the horse and demanded, "You there, stop this minute!" The people closest to her froze, stunned. Their neighborhood had probably never seen the likes of her, in all her finery.

Without thinking, she ran forward, pushing through the crush of people, who were slow to move aside. She reached the cart, saw the padlock was not secure, lifted its heavy ring from its hole, and threw it to the ground. It dented the earth where it landed. She wrenched the door aside, leaving it wide open to the occupants.

She expected a surge of people to burst forth, piling out of the cage, running for their freedom. Her breath coming quickly, she swallowed in anticipation, standing on the balls of her feet. But the people in the cage did not move. They stared at her with blank, hopeless expressions, not mustering enough curiosity to look for very long.

"What's wrong with you? Go!" she shouted. "Go! Be free! Run!" She tried to grab the arm of the boy to pull him out of the cage. He pulled back as if burned at her touch. *Why won't they leave?*

The crowd, recovering from their shock, began to laugh in derision. "Look 'ere. The birds don' wanna fly, they don'." A man leered at her, too close to her face. His smell of old onions, sweat, and cabbage made her eyes water.

A toothless woman with hair in much need of brushing breathed whiskey and cackled. "Were ya gonna take 'em 'ome with ye, love? Wash 'em up and keep 'em as pets, eh?" Her laugh pierced Amanda's ears. The crowd jeered louder and pressed closer. Fear moved from her belly to her throat as filth and stench blocked her retreat and pressed her up against the cage.

"What's a pretty thing like you doing so far east?" The man swinging a whiskey bottle said, then added, "A man could get the wrong idea about your intentions."

No one in the crush seemed to hear the constable on the horse call in a bored voice, "That's enough! Move along." Amanda moved up onto the carriage step as the crowd pressed in against her. She felt hands grasping for her cloak.

She started to panic. "You are too close! Back away—please!"

"Wassa' matter missy, too good for the likes of us? Don't want to muss your pretty gown?" Hands started to pull at the fabric.

"Yes, show us your fine clothes, miss." The hands became more insistent, trying to pull off her cloak; they began to claw at her hair.

She screamed, "Stop! Help! Oh, someone help me, please!" She started to lose her balance. Desperately, she clung onto the bars of the cage to keep from slipping to the ground where she was sure to be trampled. Her boots found precarious footing on a lower step. Frantic, she searched for any possible escape. Seeing none, she squeezed her eyes tight and tried to curl into a ball.

At last, she felt the crowd give way, and she breathed in a wave of fresh air. Her head still down, she saw the toe of a shiny black Hessian and swallowed in relief. Taking another deep breath, she looked up into the eyes of . . . "Lord Nathaniel?"

What is he *doing here?* She reached for him, leaning into his chest, looking up into his face. His eyes looked deep into hers, and he gently pulled the hood back up over her hair, covering most of her head. Then he effortlessly picked her up into his arms and began to push through the crowd.

Amanda could feel his heart beating rapidly in his chest. His mouth looked grim, and tension lines deepened along his eyes and around his mouth.

A part of her knew she was still in some sort of danger, but the security of his arms wiped all worry from her mind. She leaned her head against his shoulder and felt his hands tighten around her. *Where are we going?* He kept walking, cradling her, and the crowd behind them became more distant.

When the streets had once again grown quiet and vacant, Lord Nathaniel stopped and gently placed Amanda on her feet. They stood in a back alley, blessedly deserted. Out of habit, she tried to smooth her dress and remembered she still wore the over-large cloak. Not sure what to do with her hands inside the long sleeves, she concentrated on keeping them still.

"Thank you." She glanced up into his eyes and then quickly found his shoes.

How would she ever explain her presence here? What was he doing here? Her eyes snapped back up to his, trying to decipher his expression.

He stared at her a moment more. "You are most welcome, my lady. I had to come, you see; you have robbed me of my best cloak."

"What? Oh. I do apologize. I just grabbed the nearest one. I was in such a hurry . . ." She moved to try to take it off.

"No, please, Lady Amanda. It is quite beyond repair. Keep it."

She looked at the hem, which had been dragged along the dirty London cobblestone.

"I don't suppose we could mend it for you . . ." Her voice trailed off as she realized the futility of such an effort. "I'm dreadfully sorry. I didn't mean—I didn't know—"

He brought a finger to her mouth and placed it on her lips, quieting her. He brushed a stray hair to the side, placing it behind her ear. His fingers left a trail of tingles along her skin. He pulled out his pocket watch and looked up and down the street.

Odd. Who could he be looking for?

"Now, how to get you home."

"Have you no carriage with you, sir?"

"I do, but out of necessity I left it several streets away. These side alleys were not made for finer equipages." Lord Nathaniel checked his timepiece again, looked around them in all directions, and then started back the way they had come.

"Wait, are you sure this is the best way? What if—?"

Lord Nathaniel smiled and offered his arm. "I'm sure."

As they neared the square with the church from which they had just escaped, Amanda tensed and stilled her feet. The sounds of a crowd reached her ears and she said, "I'm not going back in the middle of that mess."

Lord Nathaniel patted her hand. "It will be just fine." He continued walking in the direction of the church. Her newfound trust in him moved her feet forward, one step in front of the other. The alternative, rushing again through London's streets alone, had lost all appeal.

Another large crowd was gathered at the church, and Amanda clenched her teeth. Her fingers pressing into Lord Nathaniel's forearm, she scanned the group for any sign of the strange cart with the cage or any of the awful people surrounding it. But this assembly and the other bore nothing in common. These people were obviously of the working class, but were dressed in clean clothes, pressed and mended, and they were standing in front of an orator on the church steps, listening raptly to everything he had to say.

Amanda felt Lord Nathaniel's eyes on her. When she started moving in the direction of the crowd, he walked with her, never relinquishing her hand on his arm and keeping close to her side. The speaker in front was handsome, with broad shoulders and eyes that would have been pleasant had they not been slightly bulging with his efforts to convince and persuade. They inched forward through the crowd until they could hear and see him well.

"We cannot be a truly great nation until we are free! ALL of us: every single maid and footman, workers from the steel mills and the hospitals."

The crowd applauded and nodded their agreement.

"Are we not all humans, come from Adam himself? Are we not all beloved of God?"

They nodded, and a few cheers joined the applause.

"We no longer want hearts crushed by power; hope extinguished with every unfair advantage of the titled classes. Our voices must be heard! Our elections noted. We would elect lawmakers to champion our cause! The nobility give us our work, they lend us their land, they give us clothes when it suits them, food when it is convenient. They give us our laws, pave our roads, and build our structures. Do not feel pacified by the rocking hand of your cradles. You are more than infants reliant on your mothers. We may feel we have no way out, that we are trapped, but are we?"

A few murmured in response.

"ARE WE?"

Some shouted, "No!"

"No, we are not. Our rights do not come from the aristocrats among us, because our freedom is not theirs to give. We. Have. Rights."

The crowd responded with a cheer. Amanda heard no one but the orator himself. Her heart opened in wonder to ideas never before considered.

"Just as Thomas Jefferson taught the French, just as they adopted in America, we each were born with certain rights that cannot be given or taken away, except we allow it! These rights were given to us by our Supreme Creator Himself. And these are the rights to life, to liberty, and not just property, but the very pursuit of our own happiness."

The crowd erupted in great shouts and cheering.

Amanda could not restrain her own applause. This stranger before her had just expressed perfectly the longtime yearnings of her heart. *Freedom.* If these people would ask for freedom, then surely she could too: Freedom to choose her own husband, freedom to manage her own estate, to decide her own marriage contract, and to make decisions for her education and future. Before she realized it, she was cheering along with the crowd and smiling joyfully at the families near her who seemed equally touched. And didn't they deserve to be free?

Turning to Lord Nathaniel after a moment, exclamations on her lips, she stopped and opened her eyes wider. Nathaniel paid no heed to the crowd around them but instead watched her with a particular intensity. His searching eyes showed pleasure and admiration. His smile lit the square and, for a moment, even the orator dimmed in her sights. She blushed and returned her cloak-covered hand to his arm. Great satisfaction filled her as she basked in his approval.

A woman from the crowd called out, "And what of women? Are we not to have a vote as well?"

Her head whipped around to find the speaker. *Women to have a vote?* Her heart ached at the thought.

Several women in the crowd nodded, but Amanda noticed most of the men wore smiles of condescension; even the orator himself looked in the direction of the speaker and responded sympathetically, "There may be a time for that, yes. Universal suffrage may include women someday." A few men in the audience grunted in disapproval. "But that time is not now. Let us gain suffrage for our working class of men first, shall we? We will all benefit! Let us not rest until we do! Let us respectfully and peaceably work *with* the law until every one of us has a vote." The crowd cheered, and Amanda applauded along with them.

The people around her began chanting, "Henry Hunt. Henry Hunt."

Amanda smiled and chanted, but her mind raced. So many new ideas to consider: votes for all, votes for women someday. How his words of freedom had stirred her, seared onto her heart. How she longed to be free. How she longed for everyone to be free. Free to pursue whatever life they chose to live. *What a beautiful thought.*

With her eyes shining and her heart beating happily, she turned to Lord Nathaniel and opened her mouth to speak when he said, "What a lot of nonsense! Universal suffrage indeed! Give this group the right to vote? And those that nearly trampled you? They were a lovely bunch, to be sure. England would be in good hands with that group, I daresay." He brushed his coat distastefully and looked down his nose at those assembled.

Amanda stared at him in shock. "How can you say that about these good people, and after hearing such a stirring message? Why, I feel my heart might never be the same."

He took her hand in his arm again and started leading her away. "Pretty thoughts, my dear. Why don't you buy your maid a new bonnet or some such frippery? Throw a few bones in their direction every now and then, and you'll have a house full of happy servants." Amanda stopped walking. Speechless, she could not even formulate a thought.

Lord Nathaniel's eyes sharpened, and he gave a barely perceptible shake of his head.

Odd. She followed the direction of his eyes. Curiously, the orator turned away at just that moment to talk to someone at his side. Amanda's eyes narrowed. "And are these your true thoughts on the matter, my lord? Because I, for one, don't believe it. Any man with half sense in his head would see that we are in brilliant company here."

Lord Nathaniel looked about to say something, but then he yawned. "Might we return you to your family, my lady?"

Amanda raised a cloak-covered hand to her mouth and then dropped it again when she felt the sleeve against her lips. "Oh yes, oh dear. I've been gone much longer than I planned." The cloak slipped off her shoulder, and she pulled it back up. She tipped her head to the side in realization. As facts connected, she asked, "How is it I am wearing your cloak?" Then as the full implications of his presence in her home returned, her face heated. "Did you happen to hear my conversation when I—?"

"Carried on about not wanting to marry? Yes, bits of it were quite audible from the drawing room where Lord Needley and I were taking tea with your mother."

Amanda swallowed with difficulty.

Lord Nathaniel continued. "And then I was also present to see you rush from the house and down the street in a careless manner, causing a household full of people to worry on your behalf. People who are even now still combing the streets of London in search of you. Parsons' hands shook as he handed me my hat, apologizing for the missing cloak."

Amanda's guilt heightened, but it was coupled with a growing sense of irritation for this pompous, self-righteous man by her side. How dare he patronize her in such a manner.

"And do tell, Lord Nathaniel, how you managed to find me? Did you run down the street, chasing the tails of your cloak?"

"Me? Heavens no! I leave that sort of effort to the footmen." He adjusted his sleeve and brushed the front of his tailcoat. "I had a meeting with a colleague a few streets over. I was headed there when I heard the sounds of the crowd and your squawking voice over the tops of them all." Lord Nathaniel looked at her with a bored expression. "What could I do? A lady in need of rescuing, couldn't resist . . ."

Amanda pulled her hand from his arm and walked ahead of him in what she hoped was the right direction. Lord Nathaniel followed behind her for a couple of blocks then turned down a different alley, calling, "My carriage is this way."

She could hear his laugh as he walked farther into the alley and out of sight. Huffing, she changed directions to follow him.

She hoped never to see this awful lord with his pompous opinions ever again. One thing she felt sure of: after today's rescue, she was certain Lord Nathaniel would drop his suit and no longer desire to court her. She pushed away a tiny pang of regret.

How could he be unmoved by that speech? The stirring orator had spoken directly to her heart some of the most important words ever spoken, Amanda was sure of it.

When she returned home, a very solemn and disappointed father and mother met her at the door. They hugged her gratefully, but no smile accompanied the embraces. Amanda felt her heart sink.

She tried to explain to her father. "I just want to be *free*. It is a feeling inside. Talking to you, the world closed in—I've never known how to control it."

Amanda's father looked at her sternly. "Your actions today spoke of complete selfishness. Your mother and I, our entire staff, and Lords Needley *and* Nathaniel have been sick with worry for you."

Amanda couldn't stop the snort of disbelief at the mention of Lord Nathaniel's worry. Her father hardened his eyes. *Oh dear, he misunderstood.*

"If you have so little regard for our watchful care and attention, then you will lose some of that precious freedom until you acquire the respect that I desire from my daughter."

"Oh, Father, no! I was not thinking of you or the staff—"

"You most certainly were not. I have never seen dear Parsons so agitated. Half of the footmen are still out there on the streets of London, searching. Your Molly asked to leave with them to search for you herself. We told her to stay. We didn't need two females lost in the city. As it is, she is up waiting for you in your room with a hot bath."

Amanda's heart warmed at the generous treatment from those whom she had wronged. Filled with remorse, eyes wet with new tears, she reached for her mother's hand. "Mother, I am so sorry." She held the other hand out. "And Father, please forgive me. I will strive to be better, to be worthy of your love and care."

She leaned in, kissed each of her kind parents on the cheek, and walked out of the main hallway and up the stairs toward her room. As she turned back to smile at her parents, she was surprised to see Lord Nathaniel folding a now dirty and tattered cloak over his arm and placing a hat on his head. He had heard the whole of her mortifying interchange with her parents. Had he no decency?

He tipped his head in her direction. Then he turned and walked out the front door.

Did she see admiration in his eyes? She shook her head. That was probably the last time he would ever be in her home. Surely, he would not want to court her after today. She told herself she was glad of it. She turned from him, her mortification, and her punishment and ran up the stairs. She rushed down the hallway and into her room, slamming the door in her wake.

CHAPTER TEN

SHE LEANED AGAINST THE CLOSED door, breathing heavily; closing her eyes, she tried to block the hurt in her father's face. A small clearing of a throat startled Amanda's eyes open. *Molly.* Dear Molly, who despite being ill-used, awaited her with a hot bath. Amanda rushed toward her and enveloped her in a desperate and tight embrace.

"I'm so sorry, Molly!" Amanda cried on her shoulder; she was sorry for hurting her maid, sorry for disappointing her parents, but more than anything, she was sorry she could not help those poor people in the cage. Were they in the Marshalsea even now? Did the young boy have anyone to care for him?

Molly patted her shoulder. "My lady, there is no need to carry on so. We will get you dressed and comfortable soon enough. Come now, let's get you into the bath, and you can tell me all about it."

"Oh, thank you."

After the dirt from London's streets had been thoroughly scrubbed from her body, Amanda sat in the soothing water and recounted all that had happened.

Molly gasped at her description of the crowd. "You could have been seriously hurt, or worse."

When Amanda described the people in the cage and their refusal to leave, Molly wiped her eyes. "Those poor souls."

Amanda squeezed water from her hair. "Why were they so without hope, so devastated that they wouldn't even budge from their prison?" After a moment of reflection, her thoughts took a different direction. She turned in the tub, chin resting on the side of it. "You'll not believe who rescued me. *Lord Nathaniel.*"

Molly gathered her things in a small pile as she talked. "He saw you run out the door, miss. He left faster than anyone else, even without a proper cloak."

Amanda considered this information against his claim of having other business in the area.

The two discussed all the events of the day, especially Henry Hunt and his great speech.

"He said so many wonderful things." Amanda stood up, reaching for the offered towel. "I am going to write them down before I forget."

"I would like to read them if you wouldn't mind sharing." Molly busied herself, gathering Amanda's clean clothing.

After Molly helped her dress in her nightclothes and left her, Amanda sat with a candle late into the night at the small table in her room. Her pen scratched on the paper as she wrote line after line, dipping again and again into the ink, recounting all the words she could remember coming out of Henry Hunt's mouth. And as she wrote, the fire of their message burned ever brighter in her heart.

She couldn't wait for Molly to read them. She was certain everyone in England should read these powerful words. As she wrote the last few lines about his message, a plan began forming in her mind, beginning with a copy made of her notes and sent to *The Times*. Surely the newspaper would want to print it as soon as possible.

Sleep far from her mind, she felt an old urge to sketch. As Amanda looked through her sketchbooks, she came across the drawings of her sparrows. She had drawn them frequently in her youth: in their cage, taking baths, eating food, singing. She smiled at the happy memories.

She shuffled through the drawings, seeking one in particular. There, at the bottom of the stack. Her heart sped up at the sight of it. She had captured the moment the birds broke free, their heads pushing forward outside the cage door, wings behind them, about to unfold in the wind. On that day long ago when the world did not seem to have a place for her free spirit, she had finally set her sparrows free. With their freedom, she found exhilaration and peace, even acceptance of the new direction her life would take.

Amanda found her charcoal and a blank sheet of paper. She began sketching, starting with the boy's eyes: haunting, desperately hollow. The longer she sketched, the greater the peace that enveloped her. She began to hum, drawing the mother and infant. Eyes furrowed in concentration, the unkempt hair and soulless eyes transferred from mind to page. Each image became more and more clear.

She put all her effort into the emotion of the faces. She tried to understand, to piece together a puzzle. As she drew the lines on the mother's face from memory, she studied her haggard expression. She saw love, but not joyful and hopeful—more of a despairing kind of love. It was as if this mother had no indication that her life could ever be different from what it was. Everyone in the cage must have felt the same.

This realization, that they had no escape from their situations, brought such an immense amount of sadness to Lady Amanda that she didn't think she could bear it. Her heart ached for the people she did not know, and she vowed then and there to make it the duty of her life to help in some way.

How would she ever be of any help to these people? Could she be of much influence? Perhaps—she still wielded quite a bit of power, and from now on, she would use it to help people.

Molly came back into the room and Amanda said, "Oh good. Could you take a look at this?" She showed her the new sketches. Molly gently touched the eyes of the little boy. When she finally looked up at Amanda, there were tears in Molly's eyes.

"Fliers, Molly! I'll draw fliers, satires. The *ton* is fascinated with them." They were mostly fascinated with gossip, but people were always talking about the next flier.

"This is a right good thing you aim to do, my lady. If I could, I'd like to help you. I don't know how we will do it, what with two men trying to win your hand and all the *ton* watching your every step, but heaven help us, I want to try."

Amanda let out a great breath of relief. "Oh! Thank you, Molly. I could never do this without you." And then she smiled a pleased, secretive smile. "I do believe we are going to have a bit of fun with this. To begin, I wonder if you could find a way to commission the creation of my own signet ring." She held up one of her drawings of the birds. "And on it, I would like the image of a sparrow."

CHAPTER ELEVEN

AMANDA SMILED A BIT BRIGHTER than she felt and laughed a bit louder than the joke merited. Her dance card was full as usual with smiling, hopeful men determined to win her hand and purse. She tired of their company, their conversation; but Molly had told her countless times she excelled at acting, and Amanda had a part to play.

She batted her eyes. Here was her test. "Lord Walter, what do *you* think of all these reformists?"

A handsome young lord faltered in his steps for a moment but soon recovered. "Why Lady Amanda! I am all amazed. That is not something you need to be worrying about, to be sure."

Amanda smiled, hiding her regret. "Oh, but I am curious! They wear such droll red hats! Is it to be the new fashion, do you think?"

Lord Walter laughed, returning to comfortable social ground. "Well, my lady, if you were to wear it, I am sure it would soon be all the rage."

Amanda laughed. "Oh, too true! Perhaps I will try it. Shall you join me?"

Lord Walter continued to laugh along with her. "Name the day, name the event, and I will join you. What a jolly joke we shall share."

Amanda's laugh carried across the room to Lord Nathaniel who, she saw with some gratification, scowled at the sound. His disapproving expressions followed them as they whirled by in their waltz.

He excused himself from the lady glued to his arm and made his way toward the dance floor. He stood, feet apart, arms folded across his chest, glowering at Amanda and Lord Walter as new ladies joined him, trying to catch his eye.

"Don't look now," Amanda said, "but I do believe we have caught the attention of Lord Nathaniel." She motioned with her head in his direction.

"What? Ho! But he does look serious." Lord Walter looked at her speculatively. "Perhaps he feels I am in his place?"

Amanda laughed at that, too. "If that were the case, I am sure he would ask me to dance. No. I will tell you his secrets. You see, I have it on good authority that—" She leaned closer to Lord Walter, breathing lightly on his neck and whispered, "He likes to be miserable."

Lord Walter burst out laughing again, and Lord Nathaniel scowled even deeper. Amanda smiled in satisfaction.

Lord Walter said, "So unexpected, my lady." He wiped tears from his eyes and returned his hand to her lower back as they continued to waltz. "I have not enjoyed a turn about the floor this immensely all Season." His eyes twinkled at her, and he pulled her closer to him as the music finished. "Thank you. Perhaps I might call on you this week?"

"It would be my pleasure to receive you, Lord Walter." She smiled deeply at him and curtsied as he bowed.

Lord Nathaniel interrupted their path off the dance floor. "Lord Walter." Lord Nathaniel nodded briefly in his direction and turned his eyes to Lady Amanda. "I believe this is our dance, my lady."

"Oh? I don't believe you have secured a set—"

"Lord Needley left to see to his mother's sudden illness. So I am here in his stead." He bowed elegantly over her hand and offered his arm to lead her back onto the floor.

Amanda shared a look with Lord Walter, raising her eyebrows as though to say, *So, he chose to dance with me after all.* Lord Walter waggled his eyebrows ridiculously in return. She couldn't hold back her laugh as she turned and placed a hand on Lord Nathaniel's arm. She hadn't spoken with him since his departure from her home two weeks ago. She willed her heart to slow. *What can he mean by dancing with me?* His silence weighed on her as they moved through the steps, changing couples and then coming back together again.

She finally broke the silence. "I trust you have acquired a new cloak?"

Lord Nathaniel's eyebrows rose. He cleared his throat. "Ah. Actually, no. I already had several others. If you recall, the one you pilfered was my *best* cloak, not my *only* cloak."

"Oh, I see. Of course." She searched for something else to say.

He surprised her by adding, "I'm having yours mended, you see. I didn't see the need to commission a new one when your cloak is perfectly serviceable."

Amanda was sure confusion showed on her face. "My cloak?" She nearly stumbled to see a faint redness rise to his cheeks. He cleared his throat again.

"Well, no, not yours." He paused and seemed to rally. "I can't help but see all the marks you left on it. You have quite claimed it as your own, with the inches of London dirt, tears from London's poor, tatters from the miles you walked in it, strands of your hair in the hood, and . . ." He leaned close to her ear and whispered, "your lovely perfume that still hovers about the thing."

Heat filled Amanda's face, and she couldn't stop it.

"I decided I cannot live without it and am therefore having it repaired." He smiled and nodded his head decisively.

Amanda could not at first respond. Lord Nathaniel waited, eyebrows raised. Finally, she said, "I am glad you will still get some use out of it." She cleared her throat. Seeing him now, she recognized her conscience had been pestering her. She said, "I know I should thank you."

Lord Nathaniel raised his eyebrow in an amused expression. "You know you should?"

She smiled and blushed. "Yes. I mean, I do. I thank you for rescuing me, again. I am still not certain what business you possibly could have had on those streets, but if you had not been there—"

"Think nothing of it, my dear. I cannot resist a—"

"Damsel in distress. Yes, I know." She found herself more intrigued by him than ever. It was so difficult to keep up with all his different personas. Who was this man? When all the layers were finally peeled away, what would she discover at his core? She realized with a start that during their past few moments together she had dropped her facade. They were the first moments of the evening when she felt completely without disguise. She felt an odd sense of relief to rest for their time together and simply respond as herself. She very much hoped the person she saw right now represented more of his true core.

Smiling, he said, "I noticed you are luring quite a few gentlemen."

She choked. "What?"

His mouth quirked in a half smile. "You have a gift, my lady. You are quite proficient as a coy debutante flirt; but . . ."

Her eyebrows drew together. "But?"

He laughed. "Well, you are currently in the presence of the master. They do not call me a rake for nothing . . ." He waggled his eyebrows at her in a most silly manner.

"Are you saying you could best me? Out . . . flirt me?"

"Shall we have a bit of a contest?"

Amanda swallowed. She knew she was no match for Lord Nathaniel, whatever his contest might be.

"A bit nervous are you? Perhaps you doubt your abilities to withstand my charm?"

Understanding dawned. It was Amanda's turn to laugh. With a challenge in her eyes, she moved closer to him, her lips parted, close to his own. "I doubt your ability to resist mine."

Nathaniel's hand tightened on her back, his fingers pulling at the fabric on her gown, but he relaxed his hands just as quickly. He leaned closer to her face, locking his eyes on hers, tilting his head, his lips a mere inch from her own. "Lady Amanda, you don't want me to resist."

Her blood raced. She closed her eyes, and she felt Nathaniel's whisper in her ear. "Do you?"

Amanda shook her head before she could stop herself.

Nathaniel leaned his head back and laughed.

Amanda's eyes opened wide, then narrowed. He was too confident. Oh, but his flirtation was effective. She felt her blood warm to him. She enjoyed his attentions too much, but she could not resist. She wanted more, and more often. And she wanted to feel his weakness in reaction to her. She chuckled a low, slow laugh and said, "Challenge accepted, my lord. But how does one win such a contest? What are the rules?"

Lord Nathaniel laughed again. "Oh, but you are fun, my lady. We shall have to come up with answers as we go along." His eyes twinkled and he stared down at her with so much admiration, Amanda almost faltered in her steps.

"How will we know whose flirting is the most effective?"

They waited their turn to skip down the line of dancers. Nathaniel locked her with his gaze. "When one of us can no longer resist."

Amanda needed something to hold to balance herself. She felt an unfamiliar yearning and a need for his arms around her. She clutched at his hands as they moved together down the line. "My Season just became much more interesting, Lord Nathaniel."

CHAPTER TWELVE

THE NEXT MORNING, SHE FOUND her mother in the breakfast room.

"Good morning, my dear Amanda. You are up early today."

"Oh, good morning, Mother. You look lovely as usual. I am off in search of a new bonnet this morning—with a feather, just so." She demonstrated where the feather would be on her bonnet. "They are all the rage, you know." She hoped her mother would believe she cared that much about a bonnet.

The duchess smiled. If she suspected anything, she didn't let on. "How diverting. You have been far too often by yourself in your room of late. You will bring Molly with you of course."

"Oh yes. And I hope to meet Miss Clarissa for tea while I am out as well. We expect the gentlemen to be exiting the street from White's at precisely the same time that we will be strolling by and feeling in great need of company." Amanda smiled at her clever idea.

Her mother watched her for a moment and then said, "I am happy to see you have taken your father's counsel to heart. You know you will have to narrow your selection significantly before the end of the Season."

They walked together into the drawing room. "I thought I was not allowed a selection. It was my impression my choices are limited to two." Her response came out sharper than she intended. She amended with a smile and kiss on her mother's cheek. "Not to worry, Mother. I am acting the perfect English debutante, wooing gentlemen, seeking marriage offers. Do you need evidence of my successes?" She waved her hand out beside her, indicating the room full of gifts.

Amanda picked up one card from the stack of callers. "Lord Walter wishes me to know I am as lovely as these roses." She grabbed another. "Sir Kenton likens my siren hair to that of burgundy silk from France." She reached across a table and grabbed a handful of cards. "They are leaving personal notes on their cards, Mother. And here is a full poem. 'Ode to Lady Amanda's Feet.'" She stopped to look again, and she and her mother burst out laughing.

"Is it really a poem about your feet? Who would write such a thing?"

Amanda's face stilled, and she smiled appreciatively. "Lord Nathaniel. He says my feet are like the tinkle of bells in the church. Their smell as odiferous as a room full of flowers. Mama, I cannot figure him out. He is at times so clever and attentive." She frowned. "At other times, he is truly boorish." Her mother scoffed at that. "No, really. He dismisses me as if I were a child."

Her mother asked, "What did Lord Needley leave you this morning?"

Amanda searched through the flowers and cards. "Here. Lilies." She paused. "My favorite." She turned suspiciously to her mother, who smiled with a convincing air of innocence.

"Maybe he knows you better than you think."

Amanda considered how true that could be and said under her breath, "I hope not."

She rose quickly. "Well, off to search out the best bonnets. I cannot allow these illustrious ladies of the *ton* to outdo my head adornment, now can I?"

The duchess smiled at her indulgently, and Amanda hurried from the room.

Molly and Amanda sat close together in the carriage as they watched London go by through the window. "We must stop on Kings Road at the milliner's shop, and then I think we can walk over to Gramden's printers on Abbey Street from there." Molly nodded in agreement, her face tightened in worried lines.

"What is wrong?"

Molly's mouth opened in surprise. "Oh nothing, my lady. I . . . I've never done anything quite like this before." She ran her hands nervously over her skirt.

Amanda watched her for a moment until Molly met her gaze. "Have you changed your mind? It is quite all right if you do. You do not have to help me in this."

"No, it's not that. I was thinking about my father, is all. He would not take kindly to this outing of ours. Taking fliers to a printer, encouraging dissatisfaction. He would not. 'Trying to ennoble the working classes,' he would call it."

Amanda frowned. "Even if we eventually win? Surely he would like our outing if it brought about more freedom and rights for you and your family."

Molly sat quietly for a few moments and then said, "I don't know, my lady. He takes great pride in serving the nobility, he does. Views it as his right and honor."

Amanda smiled. A man who took pride in his work and does it well was noble by her own definition, title or no. "He is a good man, your father."

"Aye, he is. And he would not take it kindly if I were to lose my position." Molly's eyes pleaded for understanding.

Amanda noticed Molly's hands shaking slightly. "I will make sure that does not happen. You have my word."

Molly nodded. "Thank you, my lady." Molly's hands rested in her lap and she leaned back against the carriage seat. Soon, she began to chatter about her family and her sisters and how they would react if they knew Lady Amanda's errand that morning. Most shared her father's sentiments. The young ones already looked forward to the day they too could enter a great noble house.

Amanda said, "Let us pray the man received my letter with the drawings and that he is willing to carry our fliers in his store."

"I do hope he will, my lady. He may have the first group ready for us today. If he agreed to it, that is."

Amanda nodded and hope filled her. "This idea of ours—it might work."

The carriage and its two grinning passengers arrived in front of the milliners. After purchasing the first ridiculous feathered bonnet to catch her eye, they set off on foot to the print shop.

Gramden's was busier than she would have liked. A group of well-dressed women lingered around stacks of fliers and laughed together. Amanda peered over their shoulders and was pleased at the quality of the drawings. Although these fliers were mostly in response to *ton* gossip or other news of high-society families, she had to acknowledge them as very clever and exhibiting an abundance of artistic talent.

How would her fliers appear next to this kind of talent? She tried to think encouraging thoughts, but the weight of her inexperience pulled at her hope. Her need to remain anonymous complicated things also. No one must know her new identity as the Sparrow. She needed to do everything she could to dissuade anyone from suspicion.

As she took in the full shop and considered how she and Molly were going to pick up their package, she decided to provide some kind of distraction. Just as Molly approached the counter, Amanda started laughing overly loud. The women in front of her startled at the sound immediately behind them. When they turned to see the source, their eyes rounded and mouths opened in lovely O's of surprise. She did not have to fake her next laugh as she took in all six of them forming perfectly orchestrated round lips.

Luckily, she was already acquainted with one of them. "Miss Clarissa, how do you do? I expect I will see you shortly for tea, will I not?" She gave a brief curtsy and a warm smile.

Miss Clarissa, apparently pleased at being the only one in the group with such a high acquaintance, curtsied in return and responded, "I am well, Lady Amanda, thank you." She made introductions to all the other ladies.

Amanda pointed to the fliers and said, "These are quite diverting, you know. Just look at that one right there." It was a picture of a couple waltzing. The gentleman had his foot firmly planted on the dainty slipper of his partner. "Bless her feet! You know she'll go to rest a moment in the ladies' parlor after that. Do you suppose this is meant to be someone we know?" A few nervous giggles answered her.

She tried another flier. "And this one here, she's bouncing the men away with her skirts. Why would she do that?" A few more nervous giggles responded. She could see they did not know how to respond, so she brought up a more interesting topic. Molly would be completing the transaction soon, and Amanda did not want any connection to the fliers coming back to her.

"And what of Lord Nathaniel?" She tried the only topic she knew of interest to all women of her acquaintance. All the ladies giggled at that. "What would his cartoon look like, I wonder?" A few ladies gasped in delight. "Shall we paint his image in our minds? Yes?" Several of them nodded vigorously and then blushed, looking to see if anyone had noticed their enthusiasm. Out of the corner of her eye, she noticed other patrons of the shop look in their direction, showing interest.

"I know what I would draw." A beautiful pale face with cunning dark eyes gained everyone's attention.

Amanda laughed nervously. "You do?"

The lady swallowed and continued with a laugh. "Yes! This will be perfect! Because I don't even have to make something up! I will tell you what I saw with my own eyes." They all gathered closer, including the other patrons.

This young lady had the undivided attention of everyone in the shop except the clerk at the front, who was leading Molly to the back room to pick up their fliers and to receive the art for their next order. She smiled with satisfaction, knowing that some of her fliers would also be seen amongst the drawings as early as tomorrow.

The lady continued. "I was at dinner with Lord Nathaniel just the other evening." Some of the ladies sighed. Amanda managed to refrain from rolling her eyes. "He was talking to the woman at my right across from him, flirting outrageously, planning their next rendezvous in the park, and what did I see underneath the table? His boot brushing that of the woman to his left!" The women gasped in unison. "It is true. And there's more." The women leaned closer and the other patrons hushed to silence.

Amanda shook her head, hesitating. Should she stop this defamation before it went any further?

"His hand, ladies, his right hand was resting on the hand of the woman at his right, *under the table.*" The ladies brought hands to their mouths while they uttered another gasp collectively.

Miss Clarissa sniffed. "I for one find that difficult to believe. Lord Nathaniel and I are personal friends. I do believe I am a favorite of his. And I have never found him to be anything less than a gentleman."

Aha, curious. Amanda had found a true admirer. She nodded. "We all know he is a bit . . . free with his attentions, ladies, but it is all in good fun, is it not? Nothing indecent, to be sure."

The dark-eyed beauty spoke again. "Oh come now, Miss Clarissa, everyone knows him to be one of the most outrageous rakes of the last three Seasons. I saw it with my own eyes, more or less." The women laughed. "The cloth on the tables blocked my view, but looking at the angle of their hands and the expressions on all the faces involved—well, it had to have been just as I said. Besides, we are inventing cartoons, are we not? And that one perfectly describes our dear Lord Nathaniel, does it not?" The group, excepting Miss Clarissa and Amanda, all nodded vigorous approval.

Amanda noticed a man watching and listening intently while taking a few notes on a pad. Molly cleared her throat across the room as if coming in the front door. Amanda made her way to the counter and purchased some stationary for writing letters and a new quill pen. While at the counter, she asked about the man taking notes. "Who is that man over there?"

The clerk answered, "That is Peter Hamilton. He is one of our cartoon artists. Right talented man, he is."

Amanda gulped. She hoped their conversation would never be repeated, but she suspected it might show up on a flier somewhere. She nodded at the clerk and hurried outside after her maid.

She stepped forward onto the street, a breeze picking up the curls around her face. Empty streets and fronts of shops lay before her. Turning to the left, her foot nudged something.

"Oh no!" She bent to pick up the package of their new fliers, smudged and torn at the corner. She hefted them into her arms and stood in haste, now alarmed and wondering where Molly was, but found herself staring into the face of Jack Bender, who grasped her by the arm. Her heart jolted in surprise. "What do you want?"

Bender laughed and began pulling her with him. "Well, now, that is the question, isn't it?"

"Where's Molly?"

Looking up and down the street, he hissed, "No talking until we are in private." She struggled against him as he dragged her away from Gramden's. He gestured toward a corner ahead of them, which must lead to an alley. "We'll talk there. I have something urgent I need to tell you."

"Unhand me. You can have nothing to say I wish to hear." Resting the fliers awkwardly on her hip, she continued to resist him. The fury in his eyes rose at her defiance and his free hand clenched into a fist.

He said in a deceptively calm voice, "Oh come now. There is no reason for bad feelings to exist between us. We have a friend in common after all, a friend you would not want to come to any harm."

She halted, and Bender turned toward her. "If you mean my mother, she is no friend of yours. Not after—"

"Do not speak of your mother to me." Nostrils flaring, he stepped closer, bearing down on her. "I'm talking about Charles Lemming."

Amanda stilled, and her heart pounded. "How do you know Charlie?"

"Well now, you will have to come with me to find out." Leering closer to her face, he said, "Coming, Lady Amanda?" He snatched the parcel from her hands and gave her arm a pointed tug. "You don't want to endanger two of your servants in one day." He added, "Molly is a pretty girl."

What to do, what to do! The street remained empty. She searched the shop fronts and seeing no one to come to her aid, she glanced behind her toward Gramden's. No one must have noticed the goings-on outside the printshop. Her coach and footmen were not coming back for her for several hours yet. *Would Bender really harm Molly? Or Charles?* She did not see them anywhere, but she daren't risk their well-being. And she needed those fliers. Even her generous pin money could not buy more right away. Daring not to keep Bender waiting long, she took a deep breath and allowed him to lead her around the corner and into the alley.

The light dimmed as soon as she stepped into the narrow passage. Stone walls on either side, towering up to the sky, blocked a portion of the sun. Bender turned around when she joined him and quickly pushed her back against the nearest wall. Crushing her to it, he restrained her and said, "Now, listen. I've got Charles Lemming. He works for me. Once a week he checks in, and I give him my orders. Thinks he's fighting for freedom, poor sap."

Finding it difficult to catch a full breath, Amanda coughed and struggled against him. She felt her back rub painfully against the stone behind her. "You are too close. I can't breathe."

"Do you hear me? Lemming is mine, make no mistake."

"You're lying. He's my neighbor's stable hand."

"He no longer works for that family. Gave his notice last month."

Amanda's eyes opened wide. *Charlie came to London to work for this man?*

"Didn't tell you, did he? Well, you will find there is a lot you don't know about your dear friend Charles."

"He's not my dear friend."

"Don't lie to me."

Bender pressed harder. Her head hit the wall, and she felt the ache behind her eyes. Blinking, trying to maintain focus as her vision went blurry, she turned her head to avoid his foul breath. She couldn't stop her own rapid breathing.

"Here's where this gets interesting." His hand clamped onto her chin and forced her to face him. "You see, Lady Amanda, you hold dear Lemming's fate in your very lovely hands."

A feeling of dread entered Amanda's mind. *What would he do to him? And what of Molly?*

"I see you are beginning to understand my proposal. I need something. And you are going to get it for me."

Amanda forced herself to speak. "And in return?"

Jack Bender smiled an awful grimace, his eyes black as coal. "You are quick to understand, my pet. In return, I will not harm Mr. Lemming. But if you cross me . . ."

Amanda flinched. The black dread became a heavy rock in the pit of her stomach. Swallowing, she tried to slow her breathing.

Bender shrugged. "Lemming's life means nothing to me. He will be gone before you can even think to apologize."

"What do you w-want from me?" Her knees started shaking. Desperately, she tried to focus.

Bender's chilling, grating laugh filled the alley, loud and long. "It is simple, my dear. I need your father's signet ring."

Amanda forced herself to concentrate. It wasn't a reasonable request. "You must be insane. I cannot possibly even remove it from his finger!"

The foul man backed up a half step. "Oh come, my dear. Surely he does not leave it on his hand every hour of the day."

She knew there were times he was not wearing it, but it was always kept carefully in his desk otherwise.

A person with a duke's signet ring would have great power, indeed. She shook her head. "What you ask is ludicrous, impossible." Amanda reached for courage within herself and clung to the smallest sparks she found there. She raised her chin and said, "And as soon as he saw it missing, he would simply notify his correspondence and work to make a new, altered one."

For a brief moment, Bender hesitated. His eyebrows furrowed, and his eyes glazed over as he wrestled with some inner turmoil, but then he smiled. "Then we shall just borrow it. I will need you to gain access to the ring and bring it to me at a time and location I will disclose. I will use it, and then you may return it to its place. You will tell no one, and you will perform these tasks as described with precision."

What could she do but agree? Amanda nodded. But she had no plans to actually do as he requested. Any letter sealed in wax with her father's ring would hold the weight of a directive from the Duke of Cumberland. She would breathe her last breath before she betrayed her father.

Bender stepped closer. He smelled of the gutter, and she cringed. As he leered, eyeing her lips, she could endure him no longer. Gritting her teeth, she said, "You stay away from me!"

She lifted her reticule and swung it at his head as hard as she could. He stepped back, hand on the side of his face, shock and fury distorting his features. He stumbled back another step, unbalanced. Before he could recover, she ran at him with a great shove from both of her hands into his chest. He backed up one more step but did not see the rain barrel until he was already sitting in it, water up to his chest. Pleased with herself, she snatched up the fliers and ran as quickly as she could out of the alley in the direction of the store.

CHAPTER THIRTEEN

NATHANIEL WATCHED CHARLES LEMMING AS the man readied his horse. He must make an obligatory ride through Hyde Park to be seen by the ladies of the *ton*.

He chuckled to himself. He did enjoy feminine attention, though he was likely the most innocent rake in all of London. However, the thrill of admiring eyes and conquered women lost its heady effect well into his third Season. The longer he lived, the more he tired of the same conversations with the same kinds of people. The faces in front of him would vary, but all of the women and all of the niceties blended to form one identity: the debutante. He never discovered more than her exterior of *ton* politesse and never revealed himself either.

Except for a precious few moments, he'd treated Amanda in much the same way. He knew hiding himself beneath his careless and rakish facade had hurt her. He'd belittled the very things in her he admired and it had pained him to do it. He had no choice, did he? He had lived for many years trusting almost no one with all of his secrets, not even Annesley. And he didn't trust Lady Amanda . . . not yet.

He snorted. Could he ever trust her? Where was the young and witty girl he had become fascinated with all those years ago? She seemed to have disappeared amidst a sea of dresses and bonnets and jewels. She laughed and flirted and said absolutely meaningless things to every person around her. Surely she could never grasp the gravity of all that he was working for.

Too much was at stake for anyone to recognize that he was anything other than the infamous Lord Nathaniel, the biggest rake in all of London.

Charles led Smoke toward him. The horse echoed his own feelings as he pawed impatiently at the ground. He would need to find a place for a good hard run before he walked through the park smiling and flirting and making flippant love to the debutantes.

Once astride Smoke, he eyed the new stable hand. "Thank you, Charles."

"Yes, my lord. Is there anything else you need before I finish feeding the others?"

"No, that will be all. I should return before tea, and he will need a good rub down and some oats."

Charles nodded. "Very good, my lord."

"And Charlie?"

Charlie turned, appearing surprised at the use of an old nickname. "Yes, my lord?"

"I remember you. From Lady Amanda's home in Devonshire. The day we sold Horatia."

"Yes, my lord." His face tensed, but he maintained a respectful demeanor.

Nathaniel chuckled. "You and your pitchfork were a formidable opponent."

Charlie's eyes widened in surprise.

Lord Nathaniel couldn't help the smile that came onto his face. He said, "The lady is worthy of your defense sir, and I thank you for your loyalties."

Charlie forced his mouth closed and with a bow, responded, "I thank you, my lord. My fealty remains the same and extends to those with similar loyalties."

Lord Nathaniel considered his response for a moment and studied Charlie with an appraising eye. "Loyalty is hard-won these days. I hope to merit yours, as mine are precisely in line." Lord Nathaniel reached down to offer a handshake to Charlie.

"I hope that is the case, my lord." Charlie reached for his hand and offered an open smile.

Lord Nathaniel nodded to him and nudged Smoke onto the path. Something urged him to call over his shoulder, "I will be in the far side of the park and along the northern streets."

Needing the release of a brisk run with his stallion, Nathaniel brought his magnificent animal to a gallop as soon as he was able, and Smoke did not disappoint. They tore through the hedges and across open grass. Much later than he had planned, he slowed to a walk and continued on the less-populated streets of town. Several blocks over from the shopping district, very few people walked these rows this close to the lunch hour. In one hour's time, the park and streets would be full of this Season's hopefuls out to promenade, to see and be seen.

As he turned the last street before heading back to the park, he caught a glimpse of pink in the otherwise charcoal of the buildings and cobblestone. The back of a pink gown entered Gramden's Print Shop, one of the few shops members of the *ton* frequented on this side.

He pulled back on Smoke's reins, urging him to walk then slowly return to the shop front, where several women gathered around the latest drawings advertising the gossip of the *ton*. Something about the pink figure had reminded him of Lady Amanda, and he shook his head—his mind conjured her up in the most unlikely places.

But doubts filled him. He wanted substance from her. Was he enamored with only the idea of her? Would her true essence be far from his imagined ideal? He frowned as he considered the last time he had seen her, when they were at Lord Gresham's home for dinner and cards.

Free with her smiles, accepting attention from any man willing to give it, and wearing a very alluring dress, she had quickly become the center of attention. He was quite as distracted by her as nearly every other man in attendance.

He'd clenched his fists to keep from pummeling those who'd dared to look too long or too greedily in that direction. She had spouted such nonsense he could do nothing in response but shake his head. One of her doting admirers, a young Baron Kenworthy, had never left her side—someone she would surely never consider as a viable marriage partner, and with whom she had flirted with abandon.

He remembered the conversation clearly because it had left him with his tongue frozen in shock. This baron, dolt though he was, had suggested that the group should all entertain themselves with a bit of poetry, an impromptu recitation of sorts.

Amanda's face would have been almost comical if Nathaniel hadn't been so irritated by her obvious lack of sincerity. She had said, "Oh, Sir Kenworthy! What a splendid idea! I do believe I should like to go first! May I?"

Pleased at having eliciting such a response from the recipient of his undying worship, Kenworthy had smiled and said, "Oh, but of course—you must grace us with your verse so that we may bask in its magnificence."

Amanda had laughed with false modesty and stood with her hand raised to the air, announcing to all the room,

"Why doth a sparrow fly?
Way up high,
In the sky?
Well, you see,
It is because with glee,
I set her free."

Then she had stopped, dipped a low curtsy, and returned to her seat. The room had erupted, mad with laughter and applause. There had been talk for many minutes of her cleverness, canonizing one of the most ridiculous bits of frivolity he had ever heard. She had blushed and dipped her head and acknowledged each accolade.

Could she really have fancied those few lines clever? Several other women had agreed to share as well. Instead of original poems, however, they had chosen to quote some of the great poets of the day.

He gripped the reins in frustration at the memory and dismounted from his horse. Nathaniel knew she was, in fact, very clever. So what was she playing at?

Walking beside Smoke, Nathaniel continued to wander along the street outside Gramden's.

A dark figure several corners away caught his eye. A man darted across the street and into an alley. Then a whirl of pink raced toward them, causing Smoke to rear up. The wind left his chest as the very object of his thoughts ran right into him at full speed. He looked down and saw the top of her bonnet as she stumbled and nearly lost her footing. He put his arms out to steady her.

"Lady Amanda? My dear, are you well?" He moved his hands to her shoulders and arms.

She had not yet lifted her head, but he could feel her trembling through his gloves. His protective instincts escalated as did his tender feeling. "Lady Amanda, what is the matter?" He tipped his head down so that he could peer into her face under her bonnet. Her wide eyes and very pale face stared back at him. Her lips began to quiver, and tears threatened to spill onto her cheeks. He quickly offered her his handkerchief. His eyes searched the streets around them.

"What is it? Lady Amanda, tell me what has happened."

She accepted the handkerchief gratefully enough, but she searched the street in a distracted manner, fear in her eyes. A carriage rounded the corner, and she startled. Lord Nathaniel shielded her from the street with his body, moving her between him and his horse.

"Please, Amanda, if there is anything I can do to alleviate this distress, say the word." He commanded patience in his voice, but his mind raced and tested myriad possibilities. A great protective swell began to rise inside while he studied the top of her bonnet.

She seemed to gather her strength as she took a deep breath and looked into his face. Smoothing her features, she tried to hide the nervous lines and expression around her eyes.

"Are you out walking alone, Lady Amanda? Where is your carriage? Surely you did not walk all the way out here by yourself?"

She glanced nervously up the street the way she had come and asked, "Might we walk somewhere to talk about this in a different location?"

Charlie and Lady Amanda's maid, Molly, rounded a corner then and moved toward them at a full run. Molly's face flushed from exertion.

Concern lined Charlie's face. "Lord Nathaniel, I hoped to find you here. Might we have a bit of assistance?"

"Charlie!" Lady Amanda ran to him, stopping short of throwing her arms around the lad and seemed to drink him in with her eyes. He stared at her and swallowed twice before Molly nudged him. Lord Nathaniel would have been amused had he not sensed danger.

Charles looked at Lady Amanda once more, and then his eyes sharpened again. He said to Lord Nathaniel, "Molly was threatened by a couple of men as she left the print shop a bit ago."

Amanda gasped beside him. Molly looked to her quickly in question. Lady Amanda subtly indicated the package she was carrying, and Molly seemed to relax a little. Charles continued. "I was able to hinder their pursuit, and we have been running from them until just moments ago; we lost them at the last alley."

Nathaniel looked in that direction. "Let us make haste and find a safer location."

He turned and wrapped his hands around Amanda's waist, trying not to think about how perfectly she fit in his grasp. Before she could breathe a protest, he lifted her onto Smoke. Her eyes opened wide, and he was gratified to see a bit of pleasure flash across her face. So she was not immune to him. She gracefully crossed one leg over the other, even without the proper saddle; she must be an accomplished rider. Satisfied, he stepped back to do the same for Molly, but before he could lift her up, Charlie had moved in front of him and did the honors himself.

Molly's face blanched, and her hands clutched Lady Amanda's waist in front of her. Amanda said something under her breath. Heads together, they whispered a conversation, and Molly seemed to calm.

Without time to speculate, Nathaniel took off at a run, his horse's reins in hand. He searched the streets behind them, second guessing every shadow. With a great lurch as the horse broke into a trot, the ladies clutched at each other and caught their balance. He chose less-travelled, quieter streets just to the east of the London shopping district. The last thing he needed was to be caught by their parents' friends leading Lady Amanda and her maid on his horse with a stable hand in their wake. They would become the talk of the *ton*, if only for the humor in their situation, no doubt the subject of the next satirical flier. And he could do without more attention.

After he felt they had sufficient distance from Molly's pursuers—he had seen no one following—he stopped and reached his hands back up to Lady Amanda's waist. Her lips turned in a tiny smile, her eyes brightened, and she watched him as he lifted her off the saddle and set her slowly in front of him.

Her cheeks pink, she said, "Thank you."

"You're welcome." He did not move away, and Amanda held his gaze. Nathaniel's body flooded with warmth. Tingling sensations caused the hairs on his neck to stand on end. He moved his face closer to hers.

She cleared her throat and inched backward a step.

He had led them to a quiet location merely three streets behind the busy and populated Mayfair. "Will your carriage be somewhere near here? Or shall I call for mine?"

"This will be fine." Lady Amanda broke his gaze and brushed the front of her dress with one hand, the other still clutching the brown package. "We are to take tea with Clarissa Hampton and shall catch our carriage shortly after."

"But what of those men chasing Molly? And you? Why were you running? Were you also pursued?"

Charlie jerked his head in his direction. "What?"

Amanda shook her head. "I am sure we will be fine. See? Almost to the tearoom now. And the whole time on your horse, we saw no one in pursuit."

His eyes travelled to her brown, slightly torn and smudged package. "Did you stop by Gramden's Print Shop earlier this morning?"

"Oh! Ah . . ." She seemed flustered, blushing. Then, much to Nathaniel's amusement, Amanda lifted her chin and ignored his question. "Thank you, Lord Nathaniel, Charlie, for coming to our rescue." She looked at Nathaniel again with a peculiar intensity. "Again." She gave him another small smile, and then she and Molly turned together and walked down the street toward the nearest tearoom.

Charlie and Nathaniel stood watching them in silence, each with his own thoughts. Then Nathaniel turned to Charlie with his eyebrow raised. "Just what were you doing outside the print shop?"

Charlie widened his eyes in surprise, and then his expression cleared. "I finished with all my tasks at the stable and wanted to go for a bit of a walk."

Nathaniel looked at him in disbelief. "On Abbey Street?"

Charlie smiled. "Well, I started at the park just as you did, but then found myself desiring one of those new packages of stationary. My mother is hoping for a letter. I was several blocks down the street from Gramden's when I saw Lady Amanda and Molly enter through the front door, so naturally—"

"You decided to see just what they were up to."

"Exactly, my lord."

"And what did you discover?"

"Lady Amanda appeared to be very interested in the satirical drawings in the shop while Molly went in the back with the clerk and came out with that brown package Lady Amanda was holding." Charlie appeared to be as unsure as Nathaniel about what to think of this information.

"I'll need to tell her father." Nathaniel frowned. "She should not be about London without footmen."

Charlie nodded. "She'll not thank you for it."

Nathaniel couldn't stop the grin that spread across his face. As foolish as Lady Amanda seemed to be in walking about London alone, the intrigue in her situation excited him, and his desire to know her increased. If anything, her latest actions at least proved her capable of much more than silly debutante conversation.

As soon as Amanda and Molly moved out of sight of Lord Nathaniel, Amanda leaned against Molly in nervous exhaustion. She turned to look at her. "Molly, are you quite well?"

"Perfectly well, my lady. Charlie appeared out of thin air, he did; knocked down the men, and they weren't small, neither of them. Then he told me to run! He stayed with me the whole way—said he knew where to find Lord Nathaniel. We were only just slowing right before we saw you." Molly looked at her quizzically. "And how did that come about?"

Amanda shook her head. "Bender. The men after you must have been with him. He threatened me, and you and Charlie."

"What?" Molly's face went white.

Amanda nodded. "Molly, we have grave trouble to fix. I'm not sure how we will do it. But it is too much to discuss here in the street. Let us get these fliers delivered to the tearoom, shall we?"

When they entered the shop, the delicious smell of brewing tea reached them immediately. "I've never longed for tea as I do now. Let's do have some while we wait for Miss Clarissa and the others."

Molly nodded gratefully and went looking for Mr. Tanner, the owner of the tearoom, who had agreed to carry their fliers in his shop. Moments later, she returned to the table with a big grin. Behind her, a woman about Amanda's age smiled, a hint of mischief playing about her eyes. Amanda liked her immediately. To her surprise, Molly and this young woman both sat down across from her at the table.

Molly said, "Lady Amanda, may I introduce Miss Maribel *Tanner* to you? Miss Tanner, this is Lady Amanda."

Miss Tanner said, "Pleased to meet you, Lady Amanda. I prefer to be called *Tanner* by business associates."

Amanda's eyebrows shot up and her mouth opened. She glanced at Molly, whose smile had not left.

Amanda cleared her throat. "You are Tanner, owner of this tearoom?"

"Very few know, but yes, the one and the same."

Amanda tipped her head to the side. "Of course. Maribel's Tearoom." She smiled. "Well, I am equally pleased to meet you. Thank you for helping us."

Miss Tanner nodded. "It is my pleasure, of course."

When the women had worked out a schedule for regular delivery of new fliers into Miss Tanner's hands and had laughed for a good long time, Amanda knew she had found a true kindred spirit in this woman. Just as Miss Tanner was standing up to return to work, Miss Hampton and three of her friends entered.

"Here we are, my dears! Come and sit where it's cool." Amanda waved and smiled. The four newcomers giggled and hurried over to join them. They looked curiously at the seated Molly, in servant's garb, who stood quickly and curtsied to Amanda. "I'll be seeing to things in the back, my lady." She hurried in the direction Miss Tanner had taken. Amanda watched her wink over her shoulder, knowing that of the two of them, Molly had the better company.

CHAPTER FOURTEEN

July 23, the day my revenge will at last be complete.

It was never enough. No matter who he hurt, the peace of revenge alluded. The whole class of nobles must fall. Surely, Jack Bender would have peace when England's government toppled at his feet, when he stormed their offices and placed himself and his followers at the head. His face twitched, and he rubbed it vigorously to try to make it stop. A new committee of public safety to oversee a full-scale revolution! *Long live the people!* His heart raced in anticipation.

A man in a purple tailcoat covered in gold stars, with several spyglasses hanging from his waistcoat and a watch fob as well, interrupted him. "July 23 the entire cabinet will be in the room celebrating the passage of the Corn Law. It is written in the stars as the day of victory—it is a sign."

Bender did not really like this new mystic who had joined their gang. But he was a powerful man in London. Most sought him in secret. It was rumored he had the ear of the Prince Regent himself, advising him in his choices of romantic dalliance. Emmerich's presence in the room solidified Bender's own seat of power, so he endured his nonsense.

This meeting held his most trusted members, who were seated around the table. Several wore black shrouds to cover their faces. Bender alone knew the identities of every member in his ring.

Baron Kenworthy said, "Well, thank the heavens for the stars then." Several in the room hissed their disapproval. "Has anyone else considered the lunacy of this plan? *All* members of the cabinet? Including the prime minister himself?" A few members of the group started muttering in agreement.

Harrison, a newly acquired magistrate, said, "It's bloody impossible. I don't care what the stars say."

Jack watched their reactions. Almost every face held lines of tension, their mouths pulled down in worry. His eyes stopped on Charles, who hid his reaction, his face a careful stone mask. Jack cleared his throat, and the room fell silent. "What do you say, Charles?"

Surprise flickered in the young man's eyes, but his face remained blank. He cleared his throat. "Maybe if the members of this team could hear the plan, they would feel more confident in our ability to carry it out. I think you should tell us more."

Jack felt Charles's intense gaze, and every other eye followed until the room was cloaked in a tense silence, waiting. The usually obsequious Charles surprised him. Considering the potential challenge to his supreme authority, he stood. Immediately all eyes at the table dropped, and the men closest to him flinched.

"The prime minister and the members of his cabinet, as well as their wives, have all been invited to a dinner party in celebration of the passage of the detestable Corn Law." Several of the hooded guests grumbled their disapproval of the bill.

Jack was secretly thrilled England had passed something so idiotic as the Corn Law. Nervous that the common people in England were rising in rebellion, the cabinet sought for ways to further tax the people, showing its greater power. Their recent choice, to tax the very sustenance the poorer classes survived upon, would send more to the poorhouses and the weak to their graves.

Happily for him, starving the poor would serve as excellent motivation for more to join his *cause*. The more who joined, the easier it would be to oust the nobility from their tightly held seats of power, to destroy the lives of all *William* loved, and to place himself as ruler over all. He cleared his throat to quiet the murmuring. "I feel it is so fitting, perfect really, that the prime minister will fall in the very act of celebrating one of the worst crimes ever committed against the English working class. Let it be known how the people feel about our government controlling the very source of our sustenance."

The men around the table banged their fists in support. Jack appreciated their idealism. It made his job that much easier.

The annoying baron piped up again. "But how? How can we possibly accomplish such a thing?"

Jack's eyes pierced his until the baron's gaze lowered in submission, his face losing color. Satisfied, Jack turned his attention to Charles and continued. "That is all the information I am willing to give. You will receive pertinent additional instructions as necessity dictates. We will meet again at the pub on Cato Street two days before the event. Anyone unwilling to continue on in our cause may speak now."

Jack waited placidly, staring in a deceivingly calm way at the floor. After a few moments, and when no one voiced another concern, he glared at each person around the table again and said, "Wise choice, *gentlemen*. Our inner ring is not a place for doubters." His cheek began twitching, eyes closing and opening in sporadic movement.

He pulled back his tailcoat and brought a pistol forward in his hand, studying the cocking mechanism. He turned to his right and began walking around the room behind those sitting at the table. He stopped beside each man, resting the gun on his shoulder or arm. Sometimes he let it linger along their upper back as he passed behind them. Nearing the baron, Jack tensed in irritation. He brought the gun up to the man's temple.

The baron stiffened. "Oh, hey now, Jack. No need for that. I'm in. You know I'm in for good. A little grumble now and again never harmed anyone, now did it?"

Jack whispered in his ear, loud enough for everyone in the room to hear. "Doubt is dangerous." He lowered his gun, eliciting a collective sigh. But he raised it again immediately and fired a shot into the head of the person immediately to the right of the baron. The hooded man slumped forward, his head hitting the table. Jack ripped the hood from off the man's head. Gasps showed surprise to find the face of John Scott, owner of the Adelphi Theatre.

"He was a spy," Jack said.

Harrison, the magistrate, went white. He used his handkerchief to wipe his brow. More in reaction to the possible leak of information than to the loss of life, no doubt. Charles looked equally white, but Jack assumed his discomfort was more in reaction to the lifeless expression in John Scott's eyes. Charles's idealism was his greatest weakness.

"Charles."

The boy stood up immediately.

"Dispose of the body somewhere public. Place this on his head." Jack produced a red cap of liberty, which he placed in Charles's outstretched hands. Charles motioned for one of the guards at the door to help him, and they half carried, half-dragged John Scott's corpse from the room.

Later that night, Charlie scribbled furiously across the page, informing Red of all the details surrounding July 23. Still sick to his stomach from his earlier task, Charlie held a handkerchief up to his mouth while he wrote. *If this information saves lives, it will all be worth it.* He repeated to himself over again that and similar sentiments, but the tendrils of darkness remained, stealing his peace of mind.

John Scott had been a good man. He and his daughter, Jane, had run the theatre together. She served as its main playwright. What would she do now without her father? Even though she was the true source of the theatre's success, without her father to give her credibility, she would lose patrons. Again, in his mind, Charlie saw the blank eyes of the dead John. He rubbed his hands over his face, trying to blot out the image that seared his brain.

Refocusing on his efforts, he shook his hands and picked up his quill, dipping it into the ink. He would ride all night to deliver the message himself—this news must be in Red's hands tomorrow.

CHAPTER FIFTEEN

"Lady Amanda, what are you doing?" A smile, unbidden, gracing his lips, Nathaniel muttered to himself and shook his head.

He ran his fingers over the images on the flier he had picked up in town. On it, a boy's haunting stare peered at him through the bars of the debtor's cart. The mother and nursing child, the filthy men—she hadn't missed a single person. She was remarkably talented. Their likenesses so captured, he felt himself return to the scene, and he saw Lady Amanda again, wrenching open the door to that despicable conveyance, her shoulders and hands, the very manner in which she stood, so full of hope. Nathaniel shook his head. Although he was likely the only person in the *ton* to know who drew these fliers, he couldn't help but feel a small ball of worry begin as he thought of the risk she had taken. Dangerous players toyed with the concept of liberty, and Bender had already targeted her.

"I hope someone is aware and watching out for you," he murmured. Smiling, he reached for his father's latest letter. Somehow word had reached the estate that Nathaniel had an interest in Lady Amanda, and his father expressed his full support. He shook his head. He knew too well the difficulty of guarding secrets from the *ton*.

Brooks stood in the open doorway, the letter tray in his hand. "My lord, Martin has just delivered the post."

Nathaniel looked up from his father's desk in the library and raised his eyebrows. "Very well, Brooks. Let's take care of that now."

"Yes, my lord." Brooks looked up and down the hallway and then entered the room, locking the door behind him.

Nathaniel stood up from his desk and led the way to the back of the room. He walked toward the window alcove that overlooked the east gardens and reached behind the curtains. Nathaniel felt the small, nearly invisible latch, which he depressed with his forefinger. They both waited while the adjacent wall slid silently to the left, revealing a passageway.

He glanced around the hidden office, verifying that all was in order and that they were alone. They moved to sit at the desk, Brooks setting down the tray between them and Nathaniel pulling out his signet, used only for Liberty Seekers correspondence. "I am almost afraid to read the latest news."

Brooks nodded. "The Spa Fields riots really set us back. Were it not for Bender and his men, Hunt could have finished his speech at Islington and we would be much further along."

"Exactly," Nathaniel said. "The man is a menace."

Brooks gestured to the air. "And insane. Hopes to overthrow us all. I fear the man hungers for Madame la Guillotine's reign in London."

Thinking of the boy in the cart, a desire to save him and all those like him renewed Nathaniel's energy. He reached out and gripped Brooks's shoulder. "We must plan an effective rally, a peaceful demonstration, try again without Bender's interference. Perhaps somewhere closer."

Brooks said, "God willing, my lord."

Nathaniel stood and began pacing off his excited energy while they talked. "Why not Manchester? They are the largest group of unrepresented people."

Brooks smiled. "Just so, my lord. St. Peter's Fields is a lovely large space. It could fit half the town."

Nathaniel pulled fresh paper across the desk and dipped his pen in ink. "I'll call in the men for a meeting. We can't lose momentum. We had better get the rally planned as soon as possible." After sealing his correspondence with hot wax, the image of an eagle's head betokening the letter's author, Nathaniel ran his thumb across the top of his signet ring. "I have always loved the eagle. The first time I saw one, soaring at heights no human could ever reach, I was fascinated by the bird. My first signet—do you remember?—it was an eagle in flight."

"I remember."

"But *we* are not in flight, Brooks, and we are not in battle either. Peaceful, lawful ways will excite the greatest change. The eagle in flight seemed the best image for Red at the time, until I met an eagle at rest."

Brooks raised his eyebrows in question.

Nathaniel explained, "I was traversing some old ruins near my estate in Wales and I came across an eagle's nest, overlooking the cliffs by the sea. From my place at the top of a crag on a hill, I stood mesmerized as I watched an eagle on the edge of her nest facing the wind. The majesty and calm of the creature struck me. In that moment I thought, 'This bird may fly high and far, but she is truly free only in the peace of this moment.'" Nathaniel shrugged with a smile. "That is when I commissioned this ring. Freedom became more to me that day."

"And the eagle in flight is a most appropriate signet now for our spy. I was much pleased when you asked Martin to deliver it to him."

Nathaniel said, "Brave man, he is—it is time I met him, I believe."

"There is a letter from him here, my lord." Brooks indicated the small stack of correspondence on the tray.

Finding the letter, Nathaniel broke the seal and read the first few lines. Dread settled in his gut and his fist clenched, crumpling the paper.

Brooks's eyes flew to Nathaniel's face. "What is it?"

"He says Bender plans murder—of government officials."

"Where? When?"

"July 23. He will have more information in a few days." *Oh, that he would hurry.*

"That's only a few weeks away," Brooks said gravely.

"We will have to work quickly."

CHAPTER SIXTEEN

The crush at the opera would have pushed Amanda along in a most uncomfortable way had they not given her a bit of space due to her title and the fact that her father accompanied her. Loud laughing at her left startled her from her thoughts. A group of this year's new debutantes, some she had not met yet, leaned together in a small huddle, looking at something.

The duke noticed and chuckled. "It looks like our dear artist has printed a new satire."

"Our dear artist?" Amanda swallowed, her hands shaking a little.

The duke smiled. "Surely you have seen his work. It seems that everybody's talking about it. Peter Hamilton is his name."

Amanda nodded, breathing out, "Oh yes, Father, I have seen one or two of his fliers, I believe." They continued walking toward their box. Her father's strong arm provided comfort as well as support as she rested her hand in the crook of his elbow.

He said, "Oho! I think I see one now." He reached and picked up a flier from a nearby table. "Someone must have discarded."

Her heart pounded in her chest when she recognized it. The mother and baby stared at her with hopeless eyes, along with the other passengers of the prison cart. She commanded her heart to still, and she watched her father's expression. His eyebrows furrowed as he took in all of the detail.

"No, this is not one of Hamilton's satires. I find nothing at all amusing in this drawing."

She leaned toward him to look at the drawing herself, though she had long since memorized each line.

"The artist has great talent, however," her father went on. "This young boy's eyes will haunt my dreams tonight."

A smile threatened to break through on her face. The art pleased her father and touched him. She could not receive a higher accolade. "I wonder at its purpose. Who are these people? And why are they in a cage?"

"As to its purpose, I could not say. It does make one dreary to think of people in such a condition. I wonder who the artist could be? It is signed simply, *The Sparrow*." Her father folded the paper into thirds and slipped it into his waistcoat pocket. "And here he is! Did I mention we are meeting Lord Needley tonight?"

Amanda glanced up in surprise at her father and then ahead at Needley himself as he approached.

"No, Father, you neglected to tell me." She looked at him in mock reproach. "But never mind. I find I am in the mood for a bit of fun. And Lord Needley will always provide." She left the crook of her father's arm and stepped forward to greet their guest. "My dear Lord Needley! How good of you to join us."

His smile grew as he stood a little taller. Then he placed her hand on his arm. "Shall we, my lady?"

"Thank you, my lord." She stepped back a bit as if to look over his person from boot to top hat. "I must say, Lord Needley, you are looking well." They began walking, her father following a few paces back.

He blushed, and his lip quirked in a crooked smile. "My lady, you shouldn't say such things. My head shall swell." When she pouted, he said, "But I thank you."

She flashed him her most brilliant smile. His feet faltered, and she had to slow her walk to remain by his side. She wondered at his reaction. *Surely no person is that physically affected by another.*

As she turned her head, she startled at the sight of Lord Nathaniel's big frame suddenly standing close to her small one. In the bustling crush, she hadn't been aware of his approach.

She breathed in his musky scent and felt her knees go weak. Her mouth felt full and dry as cotton, and her heart pounded in her chest. She clutched Lord Needley's arm tighter to keep herself from trembling. She dipped a low curtsy and rose slowly, watching him through her lashes.

Lord Nathaniel nodded his head at her. "Good evening, Lady Amanda. Lord Needley. If you'll excuse me, I must find my box." Lady Amanda's eyes widened. He stared meaningfully at her, directed her gaze to his hands, where he held two fliers. He angled them so she could see and then walked past, toward his own box. Her heart sank. Of course he knew she drew the fliers. She must find a way to talk to him somehow tonight.

Lord Needley gently pulled her with him, encouraging her to walk again as they made their way toward her father's box. "That man is always running off in a most abrupt way, is he not?"

She answered something in a noncommittal fashion, distracted. They arrived at her father's box and took their seats, she and Lord Needley sitting behind her father. Her mother would be arriving shortly with a couple of her widowed friends.

As the lights dimmed and the audience prepared for the performance, Amanda's cheers and applause were not at all forced. As soon as the curtain opened, she became swept up in the scenes and the beauty of the music. But moments before intermission, her mind wandered, and she found herself often looking at the profile of the man beside her. He was exceptionally handsome.

Why can I feel no attraction to him? He was perfectly kind and amiable. He was wealthy and successful, titled, and perfectly committed to her. Her father supported him. And she could tell that he would allow her many liberties other men would not. She suspected she could talk him into anything.

But would he understand her work? She tried to imagine telling him about her illustrations, about the stirring words she'd heard in the church square. She could not envision his response. She realized with a start that she knew nothing of his desires, goals, hopes. What drove him? Where were his interests and passions? She sighed.

"What is it, my lady? May I get you a lemonade?" He was ever attentive, and intermission had begun without her realizing.

"I would like that. In fact, let us go together. I could use a turn about the theatre." They were immediately surrounded by the crush outside the boxes and surrounding the refreshment tables. However, they soon found a cozy corner to stand in, drinks in hand. Amanda looked to her left where a group of ladies laughed together. Were they looking at more fliers?

She scanned faces and immediately saw young Baron Kenworthy and two other very eligible men with him, heading in her direction. "Oh, Sir Kenworthy, there you are. You walked up at just the right moment, because you see, I have quite a quandary."

He bowed over her fingertips. "Oh? And what is your quandary, fair maiden? Perhaps we can solve it." They all nodded, willing enough for the game.

She put on her prettiest pout. "Well, you see, I chose this dress especially for you, all four of you." She gestured to include Lord Needley and the three men who had just arrived. "I thought it quite fetching on me, you see." She paused and the men jumped in, chorusing her beauty and the many benefits of her gown. She nearly rolled her eyes but forbore. "But then I saw that beautiful creature onstage, singing like an angel of light and I gave up all hope. For she outshines us all."

She paused with eyes downcast for just a moment then looked up hopefully, fluttering her eyelashes at the men. Lord Needley remained surprisingly silent, but the other three lauded her charms for several moments and would have continued had she not interrupted.

"Thank you so. Hearing such undeserved praise from men as handsome as you four causes my heart to flutter." She placed a hand at her neckline and smiled. They beamed back at her.

Lord Needley cleared his throat. "I do believe intermission is almost at an end, my lady."

"I am sure you are correct. It is reassuring to have you by my side to remember such things." She returned her hand to his arm.

The girls to her left broke out in loud giggles. Amanda could almost sense the mamas of the *ton* fainting dead away. She looked up to see the cause. Her own heart stammered as Lord Nathaniel sauntered in their direction. Each of the girls fluttered her eyelashes, dipped a curtsy, and tried to get his attention.

Was it her imagination or did they seem much more obvious than usual? Amanda raised her hand to her mouth as one of the girls stepped in front of him, blocking his path so abruptly he almost ran her down. His body brushed hers before he could back away. Instead of shying away in embarrassment, the girl leaned in to him and put her hand on his chest. He took two steps back and bowed to her before moving to the side to step around her. When he did, another girl stepped in his way and curtsied deeply.

Amanda began a slow smile of amusement. What was wrong with these girls? Lord Nathaniel caught her eye as he was coming up from his bow. She raised her eyebrows in speculation, but he narrowed his eyes at her and frowned. Taken aback, she drew in a breath.

Her reaction was not lost on her companion. "Strangest man of my acquaintance, that Lord Nathaniel. What could he possibly be scowling at you about? Come, my dear. We should get back to your parents."

Amanda nodded but kept looking at Lord Nathaniel as if staring at him would help solve the puzzle. She didn't have to stare long, however, because within moments he was marching over in strong, purposeful strides.

"Needley." He stood in front of them and nodded. Lord Needley pulled her closer to him and made an effort to begin walking back toward their box.

But Lord Nathaniel stopped them. "You must wait for just a moment more."

"Oh?" Lord Needley frowned.

"To be sure. I have not yet admired this loveliest of dresses. Lady Amanda, surely you wore it just for me?"

She blushed. *Had he heard her previous nonsense?* She cleared her throat. "Why yes! I am so glad you noticed." Perhaps he was hoping to return to their previous flirtations. She stepped to the side, allowing her eyes to travel from his boots to his hair, just as she had with Lord Needley. "And that tailcoat. How well it fits you. I find I am a bit breathless of a sudden." She fanned her face and flashed him a teasing grin.

He reached for her hand and bowed over it, turning it mid bow and placing his lips on her uncovered wrist.

A puff of air left her mouth, and she swallowed slowly. He raised himself and challenged her with his expression. Though her hand still rested on Lord Needley's arm and he'd become noticeably stiff, all she could think of was Lord Nathaniel and his lips on her skin. She wanted to be pulled against his chest and to feel his strength around her. Knowing he outmatched her in this flirting contest of theirs, she could think of nothing to do in retaliation. So she admitted defeat and allowed her shy desire to show in her expression. No disguise necessary, with an open air of need, she smiled and shrugged.

He closed his mouth and then opened it again, moving his neck around in an apparent effort to loosen his cravat. He blushed, and her heart warmed to him anew. She could never have predicted such open vulnerability.

He cleared his throat, glancing at her again, and said to Lord Needley, "Have you seen the latest fliers from Gramden's?"

"I have not. I am not often in that part of town."

"Well, let me show them to you. Quite remarkable, really."

Her breath caught when he brought out her drawing.

"Not a satire, this one."

Lord Needley looked it over and then held it back for Lord Nathaniel to take, letting it fall limply down, as if he didn't want to touch it for too long. "What is the purpose of this, I wonder? Why draw something so disheartening?"

Her mouth turned down. "Wh-what do you mean?"

Lord Needley looked at her curiously for a moment. "Well . . . I mean . . . the people are so depressing. And the subject in general so morbid. I do not wish to seek out the hardships of life to dwell unhappily upon them, not when there is so much that is pleasing all around us."

Her small smile acknowledged his meaning.

Lord Nathaniel said, "Perhaps it is a motivator for change."

"It could be, yes, if it came with something to *do*. As it is right now, I am left to feel sorrow for people I don't know, stuck in a situation I do not fully comprehend, with no hopes of ever seeing them again."

She nodded and said very softly, "I see what you mean."

Lord Nathaniel's expression showed great sympathy for a moment, but then his eyes hardened. "The other flier I have is pure satire—much more amusing to some than others. In truth, many have pronounced it very humorous indeed."

She leaned forward. When she saw the flier's image, she gasped. "No!"

Another group of women walked by, and when they saw Lord Nathaniel, they giggled and smiled at him. One even had the audacity to rest her hand on his arm, letting it trail up his sleeve as she passed. He turned red and gripped the flier tighter in his fist. He put it in front of Amanda so quickly she felt the breeze from it on her face.

Looking at it more closely, she asked, "Why would anyone print such a thing?" The flier held a very good representation of Lord Nathaniel pressing his boot up against the gown of the person on is left, holding hands with the lady on his right, and making love with his eyes to the person across from him. Lady Amanda's eyes met his with sorrow.

"I don't suppose you know anything about this?"

She looked for the signature on the flier. Sure enough, it was Peter Hamilton, the man who had been listening so intently to them in the print shop.

"But how was he able to draw such an accurate likeness of you, my lord?"

He looked more fiercely at her. "So you know how this came about?"

She let her breath out slowly. "I know something about it, yes."

Patrons began rushing back to their boxes and ushers snuffed out candles to make ready for the remainder of the opera.

Lord Needley stepped away, pulling her with him. "If you will excuse us, we must return to the duke's box."

She reached a hand out to touch Lord Nathaniel's arm. "You may join us if you like. It would give me a chance to explain."

"I have guests in my own box, but I will find a way. We *will* talk, you and I."

About one quarter of the way into the second act, she felt a hand on her shoulder. Gray eyes stared into hers. His finger was up to his mouth, and he motioned with his head for her to follow him. She slipped from her chair to stand at the back of her box. Lord Needley glanced her way, but at her reassuring smile, he returned his attention to the stage.

She waited for another moment and then slipped through the curtain behind her into the dimly lit hallway. Lord Nathaniel immediately grabbed her hand and led her quickly down the hall and around the corner, where he pulled her into a small alcove almost hidden from anyone who might be out in the hallways.

"What is this little corner you have discovered? I have the distinct impression I am not the first to have been escorted here in the dark of an opera." She raised her eyebrow in question, a teasing smile on her face. She swallowed. Hopefully they would not be discovered.

He ignored her insinuation. Holding up the flier again, he said, "Explain."

She sighed. "Surely you do not think that I drew—"

"No, I do not. It is not in any way similar to the other. But you do know something about it."

"I do. I am quite ashamed of my own involvement actually." She looked down. "I was trying to distract a shop full of customers to look my way while Molly picked up our package. One of the ladies present thought up this story, and I listened. I had not thought of our ramblings ever leaving that room in such a way. I promise I never would have—"

"But what is this supposed to represent? Who are these women?"

Suddenly self-conscious, Amanda forced herself to meet his gaze. "The dinner at the Hadley's last month. The lady in the shop sat across from you. She claimed to have witnessed you giving, ah, *attention* to these women. I shed a bit of doubt on the story, and Miss Clarissa came to your defense. But as I was leaving, I noticed a man who appeared to have been intently listening, and I discovered he was none other than Peter Hamilton." Nathaniel frowned deeper at her. She continued. "You must believe me. I had no way of knowing something like this would ever happen because of a harmless story."

"Harmless? You think this image harmless?"

"Well, no, but I didn't expect it to become an *image*."

"Every word we speak paints an image in the minds of those who hear it. Her story damaged me from the moment it left her lips, and it will continue to do so with each retelling."

"But, it is an image *you* perpetuate. Are you not pleased to have painted yourself as the biggest rake in all of London?"

He shook his head at her. "Not like this."

She felt about as tall as the bottom step on her front stoop. She reached for the page again. "I should have come stronger to your defense. I don't know how to fix this. I am terribly sorry. Perhaps it would help if you, ah, settled down for a few months with someone."

His loud whisper sounded almost raspy in its strength. "I am *trying* to court *you*. If you would just cooperate for an hour's time, we could maybe progress a small amount."

Amanda blushed deeply. Pleased, she couldn't slow her heart or stop the fluttering in her stomach. So he *did* still wish to court her. Perhaps substance existed behind all of his effective flirting.

But why did he make things so difficult? Her eyes narrowed slightly. Then she retorted, "*Are* you trying to court me? Because all you seem to do is *rescue* me. When is the last time you paid me a visit? Or had a pleasant conversation with me? Or even took a turn with me on the dance floor?" She folded her arms with a challenging look in her eye.

He cleared his throat. "Would you enjoy that, my lady?"

His eyes sparkled at her. Was he teasing her? He searched her face earnestly, and she remembered he had asked her a question.

"I would, yes." Her eyes followed the line of his jaw, lingered on his lips, and then found his eyes.

"Magnificent. It just so happens that I would like to talk about this further. May I call on you tomorrow, take you for a ride in the phaeton through the park?"

He stepped closer, and suddenly she became aware of the smallness of their hiding place. His lips were eye level, his face only inches from her own. If she tipped her head up a little more and looked into his eyes, her lips would be ready for his. She forced that thought away, blushing. She looked down, finding his boots.

Lord Nathaniel put his finger under her chin and lifted her face so she was looking straight into his eyes. They were smiling at her. He ran his hands down her arms, trailing gooseflesh wherever they touched, and took both of her hands in his own. "Until tomorrow then?"

She nodded. Oh, could this really be happening? He leaned closer, her heart fearful and expectant at once. His gaze, intent, searched her own. She closed her eyes, and he brushed his lips against her cheek. Still deliciously close to her face, he rested his hand at her other cheek. She opened her eyes again as his eyes devoured her features, lingering on her lips, and then with the puff of a sigh, he stepped back. With a wink, he held her hand and led her away from their alcove.

Her emotions swirled around inside. Did all women succumb to him like she had wanted to? Her thoughts flitted by so quickly she could not hold on to one long enough to form a coherent train. The one clear, solid emotion that outlasted the rest filled her. Yearning. She wanted more. Whoever Lord Nathaniel turned out to be at his core, she wanted more.

Was he as affected as she? He walked so quickly, they almost ran down the hallway. Without another word he delivered her to her box.

Lord Needley turned when she arrived, saw her standing at the back of the box against the curtain. Although he raised his eyebrows, he said nothing about her absence and continued viewing the second act.

Amanda returned to her seat, her hand touching the side of her face where Lord Nathaniel's lips had left their invisible mark. Surely he felt something for her. The sincerity in his eyes could not be fabricated, could it? She relived the moment when his lips touched her skin. Oh, that it had been her mouth. How she had willed it to be so. The man drove her to distraction.

Her thoughts changed direction to the subject of their tête-à-tête. The stage blurred as she tried to make sense of it all. Peter Hamilton *had* been listening and had recreated the story onto fliers! She clenched her fists. The more she thought about it, the more ashamed she felt. She should have steered the conversation in a different direction.

Then without warning, the humor struck her. The silly and exaggerated reaction to the picture of Lord Nathaniel from this year's debutantes came to her mind, all those women falling all over him. She raised her hand to her mouth, shaking in an effort to stifle her laughter. *Serves him right.* He certainly would not die from over-attention. If he didn't wish to be misunderstood, he should not walk about pretending to be a rake.

CHAPTER SEVENTEEN

AMANDA TWIRLED HER PARASOL AS she walked down London Street right in the heart of the shopping district. Three men crowded around her. She felt a bit frustrated this morning, because she had not tried to attract a single one of them and yet here they were. She was in quite a hurry to deliver some new fliers, and there was simply no way to be secretive when surrounded. Molly walked about eight paces behind her, and whenever their eyes met, Molly raised hers to the sky.

Amanda hoped that Lord Nathaniel had received her note about picking her up at Mirabel's Tea Room instead of at her home. She did not know what to expect from a ride in the park with him, but she was very much looking forward to it. She turned to the nearest man at her side, Baron Worthing. "Shall we go get an ice? I am feeling quite parched."

"Your wish is my command, my lady," he said and nodded his head.

One roguish Lord Foxworthy said, "Allow me, my lady." *An ice from me is sure to be superior to one from anyone else*, he seemed to imply. He pulled her to a stop and kissed her hand, smiling hopefully.

She smiled, laughing. "But of course. I thank you."

They continued walking. She scanned the street with a moment's apprehension. Ever since her meeting with Bender, she had been wary of an attempt to talk to her again to set up their meeting place. She knew she would have to think her way out of supplying the ring, and soon. With a shiver, she wondered how he would initiate their meeting.

Sir Worthing noticed the shiver and immediately suggested they move indoors. She laughed. "Oh no, my dear Baron. It is not the chill that makes me react so. I am simply quite overwhelmed by all of you, the handsomest men this Season, escorting me the way you are." She fanned herself. The seams on their waistcoats stretched as they flexed and preened. She could have never predicted a few words of praise could have such an effect.

Lord Foxworthy returned with her ice, and she crossed the street to find a bench overlooking the park and the shops. She glanced at Molly, standing behind her as befitted her station. Amanda felt suddenly awash with indignation at the injustice. She called to her. "Molly, do be a dear and come meet our new friends."

The group stared in silence. She turned to look at her companions and noticed a few of the men belatedly closing shocked mouths.

She looked up innocently at each in turn, widening her eyes. "What? What is the matter with the lot of you? Molly is one of my dearest friends and a loyal employee. I should think you, also my dear friends, would want to meet her, and she you."

The men looked uncomfortably around, avoiding her gaze, until Baron Worthing seemed to shake himself and stepped forward. "But of course. Molly, you said?"

Amanda beamed with gratitude. "Yes, Baron Worthing, this is Miss Molly, my personal maid and dear friend. Molly, this is Baron Worthing of Gloucester."

Molly could not have looked more uncomfortable. She stammered a, "Pleased, I'm sure." Curtsying to the baron, she kept her eyes cemented to the ground.

The other men shuffled awkwardly, avoiding her gaze. Lord Foxworthy pulled out his watch and mumbled something about an appointment at White's. The others followed. The loyal Baron Worthing stayed for a moment more, asking if the ladies would be seated and then once he was sure they were comfortable, he too made his exit, a slight apology in his eyes.

"Well! How absolutely absurd!" Amanda could not hide her outrage at the men's behavior.

Molly asked, "My lady, may I be frank?" Her voice had a strange pinched quality.

"Why yes, of course. I apologize for their behavior. What a disappointment. I expected more from them. Had I known they would behave so, I would have never subjected you to such humiliation."

Molly stared at her for a moment while collecting her thoughts. "I don't blame them at all for behaving the way they did. If they were to acknowledge an introduction to me, it would open doors and allow familiarity with someone of my station. I could approach them at a later time. I could even impose enough to call on them. My lady, forgive me, but until our system of social status and class changes, we must follow society's rules."

Amanda considered her wise observations. In many ways she suspected the division between their classes would be more difficult to change than even their current electoral policies. "I did not think. I am truly sorry, my dear Molly. I guess sometimes I get so caught up in our cause that I forget others do not feel the same. At least not yet, anyway."

"And what cause is this, Lady Amanda?" Charlie approached them from behind. She wondered just how much of the scene he had witnessed. "Trying to ennoble the working class, are you?"

Amanda narrowed her eyes. Apparently, he had witnessed the whole of their interactions. They stood to welcome him. "Hello, Mr. Lemming. What has you out on the London streets at this hour of the day, spying on old friends?"

To her surprise, Molly also greeted Charlie and offered him her hand, "Hello, Charlie." And she curtsied. He smiled, wiggling both eyebrows at her and bowed over her hand in a very gallant, well-executed manner. Molly giggled, and Amanda was grateful for his ability to lighten the mood.

Amanda said, "Won't you sit with us? It is such a lovely day, and we seem to have misplaced all of our company."

"I would love to, for a small moment. I am watching that horse over there and cannot let him feel too alone. Gets right impatient, he does."

"Oh! Are you employed here in London then?" Amanda still had not heard what occupied his time.

Charlie had the decency to look regretful when he said, "I am. I work at one of the finest houses for a fine gentleman. He rivals your father in fairness and goodness, I tell you." Before Amanda could ask who his employer might be, Charlie looked to Molly and asked, "And how are you, Miss Molly? Recovered from our mad dash through London, I see."

Molly blushed. "Oh, yes, I am." She paused and then seemed to push herself to respond, "But it was quite an adventure, was it not? We gave them the slip, and that's for sure."

Charlie bent his head back and laughed with his belly. It was so infectious that Amanda joined him, and others on the street turned in their direction.

Wiping his eyes from mirth, he looked at Molly again. "You are right plucky you are, Molly. I'm glad Lady Amanda has a friend such as you."

Amanda felt a bit as though she were intruding as the two of them looked into each other's eyes for a moment. She readjusted her skirts and turned a bit to the side. His mention of work brought back all her worries from her meeting with Bender. She started to wring her hands as she pondered what she must do. Did Charlie know his very life was in danger?

Anxiety rose up in her chest at such a rate that she burst out the words, "Charlie, do you really work for Jack Bender?" And she turned to him with eyes full of equal amounts hope that he did not and dread that he might.

Charlie paused, looking from Molly to Amanda then down at his boots and answered softly, "Now, that's a complicated question for a poor chap to answer."

Amanda's heart sank. "Then it's true? How could you give your loyalties to such a low form of scum and degradation?"

Molly caught her breath. The three shared a bench in the shade of a tree. The street wasn't crowded, but now and then people passed on their way to the many shops in the area.

Charlie said, "Such language, Lady Amanda. Remember we are not at the fishing pond here."

Before Amanda felt her fury rise, she noticed the glint of teasing in Charlie's eyes, and she was mollified, but only slightly. "Answer me, Charles. I must know."

Charlie stared into her eyes. "I swore to you, and I stand by it. You and your house have nothing to fear from me."

Amanda was unmoved. "But you are not answering my question." Her eyes locked onto his and demanded an honest response.

"I do not work for him." Both ladies sighed in relief. He held up a finger. "But . . . I am associated with him and his gang and do on occasion . . . participate."

Amanda stood up in shock. "What are you saying? Do you work for that awful man, or don't you? He threatened me, you know! Came to me, forced a conversation!" Amanda began pacing in front of them. She looked up and down the street before hissing into his face, "He is at this moment blackmailing me!"

Charlie stood up in alarm, putting his hand on her arm. "What? What do you mean?" He gently guided Amanda back to her seat as more people looked curiously in their direction.

Amanda's hands began to tremble.

She wanted to warn him, to tell him to flee back to Derbyshire. But if she said anything, Bender would kill him. Never had she felt so trapped.

Charlie held both of her hands in his, waiting for a response.

She took a deep breath and realized they were drawing far too many eyes. She flashed him her most apologetic look before laughing a bit too loudly at nothing and fanning her face. "Oh how droll you both are. I have been quite diverted, I promise, but it is high time for tea, and I have a gentleman waiting in the tearoom." She stood, opened her parasol, and waited for them to accompany her across the street.

Charlie huffed. "You will not avoid this, Lady Amanda. We must talk. He is a dangerous man! What kind of hold could he possibly have over you?"

She looked down pointedly at the hand that was now grabbing her arm. "You."

"What?" Charlie asked.

"You. He holds your life over me." And with that she turned to walk away. But Charlie stopped her again. "Please."

Amanda shook her head. "He ordered me not to talk to you about it—not to tell anyone."

"Please give me one minute more. There is something you must know."

Amanda hesitated and then, seeing the pleading look in Charlie's eyes, she nodded and followed him, with Molly at her side. As soon as they had walked a few paces, Charlie said hurriedly, "We don't have time for you to hear everything fully. Please just listen carefully." He forced himself to swallow. "Try to just . . . trust me."

Amanda remained silent. She gestured for him to continue.

"I do not work for Bender, no, but I am there on assignment."

"What? Speak sense, Charles." Confusion warred with hope in her mind.

Charlie grunted in frustration. "Amanda, be quiet and I will tell you."

She nodded.

He led them farther back into the trees. "The reason I am on assignment with Bender is because I have pledged my loyalties and my undying effort, my life even, to a group of courageous men working for freedom, for equality, for universal suffrage. I would face any threat, no matter how large, if I thought it would help further our cause."

Amanda watched his chest rise and fall with greater intensity as he spoke. His eyes burned with fire. His whole countenance changed, and he was alight with passion. He turned his eyes on her and she felt nearly singed by their intensity. The words of Henry Hunt came back into her mind.

She stammered, "And this . . . this . . . group—who are they?" She shared a look with Molly.

He glanced around. "Ask me again another time. Please understand that it is for them and for the cause of freedom that I face Bender and his gang every week."

"What have they to do with it?"

"Bender is corrupting the cause. Because of him, reformists have a bad name. And people are getting hurt, my lady. Innocent meetings turn into riots. Houses of nobles are pillaged, just like your uncle's! I have only ever tried to protect innocent families."

A great warmth filled Amanda. "My coming-out ball. Your group was there! Helping us!" Such a relief washed through her she nearly hugged Charlie. Tears of gratitude filled her eyes.

Molly squeezed her hand. "We knew someone was helping. I should have known it was you, Charles."

"I'd never let you down, Lady Amanda, or you, Molly."

Amanda cleared her throat. "But this Bender threatened to harm you. And he will if I do not do exactly as he says. Already I have spoken when he ordered me to stay silent."

Charlie returned his gaze to her. "But this is why I am trying to explain things to you. You do not need to concern yourself with me, my lady. My position there is much larger than you or I. Every time I meet with them my life is in great danger. Nothing you do or don't do will change that. I am aware of the risks, and I take great care." He looked into her eyes, studying her face. "I will be fine. Do not let him control you, especially on my account." He leaned closer. "Now tell me. What is it he is demanding from you?"

"My father's signet ring."

"What! Lady Amanda, you cannot."

Amanda waved her hands at him. "I know. I know. He wants to borrow it. I made him understand he could not keep it. I will make a note of the direction on the letter, and Molly and I will intercept the letters—"

"That is lunacy. You would certainly be killed."

Charlie's intensity startled her. Not for the first time, she doubted the viability of her plan. But what else could she do? Talking about it further would not help. She shrugged her shoulders in feigned nonchalance.

Charlie was about to protest when they heard Lord Nathaniel approaching.

"Charles, please ready my horse. It seems her ladyship . . ." He stopped in surprise.

She could not imagine what he might think about their cozy threesome in such an intense conversation.

Charlie stepped back and hurried to untether Smoke, his own ride back to the estate.

Lord Nathaniel cleared his throat. "It seems her ladyship is here after all. Hello, Lady Amanda." Lord Nathaniel bowed over her hand, kissing it. He looked up at her, eyebrows raised in a slight teasing manner.

Amanda rose from her curtsy. "I apologize, my lord. You have caught me reminiscing with an old friend. I quite forgot the time." She looked around in confusion. "But where is the phaeton? Are we not to go for a ride?"

Lord Nathaniel smiled. "But of course. It is just over there, awaiting our every pleasure."

She looked in the direction he was pointing. "Oh! It's lovely." A footman stood in front of a bright red open-air conveyance.

Amanda's face filled with pleasure. How nice it would feel to enjoy a simple outing amidst all the worry and agitation. She walked toward his offered arm. Looking over her shoulder she said, "Oh and Molly dear, would you give the package to Charles, explaining what he is to do with it?" She hoped Molly understood what she was thinking. Charlie would be the perfect person to help distribute these fliers.

Her head was spinning with all she had learned today. But one thing stuck out clearly and gave her a wild exhilaration of hope. Somewhere in London was a group who felt as she did—good people fighting for equality for all classes. And she was determined to help them.

Molly smiled in confusion at first, and then her smile grew wider. "Yes, miss!" she said with more enthusiasm than was necessary, and she dipped a quick curtsy before turning to Charlie.

Lord Nathaniel wore an amused smile. "You have a very exuberant maid."

Amanda laughed. "Yes, Molly is quite a gem. A dear friend besides." Lord Nathaniel nodded as if befriending one's maid were the most natural thing in the world.

After helping her to her seat, Lord Nathaniel grabbed the reins and turned to her. "Where to, my lady? Where does our fine adventure await?"

"Surely someplace with pirates and handsome heroes and damsels in distress."

Nathaniel shook his head. "No damsels in distress today. Let us leave that behind us, shall we?"

Amanda's laughter rang across the square. With a sigh she said, "If we must. But I do insist on handsome heroes."

"Heroes! You are limited to one on this ride, and he sits beside you. It is up to you to decide if he is handsome or not." He lifted his chin, showing off his profile.

She laughed again and said, "Oh, very handsome indeed. I may faint from all of your handsomeness."

"And then we'd have ourselves a damsel in distress. It is our lot, I see. Well, if that's the way it has to be, then we must forbear."

"What a lovely day." Amanda scooted closer, placing a hand on his arm. "Thank you."

"I forget how nice it feels to take time to simply enjoy a beautiful day with a beautiful lady."

Amanda blushed. He seemed so different from any other time she had seen him. Then curious, she asked, "Do you not have much time for these pursuits? Surely you could ride out every day with a beautiful woman?"

Nathaniel chuckled and glanced at her. "A beautiful woman, yes, but not Lady Amanda Alexandria Cumberland. She is in a class all by herself."

"Oh, stop. Now you are being silly, my lord."

"I do enjoy watching the pink on your cheeks, but I am in earnest. You must know. I desire to know you, understand you, decipher what drives you on. I admit to being smitten with a terrible curiosity."

Amanda smiled and watched his face. She hoped at last to know the Lord Nathaniel beneath his usual facade.

"As to the other half of your question, no, I do not often find myself with time to frivol away an afternoon. Rides in phaetons are a rarity for me."

"So, are we frivoling away an afternoon?" She raised one eyebrow.

He searched her face, laughing. "Oh no. A ride with you is not frivolous, my dear. I am sure this will stand out as my best-spent time of the week."

A wonderful warmth and peace filled her. "Lord Nathaniel, you do surprise me. Such artlessness from you is wholly unexpected."

"So, are you saying I am a bit of a mystery? Curious, are you?" He waggled his eyebrows.

She laughed. "You are a whole book of mysteries, of which I have begun but a few pages."

Nathaniel's lips moved into a pleased smile. He urged the horses forward, and they continued a slow walk on the dirt paths that wound through the park. The air carried a light breeze. The sun was shining. A comfortable silence filled them. Five minutes passed before either of them said another word.

Amanda spoke first. "Oh! Do stop for a moment."

Lord Nathaniel pulled on the reins. "What is it, my lady?"

Amanda sighed in happiness, listening. "Can you hear the birds?" And then as if on cue, a whole group of them burst from the trees and soared up together in one mass. They continued upward for so long Amanda thought they would disappear completely. "I love to watch them." She wondered where they were going. *Wherever they wanted.*

Lord Nathaniel put a hand on hers and she turned to him. He pulled her flier from his pocket. "You call yourself the Sparrow." He let his eyes wander over her features. Then he smiled a slow, seductive smile.

She could not stop the flush on her neck. She nodded, senses tingling.

His eyes lingered on her lips for a delicious moment. "It fits." His attention returned to her flier and he ran his fingers over the faces of the people in the prison cart. "This is quite good, you know. Remarkable likeness of that moment."

Amanda smiled. "It is so nice to have someone besides Molly know I drew it." Her fingers brushed his as she reached for the drawing, closing her fingers around the corner of the paper.

He allowed her to take it from him but then reached over and grasped her hand in his. His hands felt warm and protective around hers.

He said, "So tell me, why are you creating these wonderfully meaningful fliers?" He leaned closer.

She stammered for a moment while she collected her thoughts. "I was deeply affected by those people in the cart. They seemed so hopeless." She shrugged. "I wanted to help somehow."

Lord Nathaniel looked at her with kindness and perhaps a spark of admiration. He asked, "And what else are you drawing? Are there others?"

"Oh, yes. I have a drawer full of them. The others are more satirical, however—more in line with Peter Hamilton's work. I just know there are good people who would want to help. If I can tell them, *show* them . . ." She stopped, unable to fully explain. A new insecurity stopped her. She felt bare, but Nathaniel smiled so warmly at her, her heart calmed. She felt her face heat, and she shrugged. "It is fun to try, anyway."

Lord Nathaniel nodded, seeming pleased. "You are exactly right. I believe every effort we make, no matter how small or limited, will do some bit of good. Thank you for sharing that with me." He squeezed her hand and pulled away, reaching for the reins.

As the horses began walking again, Amanda felt the loss of his hand around hers. He seemed to stare at nothing, deep in thought, and she wondered if he was distancing himself emotionally as well as physically. She was about to reach for his arm when they pulled into a clearing in the park and heard giggling.

"Oh, Lord Nathaniel! What a surprise!"

A phaeton filled with young women pulled up beside them and all of them had their eyes trained on Lord Nathaniel.

He groaned beside her and looked at her out of the corners of his eyes. "We still need to discuss this." He turned toward the other phaeton and made a graceful bow while sitting, tipping his hat to each of them. "What beauty sits before me!" He put his hand to his heart. "And where are you off to this fine morning?"

Miss Clarissa answered for them all, dipping her head sensibly. "We are just out enjoying this fine air. What a splendid day for it, do you not agree?"

"That I do. And how is your dear mother, Miss Clarissa?"

"She is well, thank you. She sends her regards."

"I receive them gladly. Will I be seeing you, and all of you fine ladies, at the Winterton Ball on Thursday?"

"You will, my lord," Miss Clarissa said.

One pretty face with blonde ringlets called out, "I'll be there!"

"As will I, my lord!" the brown-eyed beauty next to Miss Clarissa purred.

"Oh, so will I!" The remaining woman in the back seat leaned forward to be seen.

Nathaniel smiled at them all, dipped his head again and winked at Miss Clarissa. Then he picked up his reins and urged his horses to move forward. Lady Amanda nodded at the girls as they passed. Only Miss Clarissa nodded in return.

As soon as they were out of earshot, Amanda huffed. "They didn't even acknowledge me!"

"Miss Clarissa did."

"Yes, she did." Amanda sat troubled for a few moments.

Lord Nathaniel led the phaeton closer to a copse of trees, secluded and far from the eyes of most anyone who would visit the park today.

"Why did they act this way?"

"As if you don't know the answer to that . . . the flier, of course. Enjoying yourself, are you?"

"No! I am almost as disturbed as you are at this point. They have forgotten all sense of propriety."

"This behavior, wherever I go, is making things dashed difficult for me. I can't do anything without the noise and attention." He turned to frown at her. "Why choose me to distract a store full of people?"

"I should not have mentioned your name. I hoped to gain their attention, and you are an easy distraction. I knew that Miss Clarissa and all the ladies would be interested. You were quite popular even before the flier, you know."

Lord Nathaniel grimaced. "But this flier gives all the women of the *ton* permission to be bold."

"How so?"

He grabbed the other flier out of his pocket and thrust it at her. "See for yourself. I do not discriminate. I give attention to anyone who asks—even three women at once!"

Lord Nathaniel looked seriously agitated. She had obviously crossed some line of propriety he had drawn for himself when he began behaving as a rake.

She kept watching him, hoping to unravel and understand this part of his character.

"Stop studying me like that. Your deep blues could undo a man. What I need you to do, Lady Amanda, is fix this." His voice took on an endearing pleading tone.

"How can I possibly fix it?"

Lord Nathaniel ran his fingers through his hair in exasperation. "I don't know yet. I was hoping you would have some ideas."

He looked at her with such desperation that her heart went out to him at once. She reached her hand over and squeezed his arm.

"I am so sorry, my lord. I have regretted my words every day since. I was unfeeling and selfish not to intervene. And I see now, one woman's words have placed you in an increasingly unenviable position." They both sat in silence for a time when Amanda said, "I've got to draw something. Something that shows your, ah, other fine attributes."

Lord Nathaniel looked at her skeptically. "That would only increase the problem. The last thing I want to do is broadcast my marriage eligibility."

Amanda straightened. "That's it! You need to become unavailable. I need to draw something that makes the ladies feel like you are outside of their reach, at least for a time." She tapped her finger on her chin. "Hmmm. I don't suppose you could go into mourning; anyone about to die?" After a discernable, lengthy pause, she reached her hand up to her mouth and covered it in horror. "I did not just say that. I apologize, profusely, my lord."

Lord Nathaniel's face turned red and became increasingly more so. Then he started shaking. Tears forced themselves from the corners of his eyes. Amanda watched in growing angst as Lord Nathaniel broke down in front of her. She searched her memory for any news of a recent death in his immediate family. Friends? Distant relatives? She couldn't think of anyone.

And then he said with peals of laughter, "HA! HO! Amanda! I can't. Ha!"

She looked wide-eyed at him, her hands covering her mouth. He shook convulsively until he snorted, out loud, like a pig, and burst into laughter—great, loud, belly laughter.

Irritation, hot and tight, filled her chest. She folded her arms and turned away. "Well! You needn't laugh so hard, my lord." She stared off into the woods to their right, trying to ignore him.

Lord Nathaniel tried to stop. He reached for her. "Lady Amanda, it's wonderful. Please allow me to laugh. Surely you can see the humor as well." He stared at her, eyes pleading through his laughter, his expression childlike.

She grinned at him, which caused him to burst into further laughter, and she felt a chuckle rise in her own belly. Giving in to him, her own laughter filled the air around them. Her mouth felt tight and her stomach sore by the time they sat quietly again.

Wiping tears from her eyes with his offered handkerchief, she brought her hand up to her mouth, shook her head, and said, "What came over me, hoping to put you in mourning? I am sorry, Lord Nathaniel."

Her hand had found its way into the crook of his arm, and he patted it. "Think nothing of it, my dear."

She stilled next to him, and his hand froze its comforting motion. He had called her *my dear* before, but she couldn't help but notice the certain warmth it held this time.

Nathaniel leaned closer. He looked at her mouth and then back to her eyes in question.

She stared back, frozen.

Don't look at his lips! Her eyes betrayed her. She too leaned closer, seeing hope and regard, and something else smoldering beneath. Desire. She recognized it because she was filled with her own.

She ached for him, for his arms to surround her. She leaned toward him in greater urgency and when her lips found his, thought ceased. Every sense in her body began firing. Lights flashed in her head, and she felt the world spin in a dizzy whirl. He softly pressed his lips to hers again and again, then firmer and with more urgency, his mouth moving over hers, exploring each angle. She melted into him, completely overcome, enjoying each new sensation as it came.

Too soon, he pulled away, looking down at her in wonder.

She returned his gaze.

Neither spoke until he reached his hand out and tucked a stray hair behind her ear, holding his hand against her cheek. "I knew it would be like this," he murmured. With one last kiss on her forehead, he took up the reins again, and they began moving through the park.

CHAPTER EIGHTEEN

CHARLIE WATCHED IN SILENCE AS Lady Amanda and Lord Nathaniel rode off. The corners of his mouth drooped. His eyes closed in pain, and he clenched his fists, fighting the emotion rising in his chest. He dreaded the moment as much as he hoped for it, when Amanda would know she belonged with Nathaniel. A ball of misery started to grow in the pit of his stomach. Amanda had loved Charlie first. If only he had been gifted a different birth, she would love him still, and it could have grown into something lasting.

He wanted nothing more than to run after the horses, shouting, "Wait, Amanda, no!" But he knew that would avail him nothing. He unclenched his fists.

Molly folded her arms across her chest and said, "Charlie, we have work to do . . . unless you are going to stand here staring all day." Molly grinned at him, her eyes teasing.

Charlie felt his face heat. He'd had an audience, one almost as dear to him as Amanda, patient and beautiful, standing at his side. The weight in his stomach lessened, and he turned to look at Molly's face—she had been his friend through everything. She was kind and compassionate.

"Now, what would staring after a duke's daughter do for me? No, that won't do at all. Not when I have the opportunity to share the afternoon with her lovely maid." Charlie raised one eyebrow and held his arm out.

She laughed and put her hand in the crook of his elbow. "We, sir, have some deliveries to make."

"At your service, my dear. But tell me, what exactly are we delivering, might I enquire?"

Molly paused for a moment and looked coyly up at him.

His breath caught when he noticed their brilliant shade of blue.

She smiled and said, "We are delivering fliers. Stacks of them, to all the establishments who have agreed to carry them."

Charlie tapped his finger on his chin. "Fliers, eh? Well, I have just the thing." And he led her gently across the street toward the ice shop.

"I do love a good ice, but Charles, let us hurry. We haven't much time."

"Which is why, my dear maid Molly, we are going to do both tasks: eat a delicious ice on this surprisingly balmy day *and* deliver fliers." With that, he took the stack and kept her hand on his arm, while marching deliberately across the street.

Five new shops later, their ices long devoured and their feet aching, Charlie and Molly returned to the place they were to meet with their employers. Charlie commented, "What a pleasant afternoon. I thank you, Molly."

"And I thank you for your help. I could never have convinced most of those shops to carry our fliers. As it is now, half the *ton* will have seen them by morning."

Charlie frowned for a moment. "Has Lady Amanda thought of the ramifications of that kind of exposure? Is she sure no one will suspect?"

Molly nodded her head. "Who would suspect Lady Amanda? Especially now that she's nothing but pomp and fluff and flirting with all the gentlemen the way she is!"

Charlie shook his head. "I don't know how she can stomach it. Has she no enlightened conversation around her, ever?"

"Well, she has me, doesn't she? And Lord Nathaniel."

Charlie's eyes darkened at the mention of his employer. Then he sighed in resignation. "Yes, there's Lord Nathaniel. For all his cavorting with females and banding himself about as a rake, she could do much worse."

Molly eyed him in appreciation, her brows raised.

Charlie chuckled. "He is a good man. And she deserves such."

They heard horses clomping on the stone. Their lord and lady called to them from the phaeton, gesturing that they join them. Charlie helped Molly climb into the back.

He smiled at Lady Amanda and said, "I must be getting Smoke back to his paddock and fed and brushed before he forgets he's the king of us all."

"What is this, Charlie? Jealous of a bit of horse flesh?" Lord Nathaniel goaded him a bit.

Lady Amanda laughed, head back, the sound so infectious that soon they were all laughing and teasing Charlie. He warmed as a sense of camaraderie and friendship filled him.

Lord Nathaniel then extracted a stack of correspondence from the inside of his tailcoat and handed it to Charlie. "Could I trouble you to also make certain that these letters are mailed posthaste?"

Charlie nodded. Reading the direction on the top letter, he froze. It carried a seal in blue wax, the unmistakable profile of an eagle. His eyes flashed up to Lord Nathaniel, who returned his gaze with an air of nonchalance.

Charlie bowed low and said, "Of course, my lord. I will take care of these straight away." And he turned abruptly down the path toward the footman standing watch over the horse. Soon he was untethering Smoke and swinging up into the saddle. Lord Nathaniel nodded to him and then directed his attention to the ladies as he urged his horses forward. Charlie could hear the ladies' giggles as they turned the corner and went out of sight. For a long moment, lost in thought, Charlie studied the stack of letters in his hands.

The eagle seal belongs to Lord Nathaniel. He is Red. The head of the Liberty Seekers was his employer. Charlie shook his head in disbelief and wonder. Did Nathaniel know that he, Charlie, the stable hand, was his informant, his Eagle in Flight? He had not revealed that information to anyone except Lady Amanda. All of his letters were carefully anonymous. *Lord Nathaniel couldn't know.* He likely did not expect Charlie to recognize the seal.

For years, Charlie had admired Red. The idea of such a man, his very existence, had carried Charlie through moments of frustration and impatience as he tried to function in a world with so much injustice. He began to grin. His mouth stretched wider until all his teeth were showing. He kicked his heels into Smoke and took off racing through the park. As he disappeared through the trees, he let out a loud, "Wooooop!"

CHAPTER NINETEEN

STANDING IN A LOVELY TEAROOM, waiting for Lord Needley to return with their cakes, Amanda smelled Jack Bender before she felt his foul hot breath on her neck.

"Smile pretty and meet me around back in one minute." And then his sour stench left, and the air cleared.

But Amanda's throat closed and her hands shook, her breathing painfully shallow. Lord Needley returned with their fare. He said something, but she couldn't make out the words. The world tilted and began to darken. As it lightened again, she saw his concerned face. He steadied her with his strong arms and looked into her eyes. She blinked.

"There you are, Lady Amanda. Let us sit for a moment. I was afraid I had lost you."

Amanda gratefully took the chair he pulled over and accepted his solicitous offer to sit near her to lean on if necessary. She smiled weakly. What was the matter with her? Surely she had not just swooned. Fortunately, she could use her dizzy episode to her advantage.

"Oh, you are too kind. What would I have done had you not been here to catch me?" She blinked slowly at him and smiled in what she hoped was a charming manner. "And you are so strong! Your arms and . . ." She allowed the sentence to linger as she studied his broad chest. He really was a beautiful man. "I do believe I could use a moment to myself this afternoon. Do you think you could call the carriage? I'll just go into the back to splash some water on my face."

He stood immediately and went to call for his footman. As soon as he was out the front door, she stood, took a moment to make sure of her balance, and rushed through the shop to the back door and out into the alleyway. She frantically looked right and left, hoping she was not too late. Seeing no one about, she felt panic rise to her throat. Would he punish Charlie for her neglect? She stepped farther into the alley, nearly missing an awful pile of something at her feet. The pungent odors reached her as she grabbed for her handkerchief and held it over her nose.

Bender stepped out from an adjoining alley. She whirled around to face him and tried to be brave.

"You are late." His voice sounded raspy, as if he had been shouting for the better part of an hour.

"It is the best I could do. As it is, Lord Needley will be waiting with the carriage. What do you want?"

"Meet me with the ring this afternoon at three at this address." He handed her a paper with the directions scribbled on it. "Come alone."

Amanda's hands rose and waved in the air as she spoke. "How do you suggest I do that, assuming I can get my father's ring so quickly? I am not permitted—"

"I don't care how you manage it. But I had better not see another person near. I am sure I don't need to remind you whose life you would be risking by crossing me."

Amanda swallowed and nodded. "I understand." She studied him. His eyes darted every which way in a crazed fashion. He had a sheen of sweat on his forehead and several beads running down his face. And he rocked from side to side as he shifted the weight of his feet from one to the other.

Amanda felt an intense revulsion to him, and his crazed behavior filled her with fear. Her eyes widened, and she couldn't look away.

He stepped toward her erratically. "Stop staring!" His eyes started twitching. He raised a fisted hand as if to strike her.

She yelped and ducked her head, putting hands up over her head for protection. But he stopped before his fist reached her face.

He froze, staring at his raised hand for a moment, and then slowly lowered it to his side. Without another word, he turned and ran down the alley in the other direction.

Lord Needley slammed open the back door of the shop. Amanda spun around, heart pounding. Before she could do or say anything, Lord Needley cradled her in his arms, holding her against his chest. "I heard you call out." He pulled away, held both sides of her face with his hands, and said gently, "What happened?"

She tried to formulate some sensible reason to be standing behind the shop.

When she didn't immediately respond, he said, "Lady Amanda, can you hear me? You are in the back alley. We need to get you home."

She blinked slowly in confusion. Did he think her brain addled? She bit back a smile, which created an even greater look of confusion on his face. "Oh, Lord Needley. Thank you. I thought a bit of fresh air . . ."

They both glanced around them at the awful refuse that cluttered the ground.

Lord Needley raised a handkerchief to his nose as Amanda replaced hers. "Yes, quite." He shook his head.

And then she rested her head against him, cringing at the huge falsehood.

He said, "But let us leave this lovely air and get you home, shall we?" He stepped back, placing her hand gently on his arm, and walked her back through the shop.

As Amanda passed between the tables, she smiled as she saw her latest fliers in the hands of several patrons. They were laughing together and in some cases appeared to be discussing her drawings. She looked down to hide her triumph. Would her fliers make a difference? She hoped to find out tonight at Miss Clarissa's dinner party.

An awkward atmosphere in the carriage hung over them all. Lord Needley lacked his normal attentiveness. He watched out the window, appearing deep in thought. Perhaps he assumed she would need some quiet.

Molly had spent the time with Miss Tanner, she assumed, and her eyes were full of questions, but Amanda just smiled helplessly at her and knew she would have to wait.

She cleared her throat. "Lord Needley. I must apologize. I do not know what to say . . ."

He turned to her, and she could almost see a battle going on behind his eyes. He said, "You appear to be recovered. Remarkably so, I would think."

Amanda blushed. "I think so, yes."

He leaned back in the carriage and folded his arms across his chest. He raised one eyebrow at her. "And what *were* you doing in that alleyway, Lady Amanda? Really."

She raised both her eyebrows. She glanced at Molly, who responded with a confused look of her own. Amanda's eyes returned to Lord Needley, who watched her, waiting.

"Well, I . . . I'm sure I don't know, my lord," she said with a small voice. Then she lifted her chin and looked at him directly in the eyes. She wasn't sure what to tell him, but she had nothing to be ashamed of. She was doing her best to save the life of a dear friend and help free the English working class.

Lord Needley leaned forward, smiling encouragingly at her.

Amanda paused a moment longer, wanting nothing more than to share the whole of it with him. The temptation became so great she opened her mouth. "You see . . ." And then the carriage rocked to a stop. They arrived in front of her house. The footman opened her door, and the moment fled. Relief filled her.

"Thank you for an interesting outing today, Lord Needley." She swept past him, Molly right behind, before he could say another word.

He did not exit the carriage. She glanced back just before she went inside, her last sight of him, his face framed in the carriage window, leaning forward to watch her up the stairs to her front doorway.

Her father's voice called to her from a room off the entry hallway. "Amanda. You are home. Come here, my dear girl."

She hurried happily into his study where he stood to embrace her and kiss her forehead. Her body went still as she saw her latest flier on top of his correspondence on the desk.

He noticed the direction of her gaze. "Have you seen these new fliers? They are brilliant satires. You would appreciate them, for all your love of drawing."

Her heart warmed. Her father enjoyed the newest fliers, had one on his desk, was recommending it to her. She reached to pick it up—the one Charlie and Molly had delivered for her. They had certainly spread quickly. "Where did you get it? Everyone seems to have these everywhere I turn of late."

He nodded. "Yes, I have noticed that as well. This one was at White's. One of the men left it on a table. We all passed it around and had a good laugh."

In this latest drawing, she had tried to depict the work of a valet. A nobleman stood in his exaggerated wealth. He had an unrealistically large watch chain dangling from his pocket. In one hand he held a half a glass of bourbon, and in the other he was trying to place a cake into his mouth, but was dropping crumbs on his tailcoat and dribbling jam on his intricately tied cravat.

The valet was using one foot to shine a boot, one hand to brush off the shoulders of the suit coat, and the other hand to flick off crumbs as they fell. In the valet's pockets were all manner of items: a needle and thread, polish for the boots, and pomade for hair. He had extra cravats draped over his shoulders. She wanted it to be funny enough that the nobles could laugh at themselves while appreciating the tireless efforts of their valets. And from the sound of the reaction at White's, she had been at least partially successful.

She grinned. "It does remind one of your Felton, does it not?"

Her father laughed. "I would hope not! Felton is a saint of a man, but I have never spilled food on my person while he was still trying to dress me. Ho ho!"

Amanda laughed good-heartedly with her father. "No, I suppose not. Perhaps he should thank you for that," she teased.

But her father sobered slightly and said, "No, my dear. I feel I should be thanking him. A valet is an indispensable part of a gentleman's life."

A great feeling of contentment rose in her chest. A great grin filled her face.

Her father looked at her curiously. "You seem exceptionally pleased. Should I be suspicious of something? Archery lessons on the sly again? Learning to fire a rifle somewhere here in London?"

Amanda laughed again. "No! Not at all. I am happy to hear how much you appreciate Edgar is all. I think it speaks volumes about a person, how much gratitude they feel for the servants in their employ."

The duke stepped back and looked at his daughter with an appraising eye. "Now, there's the Amanda I know. I've been wondering where you had gone off to. Well thought, my dear."

Amanda blushed a little under his scrutiny. She wished she could share some of her burden with her father. She wished she did not have to act like her head was stuffed with linen. She wished most of all that she wasn't considering pilfering her father's signet ring.

Her guilt coming to a head, she considered voicing her concerns about Bender. She had yearned to do so several times over the past couple of weeks. Could she simply tell him? The idea of handing this terrifying problem to her father filled her with such relief she almost began the words. She hesitated. *What could he do?* He would call in the magistrate. He would hire a Bow Street Runner. What if Bender got wind of it all? And she was to meet him right away. Even an hour's delay could mean Charlie's life. As much as her father cared for Charlie, he would never let her be at risk to save him. No, she must move forward on her own, at least for now. She could always get help if things became worse.

Answering her father before she weakened and told all, she looked away from his searching gaze. "I am happy to hear your praise, Father. I know I have been different lately." She smiled sadly. "But you must understand I have only been trying to follow your orders." She felt her pulse speed up as she considered the injustice of what he had asked. "Insisting that I choose a suitor this Season and allowing two men to court me, even informally, with marriage in mind—I don't know how you could do such a thing." She turned from him and looked out the window.

Her father sighed and moved to stand next to her, sharing the view. "I know you don't understand, my dear. But consider. It hasn't been so bad, has it? I understand you have been quite . . . friendly, with the both of them. Surely you can see that either one would make a fine match."

"Fine? Certainly. But filled with love? Can't you see that I want what you and Mother have? With that example clearly before me all of my days I cannot possibly hope for anything less."

Understanding lit the duke's eyes, and he looked with compassion into Amanda's. "Can you not find yourself feeling affection for either of them, ever?"

Amanda blushed and looked at her toes.

Her father smiled and with his finger lifted her chin. "Hmm?"

Amanda said, "It is still so early, but I think I might, with one of them." And she couldn't stop the blush or the smile that crept onto her face. She waved a hand and began pacing back and forth in front of her father. "But that is not the point. I did not want to feel forced into such a decision, and your whole plan could very well have fallen flat. It still could. Who knows if he even feels the same as I?"

The duke's large belly laugh interrupted her. She spun to face him, indignation firing in her eyes.

"There is nothing to laugh at that I can see, I am sure." She turned from him.

But the duke pulled her around and into another hug. "I love you, my dear Amanda. It will all work out, you will see. Trust your father." Amanda was about to respond when their butler cleared his throat in the doorway. The duke said, "What is it, Mr. Parsons?"

"Lady Swanson has come to visit, and Duchess Marian has asked for your presence in the drawing room, if you please, Your Grace."

Her father drew in a fortifying breath. "Wish me luck, my dear. This will be no easy meeting. They wish to discuss the lack of decent flowers at Almack's. Your kind mother has shielded me for weeks, bless her good soul, but it looks as though it can no longer be avoided."

"Lack of flowers! What! Why can they think you will care one whit about the flowers at Almack's?"

"One never can understand the workings of the matrons of the *ton*. But let's see if we can keep them smiling, shall we?" He kissed her forehead and left the room.

As soon as he was out of sight, Amanda raced around to the other side of his desk and opened the drawer that would hold his signet ring if he was not wearing it. A part of her hoped he had it on his finger—in her distraction about her fliers and suitors, she had not noticed. Her heart pounded as she saw it resting near his melting wax and writing quill. Did she dare? Could she allow such lowly filth to even place his dirty hands upon it? She swallowed once, twice. What was a ring when compared to the cost of a man, a dear friend, Charlie? With grim determination, she reached in, took the ring, and placed it in her reticule. And not a moment too soon. Just as she was closing the drawer, their steward entered.

He stopped short in the doorway and cleared his throat. "Lady Amanda, please excuse me. I will wait in the hall." And he started backing out the way he had come.

"Oh no, please, come in. I was on my way out. I am sure Father will be in as soon as he can." Amanda almost ran from the room. She began to panic. With the steward present, her father would work on estate business of some sort, have some kind of correspondence to complete, and would need the ring. Amanda could waste no time. She grabbed her cloak, motioned for Molly, who waited in the hall, to come with her, and rushed to the door. "We are going out for a stroll, Mr. Parsons, and then Mother is aware I will be spending the evening hours with Miss Clarissa Hampton. Would you mind reminding anyone who wonders at my absence?"

Mr. Parsons nodded. "Very good, my lady. If you will wait for one moment, I'll summon a footman."

Amanda nodded and stepped out the door, Molly following behind. As soon as it was closed, she ran down the street, pulling Molly after her.

Breathless, Molly asked, "My lady, why are we rushing so? Is something the matter?"

Amanda glanced at Molly—dear, loyal, good-hearted Molly. "I can't have the footman following after"—she panted, nearly out of breath herself—"Bender came to the tearoom and demanded the signet."

Molly gasped.

"And the steward arrived. They'll want the ring and find it missing as soon as Father finishes with Lady Swanson's complaint."

Counting numbers on the homes, she stopped, and Molly nearly ran her over. "Oh, I'm dreadfully sorry, my lady!" she breathed.

"Oh no, Molly, I am sorry. I gave you no warning. We have arrived. See the numbers, just there." She glanced at the address Bender had given her.

They both stared at the neglected town house. On either side of the home, up and down the street, beautiful, well-kept fronts signified wealth. This one was a shambles. They shared a glance and then as one began walking up the steps. When they reached the door, Amanda raised her hand and lifted the knocker three times. The door cracked, and Bender's eye peered at her. Unnerved, she reached for Molly's arm. Molly placed her hand over Amanda's and squeezed.

Bender opened the door wider. "I told you to come alone."

Amanda found a bit of courage and responded, "Which I simply could not do. I will not be found alone with a man in his home. I would be ruined. Molly is my maid and has sworn to secrecy." She held his eyes, refusing to flinch.

Molly nodded, chin up.

Bender grunted and asked, "Did you bring the item?"

Amanda nodded. "But you are not to touch it."

"What?" Bender growled. He opened the door wider, reaching for Amanda. She stepped back before he could pull her inside, but nearly fell down the steps behind her.

"I will not let you touch it. Whatever business you need it for, I will seal the letter for you, and then we will be on our way."

Bender looked suspicious. His eyes flicked greedily to her reticule and back to her face.

"If we do not hurry, the duke will notice it is gone. We have only a few moments before he plans to meet with his steward, who arrived just as we were leaving."

Her words seemed to do the trick. Bender startled a bit and opened the door wider to allowed them both to pass. She heard the door close behind them, and she couldn't help the chill that trickled through her. Bender led them down a poorly lit hallway and to the right into an office. She and Molly remained standing, hoping to finish this business and leave as quickly as possible.

Bender opened a drawer in an old and scratched desk, pulling out three letters. "Seal these documents." He retrieved a wax stick from another drawer and proceeded to warm it with a candle. The wax quickly melted, and he smeared it onto the paper. He motioned for her.

Amanda gritted her teeth and pushed the signet into the wax, leaving the unmistakable mark of the dukedom of Cumberland, one of the most powerful and ancient families in England. Not for the first time, she questioned her wisdom in coming. But she reminded herself she had no other option.

As she placed her father's seal on the other two letters, she vowed to never again do Bender's bidding. He lifted the letters to speed the cooling of the wax, and she caught a part of the direction on the front side of one: King Street, Manchester.

Bender had a sharp eye and snapped, "Keep your eyes where they belong." Amanda immediately lowered hers and backed up several steps. She swallowed and reached for Molly's hand. Bender finished waving the paper around, tested the wax, and seemed satisfied that it had dried sufficiently. He again looked in their direction.

Amanda raised her chin and said, "I must be getting back before Father notices that I and the ring are missing."

"I do not care one whit if he notices your absence." His cold eyes told Amanda he spoke the truth. "I do not, however, want him suspicious that his ring has been compromised." He led them to the door and waited while they inched it open and slid through to the steps and street below. "I will contact you when I need your services again." His voice carried out onto the street.

Amanda blushed furiously and looked up and down the street, relieved at finding it empty.

Gripping each other by the hand, Molly and Amanda rushed back in the direction of the Cumberland town house. At the first alley, Amanda pulled Molly to a stop, took out the ring, and whispered, "Go. Take this with you and deliver it as soon as you can back into the top drawer of my father's desk."

Molly began to protest wildly, "No, my lady. They will think I stole it. You—"

Amanda interrupted. "I must intercept the letters I just sealed. I cannot allow them into the hands of whomever Bender intends."

Molly's eyes widened in fear. "But what will you do, my lady?"

"I do not know yet. For now, I will watch and wait for an opportunity to present itself."

With a look of determination, she pressed the ring into Molly's reluctant hand and pushed her out onto the main street, leaving Amanda alone in the back alleyway. Molly glanced once more at Amanda before walking with purpose in the direction of the town house. With any luck, no one would ever know the ring had left. At least her parents assumed she was visiting with friends this evening several streets over at Miss Clarissa's house. She had some time to intercept the correspondence.

Amanda waited in the dark of a street corner near a section of trees for something to happen at Jack Bender's town house. It felt like hours had gone by, but she was sure it was only a matter of minutes. Just as she was about to move to the back of the property, Bender's door opened and his black boots stepped onto the first step. She breathed a sigh of relief. He turned to his left and walked briskly down the sidewalk. She stepped out of the shadows to follow as a hand grabbed her elbow. She bit back a scream and whipped around.

"Amanda, what are you doing?"

Stomach in her throat, she turned with wide, desperate eyes to see Charlie, inches away, looking at her in accusation and worry.

"Let me go, Charles! We have to follow him!" When he did not release his grip, she added, "Please! We mustn't lose sight of him! He used my father's signet."

Charlie flinched. He did not release her arm, but at least they were moving now in the direction Bender had gone. She squinted into the darkness as he slipped around a corner and out of sight.

"Oh, hurry, Charles!"

They broke into a run, trying to keep their feet as quiet as possible. They followed him for several blocks, across streets and through alleys until they came to a busier part of London where he signaled a hackney carriage and went rushing through a crowded square. Amanda looked around desperately as Charles calmly signaled a driver to pick them up as well. He instructed the driver to go in the general direction of Bender's carriage.

"It's all right, Lady Amanda. I know where he is going."

She searched his face but said nothing.

On they went for the better part of thirty minutes, instructing their driver to follow, until they saw Bender jump out and make his way to an old church. Amanda looked through the carriage windows. Run-down buildings and broken windows lined the streets. Her clothing would draw attention. Charlie must have had similar thoughts because he instructed the driver to wait for him and told Amanda he would be right back.

"I am coming with you."

Charlie shook his head. "Stay here," he commanded. He hurried off in the direction of the church without looking behind him at all. She considered her options for a few moments. Could she be sure that Charlie would confiscate those letters? What if he needed her help? Bender could discover him and threaten him. Too much rested on Charlie. She told the driver to wait for her, and she followed her friend into the dark.

He had slipped in the church door, so she did as well. She peered into a small sanctuary. It was empty. At the far end and down a hallway, a door rested slightly ajar, allowing the flickering of candlelight to illuminate some of the passage. As she crept closer, voices became clear.

"What are you doing here alone, Lemming?"

She placed her hand over her mouth to stop any sound. Bender had Charlie.

She froze in her place when she heard Charlie say, "Simon was held up at home. His wife's consumption is getting worse. The doctor fears she hasn't much time left. And his lordship was extra demanding today. I just barely got away myself."

"Soon you will be able to have your own stables, raise your own horses. No more catering to the needs of someone else's animals above your own."

Is that what Charlie wanted? To own a stable of his own? She did not know. She didn't know anything about what Charlie really wanted with his life.

"I long for the day. Perhaps it will be sooner than we thought."

She heard the noise of someone searching through a sack.

"I have letters we must send by express. Tonight."

Charlie cleared his throat. "They are expecting these then?"

Amanda heard a chair scraping on the floor and the jingle of buckles clinking together. She realized Charlie and Bender would soon exit the room, and she was exposed in an open sanctuary. She turned and ran for the outside door. She tried to be quiet by running on the toes of her boots, but mostly tried to be quick. Without looking back, she burst through the door and rushed across the street, and around the corner, climbing into their hack. She stilled her breathing, hoping she had made it without being seen.

Their open-air conveyance waited down a side alley not visible from the church, but if she leaned forward at just the right angle, she could make out the entrance. The door opened to reveal Bender, who headed off in the direction he had come. A few moments later, Charlie emerged, looking up and down the street before hurrying in her direction.

He climbed in to sit beside her, his eyes furious. "What were you thinking, Amanda, entering that building? I told you to stay here."

Amanda's own fury rose to the surface, fueled by her recent danger. "And when have I ever obeyed your command, Charles? Those letters are my responsibility. I had to come in."

"And a whole heap of help you were! You could have been killed. You placed my position with Bender in jeopardy—risked my life and yours. And all because you think you know the best thing to do in every situation!"

Amanda was shocked for a moment and without words. She directed her eyes meaningfully at the driver, who was watching them curiously. Charlie noticed and asked him to take them in the direction of Amanda's home.

They spoke in hushed tones. Amanda said, "Never mind all that. We must know what the letters say, Charles. Hurry! Open them."

Charlie pulled them out of his satchel and placed them in Amanda's lap and she took them, intending to open them right away. Then as he glanced up to check their surroundings, his eyes went hard and his face white. "Get down,

Amanda. Hide your face." With no time to retrieve the letters from her, Charlie slipped out of their moving open-air hack and onto the street, stumbling from the impact of his feet hitting uneven stone. Amanda ducked and searched the streets wildly out of the corners of her eyes. Charlie ran off down a side street and was soon invisible in the darkness. On the other side of the street, Bender's jet-black hair moved amongst a crowd, all entering the same pub. Thankfully, he was not looking in her direction. But she kept her face averted and her head down until long after she approached the more familiar streets of her home.

She instructed the driver to stop several streets from her front door and paid him from her reticule. Clutching the letters, she slid them inside her reticule. She hurried up to the house, hoping to avoid Mr. Parsons, but he was right there, opening the door as soon as she reached the top step.

He whispered, "Hurry to your room. Molly is waiting with hot water for your bath." He winked at her and then stood up straight, plastering on the typically stoic butler expression. She thanked him in an undertone and hurried up the stairs and down the hall to her room without encountering anyone else. What exactly did Parsons think she was doing?

Nathaniel sat in the darkness of his carriage with fists clenched. His jaw worked back and forth as he gritted his teeth in frustration. After running his hands through his hair several times he slammed his fist into the seat cushion beside him.

"My lord?" the coachman, James, asked in hushed tones from above.

"It is nothing. Wait a moment more."

Nothing would have shocked him more in that moment than to see Charlie involved with Bender's crime ring. But to feel emotional grief for lost friendship troubled him more deeply. The man was a decent stable hand, to be sure, but Nathaniel had come to view him as a friend as well and had been certain that Charlie could be trusted. Nathaniel had very nearly invited him to join their Liberty Seekers team. When he saw the indisputable evidence that Charlie was involved with Jack Bender, he was disturbed at the level of desertion he felt.

But that felt like nothing but a pin prick when compared with the utter betrayal he felt upon seeing Amanda rush into the same church shortly after Charlie. His was such a conflicting knot of emotion he did not know how to react, then or now. Should he have stampeded in and saved Amanda from herself? Should he have carried her off and delivered her to her father? What could she be thinking, being in league with Jack Bender? Could it be that she was blinded by Bender's supposed *cause*? Did she think his methods a means to an end? Perhaps she was unaware of the depth of his evil. Her actions just did not coincide with the woman he knew. Or thought he did.

After several minutes of emotional paralysis and misery, the church door had slammed open again and interrupted his thoughts. She had come tearing out of those doors as if chased by the devil himself. He had nearly flung open his own carriage doors at the sight, stopped only by the appearance of Jack Bender and then Charlie soon after. Charlie had joined Amanda in their hired hack, and they stayed hidden. Why weren't they moving? And then a painful idea had pestered the back of his mind.

Could they be in love? Nathaniel shook his head. *Perhaps she came to help him. They are dear friends.* He ran his hand through his hair again. No, the risk was too great for mere friendship. Of course they were in love. They'd sat together in their hack for much longer than necessary. Charlie had always held feelings for Amanda, and Nathaniel had been blind not to notice that Amanda obviously cared for Charlie in return. *Else why would she be here at all?*

The betrayal and grief he had felt earlier were joined by the claws of jealousy as his fists clenched tighter together in an effort to squeeze all feeling out of his body. He was about to tell his driver to take him home when he saw Bender hurrying down a side street and Charlie and Amanda following behind. The implications of the two of them following Bender wove through him as he tried to make sense of it.

"James. Follow the hack."

After a few moments, Charlie flung himself from the hack and Amanda ducked and then continued on her own as Bender slipped into a pub.

Nathaniel followed at a distance, grateful to see the hack heading in the direction of the Cumberland town house.

"Stay back, James, give them four or five blocks."

Her conveyance stopped near her home. She stepped out, looked up and down the street, and then hurried into the opened door. Nathaniel's hands fell limply at his sides.

"My lord?" James peered down at him through a hatch in the ceiling.

"Home, James. Take us home."

Feeling emotionally spent, he leaned his head back against the seat and waited for the carriage to take him home where his bed, a hot bath, and the spinning workings of his mind awaited him. He was sure the sleep his body so desperately craved would once again elude him.

As Amanda quietly closed her bedroom door behind her, Molly came rushing out of the dressing room. Both asked at the same moment, "Did you get the letters?"

"Did you return the ring?"

Molly answered first. "The ring is in the drawer, and I don't think anyone noticed it was missing."

Amanda breathed a sigh of relief, some tightness leaving her chest. "And I have the letters."

Molly slumped to the bed. The relief pouring out of her was soon replaced with exhaustion. "I don't know if I have the energy to even hear how that miracle was accomplished."

Amanda came to sit beside her, taking Molly's hand in her own. "Charlie was there."

Molly nodded. "I sent word to him."

She pulled the letters onto her lap, and with Molly leaning over her shoulder, she broke the seals and opened the first. Her heart pounding, Amanda gripped Molly's arm with one hand while she held the letter open with her other as the details of Jack Bender's latest plan to kill the prime minister and his cabinet were spelled out as if in her father's hand. "It is an invitation of sorts. To a meeting to plan . . ." Her voice trailed off—the more she read, the more horrified she became. Molly gasped as she read over Amanda's shoulder.

Gulping in her next breath, Amanda's hands shook and her face blanched. Molly wrapped an arm around her shoulders to steady her, and she gratefully leaned against her maid. "My father could have been hanged for this."

Molly's face was grim. "Aye. Treason it is."

"I cannot believe how close we came to total disaster. If I had not—if Charlie had not come, I cannot bear to think of the consequences. My father would surely have been implicated in the deaths of our entire cabinet, their wives, and Lord Liverpool himself."

Molly said, "But the danger is not averted, my lady. Your father will not bear any of the blame, but from the looks of things, the people involved will see the plan to its fruition."

"Which would mean that this letter was written with the sole purpose of implicating Father."

Molly nodded. "Why does he hate your family so?"

Amanda shook her head, not feeling up to relaying her mother's story just now.

"We should tell the duke."

"We will if we must, but I would rather he never learned of my betrayal. If I had known the contents of this letter, I would never—no matter the risk— *never* have used my father's ring."

Molly wrapped her arms around Amanda and gave her a squeeze. "Of course you wouldn't. You had no way of knowing. But what else could you have done? He would have killed Charlie. And you never even planned for them to be delivered at all, no matter what they said."

Amanda scanned the other two letters. "They are identical." She shook her head at her own foolishness. "I don't know what I was thinking I could have done. If it were not for Charlie—" She stared unseeing at the ceiling. "Charlie was already planning to meet Bender there. He was the person who was assigned to deliver these letters." Amanda shook her head. "Oh, what is he involved in? And what will happen to him when Bender realizes the letters were not delivered?"

"Charlie can take care of himself, my lady. He knows the risks. He has been doing this a long time." Molly smiled proudly. She thought for a minute and then said, "And I don't know that Bender will discover anything at all about the letters. He would never know if they arrived or not, not until after July 23."

"You are probably right." The tightness that had wound around her heart loosened a bit as she realized her father was not headed for ruin or worse, and Charlie was as safe as he ever was without her help. Then she turned her head and looked with determination into Molly's face. "We must make sure that these murders do not happen. We have only six days."

Molly nodded. "Charlie will know what to do." Then she looked sideways at Amanda. "And Lord Nathaniel. We could tell him."

Amanda turned in surprise. "What? No. Who knows how he would react?" She thought of the times he had ridiculed her. The memory of his smug expression after she had expressed empathy for the rabble who had ransacked her uncle's home made her ill. She cringed in embarrassment anew, even knowing he was wrong. She shook her head. "He will think me such a simpleton. I can barely stand my own stupidity. And he will never help us. He would tell Father straightaway. We have to figure this out another way."

Molly reached for the letter and reread it. "At least we know where they are to meet."

Amanda jumped up. "We can trap them all, at that very meeting." She started pacing in front of Molly, her heart filled with hope. "What can we do? We could borrow a gun . . ."

Molly gasped. "No! We will not!"

Amanda turned to her with a smile. "I have excellent aim, you know. But if you are that opposed, let's think of something else."

Molly sniffed. "Thank you. Every man there will likely have a gun as well, you know. You'd be shot straightaway."

Amanda nodded and kept pacing. "To begin, we should inform the magistrate."

Molly thought for a moment. "Do you think he will believe us?"

Amanda started to respond, "Of course!" but then stopped. She wasn't really certain he would. She imagined trying to explain the whole of it to anyone and realized it sounded a bit far-fetched. They might wonder if she was daft. Her claim would be difficult, if not impossible, to prove without sufficient evidence. She would rather leave her father's name out of the story entirely.

"You know, Molly, they might not believe us. For this, I really do believe we are going to need Charlie. Again." She shook her head. As if Charlie weren't already in enough trouble because of them.

Once they had developed the beginnings of a plan and they both could see a possibility of success, they succumbed to their exhaustion, yawning, and Molly slumped on the bed.

Amanda stood and tried to wiggle her way out of her dress.

"What are you doing, my lady?" Molly giggled into her hands.

"I know you are as tired as I, so I am trying to undress without help." She sighed in frustration. "But I cannot." She turned around so that Molly had easier access to the back of her dress and stays. Molly made quick work of the lot of it and soon had Amanda ready for her bath. Amanda rested a hand across Molly's shoulders. "You really are a wonder, Molly. Thank you."

She blushed from the praise. "It is my pleasure, my lady. I'll call for some hot water—your bath has surely gone cold with all our chatter. Let us not forget that helping you is also part of my employ, one which I am pleased to have."

Gratitude warmed Amanda's heart. "I am happy to hear you say that. Now, please, go rest. I'll await my water and bathe myself. You can call for it to be emptied in the morning. We have much to do tomorrow, and there is also the dinner in the evening."

After Molly left and Amanda had finished bathing and donning her nightclothes, Amanda moaned in frustration. Attending all these events and parties and dinners and musicales was becoming a real obstacle in her ability to help spread the message of equality and freedom in England.

What a difference a month in London had made for her. The thought of men dancing and attendant upon her and the other debutantes used to thrill her. Now, the effort felt so meaningless. Had the *ton* nothing else to occupy their time?

She sat back in her chair. By this time tomorrow, everything should be set in motion to stop one of the most nefarious designs of their generation. And most likely they would be rid of the awful burr of Jack Bender as well. It felt wonderful to be involved in something important. Great satisfaction filled her as she finished brushing out her hair and then climbed into bed, pulling the covers up to her chin.

CHAPTER TWENTY

NATHANIEL ARRIVED AT HOME, AGITATED. After handing his coat and hat to Brooks, he headed toward the library. He hoped a book would calm him enough to get some rest tonight. Tomorrow promised little rest and a dinner in the evening. Lady Amanda would be in attendance. He must get some small bit of sleep tonight if he was going to manage the day successfully. Candlelight flickered in his study. His senses swung into high alert. Creeping to the door, the hallway darkened in his vision as the light inside the room became brighter. The hair on his neck stood on end as he peeked around the corner. No servant would have need to be in his study at this hour.

Alarm filled him. Charlie sat in a chair, reading Nathaniel's correspondence, several pieces in hand. If those were the wrong letters, Charlie could be a real danger to the Liberty Seekers. He strode across the threshold shouting, "What is the meaning of this?"

Charlie shot to his feet, startled, grabbing the letters on his lap, crushing them to him in a jumbled heap. "Lord Nathaniel. I'm glad you are home."

He blinked. Was Charlie smiling at him? He blinked again. Yes, smiling, and not just a small grin. The man looked almost foolish, showing all his teeth in the widest smile Nathaniel had ever seen. He stopped short of fisting Charlie's shirt in his hands and tossing him from the room and instead stared him down.

"What are you doing here?" His eyes flew over the letters in Charlie's hands and froze as he saw the broken seal of an eagle in flight. His spy now sat in the gravest danger. If Charlie were ever to take this knowledge back, the Eagle in Flight would be killed immediately. Nathaniel positioned himself to block any exit from the room and stepped closer, breathing down Charlie's chest. Nathaniel would guard knowledge of his informant with his life.

Charlie's expression clouded with confusion. His legs pressed up against the chair, and his upper body leaned back to put more distance between them.

Nathaniel leaned closer, nearly forcing Charlie back into his seat. He pointed a finger at the letters clutched to Charlie's chest. "Where did you get those?"

Charlie looked at the letters he had crushed to his chest and then he looked back up into Nathaniel's face. He smiled again.

Dashed ridiculous. "Stop smiling, lad, and answer me."

Charlie said, "They're mine, my lord."

"I recognize the seal on them. Obviously not yours. Have you read them?"

"Would you mind if we sat? I have much explaining to do."

Nathaniel huffed in frustration but pulled a chair to sit in front of Charlie between him and the door. Then he leaned forward and waited.

Charlie looked at the door and said softly, "I am your Eagle in Flight."

Nathaniel stared for a moment, digesting. He gestured impatiently with his hand. "You had better keep talking, and make it good."

"I can prove it. I am your man. I brought this correspondence with me today. The last letter I wrote to you talked of July 23."

Nathaniel breathed out a sigh of relief. If he spoke the truth, Charlie had not betrayed him. On the contrary, he was one of his most trusted allies. Nathaniel leaned back, suspicion remaining. "What is my pseudonym?"

Charlie leaned forward. "Red."

Nathaniel grunted. "What is my signet?"

Charlie said, "An eagle's profile, the *eagle at rest*, you call it—that is you. I am the Eagle in Flight."

"What was in the last correspondence you received from me?"

When Charlie again answered successfully about his last correspondence with detail, it was Nathaniel's turn to smile. He felt a rush of intense relief and euphoria. Where he had moments ago been devastated, he now felt as high as the Tower of London. He stood and pulled Charlie up and slapped him on the back, pumping his hand with vigor. And then he laughed. "My stable hand. I have hired one of the bravest men in all of England as my stable hand. Smoke is one lucky stallion." All his dark feelings from earlier disappeared. Joy filled him, loosening all the tightly wound muscles.

"I enjoy horses, my lord. I have been a stable hand since I was a boy."

"Ah yes." *At Lady Amanda's stables.* "When you worked for the Duke of Cumberland."

Charlie nodded but did not elaborate. "It was Bender that arranged for me to fill this position with you."

Nathaniel sat back down thoughtfully, a worried expression crossing his brow. "Did he? Well, that is concerning, but right now, we have more pressing matters to discuss. The first of which—what have you to tell me about your meeting with Bender this very night?"

Charlie's eyes widened, and he too reclaimed his seat. "How could you know about that?"

As Nathaniel watched closely, another emotion crossed Charlie's face.

Would he admit to Lady Amanda's company? Nathaniel continued. "I had a tip that he would be at that church. We have been anxious since your last correspondence."

Charlie nodded grimly. "I was meeting Bender to pick up letters to deliver for him. His plan moves forward as we speak." Charlie continued talking, detailing everything he knew.

Nathaniel clenched his teeth while he listened. "This is dire news indeed. Where are the letters?" He held his hand out to receive them. "Let us see if there are any clues as to how we can stop this plan from actually taking place."

Charlie shifted uncomfortably. "I believe I know the contents of the letter, but I left them in a safe location until tomorrow when I plan to pick them up again. I got into a tight spot while they were still in my possession." Charlie looked him in the eye, but his face flushed.

"What is it you assume the letters say? I need to know the exact contents as soon as possible, of course."

Charlie nodded. "They likely detail a secret meeting to be held in Cato Square. Bender plans to give out all the details of the attack at this meeting. This much I already know: the murders will take place at Lord Liverpool's dinner party with the cabinet and their wives. It is my hope the letters explain the exact day and time of the Cato Square meeting."

Nathaniel nodded. "That would be fortuitous. In the meantime, I will warn Lord Liverpool. We will see if we can get them to change the day and location, or better yet, to cancel the dinner altogether."

Charlie nodded. "I will get you the contents of those letters as soon as I am able. Tomorrow, if at all possible."

Nathaniel knew the letters must be with Lady Amanda. But Charlie said nothing more. His jealousy tried to come forward full force, but he pushed it back, allowing gratitude and admiration to replace it. He had been wrong about more than one thing this night. The happy relief that Charlie and Lady Amanda were not in league with Jack Bender overshadowed his other concerns for the moment. "Charlie, are you still safe in your position with Bender?"

Charlie snorted. "*Safe* is not a word I would ever use where Bender is involved, but he is not suspicious of me, no."

Nathaniel smiled grimly. "I don't know how I can ever thank or repay you for all you are doing."

Charlie sat taller and pulled his shoulders back. "I do not desire repayment. It is for freedom that I risk myself. I find I am in your debt, actually."

Nathaniel raised his eyebrows, waiting for Charlie to continue.

"It is because of you and the Liberty Seekers that England has any chance at all for a free society." Charlie gripped Nathaniel's shoulder. "Were it not for you, a member of the nobility, taking a stand on this issue, exerting your vast resources for something so honorable—well, I would have lost hope years ago." Charlie stood and the men gripped each other's hands with a fierceness befitting their gratitude.

Nathaniel said, "For freedom."

"For freedom," echoed Charlie.

As Charlie looked into his face, Nathaniel saw his loyalty. The man would do anything to set England free. Nathaniel felt his own doubts dissolve, his own soul recharging with energy and reigniting to the cause. He promised himself yet again to do all that he could to peacefully bring about a change in England.

CHAPTER TWENTY-ONE

As Molly dressed Lady Amanda's hair for the evening dinner party and small ball, Amanda drilled her with question after question about the day's activities.

"Do you think the magistrate believed you?"

Molly nodded, but she did not look convinced. "He said, 'Mm-hmm' and took a lot of notes. I realized when we were sitting in front of him we didn't have much to offer as proof. Charlie thought it too risky to reveal himself or his position with Bender. I didn't know what to say when he asked how a stable hand and a lady's maid had come to know of it."

"Surely they will do something. The prime minister's life has been threatened."

Molly nodded. "I suspect they will at least look into it. Charlie seems confident that all will be well. He said that others are aware, and they are helping."

Amanda frowned. "But you aren't so sure yourself."

Molly shook her head. "No, I'm not."

Amanda turned her brush over and over in her hands. "We don't have much to go on, do we? We need someone to believe that the meeting will take place."

Molly's face wrinkled in concern. "I realized, while sitting there, that we were asking the police to go in and arrest a bunch of men just for talking."

Amanda thought about it a minute more while Molly finished the last touches on her hair and stepped back to admire her.

"You really do look stunning, my lady. Perhaps take a moment to notice . . ."

Amanda stopped her musings and turned her full attention to the looking glass. She sucked in her breath. "You are a marvel, my dear Molly. It is exquisite." Her hair was up in a beautiful chignon, with ringlets framing her face. Carefully placed throughout were sparkling jewels that caught even the candlelight in her room and reflected on the ceiling. The sapphires from her father graced her neck and brought out the brilliant blue of her eyes.

Molly said, "It is you who are exquisite. This will simply bring your loveliness to everyone's notice."

Amanda narrowed her eyes just a bit and teasingly asked, "Just what are you up to, Molly?"

But Molly shrugged and said, "Nothing, my lady." Then she stopped and looked at Amanda with a serious expression. "Well, nothing besides the potentially treasonous thoughts of trying to bring greater equality to the people of England. Oh, and trying to stop an assassination."

Amanda reached for her hands. "Isn't it wonderful?"

Molly giggled. "Yes, it is."

Amanda reached for her dance card and reticule. "I suppose I had best be off then."

Her ride in the carriage gave her too much time to fill with silent fretting and anxiety. Her mother glanced at her several times but remained quiet. Amanda knew they had not done enough. An uncomfortable feeling settled in her belly and would not leave. How could she ensure that July 23 was not a day of disaster for England?

Just as they were pulling into the front drive of a beautiful home, she felt again that she would have to go herself to Cato Street. It was dangerous, yes, but not recklessly so—it was nothing worse than she had already attempted. The more she thought on the idea, the greater her determination to carry it out. She must be present near this planning meeting to ensure nothing ever came of Jack Bender's evil intentions.

If all else failed, she herself would turn them in. She planned to witness the gathering, and if no law enforcement arrived, she would bring them herself. Surely Bender had worked up enough of a reputation they would be seeking him anyway. If she had to start wailing and carrying on, if she had to cry fire, if she had to lead them personally, she would bring the magistrate to Jack Bender and his gang. And with those thoughts, she allowed herself to be handed down from her carriage.

At the touch of a man's hand under her own, she felt running tingles all the way up to her neckline. She followed the hand with her eyes along a strong arm, across broad shoulders, and into the face of Lord Nathaniel. His grin sent energy through her. She closed her open mouth and swallowed before speaking.

"Lord Nathaniel, hello."

His eyes never left her. Her heart raced and hands trembled as she stepped carefully down from the carriage. Did he know what he did to her? His finger found her glove line at her wrist, and he was gently running his finger tantalizingly, slowly, over the sensitive skin just above it. He rested on her pulse for a moment, and his eyes found hers. He knew. The desire that filled his eyes was almost her undoing as she forced herself to return his gaze.

And then the moment was broken as he gently took her hand and placed it on the crook of his arm. He led her from her carriage up the steps and into the grand house. She was vaguely aware of her mother and father following behind them. Finding a bit of her senses return, she asked teasingly, "How is it you were there, ready to escort me in?"

Was that a blush she saw? He turned to her and said, "I believe something in the heavens is speaking in my favor tonight. It was my extreme good fortune to arrive seconds before your carriage pulled up, and I waited. That is all. You look exquisite tonight, Lady Amanda."

They entered the home and greeted their host and hostess. Many curious eyes lingered on the pair of them as they were seen arriving together. Amanda lifted her chin and returned their curiosity with bold, confident looks of her own. A heady exhilaration filled her as she walked in at Lord Nathaniel's side. She allowed a moment of triumph as she inwardly acknowledged that hers was the company he sought, her hand that was on his arm.

The moment splintered as soon as they stepped farther into the room. A swarm of debutantes and their mothers surrounded them. She felt the muscles on Lord Nathaniel's arm tighten, and she sensed more than saw the change come over him as his eyes flitted to hers and then away.

"Ladies. And how are all of you lovely flowers this evening?"

Did he just call them all flowers?

"Might I have the opportunity to dance with each one of you, dare I hope?" They all giggled in return, practically throwing their dance cards at him with not-so-subtle offers. He gestured to her. "I have saved the dinner set for Lady Amanda." He turned to her with an apology and a question in his eyes. She nodded, gritting her teeth.

He seemed to breathe out in relief. He continued. "But all others are free. Let us see now." Lord Nathaniel walked forward into the mass of them without another glance in her direction, leaving Amanda. She was sure she was not hiding her irritation very well.

Walking away with a group of women? Did he think she waited for any scrap of favor he threw in her direction? She remembered the delicious thrill of her hand on his arm, the current that raced through her at his touch. And within her whirling emotions, a battle ensued. Countering her irritation, a secret sense of pleasure emerged that the dance and time together for their meal would be hers and hers alone. She sighed. What could she do but wait until he came for her?

She soon found herself equally surrounded by men of the *ton*, and she let the daring of her new Cato Street plan and her dizzying attraction to Lord Nathaniel wash over her. She restrained herself less than ever before and danced, laughed, and teased with abandon. She flirted with all, welcoming the attention and getting drunk off the accolades of the *ton*. At one point, surrounded by men, they cajoled her into sharing a new bit of poetry.

She raised her hands in the air with a dramatic flair.

"I want you all to know
Of a girl who is all aglow.
When she dances, her feet are not slow.
Flying is the way she will go,
As fun, as free, and as smart—
As the Sparrow."

The men cheered, which drew many a disapproving sniff from the matrons of the *ton* and not a few glowers from other debutantes, but Amanda did not care. She felt as high as the sparrows themselves.

Baron Kenworthy asked, "The Sparrow—Lady Amanda, do you know the identity of the famous Sparrow?"

Amanda started in surprise. She caught Lord Nathaniel's disapproving gaze boring into her own. She raised her chin in defiance. She could cover and protect herself from a perceived connection with the Sparrow. No one would ever suspect her.

Time to increase her flighty, airless manner. She said, "What? Lud no!" The nearest ladies gasped at her language. The men merely laughed some more. "I was only speaking of the bird, my dear baron." And she giggled into her hands. "I do love that Sparrow's pretty pictures, though I do not find them incredibly funny."

The men guffawed. "They are wonderful, Lady Amanda. Don't you think so?"

"Well, now I don't know. I feel I might not understand them entirely. Tut! What's so funny about a man's valet? I must know." The men only smiled condescendingly. The baron patted her hand with his own. Lord Nathaniel rolled his eyes but smiled with apparent relief. Satisfaction filled her. People surely believed her head as filled with air as any other debutante of the Season.

"But that's just it, Lady Amanda." She turned in surprise to an earnest young man at her left. "The Sparrow is pointing out some of the more ridiculous things we do, how abominably we treat our dear servants. Bless my valet. I raised his salary an extra two shillings a week after seeing the Sparrow's latest flier. He deserves it."

The men laughed and began sharing stories of how they had behaved absolutely ridiculously toward their valets. Spilled wine, drunken swaying—until Amanda cleared her throat, and they remembered they were in the presence of ladies.

She strived hard to hide her look of triumph, and she pasted on a look of confusion as she sighed. "I don't suppose I will ever understand this Sparrow person." And she waved her hands as if shooing an annoying fly. The men laughed again, the music started up, and her partner came to claim her hand for the dance.

Finally, her turn to dance with Lord Nathaniel came . . . and went. As the music started, she waited in anticipation to place her hand in his. She watched as couples all around her found places on the floor to begin the waltz. She blushed at the thought. *A waltz with Lord Nathaniel.*

But where was he? She searched the crowd in vain. And then her eyes met his across the room, his arms around Miss Clarissa as they moved together in the waltz. She felt her hands go cold and her fists tighten in anger. She whipped around and came nose to nose with Lord Jonathan Needley. "Oh! Lord Needley, I—"

He reached for her. "I couldn't help but notice that you are without a partner for this set. I cannot imagine how such a thing is possible, but I will not question my good fortune. Would you do me the honor of dancing with me?"

Amanda's mouth moved into a smile she did not feel, which grew in sincerity as she rebelliously nodded to him and placed her hand in his. "I would be delighted, my lord."

She allowed him to lead her onto the floor. She gave him her complete attention, fawning over his every word, smiling prettily up into his face, laughing at all the right moments. Inwardly, she felt a part of herself shut down. When she noticed they had come closer to Lord Nathaniel and Miss Clarissa, she stepped brazenly closer to her partner.

A new gleam lit his face. "Shall we shock them a bit, my lady?" He quirked an eyebrow at her, and she stared in surprise.

Recognizing the teasing glint in his eyes, she grinned and said, "I would love nothing more than to be a little shocking right now."

He laughed. Lord Needley *laughed aloud.* Gone was the proper and staid gentleman she had always known. He pulled her even closer. They moved toward Lord Nathaniel, who was watching with a steely glare and scowling so completely that his eyes barely opened. Amanda laughed and spun around the room.

Lord Needley weaved them in and out of couples, holding her closer as he became bolder. They moved nearer to the edge of the ballroom until they went right off the floor and out behind some of the potted plants and trees where he stopped, a bit breathless, and asked, "Would you care for a bit of fresh air out on the balcony?" He raised his eyebrows suggestively. She glanced over her shoulder. Lord Nathaniel's eyes still followed her as he danced.

She turned back. "That would be perfect."

They exited through the double doors out into the cool night air. There were very few other people out with them, most in quiet conversation together. He led her to the right, still visible through the glass in the doorway, but in the shadows enough to feel somewhat secluded.

She laughed. "Oh this feels wonderfully cool." She held her arms out before stopping in front of the railing and leaning forward to look out over the gardens. Lord Needley stepped beside her, his chest pressed against her side. She could feel him staring intently at her. He raised his hand and ran one finger along the delicate skin on her neck then he played with her sapphire necklace.

She kept her face forward, mind racing. How could she escape his attentions? Why had she allowed him to lead her here? She grabbed at anything at all they could talk about. She turned to face him, and before she could take a step back to put some distance between them, he wrapped one arm around her back, pulling her against his chest. She looked up, her mouth opened in surprise.

Before she could find a single word, Lord Needley leaned down and very nearly pressed his mouth to hers when they both heard, "Lady Amanda! There you are. I have a message for you—they said it was urgent." Charlie bowed before her, handing her a letter. As he rose from his bow, he winked, then turned and walked in the other direction.

Amanda shook her head in wonder, happier than she could express that Lord Needley had not been able to kiss her. How on earth did Charlie acquire such perfect timing? She realized that tonight she had pushed her flirting, airy facade too far. Too often, she jumped into situations, allowing her heart to rule and not her head. Hardly daring to talk to Lord Needley, who had put some distance between them, she indicated the note. "I should attend to this, whatever it may be."

"Can you not guess who it is from?" He gestured through the doors to Charlie, who was smiling and shaking hands with Lord Nathaniel before he walked the edges of the ballroom and stood in the corner.

Why is Charlie here at the ball? She allowed her confusion to show on her face.

Needley spared her further explanation. "Lady Amanda, I must apologize."

She tilted her head and raised one eyebrow. "Apologize?"

"It is not a secret that I have expressed a particular interest in getting to know you better, in courting you, in hopes of a future alliance between us." Amanda nodded, wary. "And as we have spent a good amount of time together and shared many of the same functions, you have been a constant puzzle to me."

"I imagine that's true." Guilt crept into her consciousness, and she made herself meet his eyes.

"One minute you are a brilliant, intelligent, caring woman and the next, the silliest of all debutantes this Season."

Amanda's eyebrows rose as high as they could.

He paused for a moment, searching her eyes. "Forgive me."

She nodded and smiled sadly, indicating that he should continue.

"I have seen you behave outrageously this evening. You seem far more reckless than I have ever known you to be." He pulled himself up taller and straightened his tailcoat, seemingly proud of himself. "And so I performed a little playacting of my own."

She couldn't resist a little laugh. "But I don't understand."

"I wondered just how far you would allow things to go. I must say, it was quite diverting. I've underestimated the enjoyment of the rakes among us." He looked wistfully out amongst the twirling ladies of the *ton*.

"And if we had been caught? Kissing out here?" Amanda was astounded at Lord Needley's admission.

"I cannot say I would have regretted being tied to you in any fashion." When Amanda opened her mouth in outrage, he held up his hand and continued. "And better me than some of the others who could have done the same." He looked meaningfully at her until she lowered her eyes in admission to the truth of his words. He lifted her chin with his finger and looked again into her eyes. "I would enjoy spending my life with you. The real you. The one you keep so carefully hidden away. I know you are not amorously attracted to me as yet, but we could have a good life together."

Amanda gulped. "Are . . . are you proposing, my lord?" She glanced back in the ballroom, hoping her father was not aware of this conversation.

Lord Needley considered her for a long moment. "I am not." And when she released a relieved breath, he laughed humorlessly. "I am not proposing, but I am asking if you would welcome such advances in the future if you were to, let us say, grow in your affection for me?"

Amanda smiled at him. "I admire you greatly. I enjoy your company."

Lord Needley held up his hand. "Yes or no, if you please."

She looked sadly into his eyes and said, "Not when I have those feelings for another." And her eyes found the floor. She felt the guilt of her previous flirtations hit her full force, weighing heavily.

Lord Needley cleared his throat to regain her attention. "I understand. And in a moment when he reaches us, may I wish him every happiness?" His amused expression did little to assuage her guilt or embarrassment. She turned to follow his gaze and saw Lord Nathaniel stomping in their direction. She would not have been surprised at all to see smoke coming out his ears.

"Oh dear," she said.

"Yes. Shall I protect you, fair lady? Slay the dragon?"

She shook her head. "No, I think I had best face this beast on my own." But, as he turned to go, she reached her hand out and squeezed his arm. "But thank you. I wanted to care for you in that way. I truly did. I wish you every happiness."

Lord Needley smiled. "Well, that's something at least." Then he squeezed her hand in return and slipped off to the right and in through the other doors.

"What do you think you are doing?" Lord Nathaniel's tall frame bore down on her, heating the balcony. Amanda stepped back, away from his anger.

"What do you mean?"

He waved his hands wildly about. "This whole evening. What do you think you are doing?"

She stared at him a moment. She'd never seen him so . . . flustered.

"Throwing yourself at every male who can walk! Flirting rampantly with all of them. You were mere inches—*inches*—from Needley in the waltz just now."

Amanda couldn't help the smile that grew as Lord Nathaniel grew more agitated.

"And then receiving notes from Charlie! I mean, I am grateful to the man for stopping that nonsense with Needley, but *notes*? Have you lost all sense of propriety?"

With a start she was reminded of the paper she held in her hand. "You didn't send this?"

"Absolutely not. I am shocked you accepted it. That is not the kind of deportment I would expect from the daughter of a duke. Act or no act, this has gone far enough."

Something snapped. "This, coming from you, surrounded by all your women. You didn't even have the courtesy to properly ask me for the supper set.

And then you walked off without a backward glance." She folded her arms and scowled at him. "And how do you know it's an act? Maybe this is who I am! The real me, finally revealed. I have been having fun tonight—carefree, albeit reckless, fun."

She spun in a circle, arms wide and then stepped back farther and folded her arms across her chest again. She would not be made to feel guilty again by him. She had done nothing to wrong him. Though she did feel several nagging thoughts about Lord Needley that would cause her to lose sleep tonight.

The paper was beginning to burn a hole in her hand. It must be urgent, or Charlie would not have taken steps to deliver it in the way he had.

"This is *not* the real you." He stepped closer to her.

She snorted. "Well, you are definitely a rake down to your core. Did you even remember you had demanded the supper set from me?" She could feel the heat from his chest and smelled his wonderful spicy musk. She faltered a bit, and reached for his arm to steady herself. He didn't even have the decency to look apologetic.

"Yes, of course I remembered. And here I am to collect you for the set."

Amanda opened her mouth and then closed it again. "Wasn't that just the supper set, a moment ago?"

Lord Nathaniel frowned. "No. It begins right now."

"What?" How could she have confused the dances? She clenched her fists in embarrassment. "I'm so sorry, Lord Nathaniel, embarrassed really. I thought . . . that is, I assumed . . ."

"That I forgot our set? And danced with Miss Clarissa instead?"

Amanda nodded, blinking. "It was a waltz. And you enjoyed it." She felt her indignation rising again. "And you've been flirting just as much as I."

"Lady Amanda, I have been counting the very seconds that pass, waiting until I get the opportunity to hold you."

Amanda looked up into his eyes. "You have?"

He cupped her cheek in his hand. "I could never forget a promised moment with you."

She leaned into his hand, smiling, relieved, feeling foolish. "I'm sorry for assuming something so ungallant of you."

"Too often, I give you reasons to doubt me." His eyes communicated a warmth and caring that made her knees shake.

She again noticed her message from Charlie in her hand and glanced down at it. "But I do need some time to myself. If you will please excuse me, for just a moment."

As she turned to leave, he reached for her arms, staying her. "Go ahead and read your letter here. I won't interfere." Her heart warmed toward him when his expression deepened with understanding and empathy. Perhaps he was capable of far more kindness than she ever understood before.

She'd never seen this seal before, an eagle in flight. How curious. She broke it quickly, but as her eyes swept over the page, she saw it was written in Charlie's hand. Lord Nathaniel studied her.

I am leaving town. Do not do anything rash. Stay home! We will take care of Cato. I have help. All will be well.

Trust Lord Nathaniel.

Worry filled her. She looked in the direction Charlie had gone. He no longer waited in the shadows.

Lord Nathaniel interrupted her thoughts. "Distressing news?" He watched her face.

"Yes, a bit. I feel a headache brewing." She applied pressure to the bridge of her nose.

He stepped nearer to her. "Might I help you?" She saw such earnest kindness again in his eyes and an obvious concern. She longed to share all. *Trust Lord Nathaniel.* The words repeated themselves in her mind. She opened her mouth.

"It is just silliness, my lord. A childhood prank from an old friend. He has won a bet is all." She could not bear to share her involvement—having used her father's ring—as ashamed as she felt.

A flash of disappointment crossed his eyes. "Shall we still have our dance? They are playing another waltz . . ." He waggled his eyebrows at her, making her laugh.

A bit of happiness filled her at the thought. She smiled. "That would be lovely." She folded up her letter and placed it in her reticule.

Nathaniel took her into his arms and swept her out into the ballroom. Her feet barely had time to touch the floor before she was swept in the other direction only to graze the ground before moving on again. No dance had ever felt so exhilarating. She hovered above the earth, gliding along just at its surface. Lord Nathaniel whisked her away, and they flew. Everyone faded. His gaze took in her every feature, studying her eyes, moving along her cheeks, lingering on her lips. She moved wherever he led, barely perceiving his lead at all. She had never felt such a perfect oneness. They floated and spun and whirled until the last chords were played and the couples around them had stopped. Amanda stared deeply into Lord Nathaniel's eyes, willing him to stay. With his arm still wrapped around her, he caught his breath, all the while returning her gaze.

Amanda found her voice. "Thank you, my lord."

Nathaniel blinked and then lowered his arm. "My pleasure, Lady Amanda. Perhaps I might have the next set? And the next after that?"

Amanda touched his face and whispered, "And the next." Then she laughed. "But I do believe they are calling us in to dinner."

∽

Lord Nathaniel held out his arm to escort her in to their table. This was not to be the quiet moment with Lady Amanda he had hoped. She was seated at his left, but on her other side, the Baron Kenworthy monopolized her attention. And Miss Clarissa, whom he respected greatly as a friend, sat on his right. Across from him, they were joined by two young ladies who immediately began eyeing him and giggling to each other, leaning around the poor chap who sat between them.

Lady Amanda placed a sympathetic hand on Nathaniel's arm.

He turned to her and winked, and she squeezed his arm before placing her hand in her lap.

Well into the second course, having spoken only a few sentences to her, Nathaniel thought this dinner might go down as the most aggravating of his thirty years. A young man across from him asked, "Has anyone seen the new flier from the Sparrow?" He felt Lady Amanda stiffen beside him.

He said, "I have not." And then with a smile, he said to Miss Clarissa, "Do tell us about the latest exhibits at the art museum. I hear they are much envied by even the French."

Miss Clarissa smiled and began to explain when, not to be deterred, the other young man said to the others, "The Sparrow's message is disturbing in my mind." Lady Amanda's attention now completely riveted, she raised her eyebrows in expectation. Lord Nathaniel frowned in irritation, trying again to dissuade him. The man hardly spared a glance for Nathaniel and continued. "I brought it with me. Couldn't believe it myself. See, here it is." He laid it out on the table in front of them. Several matrons a few seats down looked disapprovingly at the young man and sniffed, their noses in the air.

The ladies took note of the flier. "What is it? Oh, do show us."

Lord Nathaniel picked it up and studied it. In the center of the page, she had drawn a flag with a cap of liberty on the top. A quick glance at Lady Amanda saw nothing there to help him. His eyes moved over the paper, taking in the rest. A man dressed in livery stood next to a housemaid. And next to them someone with a soot-marked face and a young child with ripped clothing. The mother from the debtor's cart made an appearance, only now she was walking, with her babe in arms. He was astounded at the realistic expressions, full of hope the people wore as they made their way toward the cap.

He had to admit he was impressed. Then he froze as his eyes caught the description at the bottom of the flier. *Seeking Liberty. Did she know about the Liberty Seekers?* His eyes darted to Amanda's, which were glued on him, as were the eyes of everyone in their group at the table. He carefully schooled his expression.

"This Sparrow is obviously very talented. I have not seen this kind of precise detail except in the museums Miss Clarissa was discussing." He gave her a smile.

She reached for the paper. "Oh my, yes! Excellent detail. Look at the expressions on their faces."

One of the girls from across the table sniffed. "Well, I find it distasteful." She reached for the flier, and Miss Clarissa reluctantly handed it over. The girl continued. "Just look at all those women, arm in arm. Imagine! Someone from our class, sharing a sidewalk with some of them." She pointed out the more poorly dressed figures. "Why! We would soil our dresses!" Her friend leaned over and laughed.

"And our reputations."

Lady Amanda frowned at them. "Well, I find it enlightening."

When Lord Nathaniel saw the expression on her face, he braced himself, unsure what would come out of her mouth.

"Everyone wants freedom. Everyone is after that red cap of liberty. You, me, them, all of us." Then she dismissed them all and began conversing with Baron Kenworthy on her left.

The girls' faces showed their uncertainty. Lady Amanda outranked them all. Nathaniel watched with amusement as the girls struggled with their own reactions to Lady Amanda. He could almost see their minds spinning. He recognized their pained confusion. Should they stick with the truths they had always been taught, or agree with the daughter of a duke?

Miss Clarissa surprised him when she said in a low voice, "Very nice sentiments, but it screams of treason. What does the Sparrow suggest? A revolt of the working classes? Freedom is not something England offers to everyone. This Sparrow, whoever he is, would do well to keep to lighter parody of the *ton*."

Nathaniel's chest tightened. He was so proud of Lady Amanda that he could have picked her up, swung her around, and kissed her soundly for all to see. Perhaps it was time for him to add his voice. "I don't know, Miss Clarissa."

Lady Amanda turned to watch him, surprise showing on her face.

"Who can argue with freedom? Everyone could use a bit more of it, don't you think?" Warming to the subject, he asked, "Haven't you ever wished a debutante could wear something other than white? I, for one, would enjoy seeing all your loveliness in some of the deeper, dare I say, alluring shades that are available. Or property—wouldn't you love to have a bit of land to your name?" He smiled his roguish smile and raised an eyebrow, looking at each in turn.

He was pleased his efforts had an effect. After they recovered from their own reactions to Lord Nathaniel's charm, the two young ladies barely paused for the rest of the evening. They began in earnest, discussing all of the lovely colors of fabrics they had seen at their modiste and had not been able to select.

Miss Clarissa stared thoughtfully in their direction, but Nathaniel could tell her thoughts were far away. He asked, "Something amiss with the lovely Miss Clarissa?" Nathaniel smiled and picked up her hand. She shook her head and smiled in return, her eyes travelling to Lady Amanda and back to him before pulling her hand gently back and giving greater attention to her meal.

Lord Nathaniel followed suit, but not before he glanced at Amanda and found her staring gratefully into his eyes. His heart pounded in his chest, and his fingers drummed his thighs with an unused surge of energy. He vowed to do something in the near future that would inspire that same expression again directed at him.

With many questions still to answer about the enticing Lady Amanda, he found himself drawn to her all the more.

She laughed at something the baron said.

The baron's voice carried over to him. "You must, my lady, you simply must!"

"Oh, Sir Kenworthy, surely you tire of my silly poems by now."

"Oh, but no! They are my lullabies at night. I hear them in my sleep, and your angelic voice attends me. Do dream up another, won't you?" Lady Amanda looked helplessly in Lord Nathaniel's direction.

"Yes, Lady Amanda. I find I too am in need of the balm of your lovely voice and delightful musings." Nathaniel bit his cheek to keep his face appropriately serious.

She scowled good-naturedly at him and said, "Very well. I do believe something a little more lighthearted would do us all some good." She cleared her throat while she thought for a moment. "Given our recent flier, I shall call this 'An Ode to the Sparrow'.

"Does anyone know?
Where does he go?
Our witty little Sparrow.
Why does he flee,
When we know that he is free,
Flying with the red cap of liberty?"

"Bravo! Bravo!" The baron quietly cheered. And then he frowned. "But I would have much preferred 'An Ode to the Baron', if you please."

Lady Amanda laughed and said, "Then you shall have it, my dear baron! For being the most congenial of us all." She cleared her throat again and began.

"I'll sing a song of the baron,
Charming favorite of the ton."

The baron held up his hand. "But that doesn't even rhyme."

"Yes it does, now hush while I finish.

"I'll sing a song of the baron,
Charming favorite of the ton.
He loves to play,
And while dancing he will sway
With such elegance none can relay.
Our own Corinthian Kenworthay."

She stressed the last syllable and stretched it out dramatically, which brought laughs to most of the table's occupants, who had stilled to hear her latest rhymes. They were terribly concocted. Everyone knew it, but that is what made them fun, Nathaniel supposed. Allowing himself to be captivated by her along with everyone else, he laughed with the group and smiled at her in appreciation. Even the staunchest matrons smiled indulgently at her. She had a gift. Even when acting in a most ridiculous manner, she made love to them all, and they couldn't help but love her in return. Nathaniel shook his head in admiration.

CHAPTER TWENTY-TWO

Molly pulled open the curtains in Amanda's room, waking her with a start.

"What time is it?" Amanda blurted. Then she fell back into her bed, moaning.

Molly laughed. "I'm sorry, my lady. But it is approaching ten in the morning now, and we do have a mountain of things to accomplish today, including saving the lives of our dear cabinet members and prime minister."

Amanda moaned louder. "I always have to save people's lives. Can't we do something exciting for once?" She and Molly burst out laughing together.

When they had stopped, Amanda admitted, "You know, I am really very scared about this whole thing. I know I have to do something, but the idea of possibly seeing Bender again is terrifying. If only the magistrate had listened to you and Charlie."

Molly ran fingers through her hair.

"But I am determined. The magistrate cannot possibly ignore me if I tell him they are all sitting in one room together at that very moment, now can he?"

"No, my lady, especially if you have to start shouting that there's been a crime."

Molly reached for her hand and sat on the edge of the bed. "Before we start talking all about that, I've been anxious to tell you something that happened at the printer's while you were on your way to that ball last night."

Amanda opened her eyes and asked, "What happened?"

Molly said, "A man by the name of Jonathon Edward Taylor was waiting for me. He said he is interested in the Sparrow's drawings. Said he wants to publish them."

Amanda sat up. "Publish them? In the newspaper or a book, or what did he say?"

Molly laughed. "I thought you would love that. He said he wants to begin a newspaper—*The Manchester Guardian*, he calls it—that he would distribute to the homes in the London area. He is not interested in a gossip column from the *ton*; he wants real news and real issues. And when he saw your latest flier, the one with the red cap, he said he would like to print it in his paper, along with any other like it you would care to draw for him." Amanda fell back on her pillow with a smile on her face.

"It's beginning, Molly. Our message is spreading."

Molly bounced a bit on the edge of the bed. "It is, Lady Amanda. It surely is."

"What was this man like? Was he interested in meeting me? I mean, in meeting the Sparrow?"

Molly shook her head. "I discussed that with him, and he seemed perfectly comfortable never meeting the Sparrow. He would be happy to communicate with me or any other messenger we send."

Amanda sighed. "This is *such* good news. It is just what I needed to hear."

After Amanda was up and dressed, Molly brought a breakfast tray to her room, and she and Molly set about planning for the day. Molly would deliver the *Seeking Liberty* drawing and a batch of new ones to Mr. Taylor.

They had decided to ask if Mr. Taylor would also print some of her drawings into loose fliers like those she had been using. They had proved to be so favorable with the *ton* of late, and Amanda didn't want to lose the momentum they had gained. Molly was also going to try to find out where Charlie had gone, and to learn more about the Liberty Seekers and their plans. If she could just contact one of them, they could help Charlie, wherever he might be.

Meanwhile, Amanda was going to visit a park near a certain pub on Edgware Road near Cato Street, hoping to help intercept the meeting. She was certain that somewhere near there, she would discover clues as to how she should get the police involved in stopping the planned murders. Certainly, as soon as she saw the men assembled, that should be clue enough. They decided the safest way for her to travel would be by carriage with a footman. It was near Grosvenor Square, which was very close to her home, but since the chance of seeing Bender remained high, she thought it safer to take the carriage and proceed from the square to her modiste, where she was getting a new ball gown made.

The only footman available was the most taciturn of the bunch. He sat in silence with a blank expression during their short ride to the square. She informed him she would be taking a turn around the square and perhaps visiting with some friends and acquaintances. He nodded and helped her out of the carriage.

She began by strolling along the street on the edge of the square, greeting those she knew, stopping to chat with some along her path, and all the while searching the area. Her eyes passed over a man crossing the street and then immediately returned to study him closely. Her heart pounding in her chest, she recognized the long scar on the side of his face: Jack Bender. She quickly moved out of sight to the other side of a tree, ducking down low. She continued to watch him. He looked from side to side in his familiar nervous habit and then entered the pub on the corner.

She took a couple of steps out from behind her tree and yelped in surprise when she felt a strong but gentle grip on her forearm. She tried to pull her arm free while whipping around to face the intruder. She almost cried in relief to see Charlie, even though he was glaring down at her with accusing eyes.

"What are you doing here?" Charlie demanded.

She felt her ire rise. "I am merely going for a walk in Grosvenor Square, if you must know."

"And spying on our enemy from behind a tree."

Amanda lifted her chin in defiance. "I spotted him and didn't want him to notice me, so I stepped out of sight."

"And directly in the sight of everyone behind you, who is likely wondering at the beautiful back of a fancy dress, its owner obviously spying on a pub."

Amanda looked around Charlie's shoulder to see what kind of crowd was enjoying the park from that direction. Quite a few people glanced curiously in their direction.

"Well, I didn't think of that. The only thing I could think of at the moment was to stay out of sight of Bender. Which I feel is particularly sensible of me." She folded her arms and asked, "Where have you been? What are *you* doing here?"

Charlie tilted his head toward the pub. "I'm here for the meeting."

Then he hissed, "Hide!" He moved away from her as quickly as possible.

Someone called to him from across the street, "Oi, Charlie! Mate! Care for a cuppa?" This new friend put his arm around Charlie's back and led him into the pub. Amanda panicked. She had to get inside that pub. She waited a few minutes and then followed around behind the building.

She stepped into a dark hallway at the back of the pub and waited a moment for her eyes to adjust. She heard the patrons making noise up ahead and the busy kitchen off to her right. Just as she was trying to decide where to go next, the door to the public area of the pub opened, and a line of men came walking through the door directly toward her small corner in the shadows. She pressed herself to the wall, trying to breathe as little as possible.

The men took about ten steps in her direction and then turned to the left and entered through a door Amanda had not noticed before. She counted twenty men, including Bender and Charlie; after the last man entered the room, he pushed the door almost completely shut behind him. Amanda rushed to the door, hoping to learn something before she ran to grab the nearest magistrate.

The door did not fit the frame in precise lines and was cracked just enough for her to see into the room. Placing her ear to the door, she strained to hear the conversation.

"It has been confirmed. The dinner will happen in two days' time, right here in Grosvenor Square." Grumbling began, and Bender shouted, "Silence! I have no more time for your dissent. You have had opportunity enough to back out."

Someone who must have been seated at the far side of the table, where she could not see, said, "And you have weapons enough?"

Bender answered, "That we do, gentlemen. Weapons enough and more." He laughed, a noise that chilled Amanda down to her toes and sent all her arm hairs standing on end. Some of the men in the room shifted uncomfortably in their seats. How many were here by choice and how many by force? She would let the magistrate worry about that. She'd heard what she needed. If she was going to do any good at all, she must run now and find one. She turned from the door and ran four steps before she slammed into an overly large body. Gasping for air, she looked up into the face of the tallest man she had ever seen.

Behind her, she heard the scraping of chairs and a voice calling, "Who's out there?"

This new stranger looked at the door and back at Amanda. "Come with me. We must hurry." Amanda nodded, glancing behind her as she ran. He took her into the public area of the pub for a moment and then turned right, down another hallway that led to a stairway. "Up here. Quickly."

She hesitated, not knowing if she could trust the man. "I am a magistrate," he explained, and took the stairs two at a time in front of her.

A magistrate! She could not believe her luck. She heard the noises of men coming from the hallway, and so she moved up the stairs as quickly as she dared in all her skirts until she reached the top and rounded the corner. The man then led her into a room off to the right. He closed the door behind them, and Amanda felt a sharp pang of fear, wondering if he had told her the truth.

He must have seen her fear because he quickly explained, "I am here to investigate the dealings of some very rough men, and you are in grave danger. Please just stay in this room so I can get down there and do my job."

"Are you here with Jack Bender?"

The magistrate stepped closer to her, suspicion now written across his face. "What do you know of Mr. Bender?"

"I need to know if you are indeed a magistrate."

He considered her for a brief moment before answering, "That I am—Harrison, of Grosvenor Square. Now, you had best explain your dealings with a man such as Jack Bender."

"Harrison of Grosvenor Square, I am Lady Amanda Cumberland. I am no friend of Jack Bender's. That you can be sure of. He hates my family. He has been tormenting us for nearly a year. But sir, that's beside the point. Bender is at this moment planning to murder the prime minister and all of the cabinet members. His whole gang is down there in that room as we speak. If you could just apprehend them now—"

"Apprehend them now? By myself? I am well aware of his plans."

"This is the perfect moment, caught in the act of planning such a nefarious deed."

"It would be, if I had a small army with me. Each man in there is likely armed, and they are suspicious—you saw how quickly they came to investigate a tiny noise at their door."

"Then I will rally support for you."

Harrison looked at her for a moment and then chuckled. "And I bet you will, too. Do what you must, my lady. I have to get to that meeting. If, of a sudden, a team of Bow Street runners or night watchmen shows up to aid me, then I will count myself blessed. If not, I will continue with my job anyway, which is to *investigate*. A good day to you." He tipped his hat to her with a slight bow and stepped out of the room. As soon as she heard him tromping down the stairs in his big boots, she rushed down after him, through the pub and out onto the street, where she ran into Paul, her footman.

"Oof! Where have you been?" Amanda asked.

Paul answered, "My lady, I was thinking to ask the same of you."

Amanda looked at him suspiciously. Was that just a bit of rebellious insubordination from Paul, the quietest person she had ever met? She smiled at the thought.

"Paul, we must find ourselves as many watchmen as possible."

He considered her for a moment and then, seeming to make some kind of silent decision within himself, he nodded to her, motioned that she follow, and hurried down the street. They crossed over two blocks, turned an immediate right into an alley and approached a small doorway. He knocked four times, waited, and then entered. She followed and found herself in a very tiny but simple and tidy kitchen.

At the table sat the scariest person she had ever seen—his face was grotesquely scarred and one of his eyes stared permanently off to the right while the other pierced her with its gaze. Burn marks ran down his neck, and a long scar across his cheek, ending on his upper lip, which was twisted in such a strange way that his mouth remained open all the time. When he saw them, he stood and grimaced. "Paul, my boy! I'm right glad to see ya, I am!" His voice rang clear and strong.

Paul moved forward and pulled the man to him in a strong, back-pounding embrace. The awful grimace must be the man's smile, because he returned the back pounding with equal vigor.

Paul pulled away and looked into his face. "We've come for some help—Bow Street, watchmen, local yeomen—anyone who can aid us." Then he gestured for Amanda to explain.

She knew nothing about this man, but Paul seemed to trust him, and she knew no better way to round up help. She said, "There are a group of twenty men meeting in the pub on the corner of Edgware Road who are, at this moment, planning the murder of the prime minister and his cabinet in two days' time. They are all in one room. If we could get them now . . ."

The man eyed her in what she thought was suspicion. "And you are?"

Amanda curtsied out of habit. "I am Lady Amanda, daughter of the Duke of Cumberland."

"Ah, my son works in your house."

Amanda looked in surprise from Paul to this man. "And what is your name, sir, if I may ask?"

"Garth Simmons, my lady." He stared at her again with his one eye narrowed. "And how is it that you are here alone with Paul, full of knowledge of such a treasonous conspiracy and your father, the duke, not knowing anything about it?"

"Please, sir! We have no time." Amanda twisted her hands together. "It is such a long story. I will happily tell all as soon as they have been apprehended." She looked at him with her most pleading expression. Seeing no response, she realized that this man would not care one whit for any of her expressions, pleadings, or girlish ways. But surely he would respond to urgency and reason. "Have you heard of Jack Bender, sir?"

Simmons's expression sharpened. "What do you know of Jack Bender?"

"He is there, in the pub. He is the mastermind of this plan." And then she remembered the letters. She still had one in her reticule. "Wait, I have a letter written by Bender himself." She pulled out the letter and handed it to Mr. Simmons. She had scraped every last piece of wax off all three letters, wishing that its absence would somehow wipe away her awful disloyalty.

As Simmons took in the contents of the letter, he stood up in alarm. "Let's get the men together."

Amanda let out a long breath of relief. "Oh, thank you! Do you know people who can help us?"

Paul answered, "My father is a Bow Street runner."

"Oh, I am so glad!" Amanda sank to the nearest chair. "Thank you, sir! And thank you, Paul." She watched as the two men scratched a list. Then they called to a young boy and asked him to take messages to one after another of the men, and blessedly soon, men started showing up.

As soon as they had ten men gathered, they left *en masse* and hurried to the pub together. Amanda and Paul followed behind. Simmons advised her to return to her carriage, but she planned to watch from the park as soon as he was distracted.

As they walked, more men joined them, seemingly peeled from the very walls that lined the alley. When they arrived at the pub, a sizeable group of thirty or more entered together, ready to apprehend Bender and his men. Paul and Amanda moved to a bench on the edge of Grosvenor Square and waited. She had promised to stay away until Mr. Simmons indicated she would be safe.

With his men now in the pub, the street fell into silence. Amanda fidgeted with her hands, clasping and unclasping them. She stood up and began pacing in front of the bench. She started counting the cobblestones on the street, huffed out a breath, and sat again.

She and Paul jerked to their feet when they saw a man bolt out the front door and take off running down the street. She heard gunshots inside and women's screams. She grabbed for Paul's hand and squeezed with all her might. She feared for Charlie, feared for Simmons, feared that the Runners would not be successful. It was all she could do to resist tearing in after them.

And then everything amplified. From down the street came another group of what looked like local law enforcement, yeomen and a group of watchmen perhaps. Some were on horses; others were running toward the pub. Just as the new group arrived at the front of the pub entrance, seven of Bender's men charged out the door and onto the street. Immediately they collided with the group of yeomen, and in the resulting confusion and bucking horses, three of them got away and ran down back alleys.

Amanda wasn't sure, but she thought she recognized Bender's thick black hair among them. She strained to get a better look, when he turned around and caught her gaze. His steely eyes bore into hers. From all the way across the street, she felt Jack Bender's hatred. The strength of his loathing caused a shiver to start in her chest and work its way through her body. He stopped and changed directions, making his way toward her.

"Paul! That man! He's coming. It's . . . it's . . . Bender." Paul stood up in front of Amanda, blocking her view of him. She looked frantically over at the yeomen and the others who had just arrived. Many had already entered the pub. The others were involved in combat with the men still outside in the front. No one had any attention to spare them, and no one saw Bender as he walked slowly, and in plain sight, across the street. Amanda trembled. "What should we do?"

She spent one more second looking desperately up and down the street for help, and then she ran. She ran toward the nearest yeoman, knowing Bender would intercept her. She ran anyway and shouted, "Help! Oh, help me, please!"

Before she could take ten steps, she was jerked to a stop with an awful pressure and sharp pain all over her scalp as her bonnet was torn off her. Her whole head rattled as Bender shook her and pulled her closer to him. His hand tightened its grip on a patch of Amanda's hair.

Paul reached her at that moment. "Unhand her at once!" he shouted and punched Bender in the face, trying to push him backward, away from Amanda. But Bender held tight to her hair, and Amanda screamed in pain as she was sure he was going to yank it all out in one mass. She had never felt such stinging agony.

"Ow! Oh, stop! Please!" She screamed again as he jerked her closer to him, slammed Paul across the head with the butt of his gun, and dragged her off, away from the pub, away from Paul, who was now sprawled unconscious on the ground. She looked around again for anyone who would notice and help. The gunshots had cleared the square of anyone not already fighting.

And then she saw him. Nathaniel was here. Fighting with one of Bender's men, not thirty yards in front of her. "Nathaniel!" She screamed as long and as loud as she could. "Nathaniel! Help! Nathaniel!" He swung his fist at his attacker, throwing the man off balance.

"Amanda?" He seemed frozen, stunned.

Amanda shouted, "Watch out!"

Nathaniel blinked and then ducked as his attacker swung, nearly missing his head.

Bender gritted his teeth and snarled, "Be quiet, you. Or you won't live long enough to think of what you'll say next."

She shouted again in agony as a thousand pinpoints of pain fired all over her head.

"I said, be quiet!" He pulled her again, throwing her off balance.

She stumbled to the ground, knees digging into the cobblestone.

"Get up!" Bender shouted, and he swung his arm back, ready to strike her across the side of the head.

"I'm up! I'm up!" She scrambled to her feet as quickly as she could, wincing as she put weight on her feet, her knees throbbing. Bender swung his arm back, high above his head, and Amanda cowered with her hands covering her head and face. She winced, preparing for Bender's strike.

"Let her go." Nathaniel's voice sounded guttural and straining. He gripped Bender's raised arm in his hand. With one swift force, Nathaniel yanked the man down to his knees. In his fury, he shoved him again, Bender's body slamming onto the ground, his head knocking into the cobblestone. He lay still, unmoving. Amanda turned her head away from the pool of blood forming on the stone underneath his head. The street in front of the pub had emptied. All fighting seemed to have stopped. She collapsed to the ground as great waves of relief flooded through her.

Nathaniel rushed to her, cradling her head in his hands, crouching beside her on the ground. "Amanda! My Amanda. Are you all right? Where are you hurt?" His touch was gentle as he held her head where Bender had, just moments before, commanded handfuls of her hair. Then he placed both hands on each side of her face and kissed her—desperately, longingly kissed her. She laughed; she couldn't help it. They were sitting on the cobblestone, Jack Bender unconscious at her side, and Nathaniel was kissing her. He pulled away indignantly. "You're laughing?" The expression on his face made her laugh even harder.

"I'm sorry!" She hiccupped, which started her laughing all over again. "But look around us. I just don't know what else to feel."

Understanding lit Nathaniel's eyes. "Let's get you somewhere more comfortable." He swept her up, off the cobblestone and into his arms. She snuggled against him as he cradled her. They passed Paul, who was just rousing from his blow to the head. He sat up, groaning, and Nathaniel set Amanda down to stand next to him.

Nathaniel paused. "Oh, good. Man—"

Amanda said, "Paul."

"What?" Nathaniel helped him to his feet.

"He's my father's footman. His name is Paul."

Nathaniel said, "Paul. Will you sit with her on this bench and make sure that nothing happens to her?"

Amanda sat on the bench as Paul smiled wryly and said, "Impossible task." When he saw the expression on Nathaniel's face, he added an apologetic, "Yes, sir, my lord."

Nathaniel grunted in satisfaction

He kneeled before Amanda and squeezed her hands. "I'm going into the pub. I must see how they are getting along. Will you be comfortable here until I return?"

She nodded. "Will you find Charlie?"

Uncertainty, insecurity perhaps, passed through Nathaniel's eyes but he said, "You can be sure I will."

Amanda looked toward the pub. The ground where Bender had lain, empty. Fear iced through her. "Bender! He's run away!"

Nathaniel searched the square frantically in the direction she pointed. Seeing no one, he ran to the pub door, shouting inside, "You there! I need some men to go in pursuit." A group of five responded and ran in the direction Nathaniel pointed.

Amanda jumped up off the bench. Immediately pain shot up her legs, causing her to stumble and reach for Paul. Struggling to move, she leaned on his arm and hobbled after Nathaniel toward the pub. When she was at his side, she said, "I am not staying outside with Paul while Bender is loose and running about. We will just come inside with you, thank you very much." Relief filled her when Nathaniel watched the spot where Bender had been for a moment and then nodded and took her hand in his own.

"I shall retrieve the carriage, my lady," Paul said.

Amanda nodded. "Thank you, Paul." The footman then bowed and headed in the opposite direction.

Together, Amanda and Nathaniel entered the pub. The first thing she saw was Charlie. He sat by the window while one of the barmaids tied a bandage around his upper arm. He looked at Amanda with relief and winked. Happiness filled her. Nathaniel watched her with a peculiar intensity.

"Charlie is well," she explained.

Nathaniel nodded. "I'm glad to see it."

Why is he behaving in such a strange manner? She asked, "Did they arrest everyone? Well, everyone except Bender?" The thought of Bender free and hating her filled her with more fear than she wanted to admit.

Nathaniel answered, "I don't know what happened. I had just arrived when you saw me, with the group of yeomen. Good men, those employed by Lord Annesley."

He squeezed her hand. "Lady Amanda. You probably should not see into the back room. Why don't you go sit by Charlie while I ask some questions?"

Amanda wanted nothing more than to stay by Nathaniel's side forever, but she nodded. He was right. And she knew she could learn most of the details from Charlie anyway.

She approached Charlie hesitantly. But when he noticed her coming, he smiled a large, comfortable smile and reassurance calmed her.

"How are you?" Amanda stood in front of him. His clothes looked tattered and ripped in places, but he was otherwise unscathed.

He answered, "I am just fine, Amanda. And I see you are well, stayed outside—you obeyed for once." Charlie winked at her, smiling larger.

Amanda couldn't bring herself to tell him what had happened, not when he seemed so pleased. She asked, "So, were we successful? Did we stop Bender and his gang?"

"Yes. We were successful. There will be no July 23 disaster. We informed the cabinet, and they are taking security measures to prevent future attacks. Bender's gang is all but dismantled. All the major players were at the meeting, and they have been carted off to jail. They may receive a trial, or not, depending on how angry Lord Liverpool is by morning."

Amanda nodded. "So maybe we are free from his terror for now. Bender can hardly get another team together quickly, and maybe they can catch him right away before he has an opportunity to contact anyone."

Charlie stood up in alarm. "What? I saw him walk out of this room, tied up, a man on each side!"

Amanda gently pulled him back down to his seat. "All I know is that he came tearing out of the pub alone and made his escape."

Charlie studied her for a moment. "What aren't you telling me?" His eyes searched her person. "Did he harm you? Are you well?"

Amanda smiled. "I am fine. But he is gone, yes, although, men went after him." She suddenly felt tired, weary of Bender's constant menace in her life. Her head ached and her knees stung. The enormity of her circumstances seemed more than she could bear any longer. "We can only hope they will find him quickly . . ." She had tried to keep her voice from catching, but when it started wavering, she just stopped talking and looked at the floor.

Charlie reached over and laid his hand on the side of her face. She looked into his kind eyes and tried to smile. Tears welled up, and Charlie stood and pulled her up into a one-armed embrace. His hug brought back all the feelings from her childhood. She could almost smell the fields of green and the roses from the garden. She felt again the carefree manner in which she had lived and, for a moment, she sunk into the feeling, allowing it to consume her.

She heard a cough behind her, and she pulled away. Lord Nathaniel, looking uncomfortable, stood in front of them. Charlie's eyes held an apology as he nodded to him. Amanda wondered at that, and at the returning nod from Nathaniel. But she did not wait to figure them out. She squeezed Charlie's hand and then rushed toward Nathaniel, her head on his chest, wrapping her arms around his middle. Nathaniel hesitated before enclosing her inside his arms, resting his chin on the top of her head.

She closed her eyes and felt whole. She felt strong, as if she could face the world and feel protected at the same time. Nathaniel rubbed his hands up and down her back and then gently took her shoulders and stepped back enough to look into her eyes. His expression mirrored her own feelings. Joy ignited in her and filled her heart. She took both of his hands in hers.

Nathaniel asked, "Where are you hurt, Amanda?"

She winced. "My knees. But I *think* all my hair is still on my head."

Charlie said, "What?"

Nathaniel rubbed his thumb along the side of her face. "My brave girl."

Her heart filled with wonder. Smiling through her tears, still clutching one of Lord Nathaniel's hands in her own, she turned to Charlie. Startled that his eyes held tears as well, she stepped toward him with concern. "Charlie, are you in pain?"

He waved her off. "I am well. Just happy is all. Now go. I am sure Lord Nathaniel is here to see you home."

Amanda still smiled, unconvinced. "Let us take you with us."

"No, I need to stay and see to things here. I must give a very detailed description of Bender."

Lord Nathaniel said, "Come directly home when you are finished. I've arranged for a watchman to escort you. Your life will be in grave danger until we can stop Bender. Both of your lives will be, I would imagine."

Charlie's face clouded with concern as he looked at Amanda and then he nodded.

"Until tonight then." Lord Nathaniel led Amanda out into the street, where her carriage and Paul were waiting.

CHAPTER TWENTY-THREE

AMANDA'S FATHER HAD BEEN NOTHING short of furious when they had arrived at her home and explained the days' events. On the way home, in the carriage, she had begged Nathaniel not to tell her parents of her involvement, pleading and saying that her life would never be her own again. Nothing had moved him. Nathaniel had stubbornly insisted, and now Amanda had a permanent footman at her side. They had a Bow Street runner assigned to watch their home, and she was not to go anywhere without an additional footman.

"Why must I have two footmen, Father?" she had asked. "I will be a spectacle everywhere I go! Think of the gossip this will arouse."

"You think a bit of chatter amongst the birds of the *ton* will sway me? Two footmen, or you don't leave this house."

And that had been the end of it. Even while she was sleeping, Thomas, footman number one, stood outside her door. And given the incident with the window last year, she also had men patrolling the gardens in shifts below her room. It did not make her feel any better that her mother was under the same lock-and-key treatment. Only their father seemed to be able to come and go as he pleased, unencumbered. She had been tempted many times over the last week to mention the unfairness of it all, but had wisely held her tongue.

She still had to find a way to get some additional drawings to Mr. Taylor for the first issue of *The Manchester Guardian*. And she hadn't seen Charlie yet to find out what had happened at the home office or to hear if there was any news of Bender's capture. If she did not hear something by the week's end, she was determined to march herself down to whatever magistrate knew what was going on and ask him herself.

The one bright spot to the past week was the nearly constant presence of Nathaniel. She smiled, looking at the flowers he had brought with him last time. Lilies. They were the first thing she smelled in the morning before she opened her eyes and the last thing she noticed before she succumbed to sleep at night. Her stomach jumped a bit just at the thought of him.

The hour was growing later, and it was long past time for breakfast or tea. She opened her bedroom door and nodded at Thomas. He followed her down the stairs and took up his position again outside the door to their family dining room. She sighed. Perhaps the newspapers her father read every morning had printed something interesting for today. Two o'clock, the hour of her deliverance, couldn't come soon enough. She and Molly and her entire entourage would make their way to Mayfair, with the hopes of Molly encountering Jonathon Taylor to give him more drawings.

She was about to nod to the footman to open the dining room door when Nathaniel and her father entered the hallway, their faces lit with smiles. Amanda's hand went to her heart. How could one heart sustain so much love? She reached her hand out to each and kissed her father on the cheek. "Father. Lord Nathaniel."

Lord Nathaniel bowed over her hand and kissed it properly. His eyes spoke of adventure. She quirked her brow at him in question, but his smile just became wider, and he took her hand in his and placed it on the crook of his arm. They both turned to her father.

"It is good to see you this afternoon, Amanda. I feel it will be a wonderful day." The duke reached to rest his hand on her shoulder. "I must go prepare for my meetings with our steward this afternoon, if you two will excuse me." His face was full of sunlight.

As soon as he was out of earshot, she turned to Nathaniel and asked, "What is going on? You two look like cats with your mouse."

Nathaniel raised his eyebrows in question. "I don't know about your father, but I am happy whenever I see you. Can a man help it if he responds to your charm?" He raised his eyebrow, and his eyes held a hint of a teasing twinkle in them.

She laughed. "I'll let it go, but I can tell that something is afoot with you both." She gestured to the closed doors in front of her. "Would you like to join me for late luncheon or later tea? Whichever you would like to call it?"

Nathaniel shook his head. "Sadly, I too have appointments this afternoon that I must hurry off to meet, but did I hear you will be visiting Mayfair a little later?"

"Yes, Molly and I and a couple of footmen, the coachman, and possibly someone else just because the servants need more things to do."

Nathaniel laughed and patted her hand on his arm. "Amanda, my dear. Enjoy your shopping. Meet up with friends. Your father is trying to keep you safe. And grateful I am for it."

Amanda sighed. "I know. I just can't help looking at it more like oppression than protection. I don't even know what is going on with the investigation. Did Charlie talk to the Bow Street runners? Are the men still on the hunt? Where is Bender?"

Nathaniel laughed again. "Amanda. You needn't be troubled with these kinds of things. Your father and I will take care of everything." He stepped closer and looked into her eyes. She felt a thrill course up and down her center. Nathaniel leaned down and spoke softly in her ear, "You have worried enough for one lifetime. Let me protect you from all the rest of your cares." He kissed the area just below her ear and then pulled her to him, resting his chin on the top of her head.

Amanda melted into him. She loved this feeling. She loved this man. But safe in his embrace, a niggling thought that seemed far away at first disturbed her peace. The closer it came, the more it upset her until by the time Nathaniel pulled away and said goodbye, it was a fully recognizable worry and frustration. Would Nathaniel never take her seriously? Could he never confide in her? Or she in him?

She drew in a fortifying breath. Two o'clock was fast approaching. She would just have to bide her time. She nodded to the footman to open the double doors, and she entered the dining room. At the other end of the table, a newspaper hid her mother's face. Amanda stopped and swallowed. *The Manchester Guardian*, in bold black, was written across the top of the first page.

Amanda ached to know her mother's thoughts. She cleared her throat. "Good morning, Mother."

Her mother shifted the paper to see her and smiled in welcome. "Hello, my dear. I was hoping you would join me. This is awfully late for you, isn't it? Did you sleep well?" The duchess rose with concern to place a hand on Amanda's cheek and look into her eyes.

Her mother's love brought a lump to her throat. She swallowed. "I did sleep well, but there is nothing to do around here, so I put off breakfast and luncheon as long as possible so that my shopping venture will come all that sooner." Amanda shrugged in what she hoped was a carefree way.

Amanda's mother smiled indulgently and gestured toward the side table. "Do get something to eat and come join me. A new paper arrived this morning. I would love to hear your thoughts about a most interesting drawing."

As she sat with her food and began to sip the chocolate a footman had brought, she waited to hear her mother's thoughts. Sifting through the scattered pages on the table, on the second sheet, she read words that made her heart pick up in excitement. It was the speech! Henry Hunt's speech that she'd heard in the church square. Someone had printed the whole of it right there in the paper.

Her mother said, "What are you enjoying so? Your smile could blind us all. Do tell me, my dear."

Amanda looked up in surprise. "Was I smiling?" And then her mouth spread even wider. "Yes, I suppose I was." She ate another bite. "I was just reading the words of one Henry Hunt here on the second page." And suddenly she wanted very much for her mother to understand, to feel the same way she did about freedom, for her heart to be stirred. "He is quite a talent. We should invite him to one of our readings some time. He would be magnificent!"

Her mother looked at her quizzically. "You can tell all that by his speech?"

Amanda blushed. "Well, no, but his words are so stirring that I can just imagine him speaking them. Surely he would be magnificent."

"I too was quite moved by them actually."

"Were you, Mother?"

"Well, it seems right, doesn't it? That all people have the same rights."

Amanda nodded excitedly. "Exactly! Including a voice in the government. And the servants! It is very difficult for them to be educated without money. And many people here in England are without work. Some of them barely have enough food to eat!"

Her mother considered her for a moment. "You seem to have given this much thought, much more than a few moments' glance at a paper."

Amanda looked into her mother's eyes, praying she would understand. "I have, Mother. I, ah, stumbled upon these very same ideas months ago, and they have been seeping into my soul." She put her hands over her heart. "I don't always know what to do with this burning ember, but I have the biggest desire to be free." She reached for her mother's hands and squeezed them, hoping to send all her thoughts straight into her mother's heart. "And I want most desperately for everyone else to be free as well." She held her breath.

Her mother's eyes glistened and she said, "Amanda, my dear. These are noble thoughts. You have a good heart. It speaks well of you that you should care for others so. Remember, my dear, should you have a son, he will one day be the heir to your father's dukedom. Guard these desires. Keep them." She looked more intently into Amanda's eyes. "Don't let your passion dim with the passage of time. Pass these feelings on to your children, should you be so fortunate as to have many; they will be powerful people here in England."

Amanda shook her head. Generational change was not the kind of change she was working for. "No, Mother."

But her mother spoke before she could continue. "Be patient, my flower. Change takes time. But don't underestimate the power of one." She held Amanda's chin in her hand.

Everything in Amanda wanted to shout for immediate change. She wanted to tell her mother all about how that very paper she was reading had one of her own fliers on the front. She was making change right now. It was happening. But she held her tongue. Amanda had said enough for now.

She also had the nagging feeling that her mother was right. But Amanda didn't want to think about whether or not change would come quickly or slowly. She just wanted to be a part of it. Her heart leapt with excitement as her mother turned back to the front of the paper and said, "This drawing is what drew me to the paper to begin with . . . something so familiar about it."

Amanda placed a bit of bread in her mouth. "Oh?"

Her mother glanced at her. "I really looked closer, I was intrigued by it." She ran her fingers over the figures in the drawing. Amanda felt pleased that Mr. Taylor had decided to use her *Seeking Liberty* drawing first.

He mother said, "I love the women the most. All different kinds of women. It is as if dear Martha and your Molly and your old governess, Miss Tildy, and I and others—all women—are walking together."

"I can see you, as a young girl, right here." She pointed. "This whole drawing is so like you." Then she snapped her head up, finding Amanda's eyes, her own much wider. "Amanda." Her mother paused, searching Amanda's face and then smiled a wide, proud smile and gave her a knowing look.

Amanda just stared back at her, unsure just what her mother was thinking.

"Well," she continued. "Whoever the artist is, she is *brilliant*, darling. The emotion, the depth, the expressions on these women's faces. She carries me right into the drawing. I wish I were right there"—she tapped the paper emphatically—"marching along with them." A single tear spilled down her mother's face.

Amanda leaned into her, throwing her arms around her mother. "I wish that too, Mother."

As they silently embraced from their chairs, Amanda's mother wrapped her arms around her and rested her cheek on her head. She gave her an extra squeeze. "I love you, Amanda."

Parsons entered a moment later, clearing his throat. With a smile, he said, "Excuse me, Your Grace, my lady, but the carriage is ready for Lady Amanda."

Amanda kissed her mother's cheek and stepped away. "Off I go, Mother. Would you like me to get you anything while I am out?"

Her mother wiped her eyes with her handkerchief and smiled. "No, my dear. I am quite pleased with all that I have." She and Amanda shared another look. Amanda felt her heart almost burst with the joy she felt in her mother's approval. She tried to share the joy with her returning smile and then turned to take her cloak and bonnet from Parsons.

Molly was waiting in the hallway with the latest drawings wrapped in brown paper. Amanda nodded at her, and they turned to exit through the opened door, where two footmen waited and would escort them down every street and to the front door of every shop.

They visited the usual stops first. It must appear that Amanda was only out to pick up several yards of new ribbon and another bonnet and also to pay a visit to the modiste to pick the fabric for a new gown. But they both longed to be sitting at Mirabel's Tearoom table in the back corner, discussing *The Manchester Guardian* with the tearoom's owner. She hoped that Miss Tanner would be able to join them. She had not seen her dear friend in a couple of weeks, at least. They turned the corner, and she nearly walked right into Charlie. "Oh!"

His mouth immediately turned up into a grin, which lit his eyes. "Lady Amanda. Miss Molly! What a diverting surprise! Already my day is much more wonderful than before. And Miss Molly, how is my very favorite and loveliest adventurist doing this fine afternoon?" He bowed over their hands.

They curtsied in return, Molly giggling. "Adventurist? How so, good sir?"

Charlie stood up and winked at them both. "I believe our adventure involved an outing in deliveries for one young artist, did it not?" And he stared at them expectantly, eyebrows up in question.

Amanda arched her own eyebrow, eyes twinkling. "I am sure we don't know what you are talking about." The ladies moved to walk on either side of Charlie.

Amanda said in a hushed voice, "I have been so anxious to hear. What is going on with the search? Has Bender been found yet?"

Charlie turned to her in surprise. "Hasn't Lord Nathaniel told you? He stops by every blasted morning, doesn't he?"

"Told me what, Charlie? What is it he hasn't told me?" She grabbed hold of his lapels in her fists and tried to shake him, but she did little besides wrinkle his clothes. When had he become such an immovable force?

He gently placed her hands in his and said, "Bender has been captured!"

Amanda reached for Molly, embracing her tightly, and she let the relief wash over her in waves.

Then she turned back to Charlie and included Molly in her question. "Then why am I still being followed about by footmen?" She waved her hands in exasperation.

Charlie looked at her with sympathy but answered in his sternest voice. "Because, Amanda. Bender had an extensive reach. Two of his underlings were traveling in Wales last week and are still about someplace, and in all honesty, London is not a safe place even without Jack Bender lurking about."

Amanda stared at him in exasperation. "You mean, capturing Bender was not the end? You think his gang will continue?" Amanda could not believe it. She had naively thought that her life would return to normal as soon as Bender was out of it.

Charlie interrupted her thoughts. "It will take them many months to regroup and to gather their numbers. Someone would need to rise as leader. They may never recover what they once had."

Charlie tweaked Amanda's nose. "You did well, my lady. You almost devastated the whole mass of them."

Amanda felt a bit mollified. And then she gritted her teeth. "I don't suppose I will ever rid myself of these extra men."

Molly laughed and shared a look with Charlie. "No, my lady. I don't suppose you will ever lose the men who follow you everywhere." Molly's grin nearly split her face.

Amanda squinted her eyes as comprehension dawned. At that moment, Baron Michael Kenworthy appeared in front of her and bowed. Charlie and Molly laughed even louder, and Amanda surprised herself as she felt her cheeks go red. How unfair of them to tease her so. She only sought attention as it served to further her disguise, and they both knew it.

She dipped a quick curtsy and said, "Oh hello, Lord Kenworthy, how are you this fine afternoon?" She looked at Charlie and Molly for help, but they had stepped back a few paces from her, as befitted their station. She huffed in frustration. Now was not the time to entertain another round of flirtations with the man, as jolly as he was. Charlie and Molly, still finding great humor in the situation, stared at her with raised eyebrows. Suddenly she was filled with an old childish desire to stomp her foot. And just at the peak of her annoyance, while trying to maintain an interested expression on her face, her eye caught another figure coming toward her, and her eyes narrowed.

Nathaniel strolled with class, his abundant charm rolling off him. He cut such a fine figure. Her frustration heightened because she noticed. How could she avoid noticing? His shoulders seemed broader every time she looked at him. His hair was tickling his forehead as the breeze blew across his face. The sharp lines of his jaw and down his neck and his whole person emanated such a strong feeling of masculinity and power that her knees went weak for a moment.

Lord Kenworthy reached a hand over to steady her. He searched for the cause of her distraction and grinned wryly. "Ah, the man who leaves us all with little hope. Shall I leave straightaway or amuse myself just a bit at his expense?"

"Oh, don't restrain your humor on my account. He could use a little torment, I am sure." Her eyes narrowed farther as she tried to shoot daggers at Nathaniel. His face was all smiles and his body relaxed.

No more hand patting—and if she heard one more placating word from him, she just might throw her tea in his face. She laughed at the thought.

The baron turned to her in surprise. "Am I that amusing, my lady? I'm pleased to hear it. I shall attempt to do something else of great hilarity so that I might once again hear that lovely melody from your lips."

Nathaniel arrived at that moment and made a face of dread. "Melody? Has Lady Amanda been singing? I do hope you are mistaken."

Amanda bit back a laugh while the baron looked much like a stuffed bird—puffed out, feathers ruffled. He said, "Any lovely note to come from our dear Lady Amanda is to be as the sound of heaven, Lord Nathaniel, and I long to hear it." He turned back to Amanda. "Another poem, my dear? Do you have it in you? Is your muse speaking?"

Amanda bit the side of her cheek. When she felt her laughter sufficiently suppressed, she answered, "Oh, my baron. I am terribly sorry." And she waved a fan in her face, looking despondently out across the park to their left. "I feel completely without my muse, much like a bird in a cage, really."

She turned her eyes to Nathaniel, scowling at him with as much menace as she could muster in polite society.

He choked on what sounded suspiciously like laughter as he made strange noises into his hand.

The baron surprised them all. "Did you hear? Oh! This is news indeed! Come, Lord Nathaniel, I'm talking to you as well. Step closer. Did you hear? They have captured Jack Bender!"

Amanda and Nathaniel shared a quick look and then stared at him, mouths open. The baron continued.

"What? You have heard of Jack Bender, have you not? That awful rogue terrorizing all the nobility? Broke into your uncle's home? Hmm?"

Amanda nodded. "Yes, of course I have heard of him. I am amazed at the news of his capture and at your knowing of it."

Lord Nathaniel said, "Yes, Lord Kenworthy, how did you come across this information?"

The baron's voice sounded almost smug. "I have it from a good source— could never reveal who, mind you—but my source says he is locked up for good." The baron had an almost reckless air about him. "We are free from the oppression of Jack Bender forever!" He waved his arms about with a dramatic flair.

Amanda took a step back to avoid contact with her face.

The baron stopped. "And the best part is . . ." He leaned closer to them, his voice lowering in a conspiratorial whisper, and Amanda smelled whiskey on it. "We have a hero to thank for it!"

Amanda's curiosity piqued. "What do you mean?"

The baron said, "Sources say, and I cannot reveal—"

"Yes, yes, we know you cannot reveal your source. Out with it, man!" Nathaniel's face had become a bit red, perhaps from irritation or impatience.

Amanda had little time to ponder his moods, however. "Who is the hero? I am all a flutter with anticipation!"

The baron smiled at her in appreciation. "They call him Red." .

Nathaniel became very still at her side. She glanced at him. His expression blank, she turned back to Lord Kenworthy.

Filled with curiosity, she asked, "Red? That's it? Just Red?"

Nathaniel rolled his eyes and glanced in annoyance at Charlie.

Peculiar, she thought.

The baron shrugged. "That's all I know. And the story goes that this Red person came riding in with a mask over his face and a red cap of liberty on his head. He carried a pistol and fired it into the air. The pub downtown cleared in an instant, all coming out to see the masked man with the gun. He rode straight into the middle of the crowd, right alongside Jack Bender and knocked him to the ground with the butt of his pistol."

Amanda gasped. "Did he deliver him to prison across the back of his horse?"

The baron said, "He did indeed—carried him off to the magistrate." Lord Kenworthy nodded decisively.

Amanda sighed. "I would love to know such a man."

The baron continued. "That's the version I like best."

Amanda blinked. "What do you mean, the version you like best? Isn't it true?"

Lord Kenworthy said, "Well of course it is true, my lady. He either burst into the crowd on his horse, or he rescued a couple of children from the evil man himself and tossed him in the clinker."

Nathaniel snorted into his fist. Charlie pounded his back as if helping him clear a cough.

Amanda stared for a moment at the baron. "Well, which is it? *Is* there such a person as this Red? Or is all of this just some yarn you have spun to amuse yourself?" Amanda couldn't explain why she felt such a surge of annoyance, but she folded her arms across her chest and stared at the baron until he responded with hands in the air, palms toward her.

"It's true, Lady Amanda! All of it! A man they call Red saved us all from Jack Bender."

She said, "And grateful I am there is such a man."

Lord Nathaniel grunted. "We all said he would be caught, did we not?"

Amanda whirled to face him. "No, you did not. You have not said or explained anything to me in days! I only learned in this instant from Charlie that he was caught!"

Charlie turned sheepish eyes to Lord Nathaniel and shrugged.

The baron took a flask out of his pocket and drank a long draught, wiped his mouth, and hid the flask again in his coat. Noticing Amanda watching him, the baron started. "Oh, beg your pardon. Would you care for a refreshment? Could I fetch you a lemonade or an ice?"

Amanda nodded. "Yes, thank you! Either would be lovely."

Lord Kenworthy looked surprised at her immediate acceptance, but he did not say anything. He bowed and left in search of her refreshment.

Amanda whirled on Nathaniel. "How could you? How could you not say anything at all to me?"

Nathaniel's eyes widened and he opened his mouth.

She continued. "You knew! This morning you knew. You were there in my house and yet you said nothing! I assume my father knows?" Nathaniel nodded. "My mother?" He nodded again. "Does everyone in the whole house know but me?"

Nathaniel thought for a moment. "Molly didn't know either, until now." He called over to her, standing four feet away with Charlie. "I assume, Miss Molly, that you heard the lot of it. Jack Bender captured, finally in jail where he belongs."

Molly nodded and curtsied. "I did, my lord, thank you, and much relieved I am to hear it."

Amanda tried to keep her fury in check. "And why is it that everyone knows but us?"

Nathaniel stepped closer and took her hand in his. He gently patted the top of her hand.

Something about the gesture infuriated Amanda all the more.

He said, "There, my dear. You do not need to be so concerned about all of this. I was hoping you could take a step back, focus on other things—"

"Take a step back?" She yanked her hand free of his grasp. "I cannot take a step back as you call it! It . . . *concerns* . . . me! If you will recall, it was I who sent in the Bow Street runners, I who gathered the magistrate and his men." Amanda threw her hands about her. She stepped closer to Nathaniel, hissing right in his face, inches away. "This is my battle as much or more than it is yours. You don't even *care* about any of this. You and your rakish pretend act, all your parties and your swooning ladies. Why do you pretend this matters to you all of a sudden? This is my life. This is what I have dedicated my last breath to: liberty. And I stand with all efforts to support it. And against anyone and anything that tries to take it away."

Nathaniel's eyes shone with what looked like pride. But he said, "What could you possibly have done in the capture of Jack Bender? Go out with your gun in the air, shouting for him around every corner? Please, Amanda, leave these kinds of worries, these dangers and risks, to those who take care of them best."

"But can't you understand that I would want to know?"

He moved again to caress her hand, but she pulled it away and crossed her arms. He tried again, his voice low and pleading. "I was hoping we could get past all of this excitement and start planning other simpler, happier things, like courtships and . . . well, marriage. I would think there would be much on your mind. I am sure a few visits to the modiste and . . ."

His voice faltered, and he wisely abstained from completing the rest of his sentence.

Amanda had never felt so misunderstood or hurt in her life. He had proven quite soundly that he had no idea of the inner workings of her mind or heart. She didn't know how she could ever entrust either into his keeping, let alone her dowry and freedom or her children.

Nathaniel amended, "Maybe you could create more of your drawings. They seem to set you at ease, calm your worries, give you some helpful manner in which to express your thoughts."

Amanda's eyes turned to steel and she said, "That is exactly what I will do. Thank you, Lord Nathaniel." Burning fury rose inside. And she turned to walk past Molly, who followed behind her, eyes on the pavement.

Amanda would work on her drawings. And gone was the time to be careful and humorous. It was time to be bold and powerful. It was time to unsettle some people, to offend and prod. She wanted heads spinning and tongues wagging.

She needed to get home and start drawing. If all went well, she would have her first fliers out tomorrow morning.

She climbed into her carriage and almost yelped in surprise to see Charlie sitting on a bench. "What are you doing here, Charlie?"

"You misunderstand Lord Nathaniel. He has the best intentions, and he cares more for liberty than you can possibly guess."

"Intentions mean very little to me. He obviously knows nothing about me at all."

Charlie shrugged. "Or he knows you too well. But that's not why I'm here. I've come to talk to the Sparrow. I have a commission for you." Amanda opened her mouth and stopped. She didn't know what to say.

Molly asked, "A paid commission? As in, someone wants Lady Amanda to draw for them?"

Charlie nodded. "Exactly."

Amanda closed her mouth and swallowed. "What exactly does this person need? I have specific goals for my fliers, you know."

"Liberty Seekers needs some publicity."

A big grin spread across her face. "How soon do you need it?"

Charlie grinned in response and handed her a sheet of paper. "Here is an example of the information we need on the fliers. Liberty Seekers wants to have a peaceful rally. A well-known orator—"

"Henry Hunt?"

Charlie raised his eyebrows. "The very same. He will be there, and we are gathering to ask for universal sovereignty."

Amanda and Molly shared a look. Amanda said, "We will do our best." She read over the paper for a moment and said, "August 9. That's very soon."

"Yes, it is. Everything is in place. We just need to invite the masses."

As the carriage neared Nathaniel's home, where they had agreed to drop Charlie, he said, "Amanda, you need to try and understand Lord Nathaniel. He is a far better man than you know."

Amanda grunted. "When did you become such an unfailingly loyal employee, I wonder?"

Charlie looked upward and closed his eyes. "Just *try*, Amanda. Try to think the best of him. He just might have reasons for the things that he does."

Amanda scowled and folded her arms across her chest. "I would love him to be the best of men, but I am disappointed at every turn. Besides, he thinks of me as a child." Tears threatened to fall, and she blinked them back furiously.

Charlie's eyes held sympathy. "Believe me, he is fully aware you are not a child." He reached for her hand. "Thank you for helping with the Liberty Seekers, my lady. I cannot stress how important your drawings are. Educating the people is everything. This newspaper is everything."

Amanda reached out to stop his movement to exit the carriage. "Charlie, I must know. *Is* there such a person as Red? Did he really capture Bender?"

Charlie looked thoughtfully into her eyes. "He is as real as you and I. A true man and a hero. He is more of a gentleman than any I have ever met." He squeezed her hands then turned to step down from the carriage.

She said half to herself as she watched the back of him turn a corner, "*Is* he a gentleman then?"

CHAPTER TWENTY-FOUR

Water seeped through Jack Bender's boots to his toes. His body shivered in his cell, but he did not feel the cold. His soul burned with fire. Hatred and desire like bile in his mouth, he droned:

> *"Her beauty shines in the sun.*
> *Her wit is sharp as any.*
> *She climbs higher and waits at the top, straining,*
> *Yearning for the earth and the neck that is waiting.*
> *She is released, falling, slicing.*
> *And the earth is cleansed*
> *Of one more, filthy noble."*

"Shut up, I tell ya! Guard! Guard!" The noises of guards came pounding down the dark hallway. Metal slid aside on Bender's cell door.

"What's the problem in here, eh? Be quiet!"

Bender's cellmate answered, "It's 'im, I tell ya. 'E's right evil, 'e is, goin' on 'bout choppin' off 'eads and the like. I won' listen to it no more I won'."

The guards laughed. One of them taunted, "Feelin' a bit squeamish, are we? Considerin' all you've done, I'd think a little talk of Madame la Guillotine would be refreshing!"

The other prisoner humphed. "Well, it's not. Make 'im stop, I tell ya, or I might do the honors meself."

"Don't you be doing nothing yourself. He's goin' to be hanged in a couple o' weeks anyway. You'll just have to sit quiet 'til then—we won't be hearing any more fuss from you." The guards turned away, and their footsteps pounded down the hall.

Bender spoke then. "Hanged in two weeks." He broke into a screeching, maniacal laugh. "Two weeks. Two weeks." Bender stood and raised both fists to the ceiling. "The nobles must be purged. We must wipe out every last stench of them until only the enlightened remain." He kept his hands raised to the ceiling, and he closed his eyes, facing what would have been heavenward had he been praying. The man who shared his cell shrunk into the corner and pulled his knees to his chest.

⌒

Nathaniel smiled, watching his valet prepare three cravats, remembering the valet in Lady Amanda's flier. How many times had Phillips retied Nathaniel's own cravat? He turned to Phillips and said, "Thank you, man. For all these years of making me irresistible to the ladies, appropriately responsible to the dukes and earls, and lovable to the matrons. It takes a special talent, and I owe it all to you."

Phillips paused in the tying of his cravat. He almost smiled and said, "Very good, my lord."

"Oh, come now, Phillips. An ounce of emotion. I'm sure you have some in there."

Phillips merely nodded in response. But he knew Phillips was pleased, because his cravat felt comfortable. He could remember many a tight cravat in his younger, less appreciative days. Phillips had been around to see it all: Nathaniel's reckless youth, his arrogance, and his entitlement. He sighed. "Thank you for putting up with me all these years. I believe I have improved with age, no?"

His trusted valet of ten years paused and looked him in the eye, something Nathaniel had rarely ever seen. Phillips said, "You have become the best of men, my lord." And his eyes stared into Nathaniel's in such a way that he felt his own mist over.

He cleared his throat and gripped Phillips on the shoulder. They shared a moment in silence, and then Philips reached for Nathaniel's tailcoat and helped him into it. Grunting his approval, he brushed it down and smoothed the lines. Nathaniel was ready.

Mrs. Whitehouse, the housekeeper, met him in the hall. She curtsied. "My lord. The duke has arrived and is waiting for you in his study."

His father? He rarely ventured outside their country estate, preferring the milder weather, fresh air, and quieter life that the country provided.

"Well, what a surprise. I will go to him directly. Perhaps we could have breakfast in there?"

Mrs. Whitehouse nodded. "It is already done, my lord." She smiled with pride.

"Thank you." He nodded at her and hurried his steps.

Before his father noticed him, Nathaniel took a moment to scrutinize the duke. No matter how much either of them aged, he still felt like a schoolboy in his father's presence. He would strive forever to please this man, whom he viewed as one of the greats in the world. The duke looked a bit more fatigued than he had two months ago when Nathaniel had last seen him, but his coloring was healthy, vibrant even. *Curious. Why the sudden visit?*

Nathaniel cleared his throat. His father stood and Nathaniel embraced him, patting his back. "Father. So wonderful to see you!"

"And you, my son. You look to be in excellent health."

"And so do you! That country air does wonders."

The duke returned to his seat. "Everything is going well and as it should be, I presume? I haven't heard otherwise."

Nathaniel filled his plate. "Yes, my latest report contains any concerns about the estate, and how they are swiftly dealt with. I have nothing in addition to what you already know."

The duke nodded. "And what of you, my boy? How are you faring?"

"I am excellent, Father. I am pleased with the estate and how things are going—"

"Not the estate, son. I know the estate is just fine. I want to hear about you. Are you happy? Fulfilled?"

Nathaniel looked at his father curiously for a moment. "You want to know if I am happy?"

The duke burst out laughing. "Is that so difficult to believe? You are my son. Yes, I want to know if you are happy."

Nathaniel thought for a moment, chuckling. "Well, yes, I am. Very happy, if you must know. And how are you? Are you happy?"

His father laughed anew. "We aren't discussing me, but yes. I miss your mother of course, but I am happy. Although I admit to a bit of restlessness which accounts for a good portion of the reason I made the journey to London."

Nathaniel raised his eyebrow. "What is the other portion?"

His father leaned back in his chair and gestured for Nathaniel to begin his meal.

The duke continued. "As I intimated in some of my letters, I have heard through several sources, the Duke of Cumberland included, a number of things which are of great interest to me—none of which, I might add, you have informed me of in our usual correspondence."

Nathaniel paused his chewing of Cook's biscuit.

"Tell me about the fair Lady Amanda."

Nathaniel swallowed the biscuit too soon and felt it slowly and painfully inch down the back of his throat. Swallowing again and drinking some tea, he said, "You already know Lady Amanda. We have been friends with her family for years. I have been spending time getting to know her better this Season."

"And?"

"And what? That is it."

"Are you courting the girl? I do enjoy her, and she comes from the best of families. I could not be more pleased if you two married, but you have said nothing about a courtship . . . which gives me pause."

Nathaniel smiled. "I must admit I am working toward that end. But it is proving a bit . . . difficult."

The duke burst into laughter again.

Nathaniel couldn't remember the last time he had been such a source of amusement to his father.

"Women are difficult, son. They don't view themselves as difficult, mind you. She'll come around. Her father is sure of it."

Nathaniel closed his eyes for a moment. He did not have any desire to discuss the intricacies of his and Amanda's relationship—there were too many facets that he could not disclose, all of them involving life-threatening situations. But he did explain some of his uncertainty. "I am finding it difficult to treat her as she wishes. I hope to protect her, and she views it as coddling, patronizing."

The duke nodded in understanding. "Your mother was much the same way. I think all women are the same, to one extent or another. They love the feeling of protection a man provides. They want someone strong and capable to lean on when necessary. But they have a fire of independence inside, make no mistake. Some have a larger flame than others. But it burns inside every female heart—I daresay every human heart. And they guard that flame oh so carefully. Feed it, and you will win her forever."

Nathaniel considered his father's words. How could he possibly allow Amanda the independence she desired? Her idea of independence stirred and festered in a category all by itself. Different from any other woman's, he felt sure. An impetuous, headstrong girl who could quite easily find an early grave if not for his interference.

But he shared none of these concerns with his father and merely nodded and agreed to consider how to best guard her flame of independence, which Nathaniel was certain was no small candle. It was much more like the time he had seen a neighbor's house burn to the ground in a towering, blistering rage.

They finished their breakfast in companionable silence. As they were sipping the last of the tea, the duke said, "What is your engagement for the evening?

I find I am seeking a bit of the Season's entertainment, and I will attend with you."

Nathaniel tried to keep the shock from his face. "Wonderful. You will reenergize a whole group of matrons who usually hold up the east wall." Nathaniel chuckled at the thought.

His father grunted. "That is something I could very well avoid."

"Oh, come now, Father. Receiving admiring looks from a room full of women isn't all that bad." Nathaniel raised an eyebrow and quirked his lip.

The duke said, "As you well know. You have turned many a lady's head, my dear boy, and it's not just your title they are after."

Later that evening, as the two of them were sitting in the ducal carriage, approaching the Buckley ball, Nathaniel's father said, "I certainly hope you have outgrown your open manner with the ladies at these events." The duke raised his eyebrow, waiting for a response.

Nathaniel cleared his throat. "Perhaps I should explain before we enter. It is not really my doing but . . ." The footman opened the door to their carriage and as Nathaniel stepped out, a group of ladies rushed to greet him, giggling and curtsying, completely blocking his ability to move forward. His father peered around Nathaniel's back as he was attempting to exit the coach in the very little space provided.

Nathaniel's father managed to place his cane upon the ground before saying, "Ladies. What is the meaning of this? I have never seen such lack of decorum. Return to your chaperones at once."

The girls froze, stared at him with open mouths, and, after a moment, remembered to curtsy before scurrying out of sight as quickly as they had come. The duke turned to Nathaniel, ready for an explanation.

Nathaniel merely shrugged and raised his hands. "I am as puzzled and bothered by it as you. I must thank you, Father. I now recognize I have been too obliging. Your direct methods are much more effective." Nathaniel looked toward the front door. "They may be too afraid to speak to me again, but that might not be so bad."

His father humphed. "A blessing, to be sure. Who would want a little slip of nonsensical frippery by his side throughout the evening? You need substance, boy, to go along with the beauty! You would coddle a girl like them to the last of her days, and what could she give you in return?"

Nathaniel considered his father's words, comparing Lady Amanda to these women. He already knew she was a pinnacle higher in his estimation than any of them. So why did he feel so compelled to coddle *her*? He shook his head. She deserved better.

The duke, perceptive as always, asked, "Thinking of your lady, are you? Is she as beguiling and as frustrating as your face indicates?"

Nathaniel snorted. "You can't possibly understand the half of it."

The duke smiled. "Perhaps not. But it will be an entertaining evening. I can see that already." Gesturing to the front door and the line of carriages behind them, he said, "Shall we enter? Face the foxes?"

Nathaniel pressed his lips into a grim line. "Yes, I'm afraid we must. After you, Your Grace." Nathaniel bowed to his father.

The duke chuckled and said under his breath, "Coward."

When they entered, a noticeable pause in conversation spread throughout each group of people as eyes found the duke and his son standing at the head of the ballroom. Nathaniel hid a laugh behind his hand. A wave of fluttering chickens erupted as word of the duke's presence passed down the east wall of matrons. Nathaniel noticed his father stiffen, frozen to his spot, and he nudged him. "Coming, Your Grace? Not afraid, to be sure?"

The duke stood taller, squinted his eyes at his son, and said, "Come, Nathaniel. We had best be about this."

Nathaniel laughed and walked deeper into the room at his father's side.

And then his eyes met Lady Amanda's. And a tug from across the room drew him to her. He smiled as she stepped toward him also, never breaking their gaze. Urgency, filled with a new and powerful yearning to be by her side, blurred everyone else in the room.

Then the swirling forms of the dancers blocked his view. She jerked back, obviously startled when they nearly bumped into her. The room came back into focus. Between them, two lines of dancers in a fast reel blocked their path. Lord Needley gently pulled Amanda close to him away from the moving couples. Then he presented another woman to her, small, with hair so blonde it looked white. Nathaniel could tell by the way Needley hovered about this new woman that she captured and enticed him. Lady Amanda's back was to him, but she turned again to catch his eye once more, a lovely flush spreading across her creamy skin before returning her focus to the introduction.

He moved as quickly as he could through the room around the dancers. But his father's presence proved to be the biggest news of the evening, and they were stopped every few steps. He kept his body turned so Lady Amanda was in his view. At length, they approached her from behind and he enjoyed a boyish excitement to present her to his father.

She curtsied her farewells and searched the room, standing up on her toes to see over the dancers. He suspected she sought him, and his pulse raced.

He chuckled while her head swung around to the front door and then moved slowly while she looked through the groups and up the line of dancers, now facing away from him.

Backing up slowly to see better over the tops of the taller people, her soft frame melted into his.

He laughed. "Looking for someone?"

He raised his eyebrow, teasing, when she turned to them, face flushed a deeper red, eyeing him and his father equally.

"Oh, Your Grace! I am so pleased to see you again!" She curtsied deeply and offered her hand to Lord Nathaniel's father.

He smiled warmly at her and kissed it before placing it on his own arm.

Nathaniel looked from his father to Amanda and back.

Turning her attention to him finally, she raised both eyebrows and said, "Lord Nathaniel."

He bowed over her other offered hand and kissed it.

"We are enchanted to see you this evening, Lady Amanda. I see you remember my father."

Amanda beamed. "Of course I remember the Duke of Somerset. He and I are past friends. You may not know this, Lord Nathaniel, but your father suggested that I be the first to ride Horatia."

Lord Nathaniel's eyebrows rose to his hairline. "I was not aware of your privilege, no." He looked again from one to the other of them.

The duke smiled and said, "I see you are wondering how we managed such a thing."

Lord Nathaniel smirked. "I was indeed, although I do not doubt Lady Amanda's ability to charm you into submission."

"Ho ho! Maneuver me to do your bidding, did you?" He grinned at Amanda again, and Nathaniel's heart warmed at their easy manner with each other.

She said, "I did nothing of the sort, Nathaniel."

He noticed the slip of his first name, and his heart jumped at the familiarity. His thoughts leapt to future cozy moments in his study. When she too recognized the slip, her eyes flitted to his. He winked, and she continued. "Yes, I was out in the barn the morning after Horatia arrived. It was early, before breakfast. I thought I would be alone yet for another hour at least. I believe we share an affinity for rising early."

The duke nodded. "Or an affinity for the barn, or both, I believe."

She nodded. "He saw me there, looking as if I would give anything to ride the new mare, and the next thing I knew, a stable hand was saddling her up."

Amanda reached her other hand over to pat the duke's arm. "It meant more to me than you probably realize."

The music for a new dance began. Nathaniel cleared his throat. "Might I have the pleasure?" He offered his hand to Lady Amanda. She looked stunning this evening. Glorious hair framing her face, curves everywhere they should be, her eyes like beacons to his ship. He could not look away. He was physically drawn to her, moored at her side.

"I would be delighted."

When he recognized a waltz, he thanked whatever stars may have helped his luck this night, and he wrapped one arm around her back, placing her hand in his out to their sides. He pulled her to him as closely as he dared and breathed in deeply her scent of lilac. He closed his eyes in appreciation and felt all the senses in his body wake up on overload. Even his shoulder was tingling from the pressure of her hand resting there. *Steady, man.*

Her wide eyes were filled with hope. Heaven help him, he would be whatever it was she hoped for. He was lost forever to a pair of stunning sapphire eyes.

As he swirled them around on the ballroom floor, he knew he could never be happy with another woman.

"What is it you hope for, Lady Amanda?" He breathed.

She laughed. "Where did that come from?" She smiled in thought, musing. "What do I hope for?" She looked back up into his eyes and whatever playful answer she had planned was lost. He could see the change as she grew serious. She whispered, "I hope to be able to fly. With you." She blinked in surprise, probably immediately regretting those last two words, but Nathaniel's heart sang at the sound. *With you.* He, Nathaniel, was a part of her hopes.

And joy filled him as he felt it too. He wanted to know all he could about her, to fill his mind with thoughts of her.

He said, "Tell me more about your fliers, Amanda."

Amanda blushed and appeared almost unsure of herself.

When he saw that insecurity, he mentally chastised himself, knowing he had put it there, his responses to her so unpredictable.

"What do you want to know?"

Nathaniel tilted his head to the side to try to catch her downturned eyes, encouraging her to look back up into his own. "I want to know more about why they are important to you."

She paused. "So much of what we do in the *ton* is full of . . . well, nothing. It has no substance or anything of value in it. When I am home, it's different. We spend time helping the tenants. We help run a school for the children and bring donations to the orphans. But here in London, hours of my day are filled with conversation and activities that amount to essentially nothing." Nathaniel could tell she wished to use her hands as she spoke. She was flushed, and there was fire in her eyes. Nathaniel liked this side of Lady Amanda most of all.

She said, "My fliers help me to fill my life with *something*." She eyed him for a moment, and he felt he was being put to some kind of test. Finally she said, "I wish things in England were different, and I want to be a part of that change."

Nathaniel nodded. "In what way?" He felt he knew exactly what she was about to say.

"Some of our people," she said, "no, *most* of our people here in England have no way to change their immediate circumstances. They cannot become educated. They cannot hope to rise from their poverty, and they are hungry. They cannot own land, and they cannot vote. They have no voice in the laws that are enacted to keep them debased and ineffectual."

Amanda stopped to take a breath and looked up at him, waiting, he supposed, to hear his thoughts.

Nathaniel fought an inner battle. More than anything at that moment, he wanted to share with her his identity as head of the Liberty Seekers. How much could he reveal of his true nature to her, of his ultimate goals for England? He wanted to applaud her for noticing all of these injustices, for caring enough to try and do something about it. How many women of his acquaintance would attempt something of its like? How many men? His admiration for her grew tenfold in that moment.

Amanda's shoulders drooped, and she looked down at the floor.

Blast! I waited too long to answer. He gently squeezed her hand and waist to get her attention. "I'm sorry, my dear. I am thinking about all you said, that's all. I am *most pleased* to hear you say such things."

Her eyes rose to meet his, and he stared intently into them, hoping to show more than he felt he could say. "Your words are some of the most important ever spoken, I believe. This is definitely the best conversation I have had in a ballroom with a beautiful woman. You have inspired me to be better, made me wonder for a moment what I could do. Maybe make a few fliers of my own, so to speak."

She dipped her head with a small laugh.

Nathaniel nearly stopped their dance when tears welled up in Amanda's eyes. "What have I done? My lady?"

Amanda blinked rapidly and shook her head. One tear made its way in a trail down her cheek. Nathaniel could resist no longer. He tucked her hand in his arm and led her out of the ballroom and down a nearby hall. He reached out and softy wiped the tear from her cheek then handed her his handkerchief.

"Surely the thought of fliers made by me isn't so terrible now, is it?" he asked.

She laughed and shook her head. "I'm not sure what came over me. And we missed the end of our waltz. I'm sorry."

Nathaniel held her cheek in his hand. "No harm done. In fact, I quite like our present circumstance much better." He stepped closer.

She glanced around her and moved nearer, a shy desire in her eyes. She stood on tiptoes to reach him, and he was overcome by his own urgings, heightened by her innocence. His smiling lips moved to cover hers.

Her soft response compelled him to press more insistently, and her small hands tried to pull him closer. He wrapped his arms around her back and pulled her against him while his lips moved over hers with greater urgency. Her body molded to his. He focused on her lips, her face, her lips again, and moved his mouth over every part of hers, savoring the delicious feel of their kiss.

They came apart in a daze, unsure why they stopped. Nathaniel couldn't remember ever feeling so content. Holding Lady Amanda in his arms, forehead touching hers, his heart began to slow, and peace overcame him. "Marry me," he murmured while they were still touching noses.

A throat cleared behind them. "Yes, that is a good idea, I think, given the circumstances," Amanda's father said in an amused voice from behind them.

Nathaniel's father joined in. "Yes, I quite agree with you, William. They've no other choice now, to be sure. Good show, Nathaniel, my boy. Good show."

Amanda stiffened. She looked up at Nathaniel, her eyes full of accusation. "No other choice? We certainly have plenty of choice, I assure you." She took two steps back.

Nathaniel moved toward her and kept her in his arms. "Amanda, no. It's not like that. He was sharing a little jest at our expense." He turned to his father. "Please, Father, if you would, let Amanda know you were in jest."

The Duke of Somerset considered Nathaniel for a moment and said, "Well, given your location and the manner in which she was encased in your arms, I'd say your choices are very limited. How's that?" The dukes smiled at each other and burst into laughter, patting each other on the back.

They turned to walk away, and Amanda's father called back over his shoulder, "I'll expect you tomorrow, Nathaniel, to draw up the papers." And with a few more cuffs on the back and congratulatory remarks, the two men rounded the corner, blessedly out of earshot.

Amanda pulled away and folded her arms.

"Amanda?" Nathaniel reached to hold one of her hands, to untie it from her body.

"So this is how it's going to be? Forced into marriage? Did you plan this?"

Nathaniel opened his mouth like a fish, at first unable to formulate coherent speech. "Plan this? No! But I can't say that I mind . . ."

Amanda scowled at him and turned her back.

"Come now, Amanda. Let me do this properly."

He reached for her again, but she shrugged him off and said, "No! I'm not ready. And not like this. How do you know I even *want* to marry you?"

He stepped back, stunned by her cutting reply. *Does she not want me?*

She dodged his arm and ran past him down the hallway, turning the opposite direction of her father—toward the back gardens, if he was not mistaken.

He marched after her. He was going to find out just what she thought. That kiss was unforgettable. He'd felt it. She'd felt it. Hadn't she? Yes. There was no way she didn't want him. He felt her response, saw her eyes. She wanted him, at least physically. But what if she didn't want *him*, as a person?

He walked blindly past people standing or conversing. He barely took note of their knowing looks or the smirks on their faces. He didn't pause to think of the scene they were creating: Amanda rushing out, and he following shortly after. He walked without seeing any people at all. He pushed on, hoping to reach her and get some answers.

Once out the doors, leading off the veranda and into the gardens, he broke into a run, searching the area, combing through benches and cozy spots where couples chatted. His eyes flew past one couple and then jerked back when he heard her laugh.

"Oh, Lord Kenworthy!"

He stumbled to a stop. Lady Amanda's white dress flowed around the baron's pant leg, as he stepped nearer, his back to Nathaniel. He leaned in, put his arms around her back, and Nathaniel watched as he tilted his head slowly to kiss her.

"Stop that this instant!" Nathaniel shouted, in a full run toward them. He grabbed the baron by the lapels, swung back his fist and landed it right in his eye. The baron toppled to the ground, groaning and holding his face.

"You are mad," Baron Kenworthy muttered.

Nathaniel ignored him and turned to Amanda, ready to plead with her and take her into his arms. Confusion erupted immediately into Nathaniel's awareness. Looking back at him in great alarm, eyes as wide as he had ever seen them, was not Amanda, but Miss Clarissa. She stepped back twice before circling around him and running to the baron, who was still lying on a rock path, moaning and holding his face. Nathaniel heard a stick break in the path behind him. He whirled around to see Amanda staring at him, eyes almost as wide as Miss Clarissa's.

"Are you mad?" she asked.

"Yes! I mean, no. I came to find you. Would you come with me? Through those bushes in there so we can talk?"

Amanda crossed her arms defiantly. "And if I refuse? I have nothing to say to you yet."

"Yet. What does that mean exactly? If you have something to say, say it."

Amanda placated. "Nathaniel, not now. Return to the ball. We should both go, dance with others, act as though nothing has happened."

"How could I possibly do that?" He stopped and noticed Lord Kenworthy and Miss Clarissa staring at them. He grabbed Amanda's arm and dragged her through the bushes into a more secluded area.

Amanda stumbled a little. "Let go of me."

Nathaniel whispered, "How can I possibly go on as if nothing has happened? After that kiss? After what our fathers said? We are to be married!"

"Stop it!" she hissed. "I cannot do it this way! Please, just give me some room, time to think." She reached for his hand. "Go back to the ball, please."

"Not until I do this the right way." He got down on one knee.

"Nathaniel, please!"

"Amanda, I have never felt this way about another woman."

She groaned in frustration.

Nathaniel ignored her. "Would you please do me the great honor of being my wife?"

Amanda looked at him for a moment, closed her eyes, and then shouted, "Why are you doing this?"

"Amanda, answer me. Darling, please." Nathaniel tried to show all of his love, his pleading, in his expression.

She burst into tears.

Nathaniel jumped up and pulled her into his arms. "Amanda, darling. It's fine, my dear. We will make everything just as it should be. I'll take care of you, protect you. You won't have to worry about another thing."

"No." She pushed away.

Nathaniel opened his mouth in amazement. "What?"

"No," she said.

"No, what?" Nathaniel asked.

She shook her head in exasperation. "No, I will not marry you."

Nathaniel took in her stance, her clenched fists, her determined face. "You are serious?"

She nodded. "I'm sorry." And she ran away again, out of the garden and up the path.

He watched her figure along the pathway until she disappeared back inside through a side entrance. He stood frozen to the ground for a few moments. Before he could move one foot in front of the other, Charlie stepped in front of him. He breathed out in relief. "Oh, Charlie, I'm glad it is you."

But Charlie roared at him, "You imbecile!" and shoved him to the ground.

Nathaniel jumped to his feet, ready to run at Charlie. "What is the matter with you?"

But Charlie held up his fists.

Nathaniel knocked his hands down. "Charlie, put those away."

Charlie reached out and shoved his chest. "Fight!"

Something snapped inside Nathaniel, all the confusion and frustration he felt for Amanda rising up inside, and he shoved Charlie to the ground.

Breathing deeply, he tried to calm his anger. "Charlie, you do not want to do this. Let's talk about whatever this is."

"You talk. I'll smash you through!" He lunged.

Nathaniel jumped aside and reached to knock Charlie off balance, but Charlie was too quick, and he blocked the effort before doing the same to Nathaniel then saying, "Stop play fighting."

Nathaniel backed up a step and said, "As you wish." He began in earnest to try to drive Charlie to the ground. He pounded him. He swung at him again and again. He tried every maneuver he could think of from his boxing instructors over the years, but Charlie avoided or returned them all. Nothing Nathaniel did could break through Charlie's excellent defense. Finally, breathing heavily, Nathaniel asked, while parrying blows, "Are you going to talk about this?"

"You—are—an—imbecile!"

"Yes, you mentioned that," Nathaniel said between fast breaths.

"She deserves better than you! You could have married her, you idiot! I have never seen her more upset."

Nathaniel lowered his arms in shock.

Charlie reached in and connected with his jaw.

"Ahh! Careful, man!"

Charlie thrust two more times with all his might. "Do you think I am parrying for fun? You deserve this!"

"So this is about Amanda?"

Charlie swung at him a few more times, sweating and breathing heavy himself. "Love her."

"I do!"

"Trust her."

"I—" But then he hesitated.

Charlie said, "Work beside her."

"Speak sense, man."

"Let her fight for freedom."

"No."

"Let—her—fight—for—freedom." With each word, he delivered a blow to Nathaniel's hands that made his arms shake.

"Charlie, hold off. What do you mean fight? Do you want me to hand her a gun and say, 'Go shoot some sense into the House of Lords?'"

Charlie stopped and held up his hands, palms out. Nathaniel gratefully lowered his own, but kept his eyes carefully glued to Charlie.

Charlie said, "She wants to be free."

Nathaniel grimaced. "So I gathered."

"She wants to change England."

Nathaniel stared at Charlie. "By herself? She wants to do it herself?"

"She doesn't mind if you help, but she views it as her cause just as much as you or I. And when you try to control and dominate, she is afraid."

"Afraid of what?"

Charlie waved his hand in the air. "Any number of things: Afraid she won't be free. Afraid you will lord over her. Afraid that you won't work together. Afraid she won't be a part of it. Afraid you don't want to change England."

Nathaniel stared at him. "But that's mad. Of course I want to change England."

"She doesn't know that."

"But you do, so why are we swinging at each other?"

Charlie grimaced and wiped his forehead with the back of his hand. "You're a much better pugilist than I imagined."

"You're looking at the champion of Jackson's, two years running."

Charlie seemed to have calmed down, but Nathaniel was still not amused. "What could I have possibly done that is so terribly wrong? Besides kiss her and do what's right by proposing?"

"She needs to understand your true motivations and work for freedom."

"I can't tell her."

"Why not?"

"There is too much at stake." He lowered his voice. "I must conceal my involvement a little longer. Let's get past the next two weeks, and then I'll tell her."

"By then, it may be too late."

Nathaniel frowned. "It's the best I can offer. You know as well as I that we must have this rally." His eyes narrowed, calculating as he stared at Charlie for several minutes. "You love her."

Charlie's eyes darkened. "Yes."

"I should dismiss you from my employ."

"From which employ?"

Nathaniel studied him a moment longer. What did he do with a man who was technically his stable hand? But who risked his life every day for the Liberty Seekers, likely one of the most devoted to the cause, who had also just shoved his lordship to the ground and tried to pummel him? Most nobles would have him transported to Australia or hung. Nathaniel considered him a moment more and then shrugged and walked past him up the path toward the house. He called back over his shoulder, "We will address this tomorrow morning in my study."

The first thing Nathaniel saw when he entered the ballroom was Amanda dancing. She laughed hysterically, loudly, almost maniacally. But her dance partner drank it in, puffed up in pride at his ability to entertain. Nathaniel laughed in derision but watched him. The man pulled her closer, and lowered his hand a couple of inches at her waist.

Nathaniel bristled and began to walk in their direction when a young lady stepped in his path. He moved to the left and then the right, dodging her quickly, but she was persistent in her efforts to stand in his way. When she giggled at his frustration, he stopped short and stared.

"Marguerite!" he said. "You have returned."

She giggled again. "*Oui, mon ami.* I have returned, and zis is ze welcome I get?" She pouted prettily, and Nathaniel couldn't help but smile at her.

Amanda's loud laugh carried to them.

He bowed before Marguerite and asked, "May I have the pleasure of a dance with the beautiful Marguerite?"

"But of course, *mon ami*. You have but to ask. I am yours." She traced a finger along the soft skin of her incredibly low neckline.

Nathaniel swallowed and diverted his eyes.

Taking Marguerite in his arms, he led her out for his second waltz of the evening with Amanda's laughter ringing in his ears. He tried to stay far away from her, but like the siren call to the sailor men, he was powerless, and soon they were waltzing in tandem.

Amanda leaned closer to her partner, so Nathaniel pulled Marguerite near. Amanda laughed yet again, so Nathaniel laughed even louder. Back and forth they went, one engaged more intensely than the other.

Marguerite began to notice early on. She said, "You want to make zis beauty jealous, *non*?"

Nathaniel grunted. "No."

But Marguerite's smile took on a knowing expression.

When the music stopped, small groups of couples remained on the floor, waiting for the call into dinner. Amanda and her partner came to join Nathaniel. Viscount Goderich bowed to Nathaniel. "Lord Nathaniel. Always a pleasure."

Nathaniel bowed in return. "Viscount Goderich, might I present the Marchioness Marguerite Dupont?"

Viscount Goderich raised his eyebrows in great interest. "Enchanted." He bowed to kiss her hand and gently pulled her to come stand beside him, where he began to converse with her.

Nathaniel and Amanda were left to stand together. His father approached and cleared his throat, rescuing them from conversation. "Nathaniel. You remember Viscount Robert Castelreagh."

Nathaniel bowed. "Castelreagh, good to see you. Have you met Lady Amanda Cumberland?"

Viscount Castelreagh bowed over her hand and then turned to Nathaniel. "We have come for a reason. Perhaps you can help us?"

Nathaniel's eyes sharpened. "But of course. What is it you need?"

Amanda stepped closer.

Castelreagh unfolded two pieces of white paper that looked suspiciously like Amanda's fliers. "Jenkinsen is furious. He demands we find the source as soon as possible and bring the person before him."

Nathaniel glanced quickly at her. She was pale, but otherwise captivated by the viscount's hands.

When he opened up the paper and held it up, Nathaniel sucked in his breath. His teeth clenched as he looked over its contents. It showed a nobleman with a ducal crest on his waistcoat, standing opposite a dirty, disheveled man. Both were gripping a liberty cap between them, and it was tearing down the middle. Across the top were the words, *Freedom for all or none.*

Nathaniel crumpled the flier in his hands. *Dangerous, awful idea. What was Amanda thinking, quoting Jack Bender?* The group around them had grown silent, everyone watching his reaction.

Viscount Goderich spoke, and Amanda startled. "Curious that your reaction is much stronger than Castelreagh's. The *second* flier is the one that has Lord Liverpool all riled."

Nathaniel unfolded it, attempting to conceal his trepidation. He nearly stepped backward in alarm. His father's hand on his arm stayed him, barely. He examined the details, his jaw working and his teeth grinding.

She had drawn an open conveyance, full of corn. Written on the side was, *Lord Liverpool's Collections.* And to the side was a young girl, waiflike and hungry, clutching an ear of corn. A nobleman was trying to take it from her hands.

Foolish.

His father nudged him. The eyes of everyone near them focused upon him with great interest. He folded up the flier and cleared his throat, attempting a smile, and said, "Interesting."

Viscount Goderich snorted. "Interesting? My lord, it is treason."

Nathaniel steeled his eyes and said, "It is *not* treason."

Viscount Castelreagh began to sputter in disagreement.

Nathaniel held up his hand. "Misguided? Yes. Brash? Yes. Willfully inciting? Yes again. But treasonous? No." He could feel Amanda's eyes on him. He turned to lock eyes with her, for just a moment, and then he said, "Whoever drew these fliers is obviously young. Perhaps they are playing with things they don't understand. One can hope that they will be forewarned to stop on this path they are currently treading and seek another, more loyal avenue. Else the authorities step in to do the warning." Many around them nodded, and there was a murmur of consent.

Viscount Castelreagh grunted. "Well, you can be sure that Jenkinsen does not see it that way. He is determined to stifle this Sparrow fellow. And he suspects the man is nobility—someone here tonight, in fact."

Nathaniel snorted. "Why would he think that? How could he know anything at all about the Sparrow?"

Castelreagh's eyes narrowed in suspicion. "You seem more defensive than usual, and so serious. I would as soon see you with several ladies on your arm than standing here defending the sensibilities of the artist. What do you know about the Sparrow?"

Amanda laughed, her voice more tittering than usual. "Oh, but my dear viscount. He does have two ladies on his arm this evening. You men have but interrupted a great rivalry between myself and the lovely marchioness. We are all aflutter awaiting his decision."

Nathaniel swallowed his smile. Lady Amanda's ingenuity would save them all from further interrogation.

Marguerite came to stand beside her. "*Oui*, my lord. You have made up your mind, *non*?" She pouted prettily at him.

Nathaniel raised his eyebrow and looked lazily about him. "My flowers, my lovelies. How can I decide between the two of you? Why force such a torturous choice from my lips, when I cannot bear to part with either of you?"

The duke grunted in frustration. "Nathaniel, could you take this conversation somewhere else while the three of us attempt to continue ours?"

Nathaniel shrugged, a large crooked grin spreading slowly across his face. "Ladies, shall we?" He offered one arm to each, and the women giggled and grabbed hold of him as he led them away.

Marguerite whispered, "We have saved you, yes?"

Nathaniel chuckled. "It is not as serious as all that, but yes, in a way—saved from a most tedious discussion at least."

Marguerite pouted again and said, "Well, *mon ami*, I must refresh myself. I hope to see you again, when next I am in town." She leaned up to kiss his cheeks, and then she waved at Amanda before turning down the hallway.

Amanda watched her go. "She is a beauty."

He pulled her gently closer. "Nothing like the beauty still with me. I am sorry for the way things have turned out. I hope that—"

Amanda hissed, "Oh, stop! What could you mean, denigrating my work like that? Who will pay me any heed now?"

Nathaniel's eyes widened. "Surely you understand that you have committed treason in the eyes of some very important people? You are involving yourself in things you do not understand." With Marguerite gone, he hoped to impress upon her the narrowness of their escape.

Amanda's eyes narrowed. "And *you* understand them? What could you possibly know about any of this?" They had exited the ballroom and headed down a hallway.

"Do you have any idea who those men are?" Lord Nathaniel tried to soften his exasperation. "They were sent here by Lord Liverpool himself to apprehend the Sparrow and bring him to justice."

Nathaniel grabbed her by the arms and gently but firmly led her into an alcove off to the side. "Amanda, you have crossed the line, twice. What are you thinking, quoting Bender? Did you want all of his people to reactivate? *Freedom for all or none* is his watchword. You *know* that."

How can I help her understand?

"And Liverpool. You had to *name* Lord Liverpool? You are calling him out, Amanda! In a very public way, you are challenging our venerable Lord Liverpool."

They stood nose to nose. Fire lit her eyes, a fury he knew would rise up like the burning inferno he remembered as a child. The counsel from his father came back to him, but he feared he was too late. "Amanda. You are on a dangerous path, and you have pushed it too far."

Her breath huffed on his face. "Are you finished?"

Nathaniel nodded, disappointed. He really did not want to upset her, but he did hope to reason with her. She put both hands on his chest and pushed him as hard as she could.

When he didn't move, Amanda threw up her arms and said, "I am *happy* I just might have been shocking enough to reach Lord Liverpool himself. That was the point! The prime minister himself saw my flier. Why can you not understand how wonderful that is?" She started to stomp away from him, but after three steps, she turned. "Can't you see that this is bigger than you or me? We are past the time to be careful and considerate. I'm done with your protection and your coddling. And your flirting and all the nothing." She sighed and held two fingers up to the bridge of her nose. "You would understand if you were anything at all like Red." She shook her head and walked away.

Nathaniel remained, watching her go. He looked to his right and was not surprised at all to see Charlie walking toward him.

"If I were anything like Red," he repeated.

Charlie tried to hide his smile.

Nathaniel asked, "What does she know about Red?"

Charlie said, "Well, you could just tell her."

"Oh, shut up, man."

Charlie laughed again. "No matter. This will all come together in the end. She's in love with you. She just doesn't know it's you."

Nathaniel ran his fingers threw his hair and shook his head. "She hates me. And she will hate me all the more when I tell her everything." He allowed himself a moment more to stare after her. Then he brushed off his sleeves, straightened his waistcoat, and said, "I'm not sure what you are still doing here, but we have work to do, Charlie, and we had best get home to do it."

Amanda paced her bedchamber. She loved him. Amanda loved Nathaniel. How did she let this happen? How could she fall so hopelessly in love with someone who just would not suit? She could never be happy with him. Most importantly, he would never support her efforts for freedom. What aspirations had he shown to do anything with his life besides flirt with beautiful women? And then he had dismissed her fliers, tried to downplay their meaning in front of the very men she hoped to reach.

So why did she love him so? Her traitorous mind remembered the protective feel of his arms around her, recounted the times he had quite clearly saved her life. Unbidden came his smile, his concern, his sense of humor. She was not opposed to shelter and protection, especially when it came with arms such as his, and lips . . . *Oh, stop!* Amanda threw a pillow across the room. She had never felt so conflicted.

Tiring, she sat at her dressing table and began to unpin her hair. She stared at her reflection and looked deeply into her own eyes. *What do you want, Amanda?*

Her head fell into her arms. She wanted Nathaniel. But not the Nathaniel who belittled her, not the man who had just this very night humiliated her. She wanted a Nathaniel who was willing to make a change. She wanted a man who would support and uphold her, not hold her passions in derision. Ideally, she wanted someone she could work with by her side as they made a difference in this world. *Red.* She wanted a man like Red must be.

Not for the first time, her mind lingered with curiosity on Red. Charlie had let slip one time that he was a gentleman. Someone of her acquaintance? Was he young? Single? She closed her eyes to try to picture Red, and the only image she could conjure up was Nathaniel, challenging her with his eyes. "Oh, Nathaniel."

She finished brushing through her hair and rang for Molly to help her undress. She shivered a little and moved closer to the fire. She doubted sleep would come easily, but at least she could stay up half the night in her nightclothes and under warm blankets.

CHAPTER TWENTY-FIVE

THE NEXT MORNING AT BREAKFAST, Amanda felt as though a large part of the light in her life had dimmed. She'd had a proposal of marriage from a man she loved but did not want. Did she? As she filled her plate from the sideboard, she took a deep breath and attempted to put all thoughts of Nathaniel out of her mind. The Liberty Seekers needed her and her fliers. She looked forward to the rally in St. Peter's Fields with much anticipation.

As she began planning how best to advertise for the rally, the bounce in her step returned somewhat, and she sat down to eat in much better spirits than when she had first come down. A footman arrived at her side with a letter on his tray. It was addressed to Molly, and when she raised her eyebrows in question, the footman said, "Molly asked that I bring it to you, my lady." It was from Jonathon Taylor, of *The Manchester Guardian*.

Her eyes raced over the page. He knew about the rally in St. Peter's Fields and wanted her to cover it, if she was able. That is, he wanted the Sparrow to be there. And more, he wrote that the aloof personage of Red would also be there and that if it were possible, she was to get some kind of quote from him that he could use for his paper. Her smile stretched across her cheeks. Taylor explained that Red would have on the liberty cap, but he would also be wearing a red waistcoat and have red on his watch fob. A nervous anticipation filled her.

Lost in thought, she did not hear her father enter the room. When he sat beside her with coffee and a paper in hand, she startled in her chair. "Oh, good morning, Father!"

He eyed her critically. "Good morning, Amanda. You seem in good spirits. I would have thought after last night . . ."

"Why, yes I am. I have decided not to linger on thoughts of last night. There is much to be done for good in this world of ours, and I'm excited to be about doing it."

His mouth opened a bit in surprise, but he quickly schooled his emotions and asked, "And what do you plan to do today for this grand world of ours?"

She thought for a moment and said, "We will just have to wait and see now, won't we?"

He laughed at this, his familiar deep belly laugh. And she couldn't help but laugh with him. Oh, it felt so good to laugh, like she had as a little girl. And when she stopped and looked at her father, he made a silly childish face at her that had entertained her as a child, and she laughed again. She felt waves of pressure and unhappiness ease off of her as the laughter did its magic. She leaned into her father and said, "Thank you, Papa. I love you."

His eyes twinkled back at her. "I love you too, my Amanda." And then he picked up his paper and began to read. Amanda returned to her food with hope in her heart. Satisfaction warmed her when she noticed he was reading *The Manchester Guardian*.

They ate in companionable silence for a few moments and then her father said to the footman, "George." The man started a bit at being addressed. "George, my good man. What do you think of universal sovereignty? Should everyone in this country have a vote?"

Amanda dropped her fork on her plate and turned to her father, eyes wide. Then she looked at George. The poor man needed a moment to formulate some sort of response.

He stammered, "Well, I ah, I'm sorry, Your Grace." He cleared his throat and then stood up straighter and with a look of determination said, "I think it would be a right good thing, Your Grace." He stared straight ahead again as was his normal habit in their breakfast room.

"Hmm." The duke returned to his paper with a small smile.

Amanda said, "Father, are you—are you thinking about encouraging the House of Lords to give votes to the other classes in England, to everyone?" She waited, holding her breath. Could her father be motivated with the same cause as she?

He kept his eyes on his paper but said, "Oh, I don't know that England is ready for that any time soon. I would be one small voice among many dissenters. But I will say that I agree with George. It would be a right good thing." He turned to her and grinned, then looked up at George who was watching them out of the corner of his eyes. George nodded his head at her father and stared again at the wall across the room.

Amanda felt her heart ache with joy. "Oh, Papa, I agree! I wish things were different here for Molly and all the others. I wish they could get a formal education and own land. I wish life were better for the poor. There are so many sad, hungry people. I don't even know about most of them, I am sure, but I want to help them."

The duke laughed.

She leaned back in hesitation. Had she said too much? Would her father continue to make her walk around with two footmen? But when she looked into his eyes, she saw nothing but kindness.

"Your generosity does you credit. You sit here with every privilege England has to offer, and yet you are thinking of those without. You will be a most excellent mother. I feel it is your future son, not I, who will have a great ability to vote in the change that England most needs. Raise him to care for others as you do, and he will make us all proud. And maybe I'll be in heaven smiling down upon you all."

Amanda leaned in and wrapped her arms around his neck in an awkward side hug. She squeezed him as best as she could. He leaned his head to the side to connect with hers. "I'm proud of you, Lady Amanda Alexandria Cumberland."

She squeezed him even harder. "And I'm proud of you, Papa."

Amanda nearly skipped to her bedroom after such a lovely morning with her father, but as she opened the door, she found Molly sitting at her dressing table in tears, with a letter in her shaking hands. Amanda ran to her and kneeled at her side. "What is it, Molly? What has happened?" Amanda anxiously searched her face.

Molly said, "Oh, my lady! It is such bad news. I don't know what to do, I'm—oh, what is there to do?" She wailed and covered her face with her hands.

"What is it, my dear? Tell me. Let's see if we can make this better."

Molly swallowed and began the letter, "Dearest Molly," but had to stop with sob after sob racking her body. She handed the letter to Amanda and gestured for her to read it.

Amanda looked at the bottom of the letter. It was signed by Molly's mother. "'Dearest Molly, I am sorry to bring you news of the most distressing nature, but I know you would want to know as soon as possible. And I also hope there is some way for you to intervene in your father's behalf. An incident of the gravest nature occurred here last night.'" Amanda glanced at the date on the letter. Already a week had gone by. "'I am sorry to bring delicate news to your attention. Much of this is unfit for the ears of an innocent, but there is nothing to do but to share it, and I would not want you to hear the truth about your father from any other person.'"

Amanda looked up with a worried glance at Molly, who gestured for her to continue. "'There is a maid working in Lord Landown's home.'"

She stopped reading again and asked, "Your father is the butler for Lord Landown, is he not?" Molly nodded.

"'This maid has found herself in the family way, and every servant in the house is convinced the father of this unborn child is Lord Landown himself. But she has come forward claiming the father is not Lord Landown, but in fact your own father.'"

Amanda gasped and looked into Molly's face before continuing. "'But I assure you, my dear Molly, that he is not the father of that baby, nor anyone else's but your own and your siblings'.'" Amanda sighed with relief and reached out to grab Molly's hand. She squeezed it. "'But the Landowns have chosen to believe the words of the maid and have dismissed her and your father without any letter of reference. It is our suspicion that Lord Landown has pressured her to name any other man and that he has paid her handsomely to do so. She has been shipped off to some distant cottage with a midwife in tow.

"'As you can imagine, we have no recourse. No one would believe us over the word of an earl and without a letter of reference, where will your father work? How will we eat? And what of the respectability of our family? It is a blight on our name, to be sure. I write as a small warning. I know you have good standing in your own home of employ, but if word of this reaches the duke's family, your very livelihood could be in jeopardy as well. This reminds me, and embarrassed I am to ask it of you, but could you send us whatever of your wages you can spare? Ours will soon run out and with the young ones still to feed, I am sure we will need it. We love you, Molly dear.'"

Molly had stopped her tears, but her face held such a lack of hope that Amanda nearly burst into tears of her own. "Oh, Molly. Surely we can make this right. There has to be something my father could do."

Molly shook her head. "It will just spread the gossip to tell him. He may never hear of it if we say nothing. I don't want to be let go, my lady! And now with my family needing my wages . . ."

Amanda shook her head. "No, Molly, you will not be let go. You will stay here as long as you have need. I could not do without you. You make me look like the veritable angel I am not." She laughed, and she was pleased to see a smile from Molly as well. "I will talk to Father."

When Molly shook her head again, Amanda said, "Trust him. He is a reasonable man and has a great love for you and your family. I am sure we can make this right." And with that, she headed straight out of the room and back down the stairs to find her father in his study.

She knocked on the door and immediately walked in.

He must have noticed her distress and the letter she was carrying. "Now, what's this? A bit of bad news? Come, tell me all about it."

"Molly is in the worst way. She cried so much she couldn't speak."

The duke frowned in concern. "What is wrong with the girl? Surely nothing too terrible."

"She has received the most grievous news from her mother. I'll read it straightaway and you will see. I have heard stories of her father almost my whole life. He is a good man and is being used unjustly, I am sure of it."

He reached for the letter and read it himself. While he read, his frown deepened.

When he finished, he rubbed his chin in silence for several minutes more. After what felt like an hour, he rested his hands on his desk and said, "We must help the family, that is sure."

Amanda exhaled in relief. "Oh, thank you. That is what I knew you would decide. They are the best of people, and Molly is quite my closest friend in the world besides being a wonderful maid—"

The duke held up his hand for her to stop.

She smiled apologetically and held her tongue.

"Situations like this have to be carefully maneuvered. I will call for our steward, and we will work out a solution soon, don't you worry."

Amanda ran around his desk and squeezed him for the second time today. "I can't wait to tell Molly. She will be so relieved." She ran up the stairs to the sound of her father chuckling.

　　　　　　　　　　　　　ᢙ

Nathaniel's heart beat with excitement as the details of the St. Peter's Fields rally came together. He, Charlie, and Brooks were deep in the planning and locked together in his study.

Nathaniel clapped his hands together and stood up. Charlie and Brooks paused in their work.

"This is all so important, gentlemen. I cannot stress enough how much rides on this event being carried out as planned. If I can carry news of a peaceful demonstration back to the House of Lords, then some of them will be open to discussion. Some of them will join me.

"If we appear to be uneducated ruffians, the rally could be a disaster. Let us tell them to bring no weapons. And to wear their finest apparel. Let us impress upon everyone the importance of a peaceable assembly."

Charlie nodded and Brooks said, "Very good, sir."

CHAPTER TWENTY-SIX

THE PAST WEEK HAD PASSED in the slowest manner possible. Amanda had convinced the family to travel to an estate outside of Manchester to visit her Aunt Elda. Once there, all that remained to do was wait. But now, on the eve of the event, finally, Amanda sat ready to leave for St. Peter's Fields. She and Molly had packed a satchel, which she kept under her bed, full of appropriate clothing. Amanda's heart pounded at the thought that she would be there, amongst all those people, dressed as a commoner even.

The thought of hearing Henry Hunt again excited her the most. She wondered if he knew the influence he could have on a person. He had made all the difference in her life, and she would have paid any price to hear him speak again. Now the moment would soon be upon her.

Amanda's hands drummed on her dressing table as she waited for Molly to come. She had arisen earlier than usual, unable to sleep any longer.

Finally, Molly came in, flustered. "Oh! You are awake. I am sorry, my lady. I was so busy, rushing about, and thinking about my parents . . ."

"It's just fine, Molly, of course. I have been using the time to become more and more thrilled that your family will be here today."

"I am so grateful to you, my lady. I don't know what we would have done."

Amanda stood and embraced her. "I am so happy my father could help. What is the news?"

Molly waved her hands. "Your father wrote a letter of reference for mine, and he has been offered a position here in town! Not three streets over!"

Amanda jumped. "Oh, that's wonderful!" Amanda held Molly's hands in her own. "Everything is working out so wonderfully for you, Molly—for us both! Tomorrow might well be the most glorious day of my life so far."

She sat again, and Molly began brushing her hair.

"To think that we will be there with people who think like us. And perhaps we will make a difference." Amanda almost didn't dare hope.

Molly nodded, humming to herself and separating sections of Amanda's hair.

"And even Red himself will be there," Amanda continued.

Molly smiled at her. "I would imagine so, seeing as how he planned the whole thing."

Amanda turned to face her friend. "I admit to being quite taken with the mystery of Red. I find I very much want to meet this man." She blushed in anticipation.

Molly began rolling pieces of Amanda's hair around her fingers and pinning them on top of her head. Her forehead creased the tiniest bit. "Did you think to invite Lord Nathaniel?"

Amanda sighed and looked at her hands. "For a moment, I considered it. But it's not necessary. He has undoubtedly seen the fliers, and I saw him holding *The Manchester Guardian* as he left Whites, so surely he knows."

"Yes, my lady, but an invitation from you . . ."

Amanda frowned. "I admit to thinking of it, but no, I cannot. I'm going in costume, after all, and I just really think he wouldn't want to go. I told you what he said about my fliers."

The crease in Molly's forehead deepened. "Yes, you told me, but it just doesn't sound like him, not from what Charlie tells me. He was worried about you, that's all. I think he's more amenable to this whole idea than you realize."

Her heart pounded with hope at the thought, but Amanda huffed. "Charlie has become a Nathaniel worshipper. He is altogether too biased." She smiled up at Molly. "You know, Charlie will be there, I am certain."

Molly blushed. "Yes, he said he would be."

Amanda watched her, smiling. That would be a wonderful match if it ever came to fruition. "Molly, you must take the day off today. Meet your parents in town, go to their new place."

Molly finished pinning up the last few strands of Amanda's hair and said, "I do think I might, if you're sure. Mrs. Gibbons said it would be all right."

Amanda nodded. "You must!"

Molly smiled. "I'm most grateful to you. Now, let's get you in your prettiest day dress, shall we?"

Amanda nodded, and the two of them talked of Molly's family and where they would be living and how excited Molly was to see her younger brothers, until it was time for Molly to leave.

After saying goodbye and ensuring that Molly left with a basket of food for her family, Amanda walked aimlessly about the house. After strolling by the morning room for the third time, her mother called her in, "Amanda, my dear. Why don't you go for a walk? Get out of the house and enjoy the fresh air."

Amanda smiled. "Is it obvious I am so restless?"

Her mother stood to embrace her. "I cannot concentrate for wondering when you might walk by again. Now go. Enjoy the day." She gently pushed her to the door.

Amanda went in search of her pelisse. Parsons assigned Thomas to follow her as soon as she made her intentions known. She sighed. "But I am only going for a bit of a stroll. Surely I will be just fine."

The butler only said, "Hmm," and summoned Thomas anyway to join them immediately at the front door.

Amanda nodded in acquiescence. She did not want someone in the house to have any reason to hinder her activities tomorrow. She turned to Thomas. "Come, good sir, let us go make merry out of doors, shall we?"

Thomas tried to contain his grin but, giving up, said, "Yes, my lady, make merry." He swallowed a laugh, cleared his throat, and waited for her to lead the way, schooling his features into a stoic expression.

Pleased with herself, Amanda stepped out the front door and into the sunshine. She breathed deeply, and contentment entered her heart. The birds were calling, flying, and searching for food in the dirt.

Movement behind the trees across the street on the edges of the park attracted her eyes. She looked closer and watched for a moment. Someone lurked in the cover of the copse of trees. She walked closer on her side of the street, squinting to get a better view of the fellow. And as soon as she recognized him, she stood still in amazement.

There, on the other side of the street was none other than Charlie. She almost called out to him when Thomas rested a hand on her arm. "Forgive me. Look, my lady."

Amanda, surprised at Thomas's boldness, looked closer and saw that Charlie was looking in all directions and reaching down into the bushes. Whatever he was doing, he hoped to remain undiscovered. After another moment, he left the trees and began walking rapidly down the street away from them.

"Oh, we must follow," Amanda said in excitement and walked as quickly as she could in the same direction, though on her side of the street.

Charlie seemed to be full of urgency this morning. She was almost at a run, trying to keep a reasonable pace behind his longer legs. Soon he crossed over to her side of the street and turned briskly down a side alley to the right. Amanda picked up her skirts a couple of inches and ran to catch up, hoping not to lose him on the next turn. As she rounded the corner, he turned down another street to the left. Her breathing coming hard, she was grateful to see Charlie open a door and enter into what might be a flat on the right.

Amanda looked up and down the street. She couldn't see anyone but Thomas, but when she stepped out away from the corner, she nearly collided with a gentleman who was making his way in the same rapid pace Charlie had been.

He said, "Oh, pardon me." He tipped his hat to her before hurrying past and entering through the same door. She glanced up and down the street again and hurried after him.

She felt a hand gently at her elbow. "Where are you going?" Thomas stared at her with suspicion.

She floundered for a moment, not sure what would appease him and then gave up. "I am following Charlie and that other man through that door. Something is going on and I want to know what." She raised her eyebrows in a challenge to Thomas.

He searched her face for a moment and then shrugged. "After you, my lady."

Amanda did not want Thomas following her anywhere, but she did not see any other way to be able to enter that door. She hurried across the alley and pushed the door open.

After the sun outside, Amanda saw only darkness for a moment. Voices sounded from somewhere at the end of the hall, which turned to the right and opened up into a great room filled with chairs and, to her surprise, people. The chairs were mostly occupied by men, but interspersed were groups of women in twos and threes. And behind the chairs, others were standing.

She and Thomas moved quietly behind the backs of many in the room and over to the far-right corner, hopefully unseen by most. As she felt the wall with her back, she leaned against it, feeling strangely reassured by its strength and solid coolness.

Thomas stood next to her, arms crossed, surveying the room. "Lots of noblemen in here." He nodded toward a few Amanda knew.

She shrank deeper into her corner, Thomas instinctively moving to shield her. He continued. "Not just nobles, though. Many the likes of Charlie and myself as well."

Amanda was about to protest that no one was the likes of anyone when she saw him grin. She folded her arms and nodded, acknowledging his teasing.

He understood her better than she realized.

The room became very quiet. Her breath caught when Charlie stood to address them.

Thomas turned to her with raised eyebrows.

Charlie said, "Thank you for coming on such late notice. I know you are all very busy preparing for tomorrow."

Triumph filled her. Amanda quickly scanned the group. If they were preparing for tomorrow, these must be the Liberty Seekers. Her heart beat in excitement. She had found them at last. Her neck craned around Thomas, looking for anyone she knew, hoping to memorize faces so she could find them again.

Charlie continued. "We have received some alarming news. It is going to require quick action on our parts, but I am sure we can divert a disaster." The crowd rumbled in concern. Amanda leaned forward, trying to make out Charlie's expression. She was too far back to see it clearly.

He said, "Our last correspondence to Henry Hunt has been intercepted and copied by one of Bender's men."

The crowd's noise grew.

A man standing next to Charlie shouted, "Quiet, please. We must move with all haste on this."

The crowd went still and Charlie read the details from his own copy of the original correspondence, a letter signed by one Joseph Johnson:

> *"Nothing but ruin and starvation stare one in the face [in the streets of Manchester and the surrounding towns], the state of this district is truly dreadful, and I believe nothing but the greatest exertions can prevent an insurrection. Oh, that you in London were prepared for it."*

The crowd gasped collectively.

Charlie continued. "I see you grasp the implications of this. We were not in any way suggesting a revolt. To be sure, the opposite has been all that we have strived for. We all agree that only the most organized and peaceful of demonstrations will have the power to sway any opinion our way."

The crowd nodded, but Amanda could tell Charlie had more to say.

"However, this note has fallen into exactly the wrong hands, and at this moment, the magistrate is preparing for an armed revolt tomorrow in St. Peter's Fields. Because of Bender's loyal followers, who may stir up trouble, the magistrate considers our meeting to be, in many ways, too great a threat."

The crowd erupted in conversation, many shouting from the back.

"We must give up."

"Let us go home now."

Charlie held up his hands, and they quieted. "We are doing our best to relieve the magistrate of his concerns. Red is at this moment doing all he can to calm alarmed feelings up and down the ranks of law enforcement. But in the meantime, we feel it wise to postpone our demonstration at St. Peter's Fields."

Some in the crowd grumbled, but most nodded their heads in agreement.

"Right dangerous, now," someone said.

Amanda was surprised to hear a woman closer to the front call out, "What if we just give it one week? We are all gathered and prepared. If we meet next week, August 16, wouldn't that be an effective delay, as effective as any other?"

Charlie consulted with the men closest to him while Amanda strained her neck to see who had spoken. She could not see her face, only that she appeared to be a sensibly dressed younger woman with fiery red hair. Amanda liked the looks of that hair. Her eyes shifted to the right, and she was surprised to see Mirabel Tanner staring back at her with a big grin. Amanda blinked in recognition and then very subtly waved her hand. Miss Tanner nodded at her and turned back to the stage.

Charlie stepped forward. "We agree with you. We propose a delay of only one week's time for our demonstration. All in favor, say, 'Aye'."

"Aye," resounded around the room.

"Any opposed?"

One large man to the right of Amanda and a few paces to the front of her shouted, "Nay!"

Charlie looked toward the back of the room, and Amanda positioned herself out of his line of sight. "And what is the nature of your disapproval? Pray tell us, so we may consider."

"How do we spread the news? What of the people here in Manchester and all over England? It's not just the Liberty Seekers we have told, is it? The papers have been mentioning it. We have fliers about. How do we tell all these people about the change of date? And moreover, how can we warn them not to step foot in that square? No sense getting arrested for *not* protesting."

A few people around him chuckled, but his point drove itself home.

Amanda closed her eyes to concentrate. How indeed could they get the word out? People all over the room began to chatter, weighing the options. Amanda opened her eyes in a moment of perfect clarity. She could fix this. She grabbed Thomas's arm and moved toward the door. Sensing her urgency, he escorted her quickly, and in all the bustle, no one seemed to notice them, except one. As Amanda glanced over her shoulder toward the front of the room, Charlie's eyes followed her. He nodded his head.

She turned back toward the hallway to the door, allowing herself to be led by Thomas out into the fresh summer air once again. "We must hurry," she said, looking at Thomas fully in the face. "I must get to the printer's shop right away. We don't have time for me to explain, but this is an errand of the most serious nature. Can I count on your help?"

Thomas made direct eye contact. She realized she had never seen the color of Thomas's brown eyes before. But he was looking at her now, intently and with great respect.

"Lady Amanda. If you mean to go about helping that group, I will do whatever I can."

"Oh, thank you, Thomas. They are the best of people, with good intentions. I promise we will be about doing good today and probably into the night. I must warn you it could take all our sleeping hours."

Thomas nodded. "Very good, my lady. Shall I find us a hack?"

Amanda nodded. "Straightaway, Thomas."

Soon they were arriving in front of the printer's shop where Mr. Taylor ran the operations for *The Manchester Guardian*. She rushed through the door, looking around in urgency for Mr. Taylor. "Oh, where is that man?" She called, "Mr. Taylor?" She breathed out in relief as she saw a man exiting from the back room, wiping ink off his hands onto an ink-filled handkerchief that he placed in the pocket of an ink-covered apron. The man was a walking ink stain. Even his cheek had a stray mark of black ink. She didn't have the heart to tell him. Besides, they had no time.

"Oh, you must be Mr. Taylor. I am so glad you are here. We work with the Sparrow, and we are having a bit of an emergency." She proceeded to tell him what she had learned at the meeting and what they now needed. Mr. Taylor nodded every time she paused for breath.

And when she had told all, he said simply, "Let's get to work." He waved for her and Thomas to follow him into the back. "I will need your assistance to help set the type. Have you thought of a specific message?"

Amanda looked at Thomas, a bit embarrassed. "No, not yet. I am afraid we simply just rushed here."

Mr. Taylor nodded. "Think of the simplest way to say what you need, with the fewest words."

Amanda grabbed a quill and dipped it in ink. After several minutes of writing, scratching out words, and starting again, she felt satisfied.

Meeting Aug 9 cancelled. Danger there. Avoid. Please come in peace Aug 16, St. Peter's Fields.

She showed Mr. Taylor, who grunted and nodded. "Now, please sort the letters required and place them here on the setter, as if you are reading them backwards."

Amanda paused and stared at him for a moment, processing his instructions. She took a deep breath and then started pulling letters out of their boxes.

When she was sure they were all lined up in their proper places, including punctuation, Mr. Taylor sent her to a back storeroom to collect large sheets of paper. He finished tightening the frame and preparing their type for the ink. When she returned, he used what looked like a large ball of linen to dip in ink and dab onto each of the letters, covering them in black.

Amanda was so fascinated by the process she did not hear Thomas at first. He cleared his throat. "Lady Amanda."

She turned to him in surprise. "Yes, Thomas?"

"I was thinking, my lady, maybe we should talk about delivery? If you don't mind my asking, how will we go about getting these fliers to the right people? Should we post them about in public places as well?"

Amanda paused. She hoped Thomas would still want to help when she told him she didn't really know. Maybe they would have to do it all themselves. "Thomas, it might be a long night."

While they were there, Mr. Taylor called in his apprentice to help him and a few friends besides to finish the printing. He assured Amanda that all the fliers they needed would be ready and at her back door this evening.

Now, four hours after she had entered the print shop, almost unable to stand on her own feet any longer, Amanda climbed out of her second paid hackney coach of the day and, trembling a bit while leaning on Thomas's arm, she stepped out and onto the steps in front of her home.

"Please help me watch for the delivery of the fliers this evening, Thomas. I must know as soon as they get here."

Thomas nodded. "Yes, my lady." And then with his help, she walked up the stairs and through the door Parsons held open for her in concern. She must look a fright. She smiled at him in what she hoped was a reassuring way.

She'd had no idea how much work it was to set and ink the type, or lay out the papers and cut them for a print job. It was not much of a stretch to claim she was unwell and therefore must stay home from the evening's activities.

Thomas had informed her that the fliers had arrived, so she waited until her parents' carriage pulled away from the house before she rushed to the kitchen, where she found Thomas and a stack of papers coming in through the back door. He hefted them onto the table with a loud *thunk*.

Only when she saw the fliers did she realize what a daunting task lie ahead of her. She grabbed onto the back of a chair, fighting the urge to despair, fighting her body's exhaustion.

Thomas eyed her with sympathy. Whatever he would have said was lost when the door burst open, allowing entrance to Molly and behind her a line of people, overflowing with conversation and laughter.

Amanda's mouth opened in surprise. "Molly!" She ran to embrace her. "You are back! I am so happy to see you! You'll never guess what I'm about."

Molly laughed. "Oh, I have some idea, my lady." She turned to the group who had entered the kitchen and crowded around behind her. "We all do. Let me introduce to you, Lady Amanda, my family." And she swept her hands out to encompass the group of ten behind her.

Amanda smiled. "I am pleased to meet you all. Molly is one of my dearest friends."

An older gentleman stepped forward and bowed to her. "I hear I am to thank you most of all for my new position. I am Molly's father. And I am right proud she has a mistress such as you as her employer. I thank you." He bowed again.

Touched, Amanda placed a hand on her heart.

Molly blushed and said, "We are here to help. Word got 'round to us what you were trying to do tonight all by yourself, and well, we just couldn't let you do it alone."

Amanda smiled. These were strangers, really, but they had all come to help. She bit her cheeks to stop herself from crying in front of them. She inhaled deeply and said, "I thank you all. Well, then, let's get to work, shall we?"

The group nodded, and Thomas started handing out fliers and giving directions to each group of three.

Amanda watched in gratitude as the pile became smaller, and the neighborhoods covered became larger. Soon everyone was gone except for Molly, Thomas, and herself.

Thomas said, "We have a rather large stack for ourselves, but I gave us the closest locations. I just don't think your father would be happy with any other— well, I don't imagine he would be too happy with you doing any of this, would he?"

Amanda considered the question for a moment. "He definitely supports greater equality in London." She sighed. "But to have me running all over in the dark, no, I don't suppose he would like that at all." Amanda shrugged. As much as she did not want to disappoint or upset her parents, this was simply the only option. Her fliers had announced tomorrow's meeting in the first place, and she felt responsible to warn others of the danger. With that thought keeping her moving, they followed where the others had gone, out the back door and into the night.

Molly said, "Most of the others had horses, and we brought a cart as well. We will all be done in no time."

Amanda wrapped her free arm around Molly's back. "You are a miracle, Molly. An angel. How can I thank you?"

Molly leaned her head on Amanda's as they walked. "I think my father would agree it is us who should be thanking you. I've never seen him happier or my mum either."

"It's just what friends do then, I guess."

Molly nodded, her breath coming heavier as they did not slacken their pace, following Thomas to the first location where they could post fliers.

CHAPTER TWENTY-SEVEN

August 16

FINALLY, THE DAY ARRIVED FOR the St. Peter's Fields meeting. Amanda awoke as early as the sun, rushed to her washbasin, splashed water on her face, and then sat in her chair to begin brushing through her hair. Within moments Molly was in her room, grinning. "Today is the day, my lady."

Amanda smiled. "Tell me what Charlie said about last week. No one was arrested?"

Molly said, "Not a soul. Even the magistrate got a flier and viewed it as evidence of its cancellation. I think a few watchmen showed up but no one else, and since then, they have been in conversation with the magistrate to assure him we are to have a peaceful meeting."

Amanda laughed, relieved that no one had been arrested. "And is he convinced, I wonder?"

Molly shrugged. "I do not know. Charlie said that the magistrate will be there, with yeomen and perhaps even cavalry, but they aren't expecting a fight."

Amanda's brow furrowed. "Why so many? The yeomen too?"

Molly shrugged.

Amanda said, "I don't like it that they are coming—untrained lot—or the cavalry either."

Molly twisted Amanda's hair into a common style a typical maid or servant would wear. "I wouldn't worry too much about it, my lady. Charlie seems convinced all will be well. He said they are expecting quite the biggest crowd we've ever seen."

Amanda clapped her hands in excitement. She couldn't keep her feet still. "We will need to carry my spare clothes with us into the carriage. I can change in there. Are you almost ready yourself?"

"I've been ready this whole week."

Amanda groaned. "It has been the longest week of our entire existence, I am sure of it. But today shall make it all worth it. Let's not wait a moment longer."

Amanda and Molly hurried to Parsons, who retrieved her coat and bonnet for her. He had come with them to help in the discovery of a new butler for dear Aunt Elda.

"Thank you, Parsons." She surprised him, standing on tiptoe to kiss him on the cheek. "We are off then." She hurried down the steps with Molly to join Thomas in the carriage, and they were soon on their way.

The crowds of people also making their way to Manchester lined both sides of the street, leaving just enough room for the Cumberland carriage to pass through. For the most part, Amanda couldn't hear them over the clomp of the horses' hooves or the sound of the carriage wheels on the street. A throng of people walked along as if strolling through the park, with mild expressions and wide smiles. Sometimes they passed so close to the carriage, she caught a whiff of the soap in their clothes. The occasional boy ran ahead, kicking a ball away from their horses. The closer they moved to Manchester, the more crowded the streets became.

"They look to be in companies or groups or something."

Molly nodded. "Charlie said they were very organized. Each group is meeting at a different time to enter the square so as not to overwhelm the streets. When all the groups are present, they will begin."

Thomas grunted. "A good idea, that."

Molly added, "Some groups have as many as six thousand."

They passed by men marching as if in the rank and file of the military, but they did not wear uniforms. Two men led, holding a banner between them with the colors and seal of their township, Oldham.

After they passed, she leaned her head out the window. "They go on forever. I cannot see the end of these people."

Their carriage moved ahead of the Oldham group and Amanda pulled her head back inside. "Everyone looks so happy."

A mother and father stood together a few paces away with their two children. A young girl with a clean, patched, and worn dress held tightly to her mother's hand. On the father's shoulders sat an impish toddler, perhaps three in age.

"Votes for all!" the toddler called in his young voice. "Votes for all!"

Molly waved to him, shouting, "Votes for all!" She turned to Amanda. "Oh, if he's not the most darling thing I've ever seen!"

People were now walking faster than the carriage could move. They brushed by their equipage, and Amanda could have shaken hands with the lot of them. A pole, holding up a black banner, bumped along against the side of the carriage. The banner said, *Taxation without representation is unjust and tyrannical. NO CORN LAWS.*

She stuck her head out the window again, trying to understand the symbols. A hand held a balance up high, one side full of corn. Molly grabbed her arm to pull her back in as a rowdy group of men stomped past, singing and swinging sticks.

"Thank you." Amanda held a hand to her chest for a moment. She felt something strike the side of her face. "What?" she shouted in alarm. It was soft, and it fell at her feet.

Thomas reached down and held up a red liberty cap.

"Oh, Thomas! Might I wear it?"

He shrugged. "It's your head, now isn't it?"

She laughed and placed it on her head. "Yes, it is, and I thank you for reminding me."

He rapped on the ceiling, and the carriage slowed to a stop. "I'll tell the driver to park a few streets over and wait for us."

Amanda said, "Thank you. I don't think we could have moved another foot. See how quickly people are pouring in."

Thomas stepped out so that she and Molly could change their clothing. Then, exiting the carriage, she twirled in her new, plain and patched-up dress. She and Molly waited for Thomas to change out of his livery as well. When he had finished, they looked very much like a jolly trio of chums out to support a neighborhood social.

Amanda laughed. "I feel invisible. Look! No one knows who I am." She felt a sudden burst of exhilaration and grabbed Molly's hand. "Let's go, Molly!"

She thrust them both into the throng that was working its way to St. Peter's Fields. Thomas steadily followed behind, his head tall above the others. Amanda glanced back at him a few times and saw his watchful expression taking careful note, but looking pleased.

They made their way, packed with a group of strangers, down a cobblestone street. Under her breath, Amanda said, "Molly, just look at everyone."

Molly laughed and then leaned in to speak quietly in Amanda's ear. "Enjoying mingling with the commoners, are you? Had I known, I would have brought you to family dinner long ago."

Amanda blushed. "It's not just that. It's everything. Here we are, all squeezed together on this street. Everyone has such a look of hope about them. Families are here. It's just the best thing I have ever seen." She squeezed Molly's hand.

Molly wiped her eyes, "For me as well."

Just then a young girl, barely knee height grabbed a handful of Amanda's skirt.

"Look." Amanda pointed down at the blonde curls of the young girl.

Molly laughed. "Oh, but she is precious."

The girl startled and looked up at them, immediately letting go.

"It's okay, poppet." Amanda smiled and looked around, hoping to see someone the child knew.

A man reached forward to take the girl's hand, winking at Amanda. "Come here, Hannah. Your mum's right here, now ain't she?" The family continued forward.

Molly's voice shook a little. "I am feeling a little bit hemmed in, though. I didn't realize so many people would come." She glanced sideways at Amanda. "Perhaps we overdid it with the fliers."

Amanda laughed. "No, this is perfect! And you know, I feel perfectly safe."

Molly's face looked pinched. Thomas elbowed his way gently to their sides, standing between them, and the three allowed themselves to move along in the current with everyone else.

A girl near them shouted, "There it is! We are here!"

Up ahead, their street opened up into a great, wide space. The crowd picked up its pace, and they would not have been able to stop this tide had they desired it. Thomas held his arms around the shoulders of Amanda and Molly, keeping them upright and trying to shield them with his body. He said, "Let's move off to the side over there." He pointed to an area directly to the right of a stage, which sat at the head of the field, in front of St. Peter's Church.

Amanda watched the field fill with people. Each side street fed into the open space in the center. A sea of bodies, more and more tightly packed, all pushed forward and turned to face the scaffolding and the platform, where they awaited the words of Henry Hunt. The three soon became pressed together so tightly that Amanda did not think she could move at all, so great was the crowd.

Behind them, men began chanting, "Huzzah! Huzzah! Huzzah!"

Then another group took up the chant. All around them, men's voices grew louder, and the tension rose. Groups farther to their left took to hissing. It was an eerie noise and Amanda welcomed the drummers who changed the tone.

Molly continued to breathe uneasily. "I don't like this. I don't like this," she muttered to herself, fanning futilely with what little movement she could muster in her arms, so tightly bound were they to her sides by the massive throng of people.

Thomas remained, closely shielding them from behind.

Molly continued to breathe more rapidly, soon panting, while sweat streamed down the sides of her face.

Amanda watched her with concern. It was clear she would need to stand elsewhere. She scanned the crowd for a solution and saw, to their right, that people were finding places to stand along the front doors of the homes that lined the field. Those doors were on higher ground and would afford a good view even if farther away. She pointed to the location, and Thomas nodded. But how to exit? They were completely surrounded.

Molly began to cry, and Amanda said in her ear, "Cry louder. Wail if you have to!"

Molly looked up at her and then took up a wailing like Amanda had never heard. "AGGGGHHH! I can't! I'm goin' ta' be sick, I am! AAAAGGGH!!!!"

The people near them reared back as much as the crowd would allow, in concern and disgust.

Amanda said to the nearest man, "My friend is going to be sick. Can you help us through?"

The man's eyes opened wide, and he nudged the man to his left. "Hey! Let the ladies out. She's sick; let her out!" A space in the crowd opened up for them to start pushing through. The people carried their message along in front of them as Amanda pushed forward in their wake along a clear path, the width of only one person and people filled in the gaps behind them. Amanda smiled in gratitude to each as best she could and grabbed hold of Molly's hand, pulling her along. Thomas followed close behind.

They reached the edge of the crowd and rushed up the steps to the nearest home, watching the proceedings from this better vantage point. She hugged Molly. "I am sorry, my dear. Who would have thought it could get like that?"

Thomas breathed a deep breath. "Glad I am to be out of that mess."

Amanda scanned the field. "Isn't it wonderful, though?"

Like their group of three, people were now packing into the fronts of homes, leaning out windows as well as standing on doorsteps. She scanned the field, looking for red liberty caps. Perhaps she could find Red. But the throng was full of red caps. She laughed at the idea that she could find Red in this field.

Disappointed, she decided to keep her eyes open anyway. "Can the field hold any more people? I think not."

"And they're still coming." Thomas grunted.

"Look at their banners," Molly said. Many carried liberty caps on the tops of their poles.

"*God armeth the patriot*," Amanda read.

"*No Corn Laws.*"

"*Universal suffrage.*"

"What would our banner say, my lady?"

Amanda thought for a moment. "I can't think of anything better than simply—"

"*Freedom*," Molly answered with her. And they both laughed. "Freedom," they repeated louder.

Amanda couldn't get enough. The individual faces blurred, but the colors captured her attention. She followed the muted shades of the clothing, to the brighter red and pink flowers tumbling out of the window boxes of the homes lining the square. The banners stood out in brilliant colors, with the stark red caps and all different colors of writing.

And then her eyes stopped. Wonder filled her, and she knew the image would never leave. Amanda sobbed. "Oh, look!" And then she couldn't speak for the emotion that filled her throat.

Molly sucked in her breath and said, "Oh."

Entering the square, directly across the expanse from where they were standing, a field of white marched in. White banners, white hats and gloves, white full skirts, all of them, coming with the message: *Votes for women.*

The women entered arm in arm. Amanda longed to join them: Independent, taking a stand, free already in that moment. Some held hands, some waved banners. Young girls shouted, "Votes for women!" All wore smiles, many laughing.

The pride and joy Amanda felt in her fellow women urged her to action, and she found her voice again. "Votes for women!" Amanda shouted. She waved and cheered them on. Unsure what else she could do, she marched in place and called out again, "Votes for women!"

Others around her joined in the cry. "Votes for women!"

The men to their right looked at her in surprise and then shrugged. "Votes for women! Votes for us all!"

Amanda watched the women pour onto the field, filling the remaining open space. Their beautiful faces shone as bright as their clothing.

Children scrambled to get better views, and the crowd chatter rose in pitch and volume. Men, women, and children all speaking at once were trying to be heard over each other.

"Henry Hunt."

"I came just to hear him. Inspiring, he is."

Amanda's eyes travelled to the back of the field. "What's going on back there do you think?"

Thomas frowned. "The magistrates."

Groups of men in uniform gathered together up against the wall lining the field. Filing out from a building, police joined them and lined the back of the crowd.

Amanda's feeling of unease was interrupted by a great swelling sound of unified cheering. Her eyes flew to the stage. Henry Hunt and several men stepped up onto the platform. A woman joined them, dressed in white, with her banner. Representatives holding banners from each of the boroughs of Manchester joined them both. Mr. Hunt stepped forward with his hands out, trying to quiet the crowd.

After several minutes of shouting and calling, "Henry Hunt!" the crowd did quiet, and he said, "Just look at this crowd! It's as if all of England showed up."

Everyone burst into cheers anew.

Amanda's eyes were drawn again toward the magistrates at the back of the field. A small disturbance erupted amongst them. All had pronounced frowns. One man stood out because he gestured wildly and shouted into the faces of the others. She felt a nagging sense of dread. She squinted. Something about the man looked very familiar. He turned to face their direction. Her throat tightened, and her knees buckled in fear when she saw a scar down the side of his face.

She grabbed Thomas's arm. "Bender! There! I see Bender." She pointed her shaky hand.

Molly gasped, "No! How could he be here?"

Amanda tried to swallow, and she wrung her hands watching him as he conferred with the magistrates, pointing to the stage, and growing more agitated the longer he talked. He directed a group of yeomen to push a vegetable cart into the crowds, bumping people aside.

"No!" she shouted without thinking.

People near her noticed the direction of her gaze and took up the shout. "No!"

She looked out to the center of the field. The crowd move aside to let the cart through, creating a pathway from the magistrates to the stage, where Henry and the others were standing.

The cart made it about halfway through the crowd when something changed, as if a great switch had been flipped. As the cart pushed through the next line of people, they stopped moving out of the way and as one turned, locked arms, and faced the cart. It could go no farther.

"Oh, good for them. They are resisting." A great affection filled her for these people whom she did not know. In their own passive way, they were standing up for freedom.

"Stand fast!" The call ran up and down the line.

"Stand fast!"

Behind the row of people blockading the cart, other lines began to form, row upon row of people.

She bounced on the balls of her feet. Energy flowed through her. *They must stop that cart. The rally must go on, and Henry Hunt must speak.* Why shouldn't she help? Amanda's feet moved of their own volition. She leaped down the steps in front of her, pushing aside those standing directly at the bottom of the steps. She thrust herself into the throng, digging and funneling toward those locked hands. She felt caught up in their courage. But she was making slow progress. The crowd in front of her was too thick. Frustration welled up. "Let me through. Please!"

A new dark sensation sent a shiver down her neck, and she had the eerie feeling of eyes on her. She found the source. Bender glared in her direction. She shivered at the evil emanating from him. Surely he could not recognize her from this distance or in this crowd dressed as she was. But his gaze did not waver, and worse, he began to make his way toward her, slowly pushing through. She looked behind her for Thomas or Molly, but she had lost them. She had no choice but to further lose herself, from Bender's gaze. She risked another look at him. He still moved slowly, but he was honing in on her as if she were a beacon.

She frantically called to the person on her right, "Oh, do make way! Please!" The man at her right didn't even notice her shoulder as she tried to wedge herself in front of him. She struggled in the other direction, but she was completely hemmed in on all sides.

And then, arms wrapped around her.

"Amanda, I have you." Nathaniel's presence felt like the sun.

Relief poured through her, his voice filling all the voids she did not know she had. Charlie appeared also, pulling himself between two brawny men so that Nathaniel, with his arms firmly around Amanda, could follow.

"Oh, Nathaniel. Nathaniel, it's Bender. He's here. Escaped."

Nathaniel nodded. "We saw him. In fact, he led us to you. He changed direction, and we realized it was you who'd grabbed his attention so exclusively."

"Can't say that we blame him, really." Charlie grinned and winked.

A wild exhilaration rose within her. The energy of the people, the thrill of Nathaniel, Charlie's teasing; it all combined and created a feeling of invincibility.

She laughed. "Let's go form a human wall, shall we?"

Nathaniel grinned. "Right you are. Let's join hands with the best of them."

"Whoooo-eeeee," Charlie shouted, still clearing their path.

Nathaniel's firm jaw and determined expression let her know they were not out of danger yet. They moved as quickly as possible through the mass of people. He shielded her from their bodies, taking the brunt of the buffeting. She felt his arms flex as they served as her buffer. A wondrous clarity filled her. His were the arms she wanted around her forever, come what may. She felt strangely at peace and at home.

And then the absurdity of their situation seemed to strike her all at once. She glanced up at Nathaniel. "Do you think we will ever lead a normal life?"

"Not likely," Charlie called back over his shoulder, laughing.

Nathaniel held her eyes for a moment. Then his lips curled in a half smile. "Are you considering *our* life, Lady Amanda? Ours together, I mean?" His eyebrow quirked, and his eyes lit with hope.

Her breath quickened, not from their physical struggle, which was beginning to tax her. She blushed and then laughed, gesturing around her. "What lady wouldn't? I would be the envy of women everywhere."

He laughed with her. "Oh no, my lady. You are here of your own accord." His face lit in appreciation as his eyes took in the top of her head. "And I love your hat."

She brought a hand up to her head, touching the liberty cap's fabric. She felt her face heat. "I forgot it was there. A group of ruffians threw it at me."

"It suits you." Then his brow furrowed. "However, I would very much like to know how it is you managed to be here at all."

Charlie called over his shoulder again, laughing. "You will come to expect things like this after you've known her longer."

Amanda shouted over the crowd, "Really, Charlie, now is not the time." She feigned exasperation.

Charlie turned fully around to face them both. He looked at Amanda. "And you can expect plenty more freedom rallies from our good man, Lord Nathaniel, as well."

She gave a half smile and asked, "Oh?" Confusion warred with hope. *Why would Nathaniel be involved in freedom rallies?*

Charlie smirked. "Oh yes." He gave Nathaniel a meaningful look.

Amanda looked from one to the other. "What? What do you mean?"

Nathaniel turned Amanda to face him, the crowd pressing in on the three of them from all sides. He said, "What Charlie is trying to say is that all this"—he waved his hand around—"is more normal for me than you might think." He tried to begin working their way through the crowd again, but Amanda squeezed his arm.

"What do you mean?"

"Just tell her, man."

"Tell me what?" Amanda grabbed his lapels with both hands and pulled.

Nathaniel sighed and ran a hand through his hair. He gestured around them. "I believe in all this. I want a different England too."

Amanda's eyes lit up. "I'm so glad, Nathaniel." Turning to Charlie, she said, "Charlie, I knew you would get him to come around."

Charlie smirked again and winked at Nathaniel. "No, Amanda. He's the one who planned all of this." He leaned closer to the both of them and yelled in her ear, "He is Red."

Her mouth opened, and she stared for a moment. "He's . . ."

"Red. Yes." Charlie looked as though he had caught the biggest fish in the river.

Turning to Nathaniel, she asked, "Is it true?" Her eyes scanned his person. He wore a red cap on his head and a red waistcoat. She eyed his watch chain, her eyebrows rising higher on her face.

He shrugged and brought out the watch, showing a red face. "At your service, my lady."

Immediately she felt her thoughts light up with happy realization. Her mouth opened in a cheek-splitting grin. "This is tremendous!"

Then, almost as quickly, her smile disappeared, and she scowled. "All along, you were Red." She huffed in exasperation. "At Henry Hunt's speech? All those times you have belittled my efforts?"

Nathaniel winced. "I told you she would be angry."

Charlie shrugged. "She will get over it."

Amanda opened her mouth to say, "We are not finished—" but her response was swallowed up in a roar so loud from the crowd Amanda had to cover her ears. They tried to begin moving again.

Charlie called, "Make way, make way, I say!"

Nathaniel glanced back behind them and stiffened against her. "The cavalry. They've sent in the cavalry!" His eyes sharpened in fear. Amanda whipped around in his arms to see, and Nathaniel shifted to unblock her view. The men on horseback tried to follow the path of the cart into the crowd toward the stage. But they'd reached the wall of people, still with their arms linked. Horse flanks, at eye level, faced the human wall, and neither backed down.

"Stand fast!" The crowd continued to call.

Her heart went to her throat. She had never seen such bravery. "We have to help!"

Apparently many around them had the same thought, because the crowd surged toward the men on horses, and the three of them found they had a bit more room to breathe.

"We must," she urged. "Stand in those lines, help those people!" She rushed forward in the space allowed, but a hand on her arm pulled her back. She tried to jerk it away, and she turned furiously, but her words died on her lips. "Charlie?"

He shook his head. "This can only end in disaster. You must not endanger yourself." Amanda shook her head and tried again to break free, but Charlie gave her a gentle shake.

Nathaniel said, "Hey now. Let her go, Charles."

"Don't you see? You two are the change we need—nobility willing to do things differently." He turned to face them, one hand on each shoulder. "Be the change yourselves. Give your tenants rights, an education. Sell them land, all of it. Others will follow. We must leave straightaway."

The crowd pushed in closer, moving them along its current, bringing them into the path of the cavalry. In short order, despite Charlie's intent, they found themselves standing at the front of the line facing the men on horses. The crowd surged and shifted, pushing them forward, almost into the breast of a foaming, agitated horse. Amanda had one clear view of the faces at the human wall before nearly losing her footing.

Solid determination, courage, hope, and love took human form and faced the cavalry. Unflinching, they guarded the path to the stage. A husband and wife stood together, hands tightly linked, the wife beaming with pride. Next to them, the frowning faces of youth, men her own age, locked arms and squinted into the sun.

She, a frontline witness to one of the bravest acts in England's history, wanted to be part of it. As one, Nathaniel and Amanda linked hands, joining the blockade and turning to face their foe. And no one was telling her to step away or back down or warning her of the danger. Her heart soared, recognizing she stood with greatness. A part of the movement, she felt she had made her mark.

Nathaniel squeezed her hand and indicated the cavalry with his head. The men swayed in their saddles. The pungent smell of whiskey singed her nose.

"Not good," Nathaniel said. "This will turn sour."

People bumped Amanda from behind, many still trying to join in the human blockade. The man nearest them shouted from his horse. "Make way, I tell you, or we will ride through the lot of you!"

Up and down the line, the demonstrators answered, "Stand fast!"

The crowd surged again, forcing a woman up into the chest of a horse. It reared up, no doubt startled, coming down onto the heads and shoulders of two men on the front row. They crumpled to the ground, battered and at the mercy of the weight of the horse and the massive throng around them.

"For shame! For shame!" the crowd called. "Stand fast!"

As if the mistake of one rider gave permission to all, like a great wave at high tide, the cavalry stopped hesitating at the edge of humanity and crashed on top of it. They pushed aside and trampled all who would not yield. Their horses reared again and again, all of them, coming down on the heads of those blocking their way. People fell, bodies collapsing, bones snapping. Amanda's eyes opened in alarm as one of the riders, swaying in drunken song, reached for his sword and swung it carelessly about him.

"Oooh no. Oh no!" she shouted.

The man on a horse next to him shouted, "Stop, man! Sheath your sword! Can't you see they have nowhere to go?" But his desperate words went unheeded as the blade swung haphazardly about, soon joined by others.

"We have to leave, now," Nathaniel said. With an arm protectively around Amanda, he began trying to usher her away from the cavalry.

Charlie stayed close.

A man stumbled forward, holding his arm, blood soaking his clothes. Nathaniel quickly reached for Amanda and tucked her head into his chest. "Don't watch, Amanda. Don't watch this."

Amanda heard the man mumble incoherently, and she shook her head, pulling free to see him rush in the other direction. She had not seen the extent of his injuries, but they must have been severe for Nathaniel to shield her so.

Unchecked, the cavalry continued to trample and carve a path, swords drawn. Blood was spilled, and the number of bodies underfoot grew.

All around them, people shouted, "They are killing! Break! Break!"

In desperation, the crowed retreated, pushing and shoving each other to evade the cavalry's blade.

Amanda and Nathaniel exerted great effort to move but had no place to go as people swarmed past in escape. She ached for the people who were pushed underneath, trampled. A hand reached upward as its owner fell, the small, pudgy fingers of a child in her last desperate attempt for rescue. Amanda lunged toward that hand but it disappeared amongst the mass of legs and hips.

Nathaniel pulled her back to his chest. "Stay close," he said in a broken voice.

"But . . . a child," she sobbed into his chest.

Nathaniel clung to her. A river of people parted around the three, shoving and bumping them as they went.

Cavalrymen reached the stage and tore down the banners, blades severing them from their posts. They dragged Henry Hunt from the stage, binding his hands behind him and raising their hands in victory. One man pointed back into the crowd. "Get their banners!"

The horses turned toward the crowd again, chopping at banners and liberty caps with abandon. The *No Corn Laws* banner came down, people trying to move hands and fingers away from the blade.

New victims ran from the field, rushing past Amanda, some with new wounds. Amanda retched at the smell of blood. Her whole body shook, and she concentrated on remaining upright.

"Get out of here! Now!" Charlie shouted, and he shoved them toward the nearest wall of homes.

She choked back a sob, unable to wipe from her mind the brave faces of those people on the front line, unable to erase the smell of blood and drunken, sweaty men or the sight of horses plowing through the crowds as if they were cattle. She nearly stumbled. She clutched Nathaniel's arm as the only thing keeping her upright. They were swept forward with the running feet of the stampede all around them. Shoved to the side of the square, forcing and pulling each other through the moving bodies, Amanda finally pressed against a wall and found a blessed few feet of space in which to breathe.

She watched the field, humans scattering, forcing their way into crowds, cramming the streets that led out of the square. People fell under the mass of running bodies and did not rise, among them a brilliant white dress, now muddied by the dirt and reddened by blood. "They're being trampled!" She held her hands over her mouth, eyes wide.

Crowds pushed into stairwells and against railings leading to basement entrances. To their right, the crowd rushed in so quickly that bodies fell over a railing to the stone below. Soon the weight against the wrought iron bent the whole thing inward, and people tipped over the edge in mounds and piles. Across the field, similar things happened at other stairwells. A desperate feeling of helplessness filled her. How could she watch such terror and do nothing?

"This is just too terrible."

Charlie shouted, "They're still killing!"

Nathaniel and Amanda shifted their eyes to the center of the field, where Charlie's gaze was fixed. The men on horses chased down civilians, striking at them with swords, even though all were clearly in retreat.

"Oh, stop! Please!" Amanda shouted, but no one heard.

Nathaniel pulled her back into his arms and she clung to him.

Charlie moved in front of them. "The hussars have arrived. They are helping us, I think."

Nathaniel turned back to the field. "Bless the man who sent them in."

The new men moved swiftly about the field, striking the most violent of the cavalry with the flat of their swords, gesturing that they stop. The hussars were also striking at civilians, but it seemed to be more in an effort to break up the meeting, to send them on their way.

"Finally, some semblance of order." Nathaniel tightened his arms around Amanda.

But it was too late. Panic reigned. Disaster and death and injury predominated. Even though she had seen it with her own eyes, Amanda didn't know how things had deteriorated in this manner. What had begun as England's largest peaceful demonstration for equal representation was now worse than even her most frightening nightmares.

CHAPTER TWENTY-EIGHT

AMANDA TURNED HER HEAD EARLY enough to see the flash of a blade in Bender's hand come crashing toward them. Time slowed as his sword raised in the air, arced, and slashed toward Lord Nathaniel's unprotected chest. She opened her mouth to scream. Another sword blocked the blow. The world spun around them in chaos, but only three people were visible to Amanda: her dear Nathaniel, Bender, and trusted Charlie.

Her childhood friend and protector strained against Bender's sword, muscles tight and veins protruding. With a primal yell, Charlie shoved the blade away. Immediately Bender jumped forward again, furiously striking at Charlie, pounding sword against sword.

Bender looked feverish and fought like a mad dog. A line of drool dripped from his chin and he gasped for breath through his foamy mouth, sweat dripping off his face. His strikes were fast and frenzied and unrelenting. Moisture flung through the air as he whirled past. Amanda winced, wiping a drop from her lip; fear pressed her heart down into her stomach. Charlie returned blow for blow, his face a mask of concentration. She mentally thanked her father for quietly allowing those fencing lessons. But Charlie must have continued his training elsewhere. No one could hold up as he was doing otherwise.

"Look out, Charles!" Lord Nathaniel warned.

Charlie whirled around as a man behind him tried to crash an old crate on his head. Lord Nathaniel jumped into the fight, kicking the man and his crate backward into the crowd. He searched madly around him, eyes widening as he reached toward the nearest man, shoving him away from them while deftly pulling a long fisher's knife from his boot. The man opened his mouth in protest, but the retreating crowd pushed him away and swallowed him in its current. Lord Nathaniel turned to face Bender, knife pointed in his direction.

Charlie came to his side, sword still raised. "Drop your weapon, Bender."

Bender's awful, maniacal laughter raised gooseflesh on Amanda's arms. He raised his sword and with a battle scream ran at Charlie and Nathaniel, his sword swinging in all directions. Nathaniel parried his blows but was shoved backward and lost his footing.

Charlie returned Bender's swings blow for blow, and they circled each other, swords moving with lightning speed. Amanda gasped as Charlie faltered, his foot catching and stumbling beneath him. Lord Nathaniel leaped forward into the fray just in time with a thrust of his knife along Bender's right arm.

Screaming in fury and clutching at the bloody wound, Bender turned his rabid eyes to Nathaniel, sword raised.

"No!" screamed Amanda, but her shout was lost in the noise of the retreating crowd. She frantically searched for anything at all she might use as a weapon. Her eyes spotted the sharp remains of a broken pot, and she crept forward, looking for a moment of vulnerability.

Nathaniel blocked each thrust of Bender's sword with a parry of his own. His knife considerably smaller, Amanda wondered how much longer he could continue. *How easy it would be to lose a finger, or a hand.*

She scrambled back as they came close to her; Bender was now facing her. He leapt forward, slamming his body against Nathaniel's chest, causing him to stumble backward. Amanda steadied him, preventing a fall. But Bender used the moment to once again swing his blade toward Nathaniel's open chest. Nathaniel held the blade back with his knife, but he grunted and strained against it.

Sweat poured off him, and his face was turning purple with the effort. Amanda didn't think he could resist for long. His hand slipped a fraction, becoming wet with perspiration. The sword moved ever closer to Nathaniel's neck. She raced in, broken piece of pottery raised, aiming for any part of Bender. When she was steps away, ready to strike, Bender shoved Nathaniel, pushing him to the ground, and turned on Amanda, sword raised, aiming for her heart. Nathaniel scrambled to his feet, horror on his face.

The world stilled, and Amanda watched the tip of the sword rip through her dress and felt the pressure of it on her girdle and stays. Someone yanked her backward to the ground beside him. As her eyes focused, her heart froze, and her breath stopped—Bender pulled his sword from the front of Charlie's chest, and her beloved friend's body fell limp to the stones. She gasped painfully, and her eyes jerked to Nathaniel's form darting in. He thrust his knife upward into Bender's chest and with a grunt, Bender landed on Charlie.

Charlie. I have to get to Charlie. Was he yet alive? Amanda rushed forward to help him, but Bender's fallen body pinned him to the ground. With two hands, using her legs as leverage, she tried to shove Bender to the side.

"Move!" she cried in frustration.

But his frame was too large; she could not move him. Nathaniel's hand, covered in blood, reached in and rolled Bender's body to the side.

Together they leaned over Charlie, seeking any sign of life. Nathaniel put two fingers on his neck while Amanda rested her head on his chest, praying for a beat. After several moments of feeling nothing, they lowered their heads, defeated. Amanda laid her head on Charlie's shoulder, away from his wound. Nathaniel, kneeling on Charlie's opposite side, rested his hand on her shoulder. Then they heard a low groan.

"Charlie! Oh, Charlie!" Amanda searched his face and saw him take a shallow breath. "You are alive!"

He coughed, struggling for air, and Nathaniel's eyes confirmed to her that he would not be with them long. She sobbed out, "Stay. You don't deserve this. You are the greatest hero I've ever known."

His eyes focused on her, and he smiled. And with that smile she felt such a strength of light and warmth, she almost smiled in return.

And then he rasped out, "Nathaniel."

"I am here, good man." Nathaniel squeezed his other hand.

Charlie looked at Amanda. "Nathaniel is Red," he said meaningfully.

She nodded. "Yes."

He struggled, forcing out his words. "You belong . . . together." He looked at Nathaniel. "Take care . . ."—his body shuddered against the pain that must have racked his chest and he swallowed—"of my Amanda." He squeezed their hands with surprising strength. Charlie's eyes lost their focus for a moment as he stared into the sky.

"Charlie. Oh, Charlie, no!"

He blinked once more and turned to Amanda, eyes lucid again for a moment, and whispered, "For freedom." And then his head tipped to the side and his arms fell limp. He was gone.

"No. Oh, no."

Amanda's tears wet his shirt, her head on his chest. Her body heaved and shook uncontrollably for the loss of her dear friend, for the horrors she'd witnessed, and for the sudden realization that they had lost.

Nathaniel put his arms around Amanda, lifting her. At first she resisted, but her fight was gone. She allowed herself to be pulled to his chest, feeling safe for the first time since she had left his arms. She continued to cry into his waistcoat, the two of them no longer aware of the field around them.

Bender's drunken men had disappeared. The crowd had dispersed, and the last of the hussars picked their way through the bloody mass of the fallen.

Some were dead, but most still lived, whimpering or moaning. Alive, dead, attached or no, humanity and pieces of it cluttered the earth. The injured tried to free themselves from the weight of other victims; men, women, and children imprisoned indiscriminately. Shredded pieces of liberty caps littered the stone. Splintered staves staked themselves into the ground, their banners trailing to the earth.

Twenty feet from where they stood, a large white banner, torn down the middle, attempted the clarion call, "Votes for women." A fallen woman, dressed in white, clutched the staff with her white fist. Her eyes stared unseeing, and the bloody wound that now marked her dress drained into the stone beneath.

Windows shut and shuttered all around them. Within eight minutes of the start of the cavalry rush, the square had become nearly deserted, the cross on St. Peter's Church paying tribute to the fallen. A group of magistrates, huddled at the back of the field, ignored the pools of blood, the yeomen cleaning their swords, a young lad crying out in a pitiful wail, and the many injured, moaning where they lay.

Nathaniel and Amanda stood, eyes closed, unmoving, Nathaniel's arms wrapped tightly around Lady Amanda, cocooning her. At length her sobbing stopped, and yet they remained for a moment more, blocking the horror of what they must now face, blocking the despair that was sure to come.

They were interrupted by a gentle clearing of the throat. They opened their eyes reluctantly, pulled as if from a dream, to see Mr. Taylor. Amanda looked in confusion at her friend from *The Manchester Guardian*.

He bowed to them both and said, "Please forgive me, Red, Sparrow." They both widened their eyes in surprise. "Yes, I know who you are. And the roles you have played in service to this people." Mr. Taylor looked haggard, his eyes mere holes in his face, his skin dirty, his hands covered in blood.

Amanda looked away from his stained hands, fearful she might retch. She desperately tried to calm her stomach. Mr. Taylor swayed for a moment and Nathaniel reached out an arm to steady him.

"I am determined, my lord, my lady, to see that this carnage"—Taylor's eyes flitted to the field and back to them—"this injustice of the lowest kind is not for waste. I will continue your work, my lady, but I propose something more."

Amanda gaped at him. How could any human who had witnessed the events of that afternoon not give in entirely to despair? She tried to feel the tiniest portion of his hope herself and clung to it desperately.

"But we lost." Her voice sounded plaintive.

And then Mr. Taylor smiled. His face and eyes lit up with the brightest hope. He held his hand to his heart and seemed to look through her eyes and into her soul. "No. We did not. And we must do all we can, my lady, all we can"—he rapped on his chest with each word—"to ensure that the events of today are not in vain. We must tell this story as far and wide as possible. The truth must be known." He stood a little taller. "Good people died today at the hands of evil and ignorance while peaceably calling for liberty, good people who did not provoke violence, who did not defend themselves—nary a rock did they attempt to throw. And they were thrashed down in the most violent of manners. That message will resonate; carry itself across distance and through time. There may always be evil, it is true, but there can be no more ignorance. We must herald our cause so insistently that all of England shall hear it. We must." And then his fire went out, and exhaustion took its toll. Mr. Taylor's hands fell limp and his head drooped. "We must," he said again. And then he slumped to the ground at their feet.

Nathaniel looked at Lady Amanda, his face streaked with new tears.

He knelt and gently shook Mr. Taylor. "Wake up, Mr. Taylor. You must wake up."

His eyes fluttered open.

Amanda also knelt and held his face in her hands. She looked into his eyes saying, "We will help you."

At her words, he smiled and mustered strength from a seemingly forgotten reserve to stand on wobbly feet.

Amanda searched Nathaniel's eyes as they both also stood. *Was there hope?* Was there yet something they could do? She saw the beginnings of a spark of light in the depths of Nathaniel's gray eyes, and that spark lit one in her own.

"We must," Amanda said.

Nathaniel nodded, and they turned to face the square, sobered again as the full effect of the afternoon once again became visible before them. Amanda shuddered but squared her shoulders. She gestured to Charlie's body, swallowing her emotion, unable to speak.

Nathaniel pulled her to him. "I will carry him."

"Thank you."

Taylor walked with them down an alley. Carrying Charlie gently in his arms, Nathaniel banged on the nearest door, not expecting anyone to answer. He shrugged, and they kept walking. They trudged along for what felt like an eternity, and Nathaniel, weighed down by the weight of the body, shifted Charlie across his shoulders.

The wounded, struggling to leave, lined the street. Some slumped against the walls, eyes dazed. Some, crawling, inched along the pavement. Others lay face down, not moving from where they had fallen. Amanda could not bear to look, nor could she stomach simply walking past. She had never felt more helpless or hopeless.

They finally reached a home that opened up to them. Lord Nathaniel grunted, lowering Charlie's body to the ground and said, "Would you please allow these good people some rest at your table? I must see to the injured in the square." The kindly man who answered nodded and hurried them inside, gesturing to worn but blessedly comfortable chairs by his fire. He walked with the slowness of age, but an intelligent twinkle lit his eye.

Mr. Taylor fell into a nearby chair, eyes closing. Amanda reluctantly took the other chair, looking in question at Nathaniel. "I should come with you . . . help those people . . ." Her voice cracked, and she ducked her head as emotion surged to her throat, causing her physical pain. Then she jerked up in her seat. "Molly! Thomas!"

Nathaniel rested a hand on her shoulder. "I will find them. For many reasons, it is best if you remain here until I or your family come to fetch you." He turned to their host and offered a bag of coins. "I thank you. Please see to their safety and comfort. I am afraid I trust few in this town right now. Please do not allow another in, unless it is someone from the Duke of Cumberland's home or my own—I am Lord Nathaniel Halloway."

The man's eyes widened so large as to completely overwhelm his forehead. But he nodded. He refused the money, saying, "I will not be paid for doing what any respectable person should do."

Lord Nathaniel looked about to insist but then nodded. He gripped the man on the shoulder and with considerable emotion said again, "I thank you." With one more look at Amanda, Nathaniel turned and walked out the door, picking up Charlie again and heading back to the square.

Amanda felt alone without Nathaniel. She sighed, and her host's well-weathered face showed concern. She attempted a small, tired smile. "We would all greatly appreciate it if you would keep our titles a secret." She looked up, pinning him with what she hoped was a pleading stare.

He nodded and waved his hand. "Of course. I have no need for airs or noble acquaintance." And then he leaned down and patted her hand. "Let me see if I can warm some broth for the both of you, though I don't know if he'll be taking any without my spooning it down his throat." He inclined his head in Mr. Taylor's direction; Amanda looked at the sleeping man fondly and then rested her own head against the back of her chair in blissful comfort. It was amazing what a worn chair could offer.

She closed her eyes but immediately forced them open as awful images played across her mind.

Their kind host returned with a cup of broth. She sipped, allowing the warmth to spread through her. "What is your name?" she asked him.

"I am Gabriel Munston. Please, call me Gabriel. Everyone does." Amanda's eyes started to droop, but she forced them open.

Gabriel's eyes saddened in empathy. "Don't like what you see when your eyes shut?"

Amanda shook her head, eyes filling with tears. "How can I ever erase such horror?" She covered her face with one hand.

"You don't want to erase it, no," Gabriel said. "Those people should be remembered." Amanda looked up at him in surprise.

"May I suggest something, my lady?"

"Of course."

"Take those memories. Accept them, acknowledge them, and then place them on your hero shelf."

"I don't understand." Amanda blinked in confusion.

"Make a place in your mind for all the honorable people and memories in your life. The horror you saw was their tribute. Their suffering, a hero's medal."

Amanda nodded rapidly.

Gabriel chuckled and gestured to her broth. "Best get some warm nourishment in you as well. Don't you worry. I'll keep watch while you rest."

Amanda smiled gratefully and drank deeply. Pondering Gabriel's words, she replaced the cup on the table beside her, rested against the back of the chair once again, and sunk into blessed sleep, too exhausted even to dream.

CHAPTER TWENTY-NINE

One week later

THE SUN SHONE WITH A promise of hope. Nathaniel leaned closer to Amanda in their parked landau. "Look at the headline. They are calling it, *The Peterloo Massacre*. Taylor writes, 'Courage triumphed this week in St. Peter's Fields. Good men, women, and children died in hopes of a better life. They did not fight. They did not resist. They stood with hopeful courage, boldly, and were struck down by the hands and swords of our own magistrates and cavalry. Their deaths, their injuries, their very blood spilt on the stones in front of St. Peter's Church has been noted, and will be remembered. We will laud them heroes. We commend them to God as England's finest.'"

Amanda wiped a tear from her eye.

A light breeze ruffled the papers, and the sun filtered through the trees above. Nathaniel continued. "The paper gets better with each page turned. Here, Taylor printed a poem by Percy Bysshe Shelley. Apparently Shelley heard about last week's events and penned this off immediately. He calls it, 'The Masque of Anarchy'."

As Nathaniel read the poem, Amanda's hands went to her heart, and she closed her eyes. Nearing the end, Nathaniel read:

"Let a vast assembly be,
And with great solemnity
Declare with measured words, that ye
Are, as God has made ye, free."

"That is everything," Amanda said. Nathaniel took her hand in his and smiled before finishing the poem.

"Rise, like lions after slumber
"In unvanquishable number!

Shake your chains to earth like dew
Which in sleep had fallen on you:
Ye are many—they are few!"

"It is beautiful." She sniffed.

"I agree. Taylor said the *Examiner* refused to publish it. They said the public wasn't ready for such sentiments."

"Ridiculous. This kind of thing is just what they need."

"Taylor snatched it up quickly. It made the second page, *before* your latest drawing, might I add."

Amanda bumped him softly with her shoulder, and together they silently read lines of the poem once more, thinking on the brave people who had inspired it.

Tears flowed freely from both of them, neither bothering to wipe them away. Amanda broke their silence first. "God made us free, Nathaniel. That's what Henry Hunt said that day by the church. Those words burned within me, caught fire in my very soul. I knew from that moment I would never be the same."

"When I see others suffering, without food or a place to live, I feel an obligation to help them. How can I live like I do, when my very lifestyle and the laws which I help create and uphold keep men in an impoverished state, unable to rise or make anything for themselves?"

Amanda's heart lifted in hopeful satisfaction. Here was the Nathaniel she'd dreamed of: the man with her same passions and desires and view of the world. "And you are working for change. Look at all you have done already. So many people." She stopped. Memories still too close and sharp overwhelmed her. Her throat hurt from the effort to swallow the emotion. "And what's more, we can make a difference still. What Charlie said . . ." She stopped again, emotion overcoming her. She put a hand up to her mouth, squeezing her eyes together.

Nathaniel reached over and took her hand in his. "You can feel sorrow. Let it come. I miss him terribly too. He was a dear friend, and I relied on him heavily in the Liberty Seekers."

Amanda squeezed his hand. "Molly is beside herself. I do believe they would have made a life together, and it would have been a good one."

Nathaniel had found Thomas and Molly shortly after he had left Amanda. Molly had collapsed at the sight of Charlie's body. Thomas had held her and brought her safely back to the family at Aunt Elda's home. She had been incapable of work the past week. And Amanda had little emotional room to comfort her, but the two had cried together most nights.

Nathaniel, somber, nodded and put his arm around her, pulling her closer. They sat together in his landau, in the shade of some trees. The pleasant day comforted them. And as they breathed deeply the beauty of the green park and the blue sky, Nathaniel whispered, "Amanda, look up."

When she did, her heart felt lighter than it had all week. A large flock of sparrows had landed in the branches above them, some flitting from one branch to another, most resting and filling the air with their song.

"My father gave me sparrows in a cage when I was a young girl."

"If only he had known then what havoc that would cause."

Amanda laughed. "I think he's resigned to my daring ways."

"Not at all." Nathaniel humphed. "He warned me plenty and told me your life is in my hands now."

Laughing, Amanda sank back against him. "Handed me over, has he?"

"You know," Nathaniel said pensively, "Charles was the second-bravest person I've ever known."

Amanda turned to him with a slight frown. "Oh? I would think working on Bender's team for all that time and saving both your life and mine would merit . . ." She stopped, noticing a twinkle in his eye. "And who, may I ask, do you think is the bravest person of your acquaintance?"

He leaned forward and stared into her eyes. "Many rose to greatness these past few months. Terror brings forward the heroes among us. But I am thinking of one in particular, and that is you, my dear."

Amanda sat back. "Me? Well, I . . . what?" She was filled with a sort of wonder and guilt all at once. His praise felt undeserved. It was undeserved. She smiled. "Well, now we both know you are speaking nonsense."

Nathaniel shook his head. "No, I am all sincerity. Since I have known you, you have done remarkable things. You helped us capture the majority of Jack Bender's gang at Cato Street and even aided in the death of Bender himself."

She started to protest the obvious, but he held up his hand.

"What's more, your fliers have convinced a great many noblemen and commoners of the value of their own freedoms."

Amanda looked down, unconvinced.

"And what would happen if they were to discover your identity? You have risked, you do risk everything to publish those."

She waved her hand in front of them. "A trifling thing, really. What do they accomplish?"

"Don't underestimate the importance of swaying public opinion, my dear, because that is exactly what needs to be done. We need to change people's minds."

Amanda added, "And their hearts."

Nathaniel nodded. "And that is where you are most effective. But I am not finished with counts of your bravery. I understand we have you to thank for keeping the good people of Manchester and London away from the field on the wrong day. And it is because of you that we had such a large number of people come on the actual day. *The Manchester Guardian* and the *Examiner* are both printing the count to be at or around sixty thousand."

Amanda opened her mouth wide. "So many!" But then her face pinched and tears threatened. "Oh, but Nathaniel, it was a disaster. Henry Hunt didn't even get to speak. All those people, the cavalry." Tears were coming again in earnest now, streaming down her cheeks.

"But a copy of his speech is printed here." Nathaniel's eyes were wet again as well, and he continued. "Those people did not die in vain. We lost eighteen, and many more were injured, close to six hundred."

Amanda shook her head, hand over her mouth.

"But their sacrifices will bring change, just as Shelley said in his poem. When I bring my report to the House of Lords, I will tell them that good, decent, unarmed Englishmen were chopped down mercilessly and unjustly. *That* will bring change."

Amanda saw a light in his eyes and felt the power of his conviction. Something began warming inside her heart. Dared she hope? Could Charlie and Mr. Taylor and Nathaniel be right? Could good things come from something so awful? She said, "We must make sure that it does bring change. We have a work to do. The Liberty Seekers are not finished." She paused and glanced at him nervously. "That is, if you will have me?"

Nathaniel reached into his waistcoat pocket. "The better question is, will you have me?" And he pulled out a beautiful ring that sparkled in brilliance as the sun hit it.

Amanda breathed in rapidly and held her breath. "I want this, and you, with all my heart. But before I respond, I must know the answer to my question. Does the Liberty Seekers have a place for me?" She held her breath again. *Oh, please.*

Nathaniel searched her face and smiled in understanding. "You know, Amanda, I was watching you in the crowds of St. Peter's. Long before Bender saw you, I saw you. It was as if my eyes were drawn to you wherever you were."

She tilted her head, a question in her eyes.

He nodded. "When the women entered the field, all in white, they were a brilliant sight. Yet I saw your face. You shone as brilliantly as all of them. You longed for their cause; it was plain for all to see the work that you must do. I knew I was wrong. So abysmally wrong in how I'd thought about you before that moment."

Amanda reached for him. "How could you know my heart when I gave you so little to go on?"

Nathaniel shook his head. "You gave me enough. You have worked for freedom from the moment you learned it should be available to all. I should never have doubted you." He rested his hand on the side of her face. "Charlie was right."

Amanda blinked back tears.

"You have much to give. So my answer is yes, the Liberty Seekers needs you. We need someone to head up our women's efforts. We are adding a new purpose and mission to the group, and that is true universal suffrage."

"That is just the work I hope to begin." Amanda's heart soared. "I have two fliers already planned—those women in white; what an inspiration. And so easy to draw. I could start with a banner . . ." Nathaniel's eyes sparkled in amusement and pride. She stopped. "We can talk about our specific plans later."

Chuckling, Nathaniel continued. "Liberty Seekers needs you, of course, but even more, I need you. I am not the man I'm meant to be without you by my side. I love you so completely I could not even *be* me any more without you. Say you'll marry me, Amanda. Let us fly together."

Her smile nearly split her face. She felt her heart might just expand outside her chest, she was so filled with joy. "Then my answer to you is also yes! Oh yes, Nathaniel. I want nothing more than to be at your side for the rest of my days. To think that I will also be working at your side, for the cause of freedom for all . . . I cannot contain my happiness." A burst of joyful energy brought her to her feet in the landau, arms spread out to the trees above. "This is everything, everything I have ever wanted." She spun on her toes and rested a hand on Nathaniel's shoulder to steady herself.

Nathaniel laughed, startling the birds above them. He pulled her back to her seat and they watched the sparrows fly off into the sky until they were dots among the clouds.

"I have never felt more complete." Nathaniel leaned in to kiss her just long enough to leave her yearning for more but not long enough to upset the sensibilities of the *ton*. And then he reverently placed his ring over her gloved finger on her left hand. "To the future Duchess of Somerset, to the Sparrow of the Liberty Seekers. We have work to do."

EPILOGUE

Five years later

NATHANIEL AND AMANDA STOOD TOGETHER on an outcropping of rock, overlooking the sea. The wind whipped through their hair, but they were warm together. Their two sons, Charles and Jonathon, played with sticks behind them. Nathaniel pulled Amanda to him so that her back rested against his strong frame, and he wrapped his arms around her to help shield the wind.

"The Chartists have their list of requests—six of them."

"Were they sensible? How do you think the Lords will respond?"

"Their list is reasonable, and the House of Lords is starting to soften. Universal suffrage, for men at least, is non-negotiable. This is going to happen, Amanda. Not tomorrow, not next year, but forces are in motion that will bring change." He squeezed her shoulders. "It's happening, my dear."

Amanda breathed in deeply. "Would that Charlie could see it too."

Nathaniel nodded and ran his hands up and down her arms.

Amanda rested the back of her head against his chest. "It will take longer for women's suffrage, but it too is coming. Perhaps our daughter will one day cast her vote."

"Our daughter?" He felt his eyes tear up and his hand found the side of her face, turning her toward him.

She nodded. "I am with child, and I just know she's a girl." One hand rested on her stomach.

Nathaniel leaned down and kissed her until their son Charles said, "Please, Father. We've just had luncheon." He and his younger brother laughed while their nurse attempted to quiet the pair.

Amanda looked up at Nathaniel, eyes burning with unshed tears. "Thank you, for this beautiful life."

Nathaniel's joy and gratitude echoed her own.

Movement caught his eyes, and he pointed. "Look."

She turned, and they watched an eagle rise up over the ridge, wings outstretched, riding the wind. She was magnificent, with an enormous span. She hovered for a moment before turning and dipping to the side, then soaring back down the cliff and off toward the sea.

They could hear her high-pitched call echoing off the cliff wall until it was lost to the distant sound of the waves.

AUTHOR'S NOTES

As with all historical fiction, some of the elements of this story are true accounts of history and well-researched fact. I used original sources and journals whenever possible, and the setting and characters are accurate to Regency-period England. In addition, the following people and events deserve mention as nonfictional parts of the story:

- Horatia was the filly of the stallion, Eclipse, one of the most famous and desired bloodlines in England.
- There was an actual Cato Street Conspiracy, and it was in fact prevented and broken up in a meeting in a pub near Grosvenor Square similar to what was described in the book. I took some liberties with the timeline. It actually happened *after* the Peterloo Massacre.
- Jonathon and Jane Smith were real owners of the Adelphi Theatre. Jane played a huge role in the management of the theatre and was its principal playwright. The circumstances of Jonathon Smith's death were fictionalized.
- Henry Hunt was a real man who gave many a stirring oration. He was a fighter for the rights of the working classes and spent time in prison for it. His role in Peterloo and in its delay of one week is accurately portrayed.
- The quotation on page 225 is an excerpt from the intercepted letter written by Joseph Johnson, Secretary of the Manchester Patriotic Union, to Henry Hunt (Robert Reid, *The Peterloo Massacre*, [London; William Heinemann, 1989], 115).
- Jonathon Edward Taylor was the owner of *The Manchester Guardian*. All other information about him was strictly fiction.
- *The Manchester Guardian* is a real press, founded during the events of Peterloo. It is still actively publishing news today in Manchester, England as *The Guardian*.

- Percy Bysshe Shelley was travelling and heard of the events of Peterloo and penned his poem, "The Masque of Anarchy", in sorrow and tribute to those who demonstrated. I took liberties surrounding its publication, which occurred in 1832.
- The events of the Peterloo Massacre and those leading up to it are as accurate as I could make them, down to the colors on the banners, the influence of the women and their white clothing, the crowd, the numbers, the order of events, the cavalry's behavior, and the peace of the general populace of demonstrators. I took small liberty with its location. St. Peter's Fields is in Manchester, which is not located as near to London as I allude.
- Chartism, briefly mentioned in the Epilogue, didn't occur until 1836.

My inclusion of these specific, true details is my tribute to a group who bravely stood for freedom and sacrificed for it.

ABOUT THE AUTHOR

JEN GEIGLE JOHNSON DISCOVERED HER love for uncovering obscure and fascinating pieces of history while kayaking on the Thames near London as a young teenager. Now an award-winning author and mother of six, she loves to share bits of history that might otherwise be forgotten. Although she married a man whose substance is the stuff with which heroes are made, thinking up stirring matches for everyone else keeps her riveted to the keyboard—whether in Regency England, the French Revolution, or Colonial America. Her romance novels are much like life is supposed to be: full of adventure. They start with a grand entrance, immediately get pretty bumpy and difficult, are full of hills and valleys and some ravines, but always end happy. You can follow all her news at jengeiglejohnson.com.